Peter May was born and raised in Scotland. He was an award-winning journalist at the age of twenty-one and a published novelist at twenty-six. When his first book was adapted as a major drama series for the BBC he quit journalism, and during the high-octane fifteen years that followed, became one of Scotland's most successful television dramatists. He created three prime-time drama series, presided over two of the highest-rated serials in his homeland as script editor and producer, and worked on more than 1,000 episodes of ratings-topping drama before deciding to leave television to return to his first love, writing novels.

In 2021, he was awarded the CWA Dagger in the Library Award. He has also won several literature awards in France, received the USA's Barry Award for *The Blackhouse*, the first in his internationally bestselling Lewis Trilogy; and in 2014 was awarded the ITV Specsavers Crime Thriller Book Club Best Read of the Year award for *Entry Island*. Peter now lives in South-West France with his wife, writer Janice Hally.

Also by Peter May

FICTION

The Lewis Trilogy

The Blackhouse
The Lewis Man
The Chessmen
The Black Loch

The Enzo Files

Extraordinary People
The Critic
Blacklight Blue
Freeze Frame
Blowback
Cast Iron
The Night Gate

The China Thrillers

The Firemaker
The Fourth Sacrifice
The Killing Room
Snakehead
The Runner
Chinese Whispers

The Ghost Marriage: A China Novella

Stand-alone Novels

The Man With No Face
The Noble Path
Entry Island
Runaway
Coffin Road
I'll Keep You Safe
A Silent Death
Lockdown
A Winter Grave

NON-FICTION

Hebrides (with David Wilson)

PETER MAY

A SILENT DEATH

riverrun

First published in Great Britain in 2020 by riverrun
This reissue paperback edition published in 2025 by

riverrun

an imprint of
Quercus Editions Ltd
Carmelite House
50 Victoria Embankment
London EC4Y 0DZ

An Hachette UK company

The authorised representative in the EEA is Hachette Ireland,
8 Castlecourt Centre, Dublin 15, D15 XTP3, Ireland (email: info@hbgi.ie)

A CIP catalogue record for this book is available
from the British Library.

Reissue PB ISBN 978 1 52944 398 1
eBook ISBN 978 1 78429 500 4

1

Typeset by CC Book Production
Printed and bound in Great Britain by Clays Ltd, Elcograf S.p.A.

Papers used by riverrun are from well-managed forests and other responsible sources.

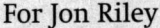
For Jon Riley

Here's to the crazy ones, the misfits, the rebels, the troublemakers, the round pegs in the square holes. The ones who see things differently. They're not fond of rules. You can quote them, disagree with them, glorify or vilify them, but the only thing you can't do is ignore them because they change things.

Steve Jobs

PROLOGUE

He has not the least idea as he turns off the lights, that what he is about to do will lead to the spilling of blood on this warm May evening. And, ultimately, to death. Innocence is so often the precursor to calamity.

It is the moon that first catches his eye. A gibbous moon, lifting from the black of the Mediterranean to cast its reflection on a surface like smoked glass. He could not have said whether it was waning or waxing. The weather in the last week has been uncharacteristically overcast, and it seems like an age since he last stood on his terrace gazing up at a firmament fighting to make itself evident beyond the light pollution of this congested Andalusian coastline. But those clouds have dropped their tears on arid soil and moved on, green shoots of renewal rising almost immediately in their wake.

The heat has resumed. With the promise of a return to the daily ritual of endless sun. Why else would they call it the Costa del Sol? It is a prospect that stretches off towards summer, and the distant autumn, unpunctuated for the most part by rainfall. A fierce angry heat reaching its crescendo as the tourists arrive en masse to spoil the beaches, turning white skin red, then brown, whilst locals move among the shadows cast by tall buildings in narrow streets, sleeping in the heat of the day, eating in the cool of the evening.

It is fresh now in this midnight hour, the faintest of sea breezes rattling palm leaves in the garden beyond the pool, the *chirr* of cicadas pervading the night air. And it isn't until he flicks a switch to extinguish underwater lighting that he notices a glow beyond the wall, where he expects the neighbouring villa to simmer in darkness. Light spills across the terrace from sliding glass doors casting the long shadows of pool loungers across terracotta tiles.

He tenses as a silhouette moves in the open-plan living space beyond the glass and momentarily passes through the light. His heart rate increases. A pulsing in his head as his blood pressure soars, and he imagines his doctor's disapproval. Has he not been taking the diuretics prescribed? A man of his age must be careful.

His mouth is dry. He recalls the handful of occasions he has sat with Ian on the terrace opposite sipping Harris gin, large chunks of ice jostling for space in his glass with the grapefruit. A nice young man. Scottish. But an educated accent, a pleasant lilt. And not so young, perhaps. But then, when you have reached your seventh decade everyone else seems young. He has never really thought about what age Ian might be. Forty? It is so hard to tell these days. But there is little grey in his hair. His body is lean and fit and evenly tanned. How

2

he wishes he were Ian's age again. Even though he knows he never looked quite that good when he was.

He recalls the cheery wave of his neighbour only that morning, calling across the wall that separates their gardens. He and Angela would be gone for a few days. A spring holiday. Barcelona. And a night or two in Sitges.

Really? A holiday? When you live in a place like this who needs holidays? And he thinks back briefly to the years he spent working in the City. The daily commute through the dark of cold English mornings, to sit in a steamy office, eyes fixed on scrolling screens, watching the rise and fall of financial charts like the swell of an ocean after the storm. It's the one thing he and Ian have in common. Their single topic of conversation before they run out of it and lift drinks to lips to fill the silence with the rattle of ice against glass.

Now there is someone in Ian's house, and there shouldn't be. He thinks about walking down through the garden in order to get a better look. But what if the intruder sees him? If only he knew Ian's mobile number he would call and ask him what to do. But they have never swapped numbers. Why would they?

For a frozen moment he stands on his terrace and wonders why the alarm has not gone off. Then once again a shadow passes through the light. Quite brazenly. And he turns quickly and heads inside to find his phone.

There are three officers on duty in the squad room when the call is picked up by the duty officer at the desk. He thinks that Cristina has been watching him through the glass before averting her eyes when he looks up. He has always thought that women find him attractive. Even though he is long past his sell-by, and a succession of relationships have invariably broken down when the women have got to know him.

In truth, Cristina had been looking at her own reflection, and might have been surprised had she jumped focus to see him watching her with appraisal. For she has just been thinking how old and frayed she looks. Now in her thirtieth year, middle age is only a decade away, and already there are shadows beneath her eyes, crow's feet at their outer extremities. With her hair pulled back severely in its habitual pony tail, black roots are showing and she regrets ever having opted to dye it blond. Too much maintenance. And soon, she supposes, those roots will start to grey. At least she still has her figure, even after childbirth. She remains slight, petite. Her male colleagues tower over her – even the smallest of them. She looks away just as the duty officer speaks.

'Suspected break-in. Out at La Paloma.'

Diego's eyes flicker up from his card game. From the cant of his head and the appeal in the faintest arching of his eyebrows, she knows that he wants her to go with Matías in his stead. Just thirty minutes until the end of his shift, a wife at home with a new and fractious baby awaiting his return, exhausted from giving birth only days before, and desperate for sleep.

Cristina sighs. She knows very well that her job here in this men's club simply pays lip service to the requirement for

4

quotas. And to the need for a policewoman to conduct the body searches of female suspects. She will never, by choice of her superiors, be entrusted with much more than traffic duty. Although she has graduated with distinction from the police academy at Àvila. Even though she is consistently the best shot at target practice in Estepona. But if Diego goes out with Matías he likely won't be home for hours. Even if it's a false alarm the paperwork will take forever.

'Okay,' she says, unaware in this counter-serendipitous moment that her act of generosity will ruin her life.

The streets of Marviña are deserted as the white Nissan four-by-four with its rack of blue and white and orange lights on the roof pulls out from the underground car park beneath the offices of the Policía Local. Matías is at the wheel, guiding them towards the roundabout at the top of the hill, through the pools of darkness that lie between the feeble lights of street lamps. From here, moonlight washes across the acres of vineyards, newly in leaf, that fall away across undulating fields towards the distant shimmer of the sea. Ugly urbanizations cluster darkly on once virgin hillsides, some abandoned, completed but uninhabited, victims of the financial crash that brought an end to the building boom that once swept this coastline. Above them the Sierra Bermeja mountains cut sharp shadows against a starry night sky. Below, the lights of Santa Ana de las Vides twinkle around the curve of the bay.

Matías drives at speed around the perilous bends of the road that descends to the sea, past the gathering of brick-red apartments that sit above the father-and-son fruit and veg store on the hairpin, and the jumble of white houses that nestle among the folds of the hill away to their left. It takes less than fifteen minutes heading west on the A7 to reach the roundabout from which the road climbs steeply into La Paloma, where wealthy northern Europeans, and more recently Russians, have built multi-million-euro villas with spectacular sea views.

The villa at the address on the call sheet is registered as belonging to the British expat Ian Templeton. It sits proud above a sheer rock face that drops 17 metres to the road below, and has an unbroken view across the Mediterranean to where the mountains of North Africa are darkly visible on clear winter mornings. To the south, the Rock of Gibraltar dominates the skyline, rising into the moonlight, its silvered face tracing a towering outline against the stars.

A light burns in the neighbouring property. The villa belonging to the caller who reported the break-in. But Matías and Cristina are pre-empted from making him their first port of call by the fact that the gates of Templeton's villa stand half-open. Tall black-painted wrought-iron gates. A Mercedes A-Class saloon car sits pulled up half on to the pavement outside. If asked, Cristina could not have said what it was about the gates that struck a discordant note. But when they pull up to take a look, Matías jumps out of the SUV and finds that they have been forced.

He slashes a finger from left to right across his throat and

6

she reaches over to turn the key in the ignition and kill the motor. The silence that follows is quickly invaded by the creak of cicadas. She slips out of the vehicle to join him at the gate. A glance through the window of the parked Mercedes reveals a wheel brace lying on the passenger seat. Neither stops to consider the obvious: that few burglars drive Mercedes A-Class sedans.

Matías unclips his holster to draw his standard-issue 9mm SIG-Sauer SIG Pro pistol. Cristina's mouth is dry as she follows suit. The gun feels familiar in her hand, but somehow heavier than during target practice. Fear lends it weight. She has never fired it in anger. Has never expected to.

Matías steps through the gate on to a driveway of crazy paving that wends its way through tall palms and a profusion of flowering shrubs. Cristina moves carefully in his wake, the barrel of her pistol pointed toward the night sky, her elbow drawn in at her side. She breathes in a heady fragrance that lingers in the warm air, and identifies it as jasmine. Off to their left a double garage is attached to the house, and a path leads around it towards the front garden where hectares of paved terrace overlook a shimmering infinity pool. Ahead, steps lead up to a porticoed porch, and a large studded front door lies ajar. The faint glow of yellow light suffuses the stillness beyond. Matías waves Cristina around the far side of the house, off to their right, while he heads in the other direction towards the pool. He hopes to catch a glimpse of the intruders through the glass doors that open on to the terrace. Better to establish what or who they are dealing with before entering the property.

Cristina reaches the far side of the terrace. Slabs of light fall across the paving stones towards the pool. She moves cautiously around its perimeter to steal a look inside. A sprawling split-level room is illuminated by lighting concealed around the ceiling. There are large, soft armchairs and a settee, an enormous, luxuriant white rug spread across a marble floor. An eclectic display of modern artwork breaks the monotony of shadowed white walls. But the room is empty, with the hallway beyond it mired in gloom.

Her eye catches a movement on the far side of the terrace and she sees Matías lurching forward as he stumbles on something unseen in the darkness. There is a resounding clatter, and then the sound of his SIG-Sauer skidding away across the paving stones. Cristina's heart fills her throat and pushes up into her mouth.

Inside, the man who calls himself Ian Templeton is emerging from a bedroom converted to a home office when the clatter from the terrace outside brings him to a dead stop. He has several folders in his hand. He stands completely still, heart pounding, as if someone inside were trying to punch their way out. Turning back into the office he crosses to the desk and extinguishes the desk lamp. He lays his folders on its polished surface and quickly opens a drawer to remove a Glock 17 semi-automatic pistol. A window on one side gives on to the garden and he moves towards it, pressing himself against the wall before daring to turn and peer out into the darkness.

By the light that spills across the terrace from the living room he sees a figure moving among the shadows, heading towards a copse of dark palms. A strange, loping run. He spins away again from the window. His face stretched taut with tension, and he presses himself once more into the wall. He has always known this might happen. That one day they could find him. That someday they would come for him. And he has always known that he would not go down without a fight. That he would rather die than let them take him.

But still, he is very nearly overcome by regret. Just a few short years ago he had lived his life without fear. When death means nothing, fear has no traction. But now . . . Now he has everything to live for, everything to lose. Undreamed-of happiness. How could he ever have known that such a thing was possible?

He wonders if he should alert her. She went to the bedroom. But he decides it will be safer for her if she does not know. She will hear the shots, of course. But by then it will all be over. And they have no reason to hurt her. She is the one innocent in all this.

He can feel sweat moistening his palm as it grips his gun more tightly. And he slips quietly into the hall, past the master bedroom, to switch off the lights in the living room. The house and garden are plunged into darkness, and beyond the shimmer of moonlight on the surface of the pool he sees silver coruscations on the black lacquered surface of the Med. He starts cautiously back along the hall towards the open front door where a narrow shaft of light from the street falls across the tiles.

Outside, Cristina is retracing her footsteps to the back of the villa where they entered from the street. She expects to encounter Matías circling around to meet her. No reason for stealth any more. Whoever is inside knows they are there. But there is no sign of him. She runs her tongue lightly across dry lips and climbs the steps one by one to the portico. The door still lies ajar, and she sees her shadow from the streetlights stretching into the hallway beyond, announcing her presence to whoever might be waiting there. Where in God's name is Matías?

She hesitates by the door, paralysed by her own fear, becoming acutely aware of a presence just beyond her line of sight. Nothing in her training or years of service has prepared her for this. She glances towards the garage, willing Matías to appear, but still there is no sign of him. Then she hears the sound of soft footfalls on marble from within, and knows that she must take the initiative.

'Police!' she calls out, and her voice sounds both feeble and inordinately loud at the same time. The echo of it propels her forward. Swinging her pistol level with her shoulder in a two-handed shooting stance. She pivots through the open door to point her weapon straight into the dark.

He sees her in silhouette. An easy target, even if he were not a crack shot. His finger caresses the trigger as light floods the hall behind him, and he realises he has been blindsided. The danger has come from another direction altogether. He spins around to see a figure caught in the light from an open door, and he fires. One, two, three times.

He hears her gasp of surprise. Then shock. And the long sigh as she falls to the floor, a final breath before her skull strikes the marble with the sickening force of a dead weight. A crack like a rifle shot. And he cannot prevent the cry of anguish that tears itself from his throat.

His hand falls to his side, fingers losing their grasp of the Glock. It too hits the floor like a gunshot. Barely aware of the pungent stink of nitroglycerine that suffuses all the air around him, he covers the ground towards her in three paces and drops to his knees, immediately aware of her blood soaking through his trousers. It seems almost black as it pools on the marble. Red lost in darkness. Though there is light enough for him to see her face, eyes open, disbelief in their sightless gaze.

He draws her into his arms, exhorting her not to leave. This woman who carries his child and all his hopes for the future. But his words fall on dead ears, and in a sudden flood of light he sees the vivid red of her blood as it spreads across the cold tiles. He inclines his head to look back over his shoulder. A young policewoman, arms extended, points her pistol directly at him. He sees how pale she is, all colour drained from a face like a ghost. He sees how her hands tremble as they struggle to hold her gun steady.

'Don't move!' she shouts at him and he thinks, how absurd! Move? Where would he go? And why? What point would there be now? In anything. Angela is dead. And a sudden anger fills all the empty spaces inside him.

'You killed her!' He hears his own voice as if it belongs to someone else. Words shouted in English. In torment. Is it really him? Surely to God none of this is actually happening. Then a second wave of fury consumes him and he screams again at this scrap of a woman who points her gun at him. 'You fucking killed her!'

Cristina trembles from head to foot, fighting to keep control. She shakes her head in denial. 'You did it!' Words in Spanish. 'You shot her.' And just like the man on his knees at her feet, she feels as though someone else has spoken.

Her focus is momentarily distracted by Matías hobbling into the hall behind her, pistol pointed unsteadily towards them. An eternity too late.

Now the man is speaking in Spanish, his voice filled no longer simply with pain and anger, but with hatred. 'You *made* me do it. *You* killed her. *You!*'

CHAPTER ONE

Mackenzie felt the pressure of being late. He hated being late. He built his life around never being late. To the extent that he would set all of his clocks, even his watch, five minutes fast. Despite knowing that his world was five minutes ahead of time, it placed a psychological pressure on him. To go faster. To ensure punctuality.

Although it pained him to admit it, the habit was borrowed – or, perhaps, inherited – from his uncle, who also set every timepiece five minutes in advance of real time, and would punish lateness with a stick. Actually, a cane. An old-fashioned walking cane with a curved onyx handle and knuckles on its shaft at six-inch intervals. *Mr Kane*, he had called it, emphasizing the *K*. His idea of a joke, a play on words. It hurt like hell.

Today Mackenzie had been delayed by Thursday traffic. Roadworks on the A4020. Circumstances beyond his control, and although his watch told him he was twenty minutes late, for once he was relieved to know it was just fifteen.

An overactive imagination conjured a picture of Alex waiting at the school gate, a few stragglers pushing past him on to Oaklands Road. Long gone the parental SUVs and people carriers and four-by-fours which ten minutes ago would have choked this narrow street.

Turning off Boston Road, beyond the Hanwell Royal Mail delivery office, he accelerated past rows of terraced houses with mean little front gardens. Already he could see the forlorn figure of his son standing outside the gates of the red-and-yellow-brick Edwardian-era primary school. His blazer was too big for him. Susan's idea of economy. If it was too big for him this year, it would fit him next. And if he didn't suddenly sprout, they might also get away with it the year after. Had it been warmer Alex might have taken it off and draped it through the strap of his sports bag. But there was a cool wind from the north-east, and he stood hunched against it, drowned by his blazer. To his already distressed father it made him seem all the more pathetic.

Mackenzie had been wrong about the stragglers. The street was deserted. Amazing how quickly an entire school could empty itself. Motors idling at the kerbside, pulling away each in turn, a well-practised daily choreography. In his day, Mackenzie had been made to walk to school, regardless of weather. Wet wellies chafing at red calves, shorts clinging to stinging thighs, coats draped over radiators to fill classrooms with steamy damp air on wet winter mornings.

Alex would be distressed, he knew, and late for his team's five-a-side game with the club from Hayes. Although it was just a ten-minute walk to the sports centre, he had been drilled always to wait for one parent or the other. But today his unhappiness went deeper than simply being late for a game of football. Mackenzie saw it the moment he drew up at the gate. Head down, Alex opened the door, threw his sports bag into the back, and slipped into the passenger seat without a word.

Mackenzie stared at him. 'What's wrong, son?'

'Nothing.'

'I'm sorry, I'm late.'

The boy shrugged and his father frowned.

'What's wrong?'

'I told you. Can we go, please? Like you said, you're late. So *I'm* late.' Eyes still turned down towards the footwell.

Mackenzie cupped his hand around the boy's jaw and turned his face towards him. The salty tracks of dried tears were clearly visible on pale cheeks, eyes red-rimmed. 'We're not going until you tell me.'

The boy pulled his head away, but his lips remained pressed tightly together.

'I'm serious. If you want to play football today . . .' Just nine years old, and already showing great talent with both feet.

Alex drew a deep breath and released it in a long, tremulous exhalation. He opened his satchel and pulled out a sheaf of three crumpled sheets and thrust it towards his father without looking at him. Mackenzie could see that the pages were filled on both sides with his son's characteristic scrawl. The top page bore the title of the piece. *What I Did In The Holidays*. Big red numerals at the head of the page read *0/25*, and beneath them in a tight hand, *Hand-writing too big and untidy!!!*

'She didn't even read it,' Alex said.

Mackenzie's anger was already manifesting itself in a trembling of the papers in his hand. He snatched the key from the ignition and opened his door. 'Come on.'

Alex looked at him, startled. 'What are you doing?'

Mackenzie waved the essay at his son. 'We're going to see about this.' He strode around the car and opened the passenger door.

'No, Dad, please. Just forget it.'

'I will not.' He took Alex by the arm, and pulled the reluctant boy from his seat. He had met his son's teacher once at a parent–teacher's meeting. A young woman. A girl, really. Miss Willow. Couldn't have been any more than twenty-five, and he had thought at the time that she was far too preoccupied with her appearance. He grabbed Alex's hand and pulled him in his wake as he strode through the gates and into the school through the side entrance.

It had the same institutional smell that he remembered from his own schooldays. Perhaps it was the detergent they used to wash the floors.

Alex's classroom was at the end of a corridor on the second floor. The door stood open, and Miss Willow was still at her desk, wading her way through a pile of children's essays. She looked up in surprise as Mackenzie dragged his son into the room behind him. Her surprise turned to alarm as he strode up to her desk and banged Alex's essay down on top of the others.

'What's this piece of shit?'

'I'm sorry?'

'You should be. Alex tells me you didn't read it.'

'I . . .'

'Zero out of twenty-five because his handwriting was too big? Are you serious?'

'Dad, please!' Alex pulled his hand free of his father's, his face pink with humiliation.

But Mackenzie was oblivious. 'Would you dismiss Einstein's theory of relativity because you didn't like his handwriting? And it wasn't too big, you know, it was too small. Notoriously mean. Oh, and, by the way, handwriting is *not* hyphenated. I can't believe someone who doesn't know this is teaching my son English. I take it you do have a degree?'

'Of course.' Miss Willow was recovering from the initial assault and gathering her defences.

'In what?'

'English and drama.'

'Oh, drama?' he said dramatically. 'That must be where you discovered the propensity for overuse of the exclamation mark.' He picked up Alex's essay and waved it at her. 'Not one exclamation mark, not two. But *three*. Oh, yes, very dramatic. Alright in social media, perhaps, but not in my son's classroom. Oh, and another footnote. Exclamation marks were originally called the *note of admiration*. Perhaps if you had taken the trouble to read this you might have been awarding him many notes of admiration. He took the trouble to write it, the least you could have done is read it.' And he slammed it back on top of the pile.

Colour had risen high on Miss Willow's cheeks, her lower lip trembling as she fought not to spill her tears. Mackenzie turned to take Alex once again by the hand, and march him back out into the corridor. It wasn't until they reached the gate, and his anger had subsided a little, that he saw the tears streaming down his son's face.

'What? What's wrong?' He was genuinely mystified.

'I hate you,' the boy spat at him. 'I really hate you. I'm glad you've left. Mum'll have to find me another school now.' He thrust his jaw in the direction of the building behind him. 'I can't ever go back there.'

Mackenzie was filled with sudden regret. He had only been standing up for the boy, as any dad would. He glanced back at the school and saw Miss Willow standing at her classroom window and knew that she was crying too. He opened the car door. 'Come on,' he said. 'We're going to be late for the football.'

The boy threw himself into the seat and folded his arms across his chest, pouting through his tears. 'I might just be in time for the final whistle.'

He was almost at the turn-off to Westlea Road when he saw the blue light flashing in his rearview mirror. It was the lull between the end of school and the start of rush hour. And Boston Road had been almost empty. A wide road lined by plane trees in spring leaf, mock Tudor semis set back behind redbrick walls. He saw the officer behind the wheel indicating that he should pull over.

Mackenzie sighed. The speedometer had crept above thirty without him realizing. He had been replaying his confrontation with Miss Willow. Again and again. And each time had failed to see how he might have handled it differently, although he knew by now that there must have been some other way. Alex was a black hole in the passenger seat, radiating hatred, draining his father of all his energy.

He wound down the window as the uniformed officer leaned in.

'Driver's licence and registration document.'

Mackenzie fished them out from an inside pocket and sat silently while the officer examined them.

'Are you aware, sir, that you were doing forty in a thirty zone?'

Mackenzie was contrite. 'I wasn't. But I realized it as soon as I saw your light in my mirror. I am truly sorry.'

'You would be if you'd hit a child at that speed.' The officer glanced across at the sullen boy in the passenger seat and took out an official pad and a pen. 'Occupation?'

'Police officer.'

The uniform's head snapped up in surprise. 'A cop?'

'Fifteen years with the Met. Starting with the National Crime Agency next week.'

The officer slipped the pad back into his breast pocket. 'You should have told me straight away, sir.'

'Why?'

'Because I wouldn't have booked you, sir.'

Mackenzie frowned. 'I don't know why not. I'm not above the law just because I'm a cop.' He paused. 'Are you telling me you would have let me off?'

The policeman threw him an odd look, as if he were not entirely sure if Mackenzie was being serious. 'It had crossed my mind,' he said, evenly.

'In that case, I'm going to have to report you.' Mackenzie reached across Alex to open the glove compartment and retrieve a black notebook and pen. 'I'll need your name and number . . .'

The traffic cop's look might have turned him to stone. He said dryly, 'Perhaps, sir, if you had spent any time on traffic duty you would know that whether I book you or warn you is entirely discretionary. In this case, I am warning you.' And there was something almost dangerous in the way he said it. He turned abruptly and walked back towards his car.

Mackenzie turned his head to find Alex looking at him with something like contempt in his eyes. 'I'll be lucky if I even make next week's match now.'

Hanwell had changed during the years that Mackenzie and Susan had lived there. An influx of Polish immigrants leading to the opening of Polish shops in a High Street which had seen better days. Everywhere you went now you heard Polish spoken. There was even a Polish school in the suburb. Ealing had always been that bit more upmarket than its less well-heeled neighbour. But as Susan had been keen to point out when Mackenzie suggested moving, everything would change when the Crossrail project was completed. Hanwell would have its own station, and direct access to central London in just twenty minutes. Property prices would skyrocket. Something from which she would doubtless benefit if she succeeded in having the house put into her name.

As usual, he was unable to find a parking place outside the house, and Alex refused to take his hand on the 50-metre walk along the terrace to number 23, marching two paces ahead of his father, half a step away from a run.

Alex had arrived too late at the sports centre to be picked for the starting eleven, spending almost the entire game sitting on the bench before coming on as a substitute for the last five minutes.

Now he couldn't get home fast enough. As soon as Susan opened the door, he pushed past her and ran straight upstairs. Susan folded her arms, standing full square on the doorstep, making it clear that Mackenzie was forbidden entry to his own house. Or her house, as she now saw it. The house whose mortgage Mackenzie had paid for more than ten years.

'What the hell did you think you were doing?'

He looked at her, surprised by her tone.

'I got held up in traffic. We were only twenty-five minutes late in the end.'

She tutted theatrically. 'I'm talking about threatening Alex's teacher.'

He frowned. 'Threatening? I didn't threaten anyone. Certainly not Miss Willow.'

'That's not what she says. I've just had the headmaster on the phone. He was livid! She went to him in tears, apparently, after your visit.'

Mackenzie sighed. 'Oh, for heaven's sake. The woman refused to read the boy's essay. Gave him a big fat zero because she said his handwriting – hyphenated – was too big. Exclamation mark, exclamation mark, exclamation mark.'

Susan just shook her head. 'You never change, do you? And you just don't get it. You can't speak to people that way, John. How many friends have you lost? How many bosses have you pissed off? Maybe you do have a brain the size of a fucking football, but you're a bigger idiot.'

She raised a hand to pre-empt his protestations.

'I know, I know. Sometimes they've got it coming. But Jesus, John, you have to employ a bit of common sense. A little tact. Filter your worst excesses.' She sighed. 'Not you, though. Not our John. He's always right, even when he's wrong, and damned if he's not going to tell everyone so.' She paused only to draw breath. 'You're a bloody misfit, that's what you are. And what's the point of all those stupid degrees when you don't have the first idea how to be civil to folk, not a Scooby when it comes to what's socially acceptable.' She nodded her head towards the stairs inside. 'And in front of Alex, too. How humiliating was that for the boy?'

'He was in tears at the school gate,' Mackenzie said. 'What was I supposed to do?'

'Leave it to me. In fact, leave everything to me. Don't bother picking the kids up from school anymore. I'll do it myself. I don't want you going anywhere near them.'

She started to close the door on him, but he thrust a foot across the threshold to stop it. 'I want to see Sophia.'

'She doesn't want to see you.'

Which took him aback. He recovered. 'Let her tell me that.'

'She's busy. She says she's fed up with you.'

He gasped his exasperation. 'She's seven years old for Christ's sake. Seven-year-olds don't say they're fed up with their dads unless their mums plant the thought in their heads.'

Susan sidestepped the issue. 'I'm going for full custody with limited access. And if I had my way, it would be none at all. Now move your bloody foot.' And she kicked him on the shin.

As he pulled back his leg she slammed the door in his face.

For several long moments he stood smarting on the doorstep, his leg throbbing where she had kicked him. He thought about hammering on the door with the big wrought-iron knocker. Shouting, making a fuss, bringing the neighbours to doors and windows. But even he realized he would only humiliate himself.

With clenched fists he retired to the pavement and glanced

up. The house was pre-war, roughcast brick, white paintwork streaked brown and in need of a fresh coat after a long winter. It had cost him a small fortune to have it double-glazed. He and Susan shared the large double bedroom at the front, Alex had the room at the back, and Sophia occupied the box room that looked down on to the front garden, such as it was. Net curtains at her window twitched, and a tiny sad face appeared behind the glass, almost obscured by reflections. Mackenzie gazed up at his daughter, consumed by hurt and frustration. Of all the people in the world, it was with this little girl that he had the strongest bond. He tried to smile and raised a hand to wave. After a moment her hand came level with her face and waved tentatively back. And then she was gone.

CHAPTER TWO

Cristina sat in the interview room, elbows planted on the table in front of her, head tipped forward into her hands. She rubbed thumbs into her temples trying to alleviate the ache. Her eyes were stinging. Although they had sent her home after the initial debriefing, she had been unable to sleep.

Miguel the station chief – or *Jefe* as he was known to everyone – had been roused from his bed, along with her immediate superior, to take both Matías and her through separate debriefs. It mattered that their stories were in sync, and Cristina saw no reason why they wouldn't be. Still, she had the feeling that somehow blame was being attached to her, and she had no idea what it was that Matías had told them.

After the debrief, she had written her report on the computer in the administration room. A blow-by-blow account of everything that had happened from the moment she and Matías left the building here in Marviñas to the shooting at La Paloma. She'd not had sight of the report turned in by her fellow officer.

A little after 08.00 a call at home asked her to return to the station. There, a ballistics expert from Malaga accompanied her downstairs to the gun room, where she unlocked and removed her gun from its drawer. It was routine, he told her. A check to ascertain whether or not her weapon had been fired.

'I never pulled the trigger,' she said. 'There was no reason to.'

He had smiled and nodded, and placed the SIG Pro in a heavy-duty plastic envelope.

She had been at the station most of the day since. Much of the time spent here in the interview room. Senior officers were coming from Malaga to question her, the *Jefe* had told her. But they didn't arrive until mid-afternoon. Two men in dark suits. One around fifty, with crisply cut steel-grey hair, the other younger, with hair that touched his collar and fell untidily across his forehead.

They were gone now, after what had seemed like hours. Cristina repeating the story she had already told in detail several times over. She had been exhausted, her mind starting to wander. To her row with Antonio over breakfast when she had told him he would have to drive Lucas to school. To the call she had made to her sister late afternoon, asking her to pick Lucas up at the end of the day. A call she'd been reluctant to make, given all the troubles poor Nuri faced herself.

Now, all these hours later, she was just numb, wondering who was watching her through the two-way mirror on the wall opposite. There would doubtless be further rows when finally she got home. Issues that could no longer be ignored, but which she had no desire to confront – especially after the events of the last twenty-four hours.

She sighed, and wondered why she was still here.

And where was Matías?

She turned her head as the door opened and a grim-faced *Jefe* strode in. He was a small man, inclined to portliness, with cropped silver hair that bristled across his scalp. He had a habit of standing with his thumbs hooked into his gun belt, or with his arms folded across his chest. He never pulled rank. Didn't have to. The insignia on his shoulder, with its single baton and two stripes, spoke for his status. But he carried his own authority with the same ease he wore the cross around his neck, or the Ray-Bans dangling from his breast pocket. He had never been anything but scrupulously fair with Cristina, and courteous, verging on avuncular, and she liked him a great deal. She got to her feet.

'What's happening, *Jefe*?'

'Sit down, Cristina.'

'I've been sitting on my ass all day, sir.'

He forced a smile and folded his arms. 'Malaga have come back to us with an identity on the man who shot the girl in the villa last night.'

Cristina frowned. 'But we know who he is. Ian Templeton. The villa is registered in his name.'

The *Jefe* nodded gravely. 'Yes. But that's an assumed identity, Cristina. His real name is Jack Cleland, and he tops the fugitives list of the British National Crime Agency.'

Cristina couldn't stop her mouth falling open just a little. 'What's he wanted for?'

'Trafficking in Class A drugs – and the murder of a police officer.'

CHAPTER THREE

Mackenzie's bedsit was in the attic conversion of a house in a run-down terrace on the outer edges of the borough. It was owned by an elderly couple who had lived there all their married lives and were supplementing their pension by letting out the room their youngest son, now deceased, had occupied as a teenager. When Mackenzie moved in there had still been posters on the walls. Of Nirvana, and the Red Hot Chili Peppers, and Pearl Jam. The couple said they hadn't had the heart to take them down, but that it was okay if Mackenzie did. He hadn't had the heart either, so images of Dave Grohl and Flea and Eddie Vedder still presided over the shambles that was now his living space.

All the furniture had seen better days. An armchair with foam bursting through threadbare upholstery, a Seventies throw disguising the damage wrought by a long-dead dog on an ancient settee. A scarred old office desk stood pushed in beneath the dormer window, books and notebooks and well-thumbed reports accumulating in drifts around a computer screen, its keyboard and mouse buried somewhere deep beneath the disorder.

The bed was unmade, sheets and pillowcases long overdue a spin in the washing machine. He could see the impression of his head still pressed into the pillow, the grease stain left by his hair. It took an effort of will to get into bed at night.

There was a chipped porcelain sink in one corner with a mottled mirror above it. His shaving gear and soap and deodorant crowded a tiny shelf along with his toothpaste and brush and an aggregation of hair and whiskers.

It was only fifteen minutes from his family home, but a world away from the life he had known until just a few weeks ago, when Susan had finally insisted he move out.

He had his own toilet on the landing outside his room, which his landlady insisted he clean himself, and he shared the kitchen on the ground floor. Although he never used it. He had quickly developed a dread of being engaged in conversation by the couple, and came and went as discreetly as possible to avoid bumping into them on the stairs or in the hall. He had cornflakes and long-life milk for breakfast in his room, grabbing a coffee at Costa's on the way to work, and bringing a carry-out home with him at night.

Home! He was unable to think of it like that. It was a space he inhabited, striving to avoid actual physical contact with it whenever possible.

It was dark when he got in, two hours spent brooding in a pub before summoning the energy to take a Chinese back to his room, tiptoeing up a gloomy staircase so they wouldn't hear him.

He never used the overhead light. A gathering of 100-watt bulbs that pre-dated the ban and somehow survived illuminated the room like floodlights in a football stadium. He remembered how his aunt and uncle had lived their latter years, too, under the insufferable burnout of overpowered bulbs. Mackenzie preferred not to confront the reality of life as it now was, and an old standard lamp and a bedside anglepoise splashed dull light among pools of darkness in his room.

He placed his carry-out on the desk and cleared away some papers and a copy of Sun Tzu's *Art of War* from his armchair. He slumped into the seat to open the mail he had collected from the hall table on his way up. Circulars. And letters that Susan had redirected. A utility bill for him to settle. A letter outlining pension entitlements from his former employer. An envelope edged in black, embossed on the flap, weighty and silky smooth between his fingers. He didn't have to open it to know what it was, and depression settled on him like dust.

He had never counted the years since turning away from his native Glasgow. Never wanted to. If life could be said to have chapters, then the first seventeen years of his were a prologue he would rather have cut from the text. For him, real life had begun on chapter one, with his arrival in London.

It was with a sick feeling in his gut that he ripped open the envelope. He ran his eye down the order of service. He had never disliked his aunt, or had much in the way of feelings for her one way or another. Unlike the hatred aroused in him by his uncle. She had always done her best in the difficult circumstances her husband created. He couldn't say why, but somehow he felt obliged to attend her funeral. Or maybe, somewhere deep down that he didn't like to admit, knew that there would be some satisfaction in going back twenty years on, just to stick it to the old man.

If only his career in the Met hadn't come to such an ignominious end. Of course, there was no way that his uncle would know that.

Still . . . it would be a fresh beginning after the funeral next week. Another chapter. And maybe this would be a better opening to the book of his life. Although there was a limit to how many times he could fashion a new beginning, and he couldn't help dreading the turning of yet another page. A new job, a whole raft of new colleagues to alienate. Life would be so much easier if it weren't for other people. He remembered with a jolt that he had not yet informed HR that he couldn't start until Wednesday, and made a mental note to call tomorrow.

And then, of course, there was the breakdown of his marriage. It would be only too easy for his uncle to point the finger of failure in his direction. But the old bastard didn't have to know about that either.

Mackenzie and Susan had met during the early years of his career in the police while she was working as a researcher for a Member of Parliament who sat on the Justice Select Committee of the House of Commons. It had been lust at first sight. Six months of non-stop sex – or so it had seemed looking back on it. Brought to an abrupt halt by her first pregnancy, only to resume again soon after the birth of Alex. The arrival of Sophie, though, had changed everything, their appetite for sex diminishing along with the constant crying and sleepless nights. Family responsibilities had predominated, and it was only then, during long nights and weekends and holidays at home, that they had really started getting to know each other. Neither of them, it seemed, had cared much for what they learned.

Susan began to find fault with everything he did and said, as if only now noticing how socially ill-adjusted he was, counting up the friends they had lost, the people he had insulted, the senior officers who had promoted him sideways to claw him out of their hair. Where the children were concerned she had become increasingly possessive, coveting their affections and excluding him from the mother–children trio.

His response had been to retreat into himself, sitting up late at night alone in his attic office – when not on shift – immersing himself in study, as if somehow knowledge could fill all the empty spaces he had inside. It had become an obsession, from which only little Sophia was able to distract him. For some reason, she loved him, and Mackenzie knew only too well how love for a father had neither rhyme nor reason.

He felt his phone vibrate against his chest, and retrieved it from the breast pocket of his shirt with thumb and forefinger. It was Sophia on Facebook's Messenger app.

– Hi daddy.

He wedged the phone between his hands and typed with his thumbs.

– Hi darling.

– Miss you.

– I miss you, too, sweetheart.

– Sorry mummy's not speaking.

He paused on that one.

– Well, I'm sure she will in time.

She posted a sad face. Kids are not easily fooled.

– Will you be at my school concert on Tuesday night?

He hesitated, and almost as if she had read his mind, added,

– I'll tell mummy it's ok. Everyone else's daddy'll be there.

– Of course I'll come, darling. I wouldn't miss it for the world.

– Got a whole song to myself.

– I can't wait to hear it. Pause. *Baby, shouldn't you be in bed?*

– I am. A happy face.

– Under the covers?

– Shhhh. Several happy faces.

– You put your phone on the charger, baby, and go to sleep, and I'll see you on Tuesday.

– Okay, daddy. Pause. *Love you.*

– Love you, too, darling.

In so many ways he didn't want the conversation to end. If he'd been at home, he'd have sat on her bed, running his fingers gently through her baby-soft hair until she closed her eyes and drifted off. He waited a long time, almost willing her to say something more. But the cursor blinked emptily, and finally he slipped the phone back into his pocket.

He eased himself out of the chair and crossed to the desk to open his takeaway. It would be cold by now, and his appetite for it had passed. Still, he needed to eat.

It was only then that he noticed a red light winking on his desk phone, almost obscured by a stray sheet of paper lying across it and diffusing the light. He picked up the phone and thumbed the message-replay button.

'*Mackenzie, it's Bill Beard here. I know you don't start with us until Monday, but I wonder if you could come in tomorrow morning for a briefing?*'

CHAPTER FOUR

The London headquarters of the National Crime Agency was tucked away in Citadel Place in a sprawl of industrial buildings south of the railway lines between Vauxhall and Lambeth. It was an unremarkable structure of brick and steel and glass. It came into view as Mackenzie walked along Tinworth Street, and he was overcome by the same depression which had afflicted him the previous evening. And not a little anxiety. Whatever he had believed or imagined when first joining the Metropolitan Police, he could never have envisaged ending up here.

Spring sunshine sprinkled light across the floor tiles in reception and he told the girl behind the desk that he had an appointment with Director Beard. She asked him to wait and lifted a phone. 'Someone will be down in a few minutes.'

Six minutes and thirty-three seconds, to be exact. Mackenzie had watched every passing second counting itself off on his watch. He had arrived on time and was aggrieved that his new boss could not organize his schedule to reciprocate.

It was a woman in her early thirties who came through the

door to greet him, offering a firm dry handshake. She was thin, with an awkward gait, blue tights beneath a grey skirt, and hair drawn back untidily. 'Ruth Collins,' she said. 'You're here to see Mr Beard.'

It seemed more like a statement to Mackenzie than a question, so he didn't respond.

They entered the lift in an awkward silence, and Collins made a brave stab at breaking it as she selected a button for the third floor. 'You start next week,' she said, as if he might not have known. Again he felt no need to reply and she seemed a little disconcerted. She tried again. 'Have you met the boss before?'

He nodded. 'At the interview.'

She smiled. 'Tread carefully, then. He can be unpredictable. Everyone calls him Mr Grumpy, and he's not in the best of moods this morning.' Mackenzie nodded, and they lapsed again into silence until they debouched from the lift on to floor three.

Beard had a corner office with windows on two walls. He was on the phone when Collins showed Mackenzie in, and he raised a finger to indicate that they should wait a moment. They stood uncomfortably just inside the door, unable to avoid eavesdropping on his side of the conversation.

'Well, fucking tell him to get the finger out!'

And as Beard listened to the response from his caller Mackenzie took a moment to make an appraisal of him. His new boss was a big man, a mop of curly fair hair above a florid round face. It was clear he was running out of patience. Steel-blue eyes turned chilly.

'If the report's not on my desk by noon I'll squeeze his balls till his eyes pop.' He slammed down the phone and looked at Mackenzie. But his mind was elsewhere. Then suddenly he was with them, and his expression changed. 'Mackenzie. Grab a seat.'

Mackenzie nodded and sat down. 'Good morning, sir.' He attempted a smile. 'I can see why they call you Mr Grumpy.'

Beard's eyes narrowed. 'Who fucking calls me Mr Grumpy?'

'Everyone, apparently.' Mackenzie glanced at the flushing Ms Collins, who appeared to have found a spot of extraordinary interest on the carpet.

Beard cocked an eyebrow and managed a tight little smile. 'Do they, now?'

Collins decided to meet his eye and brazen it out with a grin. Beard flicked his head towards the door. 'I'll see you later.'

As she turned her back on Beard she darted a venomous glance in Mackenzie's direction before slipping out into the hall. Beard leaned back in his swivel chair and eyed Mackenzie cautiously.

'You're a bit of an arsehole, Mackenzie, aren't you?'

'I have been told that, sir.'

'Have you?'

'But I'm not sure you can describe an arsehole in increments, sir. *Which* bit of the arsehole are we talking about? Is it a big bit, or a small bit?'

'In your case, Mackenzie, quite clearly it's the whole fucking thing.'

Mackenzie looked as if he might respond, but was overcome by a rare moment of restraint. Beard reached across his desk to lift a folder from an untidy pile of them. He pulled it towards himself and flipped it open.

'So what persuaded you that the NCA should be your next career move?'

'I think I explained that at the interview.'

Beard flicked him a look of irritation. 'You got the job, Mackenzie. This is not an interview. I want the real story.'

'I'm a cop, sir.'

'So why did you leave the Met?'

'Not really my choice.' He corrected himself. 'Well, it was. But one I was forced to make. In the jargon I think they call it constructive dismissal.'

Beard sat back and laced his fingers across his ample belly. 'Tell me.' Although he surely already knew.

Mackenzie drew a deep breath. 'They put me on every shit shift going, sir. I was spending most of my life behind a desk doing paperwork rather than police work. I have been repeatedly denied promotion.'

'Why?'

'Because nobody likes me very much.' There was neither rancour nor resentment in this. It was just a simple statement of fact.

Again, 'Why?'

'You would have to ask them that.'

'I'm asking you.'

Mackenzie took a moment to think about how he might frame his response. 'I think, sir, because I say it as I see it. My wife says I have no filter. That I lack tact.'

'Does she? And I suppose she would know. What kind of relationship do you have?'

'Fractured, sir. We're separated.'

This was clearly news to Beard. 'And whose idea was that?'

'Hers.'

Mackenzie's boss made a thoughtful moue with his lips. 'So . . .' he said, 'you think you know better than everyone else and aren't afraid to say so.'

'I think, sir, you'll find that in most cases I do know better than everyone else, and I am never afraid to say so.'

Beard cocked an eyebrow in surprise. 'Some people might characterize that as arrogance.'

'Yes, sir.'

'But not you.'

'I'd characterize it as honesty.'

Beard sat forward suddenly. 'Well, let me be honest with you, Mackenzie. You were not my first choice for this job. But other members of the recruitment board were impressed by your . . .' he swept his hand above the open folder in front of him '. . . credentials.' He lifted the top sheet. 'For my part, I have to wonder why a man with degrees in quantum physics and mathematics would want to be a cop.'

'I never wanted to be anything else sir. The degrees are just a hobby. I study at night on the Open University. I'm planning to take another.'

There was an almost imperceptible shake of Beard's head. 'And what might that be?'

'Astrophysics, sir.'

Which left Beard temporarily speechless. To recover himself he lifted another couple of sheets from the file. 'It says here your father was a police officer.'

'In Glasgow, yes. He was killed in the line of duty when I was two years old.'

Beard looked again at the sheet in front of him and a frown, like a shadow, passed momentarily across his face. His eyes flickered towards Mackenzie then away again, before he slipped the papers back in the file and closed it. He reclined in his chair once more. 'Well, the reason I asked you here this morning is because of your talent for languages. According to the file you are fluent in French, Spanish and Arabic.' He spat out each language as if it left a bad taste in his mouth.

'I took French and Spanish at school, sir. Quite easy really. Latin roots. I'm just starting on Italian. Arabic was much harder.'

'Ye-es,' Beard said, 'I can imagine.' Not a flicker of a smile. 'At any rate, it's your Spanish I'm interested in. It's two weeks since you finished up at the Met, yes?'

Mackenzie nodded.

'I know that technically you don't start with us until Monday.

But I want to farm you out on loan to my counterpart on the Fugitives Unit for a small job at the beginning of the week, and I need to brief you on it now. I owe him a favour, so I'm in his debt. If you do this for me I'll be in yours.'

'A little like *guanxi*, sir.'

Beard frowned. 'Gwanshee?'

'It's a concept in Chinese culture. A favour given is a favour owed.'

'Exactly. And a good way for you to start off on the right foot, don't you think?'

'Not really, sir. I'm assuming we operate on a command basis here, not an exchange of back-scratching. Since you are my boss I will do what you order me to.'

Beard held him in his steady gaze for a moment. 'I can see why nobody likes you, Mackenzie.' He sighed. 'I want you to go to Spain to accompany a prisoner back on a flight from Malaga. His name is Jack Cleland. Number one on our most wanted list. He pretty much ran the traffic in cocaine here in London until a deep-cover sting operation went wrong and he killed an undercover cop. Unfortunately he got away. We've long suspected he was hiding out somewhere on the Costa del Crime. We still have a good relationship with the Spanish police. Ran a joint operation for several years called Operation Captura. It netted us quite a few villains who'd secreted them-selves away on the costas, but we've never had so much as a sniff of Cleland.' He paused. 'Until now.'

'How did they get him?'

'Pure fucking chance. A couple of local cops in a district not far from Gibraltar went to investigate reports of a burglary at a villa in a very upmarket development overlooking the Med. Turned out not to be a burglary at all. It was Cleland's place. He'd been living there under an assumed name. Ian Templeton. His idea of a joke, apparently, since that was the name of his old headmaster at Glenalmond College.'

'He's Scottish, then?'

'You've heard of Glenalmond?' Beard clearly hadn't.

Mackenzie said, 'Of course. It's in Perthshire. They call it the Eton of the North.'

'Do they,' Beard said dryly. 'I take it you have no objection to nicking a fellow Scot?'

'None at all, sir. Particularly a toff. They teach them to be like little Englishmen up there.'

'Not like this fucking Englishman.'

'No, sir. I did say toff.'

Beard glared at him, but could detect no irony. He supposed that Mackenzie was probably incapable of disingenuity. 'Anyway, he and his girlfriend had left the house earlier in the day, telling neighbours that they were taking a short holiday. But it seems they'd left something behind, and returned only to discover they'd mislaid the keys. So they broke into their own place, and disabled the alarm before it went off. A neighbour saw lights in the house and called the police. Of course, when the cops arrived they had no idea that the couple in the villa weren't burglars. There was a shoot-out, and somehow

Cleland managed to gun down his own girlfriend. Shot her dead. A British citizen. Angela Fry. He was arrested, we were alerted, and a European Arrest Warrant was issued. He hasn't contested it in court, and the Spanish are happy to offload him on to us, since there were no Spanish casualties. He'll come back here to face charges of drug trafficking and murder.'

'When is it you want me to go, sir?'

'Fly out Tuesday afternoon. The Spanish will hand Cleland over at the airport. Armed escort on to the plane. Just a few formalities to be dealt with in Spanish, then you'll come back with him on the return flight. It'll get you in around eleven pm, and officers from the Met will meet you off the plane to take him into custody.' He smiled. 'Not too difficult for you?'

But Mackenzie was already wrestling with demons. He had realized at once that if he agreed, it would mean missing Sophia's school concert. Though much as it pained him, even he realized he could hardly offer that up as an excuse for not going to Spain. He fell back on a more valid pretext. 'I am afraid I have a family funeral in Glasgow on Monday, sir. I was going to alert HR. My aunt. I'll be there until Tuesday.'

Beard stroked his chin thoughtfully then reopened the file and sifted through the top sheets until he found what he was looking for. 'You were brought up by your aunt and uncle after the death of your father.'

Mackenzie said nothing.

'Is that right?'

'I was fostered by my father's brother and his wife after I was removed from the care of my mother.'

'Why were you taken from your mother?'

'She was an alcoholic. Apparently.'

'What happened to her?'

'I have no idea, sir.' He paused. 'And I don't really care.'

Beard regarded him curiously for a moment, then closed the file. 'I'll get them to reserve you a seat on a flight from Glasgow to Malaga on Tuesday then, and you can get the London flight back.' When Mackenzie did not respond immediately he canted his head to one side. 'Is there a problem?' Almost daring him to say that there was.

Mackenzie closed his eyes for a moment. An image of Sophia's sad little face creased with disappointment floated up through dark red, and he felt tears welling up behind the lids. He blinked several times. 'No, sir.'

CHAPTER FIVE

A smell like old socks drifted from the kitchen and followed him up the stairs. He had no idea what it was the old couple fried up in there, but it seemed only ever to reek of cabbage and onions. It was a depressing smell, one that had become synonymous with this house. And his unhappiness.

Earlier he had walked the length of Oxford Street in search of a black tie. Perhaps, he thought, black was no longer *de rigueur* at funerals. He was unpractised in contemporary burial rites.

The sun was out, the wind had swung to the south-west, and it was a balmy warm spring day. Pavements in sidestreets were crowded with tables and chairs, Londoners enjoying the promise of summer over the first premature salads of the year. Mackenzie had found a dark pub and ordered Scotch pie and beans, sipping on a beer, and putting off the moment when he would have to face the inevitable.

Back now in his gloomy bedsit, he indulged in further procrastination. The dormer faced north, so while sunshine washed across the rooftops beyond it, none found its way into

Mackenzie's room. He turned on the anglepoise and settled himself in his armchair with the file on Cleland that Beard had provided to brief him.

Cleland was thirty-six years old. Just eighteen months younger than Mackenzie. But while they belonged to the same generation, their experiences throughout what Mackenzie still thought of as his prologue years could hardly have been more different. Nor did they share a name, as might reasonably have been deduced. For while Jack was commonly a diminutive of John, it was what Cleland's parents had actually christened him.

Although his family lived in Edinburgh, he was boarded from the age of seven at Fettes, one of the most prestigious schools in the capital. Almost as if his parents had wanted him out of the way. And as soon as he turned twelve they sent him to Glenalmond. Neither school came cheap, and while there was nothing in the file about his family background, Mackenzie could only assume that his parents were independently wealthy.

From Glenalmond, Cleland had gone on to Oxford, where he read economics, and took a master's in Business Administration. Then followed a stellar career as a trader on the floor of one of the biggest investment banks in London, where he carved out a reputation for himself as a man with a keen eye for the deal. Then somehow, somewhere along the way, he had been presented with the deal of a lifetime. One that he simply couldn't resist. Only it wasn't currency or gilts or bonds that changed hands. It was cocaine.

He was hooked. Not on the drug itself, but the money it could make him. No one can deal drugs with impunity though, and soon enough he found himself trespassing on dangerous ground. Territory controlled by the biggest name in London's drug-trafficking underworld, a larger-than-life character known simply as 'The Boss'. The Boss was a fifty-something former cop called Ronnie Simms, so well connected he was regarded as untouchable. He laundered his illicit profits through the two dozen clubs and restaurants he owned around the capital.

According to sources, Simms took exception to Cleland's activities and ordered him 'taken out'. But the two thugs he sent to do his dirty work were no match for Cleland, who had long been a member of a gun club and possessed an impressive collection of firearms as well as an unerring eye. Legend had it that he shot one dead in his apartment then tortured the other into revealing who had sent them.

It was said that on learning the truth he took his favourite shotgun, with which he had won numerous clay-pigeon competitions, and walked boldly into one of Simms's private clubs. There he discharged both barrels into his would-be killer at point-blank range in an office above the dance floor. Afterwards he was alleged to have said to a gathering of Simms's ex-employees, 'The Boss is dead, long live The Boss,' and offered them continued employment in return for their absolute loyalty.

No one turned him down, and as Simms's successor Cleland earned himself the nickname 'Mad Jock'.

The circumstances in which the undercover operation went wrong were sketchy, and Mackenzie surmised that someone, somewhere, wanted as few details on the record as possible. Armed police officers stormed the same club in which Cleland had shot Simms. But Mad Jock had been tipped off. He killed the undercover cop who betrayed him, and got away through an adjoining building that he'd bought solely to provide an escape route in an emergency. No one outside of a tight inner circle even knew he owned it.

It was the last that anyone had seen of him. Until now.

Mackenzie closed the file and tossed it on to the settee. He felt suffused by a strange sense of anger. Cleland had been given every advantage in life. One of the best educations money could buy. As a trader he had no doubt made more money in a week than Mackenzie earned in a year. And yet in order to make even more he had turned his talents to trading in misery. His disregard for the law, for human life, his obvious sense of entitlement, made Mackenzie ashamed to call himself a fellow Scot. There would be a considerable sense of satisfaction, if not pleasure, in bringing this *toff* back to face justice.

He sat for some moments stewing on the thought, until he could no longer keep other considerations from displacing it.

Most of all Sophia.

His heart broke for her. And he could only imagine what

Susan would find to say when she learned that he was about to let one of his children down again. He drew his phone from his shirt pocket and held it in his hand for two, three minutes, maybe more. It wasn't until you had committed a thought to words or action that it took concrete form. He closed his eyes and wished he had some better excuse. But he would never lie to her.

He tapped on the Messenger app and reopened last night's conversation. She would be back from school by now, but there was no guarantee that she would be online. The coward in him hoped she wasn't.

– *Hi darling. Got bad news, I'm afraid.*

He waited, and his heart sank as her face appeared in a tiny circle beside the message to indicate that she was there and had read it.

– *What is it?* No preamble.

– *Daddy's not going to be able to make it to the concert on Tuesday night.* He didn't know how to frame it any less bluntly.

He waited, and the cursor blinked back at him for a long time before she finally responded.

– *Why not?*

– *It's work, baby. They're sending me to Spain, and I won't be back in time.* Not his fault. Surely she would see that?

Another wait. Longer this time. The blinking of the cursor was almost hypnotic. Then finally her response appeared on the screen.

A large sad face.

– Honey, I'm so sorry. Maybe I could take you out somewhere on Wednesday night, and you could sing your song just for me.

When he hit return this time, her face in the tiny circle was gone, replaced by a tick. The message had been sent, but not received. Sophia had gone offline.

CHAPTER SIX

Ana can feel the heat of the sun on her skin as it beats through the window. Although she has many fewer olfactory receptors than her guide dog, those she has are more sensitive now. She has his scent stored in some inner filing cabinet, easily accessed, and can tell that he is not far away. Almost certainly lying basking sleepily in the heat where sunlight falls in warm wedges across the floor.

She can smell Cristina's shampoo. Some floral scent. But chemical somehow, like nothing found in nature. She can separate it from her niece's perfume. But above all she can smell her gun. An unpleasant metallic smell. Sharp. Disagreeable. Cristina said they had taken it away for tests and only given it back to her today. Perhaps they had discharged it to check the ballistics, for Ana is sure she can identify the acrid reek of nitroglycerine – something she remembers from the chemistry lab at her secondary school. How long ago that seems now.

Outside, there are children playing in the Plaza de Juan Bazán, among the flowers that hang in profusion from pots fixed around its whitewashed walls. But she can't hear the children. And will never see the red and pink blooms, or the shrubs that grow green around the tiny fountains catching sunlight in the late afternoon.

But though she can neither see nor hear she senses something else. Something in the air. Something that can only be felt. Divined in some way beyond her understanding.

It is fear. And it seeps, it seems, from every pore of the young woman sitting opposite.

In the normal course of events Cristina would come every other day, alternating with her sister. But since Nuri's illness she has been more often. Taking her sister's place on the days that Nuri is at the hospital in Marbella, or just too sick to get out of bed. Ana appreciates the visits from her late sister's girls. A sister ten years her senior, and ten years dead, leaving Ana as her surrogate, a focus for the love of daughters for their lost mother. They are bright moments in the darkness that fills her each and every day, a delicious relief from the monotony of incarceration. Though it is technology which has released her finally from the confines of her physical self, her own body having raised an impenetrable barrier to the outside world, trapping her within, denying her sight and sound.

Sitting here in the window, with the sun warm on her skin, she now has that world at her fingertips. Literally. A keyboard linked to a computer that powers a screen that can generate Braille. She can surf the internet, reaching out to interpret the dots on her screen with long sensitive fingers, reading of world affairs, of history and scientific advance, or even just of family gossip on Facebook. With her keyboard she can interact with others online. She can place phone calls through a special operator, speak to someone at the other end, and have their responses relayed to her in Braille by the operator. The whole universe reduced to raised patterns of dots on a screen.

Sometimes she remembers what it was like to see and hear, but it is too painful to dwell upon it. You can never regain what is lost beyond retrieval.

Accept and adapt. That has been her constant mantra through most of the last twenty-five years, ever since she first learned of her impending self-imposed prison sentence. But even after all this time, acceptance of that life sentence is still the hardest part.

The anger has never subsided.

People think she has found solace in God. Her daily pilgrimage with Sandro to the church, holding his leash with a trust she would find it hard to place in any human being. Along to the end of Calle San Miguel, feeling the cobbles under her feet, the smell of meat that comes from the *carnicería*, fresh bread from the *despacho de pan*. Left into Calle Portada, heat spilling from the open door of the *peluquería* along with the acrid smell of peroxide and the pungent faux fruit of fresh shampoo. Careless people in a hurry, brushing past her, breathing garlic and smoke into warm morning air. Then right into Calle San Antonio and the long descent to the Iglesia Nuestra Señora de los Remedios in the Plaza San Francisco, inhaling the perfume of the flowers, the delicious aroma of fresh-ground coffee, the snacks in preparation in tapas bars near the foot of the street.

She feels the cool of the church the moment Sandro leads her through the doors. People come here to light their candles and kneel before the Virgin, praying for many things: a better life, pregnancy, wealth, good health. Ana kneels on the cold slabs, eyes closed, and silently vents her anger at the god who took away what others take for granted. Her sight, her hearing. Her life. If only she had been born deaf and blind she would never have missed those senses, would have known nothing else. But what cruelty was it to give her both, then take them away? What kind of god plays a trick like that?

So what others take for devotion is really recrimination, the anger she cannot let go. And after all, who else is there to blame?

Now she sits in her accustomed seat, feeling Cristina's anxiety in the patterned dots that raise themselves on her screen. The whole sordid story told in graphic detail, from her fateful decision to answer the call in place of Diego, to the shooting of the girl in the villa. Sitting opposite, with her own keyboard and her own screen, she is typing almost faster than Ana can read, tension in every keystroke, apprehension in every word.

Ana is puzzled. She says, 'But none of it is your fault, *cariño*. You hurt no one. This man killed his own lover.'

Cristina types rapidly.

– *But it is me he blames, Aunt Ana. He says if I had not entered his home illegally with my weapon drawn there would have been no shooting. His Angela would still have been alive.*

55

'But it was him who broke into the house, not you. He was the one in possession of an illegal weapon. And it was him who shot the poor girl.'

– *And it's him who's threatened to kill me and every member of my family if he ever gets free.*

'Oh, my darling girl, people say things like that in the heat of the moment, overcome by anguish and anger. Deep down he must know it's his own fault. And, anyway, he's in custody isn't he? In no position to do you any harm.'

– *He is to be extradited back to the UK. The courts have agreed to it and he has not contested the decision.*

'Well there you are then, *cariño*. Soon he'll be back in his own country and will forget all about you. When do they take him away?'

– *They bring him back from Madrid today, and a police officer from the UK will come to Malaga tomorrow to take him to London.*

Ana senses there is something more. It is impossible to say how she feels such things, but they gather somehow in the air around her and she can almost touch them. 'And?' she says.

– *It's ironic, Aunt Ana. The Guardia will take him in an armoured truck to the airport in the afternoon, and Paco told me today that he will be among the detail assigned to guard him. My own brother-in-law! It is just as well that this man Cleland will never know.*

Ana smiles. 'Well there you are, then, *mi niña*. He couldn't be in safer hands.'

CHAPTER SEVEN

The Linn Crematorium sprawled across a hill on the south side of the city to the west of Castlemilk, a housing estate built in the 1950s to accommodate people cleared from Glasgow's inner-city slums. It was built around an old mansion called Castlemilk House, constructed on the site of a thirteenth-century castle. But there was nothing in the rows of drab pebbledash blocks that bore any resemblance to the castle which had inspired their name.

When Mackenzie stepped off the plane at Glasgow Airport it was overcast and drizzling, what Scots called *smirr*. It was in stark contrast with the sunshine he had left behind in London.

He felt an odd sensation returning to the city of his birth, the place where he had spent the first seventeen years of his life. Unhappy years remembered now as having passed entirely on days like this, grey and sunless and wet. He wore a dark suit, a white shirt, and the black tie he had eventually found in a men's outfitters in Fleet Street. In a holdall he carried a change of underwear and his toilet bag. Just one night in this haunted town before flying out tomorrow to Spain.

Through the window of his taxi, he watched rain-streaked red sandstone tenements drift past, the colour leeched from them somehow by lack of light, like watching a black-and-white movie of his childhood spool by. None of it seemed familiar and he had not the least sense of belonging.

The south-side suburbs were greener, tree-lined streets in leaf, the huddled hulk of Hampden Park floating past as they climbed the hill towards the crematorium. Through wrought-iron gates bearing the city crest and the date 1962, then down a long curving drive, past the departing mourners from the previous cremation, to the concrete and coloured glass structure that offered faith and flames in unequal measure.

Mackenzie felt self-conscious, still clutching his overnight bag as he stepped from the taxi. No time to drop it off at his uncle's house before the funeral.

There were only three vehicles left in the car park, and just five souls in the waiting room. At first he thought he'd made a mistake with the time, for he didn't recognize any of them. But then was shocked to realize that the white-haired old man with the stoop and the silvered bristles on a cadaverous face was his Uncle Arthur. The old man's suit looked several sizes too big for him, the collar of his shirt curled up at both sides. The knot in his tie pulled far too tight. The colour seemed washed out of his once bright blue eyes, leaving them a pale, insipid grey. He was diminished in every way. Mackenzie remembered, with guilty regret, almost relishing the opportunity to confront his uncle at his aunt's funeral. No pleasure now in *sticking it* to this shadow of a man who had once been a vigorous and robust teacher of physical education. Almost as if his uncle had contrived to deny him even that.

The old man extended a big hand, deformed by arthritis, and Mackenzie felt obliged to shake it. Shiny reptilian skin like crêpe paper crinkling in his palm. He was anxious to let it go, but his uncle held on and placed his other hand over the back of Mackenzie's.

'Good to see you, John. I'm glad you could come.'

Mackenzie had no idea what to say. He had harboured such hatred over all these years, he was unprepared for the warmth in his uncle's handshake and the apparent affection in his watery washed-out eyes. Had the old man forgotten how much he disliked his nephew, how often he had dished out discipline with Mr Kane, or with the tawse that he sometimes brought home with him from school – half an inch of thick leather strap divided in two at one end, and delivered on to the palms of outstretched hands, leaving stinging weals on the inside of the wrists?

Had he forgotten all the harsh words, the derision, the contempt, perhaps even jealousy, for the prodigy his brother had bequeathed him? Had he forgotten that final shouting match which had sent Mackenzie running to his room to pack a bag and leave, never to return?

'Your Aunt Hilda missed you, you know. A wee card now and then wouldn't have gone astray,' he said, and Mackenzie realized that nothing had changed. The hurt was just delivered in a different way.

They arrived back at the house in Giffnock mid-afternoon. The bungalow was as gloomy as Mackenzie remembered it. There must surely have been sunny days, but he had no recollection of them. The first thing he saw in the hall was the umbrella stand, crowded with old brollies and walking sticks – and the onyx-handled Mr Kane. Mackenzie could barely take his eyes off it. He wanted to take the damned thing and break it over his thigh, as if somehow that could erase the pain it had been used to administer through all the miserable years he had lived in this house. Instead, he followed the handful of mourners past the coat-rack and into the front room where whisky was poured into cut crystal glasses and sipped in a silence broken only by the odd mumbled reminiscence.

They didn't stay long, and Mackenzie was glad to see them go. In spite of the rain he thought he might go for a walk. He wanted to spend as little time in the house as possible, and even less of it in the company of his uncle. When there were just the two of them left he said to the old man, 'I'll put my stuff in my room. The same one, I take it?'

His uncle nodded. 'You'll find it pretty much as you left it, son. She kept it for you just the way it was, in case you ever came back.'

He spoke of his wife in death with a respect he had never shown her in life. Mackenzie remembered how she had always lowered her voice in his presence, tiptoeing around his unpredictable sensibilities, bearing with extraordinary fortitude the words he flung at her in frequent rage.

Mackenzie found the pole with the hook on the end of it leaning in the corner of the hall where it had always stood. He raised it above his head to open the hatch in the ceiling and pull down the ladders that led to the attic conversion they had made for him. Although there were two bedrooms in the house, Uncle Arthur used one of them as a study. A place on which he could close the door to be disturbed only on pain of punishment.

There had been no space in the hall for a staircase to the new attic room, and so the pull-down ladders had been the compromise solution. One that his uncle had grown to regret when the young Mackenzie retreated to his room after rows, pulling the ladders up after him like a drawbridge, so that neither his aunt nor his uncle could reach him. He had once spent almost forty-eight hours barricaded in his room after a particularly tempestuous argument, pissing and defecating in a porcelain chanty kept under the bed.

He climbed the ladder now, ascending to his past. And as he stood and took in his old room, goosebumps raised themselves on the back of his neck. The old man had been right. Almost nothing had changed. There were even hairs still trapped among the bristles of his old brush on the dresser. He felt like the ghost of himself haunting his own childhood. Everything about this room – the very air he breathed in it – took him back. He sat on the bed and wanted to weep for the unhappy child he had been, but no tears would come. Just cold, hard memories.

For an adult so disinclined to violence, as a young boy he had fought and usually beaten every bully who took him on. The young John Mackenzie was incapable of backing down. So often returning home bloodied and bruised.

If it wasn't physical fighting with other boys, it was verbal conflict with his teachers. He had lost count of the number of times he received punishment for his insolence, for his inattention, or the failure to do his homework. And then they had wondered how it was possible that he could score straight A's when it came to the exams. No one ever gave him credit for his achievements, expressing instead only astonishment.

How stupid had they been not to realize how much smarter he was than them? That the only reason his attention wandered was *their* mediocrity, *their* inability to engage his interest? That he only ever questioned them because *he* almost always knew better?

Looking back now he thought that his uncle must have realized early on that Mackenzie was his intellectual superior, and that if he couldn't best him mentally he would do it physically. He had been a powerful man then, a professional footballer in his youth before qualifying as a gym teacher, a job that had given him carte blanche to bully the physically inferior. Boys that were overweight, or had flat feet, or were just *soft*. Or his brother's fatherless son given in to his care. He was unused to children answering back, unaccustomed to contradiction, traits he was determined to beat out of his young nephew.

But there had come a time when Mackenzie could match him physically too, a hormonal teenager pumped up by testosterone and anger. And his uncle had no longer been able to dominate him in any sense.

Still, he'd had one devastating card left to play. One that he had been saving for just the right moment. One that could deliver pain far beyond any corporal hurt.

He had played it, finally, when Mackenzie announced that he wasn't going to university, despite having achieved A grades in each of the seven Highers he had sat at the end of fifth year. He was going to join the police, he said.

His uncle had railed at him claiming, not unreasonably, that it would be a criminal waste of his academic abilities – some kind of pun intended. But the young Mackenzie hadn't wanted to hear it.

Now, as he sat on the bed, he heard the distant echoes of the shouting match in the hall downstairs.

'You're a bloody idiot, boy! Christ knows, you've been a pain in the arse all through school, but you've a God-given talent. Don't throw it away. Why the hell would you want to be a policeman?'

'Because that's what my dad was.'

His uncle had exhaled his contempt through pursed lips. 'Your *dad*! For Christ's sake, don't go wasting your life like he did.'

'He didn't waste his life!' Mackenzie had been incensed.

'Yes he did. He was a total waster, your father. Mr High and Bloody Mighty. Thought he was better than everyone else. Just like you. Thought he knew it all, that nothing was beyond him. Well he learned the hard fucking way just how wrong he was.'

Mackenzie remembered being shocked. In all the years his uncle had beaten and berated him, he had never heard him use the F word. He screamed back, 'You're just jealous!'

'Jealous?' The old man almost laughed. 'Jealous of what?'

'That he sacrificed his life to save someone else. While you frittered yours away. A lifetime bullying boys in school gyms, picking on the weak to make yourself look big.' Mackenzie had caught sight, then, of his aunt standing in the kitchen doorway, the blood drained from her face, apprehension in her eyes. 'Well, no one's fooled, Uncle Arthur. For all your size you're a little man, and everyone knows it.'

An index finger like a rod of iron extended from his uncle's fist and jabbed into his nephew's chest. His eyes were wild and he leaned in close, so that Mackenzie could smell the whisky on his breath and see the spittle gathering on his lips. 'Don't you speak to me like that you little runt. Time you got your fucking facts straight.'

'Arthur, don't!' Mackenzie could hear the fear in his aunt's voice, but there was no strength in it, and her husband would ignore her as he always did.

'No one ever disavowed you of the crap you were told about your dad. Don't tell him the truth, they said, it could scar him for life. So we didn't. All this fucking time, and we let you go on believing what a hero he was, just in case you might be *damaged* by it.' He couldn't hide his scorn. 'Well, you're a big boy now, sonny. Big enough to handle the truth, I'd say. How about you?'

For once in his life Mackenzie found himself suddenly at a loss for words. A sick sense of dread began to weigh like lead in his gut, then slowly suffused his entire being like a fast-acting poison. It robbed him of his ability to speak.

'Please Arthur . . .' A pleading in his aunt's voice now, but there would be no stopping him. The dam which had held back the bile for all these years was finally bursting. The finger stabbed into Mackenzie's chest in time to the rhythm of his uncle's anger, which had now achieved an oddly lyrical cadence. 'You think he was a hero, eh? A brave man risking his life to try and save that poor fucking woman?' He sucked in air to fuel his fury. 'Well, there's nothing brave about suicide, sonny. That's the coward's way out.'

A noise like tinnitus filled the teenager's head, trying to drown out the words. But still, above it, he heard the wail that escaped his aunt's lips, a strangely feral sound.

'He screwed up, your dad. Disobeyed a direct order. Because, of course, he knew better. Like he always fucking did. Went charging in to try and rescue her, only to get her killed.' He was breathing stertorously now, as if he had just sprinted the length of a football pitch to score a goal. 'Some hero, eh? It was in all the fucking papers. And everyone knew he was my brother. You wouldn't believe the shit I got at school. And then he goes and makes it worse. Cos, being your dad, he couldn't stand it that he was wrong. That he had fucked up. So he took a rope, tied one end around his neck and the other around the top rail of the stairwell, and jumped off.'

Mackenzie stood, eyes blazing, tears blurring vision. Anger, fear, disbelief, pain, all filling the chaotic space that was his mind. He lashed out, knocking his uncle's fist away and pushed him hard in the chest with both hands. Big man though he was, his uncle staggered back. 'You're a liar!' Mackenzie screamed at him. 'You're only trying to hurt me.'

'Nothing hurts quite as much as the truth, sonny,' his uncle said, and he seemed suddenly calm again, anger replaced by triumph.

The teenage Mackenzie lunged for the umbrella stand and pulled out Mr Kane, holding it by the capped end, and swinging the onyx handle at his uncle's head. He heard his aunt scream as her husband drew back in alarm, and the handle buried itself in the wall. His uncle snatched it from him, and Mackenzie prepared himself to be on its receiving end, as he had been many times before. But his Uncle Arthur just stood, clutching it in his white-knuckled hand, and screamed, 'Get out of my fucking house, you little bastard.'

The words reverberated through Mackenzie's memory as he sat on the bed and saw his seventeen-year-old self climbing up through the hatch to stuff whatever clothes he could grab into his sports holdall. They were the last moments he had spent in this room until his return today, twenty years later. The hurt had never gone away, even though he had learned to sublimate it, locking it up in the darkest recesses of his mind, in those places that everyone keeps for hiding their demons.

The last sight he had of his aunt was caught in a backward glance as he slammed the front door behind him, a fleeting glimpse of the tears that wet her cheeks. He had never seen her again, until watching her coffin today as it slipped through the curtain towards the flames.

His first stop before buying a one-way ticket to London at Glasgow Central railway station had been the cuttings library of the *Glasgow Herald*. It took very little time, searching the archive, to find the report on the suicide of a Glasgow police officer found hanging by the neck in the stairwell of his tenement home in Partick. He had gone almost straight to it, because he knew that his father's death had fallen just two days before his thirty-first birthday. Without making a direct connection, the single-column piece referred to his attempt the previous month to rescue a woman taken hostage by an escapee from a psychiatric prison in Lanarkshire.

Flicking back through the editions of the paper, he had found the original report. The police officer concerned, unnamed in this story, had defied orders to await the arrival of an expert in hostage situations, deeming the threat to the woman's life imminent. His attempt to rescue her, at the risk of his own life, had failed. Her captor had slit her throat with a butcher's knife, so forcefully that he had very nearly decapitated her.

Mackenzie rose stiffly from his old bed and knew that there would be very little sleep for him tonight. He opened the Velux window in the slope of the ceiling and looked down into a back garden grown wild with neglect. It had once, he remembered, been his Aunt Hilda's pride and joy. Hours spent weeding borders, planting annuals, pruning her precious roses. And it only occurred to him now that all that time spent in her garden was her way of escaping from Arthur.

An odd sound rose up from the house below, like a muffled cough, repetitive and raw. Curiosity got the better of him and Mackenzie climbed carefully down the ladders into the gloom of the hall. The light outside was fading.

But it wasn't until he pushed open the kitchen door and saw the old man seated at the table, head in hands, that he realized it was sobbing he had heard. A painful retching sob that tore itself with involuntary regularity from his uncle's chest.

Mackenzie stood watching him impassively for several long moments before the old man became aware of his presence. He turned red-rimmed eyes towards his nephew and swallowed to catch his breath. He said, in a voice like torn sandpaper, 'I don't . . . I can't . . .' He sucked in a trembling breath. 'I don't know how I can go on without her.'

CHAPTER EIGHT

It's a hot one. The words of Santana's 'Smooth' reverberated around Cleland's head like an earworm. And he tried to stay *cool* just like in the song. But it was hard in the olid airless space of this armoured truck. He wore a pair of freshly pressed linen trousers and a crisp white shirt, brought to his cell first thing that morning by his *abogado* before they transferred him to the truck. He had showered, shampooed and deodorized, determined to look and feel his best. But already his thick, blond-streaked brown hair had fallen across a forehead beaded by sweat. He felt a trickle of it run down the back of his neck.

If he could, he would have held his breath. Neither of the armed Guardia who sat with him in the back of the truck had showered this morning, of that he was certain. The stink of stale body odour and last night's garlic filled the air. But he tried hard to remain impassive, keeping his own counsel.

He could feel the smooth surface of the AP7 motorway beneath the tyres. They had not yet, he knew, reached Marbella, a town classier than most along this stretch of coast. The Cannes of the costas, he had heard it called. It was here, and in Puerto Banus, that he shopped for his clothes in the best boutiques, where he bought his wines in the most discerning stores – Priorat a favourite, a Catalan wine rarely available in this southern part of Spain, its grapes cultivated in a unique *terroir* of black slate and quartz soil many kilometres to the north.

He sat on the bench opposite his two guards, leaning forward, elbows on his knees, hands cuffed together between his thighs. He endeavoured not to look at his captors for fear of igniting the rage that burned inside him, a rage that he had kept tamped down with reluctant restraint, a patient biding of time.

The truck slowed. One of the guards stood up and slid aside a small hatch that opened through bars to the front cab. 'What's happening?'

'*Peaje*,' the driver called back. They were approaching the tollbooths at the San Pedro turn-off.

The Guardia slid the hatch shut and resumed his seat. But instead of coming to a stop immediately, the van swung right and made a long looping curve down the off-ramp before coming to a juddering halt.

'What the hell . . . ?' The officer was on his feet again and pulling the hatch open. He could see quite clearly that they were at the tollbooth on the exit road. 'Where are you going?' They were all jumpy.

'Diversionary route,' the driver shouted above the rumble of the engine. 'They said the *autopista* would be too risky.' The guard glanced at the armed officer who sat up front with the driver, but all he did was shrug. Nothing to do with him.

Again the hatch slammed shut and the officer sat down heavily as the truck lurched off on the uneven surface of the road. This would not be as smooth a journey as the motorway. He glanced at his fellow Guardia then glared at Cleland. The prisoner sensed eyes on him and raised his own to meet them. The guard immediately looked away, uncomfortable.

They bounced and bumped over a deformed and potholed road, the truck leaning dangerously at times on its camber. Ten or fifteen minutes passed before Cleland felt the driver turn the wheel sharply, and the tarmac beneath them gave way to a rutted uneven surface. Cleland's eyes were fixed now on the guards opposite. He could see that they knew there was something wrong. Then apprehension morphed to alarm as the truck skidded to an abrupt halt. The guard nearest the hatch was on his feet again. But before he could open it, raised voices and gunshots resounded from the cab beyond. And then silence. His hand withdrew from the hatch as if his fingers had made contact with red-hot metal, and it moved instead towards his holster.

He caught Cleland's eye and the almost imperceptible shake of the prisoner's head caused his hand to freeze on the leather. Slowly he sat down again, and lowered his gaze to stare at the floor. Perhaps, Cleland thought, like a child this guard believed that if he couldn't see he wouldn't be seen.

There were more voices now, shouting beyond the rear

doors of the truck, before a single gunshot reverberated around its interior and the doors swung open. Sunlight flooded in, blinding the three men inside. Half a dozen men clustered in silhouette at the back of the vehicle, the dust of a dry dirt road still hanging in the air behind them. Cleland rose calmly to his feet and walked to the open doors. He held out his hands for someone to unlock and remove the cuffs. Then someone else placed a pistol in his open palm. He weighed it for a moment, checked that the safety catch was off, and that there was a round in the chamber before turning back into the darkness.

The two guards remained seated, side by side, inert with fear.

'Hey!' Cleland shouted at them, and both men reluctantly looked up to meet his eye. 'Which of you is Paco?'

Paco's eyes opened wide with alarm, and he glanced at his fellow officer, the one who had been so preoccupied with the hatch. Then returned them to meet Cleland's. Paco was a young man. Twenty-six or twenty-seven. Short dark hair, a well-defined jaw shaved to a shadowed shine. His mouth was as dry as desert sand. He could not summon enough saliva even to swallow. His voice came in a whisper. 'I am.'

Cleland nodded and raised his pistol to shoot Paco's colleague in the head. Warm blood and brain tissue spattered across Paco's face and he released an involuntary cry as his fellow Guardia slumped heavily to the floor.

Cleland leaned in, using the barrel of his gun to force Paco's face around to meet his. He said, 'You tell Cristina that I'm coming for her. You understand?' Paco nodded. 'Good.' Cleland raised his gun to point it at Paco's head and for a moment the young man thought he was going to die. Then Cleland smiled and lowered his weapon to shoot Paco in the thigh. Paco screamed and Cleland leaned in again. 'Don't forget now.' And as he straightened up. 'Better get that seen to before you bleed to death.'

The last Paco saw of Mad Jock was his shadow as he jumped down into the blaze of light beyond the truck, and the callused hands that reached up to grasp him.

CHAPTER NINE

Sunlight cut sharp shadows into the mountains that spread their volcanic tendrils down through the coastal plane to the sea. Malaga gathered itself around the long curve of the bay and spilled out along the coastline east and west, as well as reaching back through fertile valleys into the plantations that climbed up into the Andalusian interior.

Mackenzie's plane banked as it came in to land, and he saw the vibrant blue of the sea shimmering in the afternoon light. The plane had encountered some gentle turbulence as it descended over the mountains, but the sky was cloudless, and the pilot had told them that the temperature on the ground was in the high twenties. It was hard to believe that just over three hours ago he had been standing in the departure lounge at Glasgow watching rain run like tears down the glass, blurring the runway and reducing the sky to a grey smudge.

He tried not to think too much about his uncle, or the strange compassion which had overcome him as he watched the old man weeping at the kitchen table. He had not, Mackenzie was certain, deserved his nephew's sympathy. And yet Mackenzie had found himself making a pot of tea, sitting down with him at the table, talking him through Hilda's illness, the life that lay ahead, and how he would have to adapt to it.

Advice, he thought ironically, that he might have given himself in the wake of his separation from Susan. But separation was not death, even if it felt like it.

He had phoned to order a delivery of Indian from the restaurant at Clarkston Toll, and the two of them had shared a bottle of cheap white wine and eaten lamb bhuna Madras in an oddly comforting silence.

As suspected, he had barely slept, and climbed stiffly out of his bed to dress while it was still dark. At the foot of the ladders, he had heard the old man breathing heavily through his sleep in the back bedroom, and crept into the kitchen to leave him a note. He thought for several long minutes with the pen in his hand before scribbling his address. Then, *I'll be here for the next few weeks if you need me*. And signing it simply, *John*.

He did not expect to hear from him, and hoped that he would not, but something had compelled him to make the offer. He had no idea what or why.

The terminal building was crowded with holidaymakers. Men in cargo shorts and brightly coloured shirts wheeling enormous suitcases, women in short skirts and print dresses and oversized sunglasses, anticipation in their raised voices of sunshine and sangria. Mackenzie felt conspicuous in his dark suit, and although he had dispensed with the black tie, he wore his depression like a shroud. Had anyone paid him the least attention, they would have known he was not here on holiday.

In his briefing he had been told he would be taken to a secure room at the airport where Cleland would be held under armed guard. There would be paperwork to be signed. A formality. But it was important that Mackenzie read it all carefully before signing. Which is why they had wanted someone fluent in Spanish. He and Cleland would then be escorted on to the aeroplane by armed officers who would leave the aircraft only when all other passengers had boarded and it was ready to depart. Cleland would be hand and leg-cuffed, and be removed from the plane on landing by officers of the Metropolitan police. Mackenzie, Beard had told him, would be no more than a glorified babysitter.

Mackenzie was expecting to be met by someone at the gate. He stood waiting impatiently for fifteen minutes, during which time his fellow passengers disembarked and headed off along a concourse that vanished into a lost and echoing distance. Announcements over the public address system made no reference to him in either English or Spanish.

Finally, reluctantly, he set off along the concourse himself. He had not anticipated having to clear passport control, remaining airside and never officially entering Spain. But in the absence of any information to the contrary he joined the queue at international arrivals and took out his iPhone. To his annoyance he found that it was not yet logged into the local server. He could not even call London to clarify his situation. He sighed his frustration and felt his blood pressure rising. Why was it that people were incapable of making plans and sticking to them?

He supposed that maybe someone might be waiting for him beyond passport control, but if so why had he not been told? It was a further ten minutes before he was syphoned off with others from the lengthening queue for the automatic passport readers, and invited across a white line to face an immigration officer who glared at him through a glass screen. Mackenzie slipped his passport through the hatch and glared back. An electronic reader below the counter scanned his biometric details before his passport was pushed back at him, and a flick of the head welcomed him to Spain.

There was no one waiting to greet him on the other side. No one raising a card with *Mackenzie* scrawled on it. Mackenzie was at a loss. He checked his phone and saw with relief that he now had a signal. He dialled the NCA and listened to it ringing two thousand miles away.

'National Crime Agency, how may I help you?'

'This is Investigator John Mackenzie. Could you put me through to Director Beard?'

'The Director is not here today.'

'You must have an emergency number for him.'

'Is this an emergency?'

'No, I want to wish him happy birthday. Of course it's a

fucking emergency!' He closed his eyes and cursed himself for swearing.

'One moment.' Not a hint in the voice at the other end that his sarcasm had even registered.

Mackenzie sighed again. Why bother asking him to wait *one moment* when they both knew it was going to be much longer than that. In fact it was almost three minutes before the operator got back to him.

'I'm sorry, Director Beard is not contactable right now. Can I take a message?'

Mackenzie fought to control his anger. 'Tell him that John Mackenzie called and that it is very important he call me back as soon as possible.'

He returned the phone to his shirt pocket and looked about him, at a loss for what to do now. This was not going well. On an impulse he decided to follow the signs to baggage reclaim. From there he knew it would be possible to exit the terminal building itself. Perhaps someone would be waiting there.

As he cleared the customs hall, Mackenzie found himself confronted by a crowd of taxi and shuttle drivers all holding up cards. He scanned them quickly to establish that his name was not among them, then stepped through sliding glass doors on to a concrete apron thick with boisterous holi-daymakers. Streams of people headed off towards a tunnel where taxis and shuttle buses and private cars came and went with relentless frequency. Others crossed a roadway to a multi-storey car park.

Mackenzie felt a rush of insecurity. He remembered his first day at school, taking a wrong turning on the way home after what had felt like an endless day. In all the years since, he had not experienced such a complete sense of loss and bewilderment. He had absolutely no idea what to do. The flight to London was scheduled to depart in two hours. If no one had contacted him before then, he decided that he would simply fly home. He carried the electronic ticket in his inside jacket pocket.

Across the concourse he spotted a tapas restaurant called Gambrinus and realized quite suddenly that he was hungry. Breakfast had consisted of coffee and a croissant at Glasgow Airport, hours ago now. He was about to head for the restaurant and get something to eat when he spotted the blue and white chequered stripes of a white Nissan SUV pulling up at the kerb short of the tunnel. *Policía Local* was painted across its doors. A petite uniformed policewoman scrambled out of the driver's door, reaching back for a square of white card. She slammed the door shut before hurrying across the concourse towards the entrance to the arrivals hall.

Mackenzie inclined his head as she scurried past him and saw the word *MCKENZEE* scrawled on her card in the blue ink of a felt-tipped pen.

'Señora,' he called after her, and she glanced back without stopping. He raised his voice in fluent Spanish, although he had not actually spoken it in some time. 'I think maybe you're looking for me.'

This time she stopped and looked at him a little more closely. She raised her card at the same time as her eyebrows, silently asking if he was the *MCKENZEE* she was looking for. The card was upside down. He indicated as much with a turn of his finger. She looked at it and quickly turned it the right way up. He walked towards her.

'Only that's not how you spell it. It's M-A-C, with an I-E at the end.'

She frowned, and he saw that she was flushed and flustered and perspiring freely.

'And you're late. I mean is this really how you people operate? I expected to be met at the gate by . . .' He glanced at her uniform for some indication of rank. But there was none, just a police insignia to the right of the reflective yellow across her chest, the word *Policía* in grey on the left. A checkered black and white strip beneath the yellow of her otherwise black uniform suggested that she might be nothing more than a lowly constable. The only marking on either sleeve was a green and white patch sewn on to her upper left arm and bearing the legend *Policía Local Marviña*. He hesitated. 'By . . . someone more senior.'

She bristled. 'Someone other than a woman, you mean?'

Mackenzie bristled back. 'Armed guards, I was told. I should have remained airside the whole time. And where is Cleland?'

Her face coloured, and a little of her self-assurance drained away. 'The exchange has been cancelled.'

'Why?'

'Señor Cleland escaped.'

Mackenzie was momentarily speechless. Then, 'Escaped?' It hardly seemed possible. And all that went through his mind was that he had missed Sophia's school concert for nothing. 'Jesus Christ!' He rarely blasphemed, believing it to indicate a paucity of vocabulary. But in that moment, as when he had sworn at the receptionist over the telephone, he lacked any other words to give adequate expression to his feelings.

She was defensive. 'The armoured vehicle bringing him to the airport was attacked by armed men. Three of his guards were shot dead and a fourth seriously wounded.' She thrust a hand towards him. 'My name is Cristina Sánchez Pradell, an officer of the Policía Local at Marviña. I have been sent by my *Jefe* to bring you to our police station.'

Mackenzie ignored her outstretched hand. 'No, no, no. My instructions were to accompany Cleland back to the UK aboard the British Airways flight to London that departs in' – he looked at his watch – 'just under two hours. If you don't have him, I'm going back into the airport to get myself something to eat, and then catch that flight home on my own. Nothing I can do here.'

Cristina withdrew her hand, her face hardening as she thrust her jaw towards him. 'My instructions are to take you to Marviña.'

'Why?'

'I'm sorry, señor, as a low-ranking police officer of the female gender, that's above my pay grade.' She had no idea how senior an officer Mackenzie might be, and realized she was sailing dangerously close to insubordination.

It was not lost on Mackenzie. He glowered at her. 'Well I don't care what your instructions are. I am not answerable to you or your *Jefe*.'

'No señor. But as I understand it, this has been agreed by your *Jefe* in London.'

'What?' Mackenzie was startled. 'Rubbish!' He pulled out his phone and hit redial. But after further dialogue with the operator at the NCA, and more waiting, it was established that Beard was still unavailable. As was his deputy. Mackenzie ended the call in frustration. Cristina watched him implacably, though he was convinced he saw something like satisfaction lurking behind her dark brown eyes.

'Maybe you'd like me to take your bag,' she said, reaching for the handles of his holdall.

He held it away from her. 'I'm quite capable of carrying it myself, thank you.' And he set off walking briskly towards where she had parked the police SUV.

Cristina pursed her lips in annoyance and followed.

They drove in silence out of the airport, past rows of cheap car rental firms and long-term parking sheds, past the San Miguel brewery and up the ramp on to the A7 to join the traffic heading west.

The sun beat relentlessly through the side windows of the Nissan as the road climbed up out of Malaga, and sent light coruscating across the Mediterranean below. A gentle sea breeze blew hot among the fronds of the tall palms that sprouted from every housing development along the clifftops.

It wasn't until fifteen minutes had passed, and they swung off on to the AP7 toll motorway, that Mackenzie finally asked, 'Where is Marviña?'

'Beyond Estepona.' Cristina glanced across to the passenger seat and saw that this meant nothing to him. She added, 'Another forty-five minutes.'

Mackenzie sat gazing into the heat haze shimmering in the distance, nursing mixed thoughts, before squinting to steal a surreptitious look at the young policewoman behind the wheel. She was not what he would have described as pretty, but not unattractive, although he was not attracted to her himself. Her tanned face was unlined and bore no trace of make-up, hair drawn back in an austere ponytail. No attempt had been made to enhance her appearance, and he realized he liked that about her. Her fingernails were clipped short, but well cared for and polished to a shine. She had fine, long-fingered hands, but they gripped the wheel too tightly, pale knuckles revealing the tension in them. He noticed how she was chewing on her lower lip. And although her eyes were fixed on the road ahead her mind was clearly elsewhere.

He replayed their meeting at the airport and pulled her name back from memory. Cristina Sánchez Pradell. And in recalling it he realized he had not shaken her outstretched hand. Regret stabbed him in the chest. Susan would have said it was typical of the way he alienated people. Sánchez Pradell . . . He ran the name through his mind again and realized why it was familiar.

'Officer Sánchez Pradell.' She turned to look at him. 'You were one of the arresting officers.'

She nodded and turned her eyes back to the road.

'You saw him shoot the girl.'

'Yes.'

'He blamed you.'

'Yes.' She pressed the heel of her hand to the horn and pulled out in front of a car that was threatening to trap her behind a truck. 'He threatened to kill me and every member of my family.'

Mackenzie said, 'Which wasn't much of a threat while he was still in custody.'

She shrugged.

'And now?'

'The surviving Guardia from the attack on the truck this morning was my sister's husband, Paco. Cleland told Paco to tell me that he was coming for me, then shot him in the leg. I think the only reason he didn't kill him was so that he could deliver the message.'

Mackenzie reran the briefing notes he had read on Cleland. Mad Jock, they called him. Not, apparently, without reason. 'Are you scared?'

Cristina flicked him a glance. 'Yes, I am scared. But I also have a husband, a ten-year-old son, a sister with cancer, an aunt who is deaf and blind. And I am scared for them, too. I looked this man in the eye, señor. He is *loco*. Quite mad.'

Mackenzie closed his eyes and regretted everything about the way he had spoken to her at the airport.

CHAPTER TEN

From Santa Ana de las Vides, the road wound up into the hills through vineyards that covered the south-facing slopes, vines producing sweet white Alejandria Muscatel grapes and even sweeter wine. The coastline fell away below them as they climbed, and the old whitewashed adobe houses of Marviña spread themselves across the undulating hilltop. On the round-about at the entrance to the old town stood a road sign the like of which Mackenzie had never seen before. A red No-Entry sign in the shape of a broken heart above a plaque that read *No Violencia Machista*.

Cristina glanced at him and his consternation produced a smile. 'A campaign against domestic violence,' she said.

They turned right into a development of modern apartment blocks, and then right again into a street that led down into an underground car park. There were several police vehicles here, including a number of motorbikes, and Mackenzie followed Cristina through a door leading directly on to the lower floor of the police station.

This was a building of recent vintage, with freshly

white-painted walls. Cristina and Mackenzie started up a staircase but were halted by a call from beyond an open door at the foot of the stairs. A gruff voice that carried the clear weight of authority. 'In here, Cristina.'

They turned back and entered what Mackenzie quickly gathered was the evidence room. Racks of metal shelving stood in rows. At one side of the room the shelves were lined with box folders, labelled and annotated. Files on hundreds of cases. On the other they groaned with cartons containing evidence collected from crime scenes or seized from the homes of suspects. The *Jefe* was sorting through an ugly collection of weapons.

He swung around as they came in, and started laying them out on the nearest shelf for Mackenzie to see. A long ceremonial sword, another shorter blade in a sheath, a well-worn blue-painted baseball bat, a sledgehammer, a long-bladed knife set in a wooden block that doubled as a club. There was dried blood on it. He said, 'All seized this morning during a raid on an abandoned housing development on the edge of town. The place was being used as a clubhouse by a gang dealing drugs in the district. *My* district. They are like rats, these drug dealers. You flush out one infestation, another appears. You cage them for a while, then the courts set them free and they're back, thumbing their noses at you.' He stretched out a hand towards Mackenzie. 'Sub-Inspector Miguel López. Station chief. *Jefe* to you, and everyone else under my command.' He grinned. 'We don't stand on ceremony here – as long as everyone understands I'm the boss.'

Mackenzie accepted the *Jefe*'s firm dry handshake. 'Not my boss,' he said.

The *Jefe* inclined his head and a tiny smile played around his lips. 'I think you'll find that I am. At least for the moment.' He glanced at Cristina. 'Did the young lady not tell you?'

'The young lady,' Mackenzie said, giving equal and disapproving emphasis to each word, 'told me virtually nothing.'

The *Jefe* nodded his approval. 'Good. Just as it should be. Let's go up to my office.'

Mackenzie followed the *Jefe* upstairs, Cristina tramping in their wake, as if her big black leather boots were too heavy for her. They stopped on the first landing and the police chief raised his hand towards a large framed photographic collage hanging in the stairwell. Photos of police officers from the past standing in groups and ones and twos. Some in colour, others in black-and-white. A large red-lettered caption read, *POLICÍA LOCAL DE MARVIÑA SIEMPRE AHÍ*. Always there. Mackenzie wondered where they had been when Cleland's people had shot three Guardia dead and helped him escape. But for once did not give voice to the thought.

The *Jefe* jabbed a finger at a black-and-white photograph of a good-looking man in uniform. An abundance of silver hair curled from beneath his cap. 'My father,' he said. '*Jefe* before me, as his father was before him.'

A family dynasty, Mackenzie thought, before realizing that he had said it out loud. But the *Jefe* just laughed. 'No one messes with the López family,' he said. He pointed towards a collection of firearms mounted on the wall above the collage. Old flintlock pistols, a bolt-action rifle, a revolver fitted with a rifle butt, several more modern pistols and a hand-grenade in a glass case. 'Police weapons through the ages.' He slapped his hand against his holster. 'And now it's a joint German-Swiss venture which provides us with guns to keep the peace. Strange bedfellows don't you think?'

Mackenzie did, but not in the way the *Jefe* intended. 'Guns and peace, yes. That seems like an oxymoron to me.'

The *Jefe* gazed at him for a thoughtful moment then smiled. 'What amazes me, señor Mackenzie, is that you would know such a word in Spanish.'

Mackenzie shrugged. 'It's virtually the same in both languages.'

The *Jefe* turned to Cristina. 'Do you know what an oxymoron is, Cristina?'

'No, *Jefe*.'

'It's a figure of speech in which apparently contradictory terms appear in conjunction. What our British friend is telling me is that he doesn't believe that guns *can* keep the peace.'

It was Mackenzie's turn to smile. 'And what you are telling me, *Jefe*, is that you are no uneducated country cop.'

The *Jefe* laughed heartily. 'After a lifetime in the police force himself, my father thought I should aspire to something better. So he sent me to university in Madrid, where I studied Spanish Literature. I wrote my thesis on the contradictions of Federico García Lorca.'

'But you joined the police anyway.'

The *Jefe* made a face. 'It was in my DNA.'

Mackenzie nodded. 'My father was a policeman, too.'

'Was he?' The *Jefe* grinned approvingly. 'Then you and I have much in common, my friend.'

The *Jefe*'s office was an unassuming room with worn carpet on the floor. Framed photographs and commendations covered the walls. Sheafs of pinned paperwork sprouted from a notice board above his desk. A row of silver sports cups stood along the top of a bookshelf on the back wall, and charts lay strewn across a long conference table in the middle of the room. A detachable blue light and the corkscrew cable that connected it to the mother vehicle had been placed on one corner to hold them down. Windows on two walls gave on to adjoining offices. Not, perhaps, so that the *Jefe* could keep an eye on junior officers, so much as making them aware that he could. He slumped into a comfortable chair, unhooking the sunglasses from his shirt and tossing them carelessly on to the desk. Mackenzie noticed the cross hanging ostentatiously around his neck, making a mental note to resist any further temptation to blaspheme. He was not religious himself, but knew that Spain was a devoutly Catholic country, particularly here in Andalusia where Christianity had sunk its roots deep to stand firm against Islam and the Moorish occupation.

The *Jefe* waved him towards a seat on the other side of his desk. Cristina remained standing. A tangle of sun-bleached and silvered eyebrows animated the *Jefe*'s face. 'You're probably wondering why you are here.'

This did not seem like a question to Mackenzie, but he understood that a response was required. 'It had crossed my mind,' he said.

The *Jefe* leaned forward. 'There is a massive search under way, Señor Mackenzie, for your fellow countryman. All the way from Gibraltar to Malaga, and beyond. Every agency is involved. The Policía National, Policía Local, Policía Judicial, the Guardia . . . It is a matter of national pride, you might say, that we recapture this man. When we do – and I say when, not if – there will no longer be any question of extradition. He has murdered Spanish police officers and will face justice here in Spain.' He paused. 'But Cleland has been living here among the English-speaking community. It is where he has left all his traces, made all his friends. And your National Crime Agency has graciously agreed to lend us your services to help us find him, since you are fluent in both languages.'

Mackenzie stared at him in disbelief. 'But I don't have any underwear,' he said.

The *Jefe* stared back at him for a moment, frowning. Before his face cleared, eyebrows shooting up on his forehead, and he laughed. 'I like you, señor. You have that famous British sense of humour.'

Mackenzie was not at all sure what was humorous about a dearth of clean underwear.

The chief of police lounged back in his seat. 'Underwear we

can do. Hopefully you won't require *too* many pairs of socks.' His smile faded. 'We want to catch this man sooner rather than later. All the intel we're receiving leads us to believe that Cleland has a major drugs deal going down sometime within the next week. Which is why his friends were so keen to spring him. The drugs squad in Malaga think that there is a massive haul of cocaine stashed somewhere, probably in this area. They are also of the opinion that Cleland could be key to an exchange being successfully completed. Cash for cocaine. And we're not just talking millions. We're talking a street value running to tens of millions. If Cleland accomplishes this exchange he will be wealthy, beyond even his wildest dreams. He will be gone. And with that kind of money, señor, we will see neither hide nor hair of him ever again. So, you see, there is a certain urgency.'

Mackenzie nodded. An urgency that would apply equally to his need for fresh underwear. But he refrained from saying so and thought that Susan would have been proud of him.

Almost as though reading his mind, the *Jefe* said to Cristina, 'You can take him shopping for underwear, and then up to Cleland's villa to let him take a look. I'll get the front office to reserve him a room at a hotel in town.' He returned his gaze to Mackenzie. 'It won't be five-star I'm afraid, señor.' He smiled. 'I have a limited budget.' He got to his feet. 'You two will work together.'

Mackenzie glanced at Cristina and saw that this was news to her. And a not entirely welcome revelation.

'Cristina will be your authority when it comes to interviewing witnesses or getting access to whatever you might need. But you will have no authority yourself, nor will you carry a weapon.' He grinned. 'Which should be no hardship, since you do not believe that guns keep the peace.' His smile faded. 'Your role will be purely advisory.' He raised a finger in the air. 'But if you need anything, anything at all, you come to me.'

Mackenzie could barely keep pace with Cristina as she marched across the underground garage to where she had parked the SUV. She slipped into the driver's seat and slammed the door shut, turning her key in the ignition and revving the motor before Mackenzie had even opened the door on the passenger side. He threw his holdall in the back and climbed up into the passenger seat. Without looking at her he said, 'I'll need some trousers and shirts, too. Shirts with pockets here on the left side.' He placed a hand over his heart. 'It's where I always keep my phone so I can take it out with my right hand.'

She turned her head to glare at him. 'I did not join the police to play nanny to some foreigner with dirty underwear.'

Mackenzie nodded, ignoring her ire. 'And they'll need to be cotton. I react to man-made fibres. Particularly my feet. I get heat blisters between the toes.'

Her glare turned to incredulity. 'Do you really think that is something I want to know?'

'I'm only providing you with the information that will allow you to make an informed decision about where to take me.'

'I'll take you where it's cheapest. And you'll take what you get.'

He nodded. 'As long as it's cotton, and the shirts have pockets. Two's fine, but I must have one on the left.'

She blew exasperation through pursed lips and shook her head. 'I always knew I didn't like the English.'

Mackenzie smiled. 'Don't worry. Neither do I. I'm Scottish. And I don't much care for the Spanish either.'

The squeal of tyres echoed around the car park as Cristina accelerated towards the exit, leaving rubber on concrete.

CHAPTER ELEVEN

Cleland's villa – actually Templeton's villa, since it was rented in that name – sat in its own extensive gardens in an elevated position above cliffs that fell away to the A7 below. From its terrace it appeared as if the infinity pool poured itself in a long waterfall over the edge of the cliff, and the house was set far enough back for almost none of the traffic noise from the road to reach it. In fact, from the house you would not have known there was a road there at all. The view was straight out to sea towards North Africa.

The sun was dipping now towards the west, throwing a pink cast across the few feathery clouds that stretched along the horizon. Palm trees in twos and threes were dotted around the grounds, among a profusion of flowering shrubs: bougainvillea, jasmine, oleander. Pink, red, white. A large Mediterranean pine cast a deep shadow at the end of the garden. The warm evening air was heavy with its fragrance.

It was the first time that Cristina had been back to the villa since the night of the shooting. She drew in behind the Guardia jeep parked outside the gate, and waved acknowledgement to the two officers sitting smoking inside it. She and Mackenzie stepped over the crime-scene tape stretched across the open gate and started up the path towards the porticoed main entrance which was at the back of the house.

They had taken a diversion into Estepona on the way here for Mackenzie to buy what he needed for a stay of indeterminate length. Cristina had driven the police SUV along the pedestrian Calle Real and parked, lights flashing, outside a shop selling men's clothes at budget prices.

Mackenzie had given her a look. 'Is it legal to park here?'

'We're the police.'

'Which doesn't mean we're above the law.' He recalled being on the end of a similar look from the traffic cop on Boston Road in Hanwell just a few days earlier.

'It's an emergency,' Cristina had told him dryly.

And he'd frowned. 'What emergency?'

'An *underwear* emergency. Apparently.'

Mackenzie had emerged ten minutes later with two large plastic carrier bags bulging with his purchases, and presented her with a receipt to be reclaimed on police expenses. He had asked if she would like to see what he'd bought. She had not even thought it worthy of a response and driven off in silence.

Now she was filled with apprehension. Just being here, albeit in daylight, brought back the full horror of that night, whose consequences had not yet played themselves out.

Mackenzie caught her by the arm to stop her on the path. 'Tell me exactly what happened,' he said, and reluctantly she took him through the events which had unfolded in the dark that fateful night. From the discovery that the gates had been forced, to Matías's stumble on the front terrace, over what later turned out to be a heat lamp, to Cristina's entry through the open door. Her recollection of the moment that had almost certainly saved her life was unbearably vivid. Cleland silhouetted suddenly in the inky dark by light spilling from the bedroom behind him. His panic as he swung around to discharge his weapon three times at the figure who had stepped into the light. And then the realization that he had just shot his lover as she emerged in all innocence from the bedroom. Cristina could still see the blood pooling on the floor around the dead girl's body, and hear the anguish that ripped itself in anger from Cleland's throat as he directed blame for his actions entirely at her.

She relived every moment of it before returning to the present and becoming aware of Mackenzie's eyes on her, his fingers still wrapped gently around her arm. She saw intensity in his hazel eyes. And something else. Not pity. Sympathy. But she was not sure she wanted the sympathy of this big Scotsman who towered over her, taller than most of her colleagues. Freckle-spattered skin, strangely pale as if it never saw the sun. She retrieved her arm from his grasp.

'Do you have the key?' he said.

She nodded.

'Then let's go in.'

*

The door opened into a strange stillness, the air dusted with dusky light from all the windows that let it in from every wall and ceiling. The hall was wide and ran the length of the house from back to front, leading into a main living area on two levels, and acres of sliding glass that opened on to the terrace beyond, with its view of the sea.

Cristina found herself almost afraid to breathe, and could barely bring herself to look at the large patch of red-brown that stained the marble tiles. She could not help stepping over it, almost as if the body were still there, haunting her, blaming her as Cleland had done.

'Is this the master bedroom?' Mackenzie asked, as he pushed open the door to their left. Cristina nodded mutely and followed him in. It was where Angela had passed the last moments of her life.

It was a large room, its cold marble floor strewn with hand-made Chinese rugs. Through French windows it had its own terrace that gave on to the garden at the side. A glass table and two chairs stood on the terrace. Cristina imagined Cleland and Angela sitting drinking coffee first thing, enjoying the warmth of early morning sunshine on this east-facing side of the house. She wondered what they had talked about. How much Angela had known about what he did, or who he really was. They would probably never know.

Mirrored wardrobe doors that rose from floor to ceiling reflected a king-size bed, fully made up. The couple had left earlier in the day, not expecting to return that night. Why had they come back? Forensics officers had been through every centimetre of the place, every cupboard, every drawer, every hidden space, but all they had found that might have brought Cleland back was a folder lying on the desk in his study. And all it contained were colour catalogues of luxury yachts, pictures and prices, names, addresses and phone numbers of agents. Had Cleland been a prospective purchaser?

Mackenzie slid open the wardrobe doors. Angela's clothes hung on one side, Cleland's on the other. She had far fewer than he. 'Looks like he'd been living here longer than her,' he said. 'Do we know where and when they met?'

Cristina shook her head.

Mackenzie ran his hands along the softness of the hanging trousers and jackets, stopping from time to time to examine labels, then crouching to cast his eyes over the rows of polished shoes tilted along racks on the floor. He could feel Cleland here, smell him. The body oils exuded by the skin, his aftershave, his cologne, as though he had just stepped out a few minutes earlier.

'He liked his clothes,' he said. 'Image-conscious. Designer labels. Italian shoes. Not cheap. How much did he pay in rental for this place?'

'Five thousand a month.'

Mackenzie raised an eyebrow. 'And maybe as much on clothes by the look of it. What was he driving?'

'Mercedes. A-Class.'

Mackenzie nodded. 'If they haven't already done so, it would be a good idea for forensics to check the addresses listed in his sat-nav. I wonder where he did his banking.'

'The financial people said Templeton had an account at the Banco Popular in Sabanillas.'

'I bet there wasn't much in it.'

'About twenty thousand apparently.' Which seemed a lot to Cristina.

Mackenzie nodded again. 'It's not where Cleland did his banking though. He would almost certainly have had several accounts at different banks under various names. I don't suppose forensics found bank statements?'

'Only for the account in Sabanillas.'

They moved on, then, to the living space at the front of the villa with its open-plan dining area and an impressively equipped kitchen. Mackenzie crouched to bring his eyes level with the black granite work surface on the island, then stood up to sheaf through the chopping boards stacked at one end. He removed several kitchen knives from their wooden block and examined the cutting edges.

Cristina watched in silence as he looked in each of the drawers and opened the doors of all the wall cabinets, before examining the contents of the big American fridge plumbed in for ice on tap. She had no idea what he was looking for.

'I would have loved a kitchen like this,' he said. 'I'd have made better use of it than Cleland.'

'How do you mean?'

'I mean he was no cook. The work tops are pristine, chopping

PETER MAY

boards unused. His knives are razor-sharp, suggesting that unless he was obsessive about keeping them sharpened, they've had only very occasional use. There's precious little in the way of food in the house, so apart from breakfast they probably ate out most of the time, or had food delivered. If we find out where he ate, we might learn who he ate with – apart from Angela. Known associates. It's a starting point.'

None of this, Cristina realized, would ever have occurred to her, and she found herself grudgingly impressed.

Mackenzie spent the next twenty minutes just wandering around the house, touching things, picking them up, laying them down, absorbing Cleland through his personal possessions, while Cristina followed at a discreet and silent distance.

In the study he went through all the desk drawers. The shallow topmost drawer contained pens and pencils, an eraser, a sharpener, paperclips, a small screwdriver and some loose coins.

Cristina said, 'Forensics took his computer, and the folder, and all of his documents, as well as the contents of the bin. Apparently it was full of strips of paper from a shredder.'

Mackenzie ran his eye quickly around the room and spotted the shredder sitting on a cabinet against the back wall, next to a laser printer. Beside the printer a white cylindrical object with rounded edges encased in a fine mesh, stood about seven inches high. He crossed to examine it. Coloured lights flashed on its top surface when he touched it.

'What is it?' Cristina came to stand beside him, inclining her head to look at it with curiosity.

'It's an Apple HomePod. They might have taken his computer, but if this is still connected to the internet his music is probably in the cloud.'

Cristina had no idea what he was talking about.

Mackenzie said suddenly, 'Hey, Siri. Resume.' And immediately the room was filled with the sound of a dead man's voice. Luciano Pavarotti's soaring rendition of Puccini's 'Nessun Dorma'. The last thing Cleland had been listening to. 'Stop,' he said. Then, 'Let me hear my favourite playlist.'

Now the room resounded to strains of Gaetano Donizetti's *Lucia di Lammermoor*. And it only served to underline for Mackenzie the difference between the two men. Cleland with his private education and privileged upbringing, schooled in the appreciation of classical music and opera, while Mackenzie had been listening to Skid Row and Tom Petty and Sheryl Crow.

As Gaetano evoked the windswept slopes of Sir Walter's Scott's Lammermuir Hills, Mackenzie turned his attentions to Cleland's shredder. Sometimes when a shredder's bin was full, the shredding device itself would jam. He removed its bin. Empty. But several shreds of paper hung loose from the mechanism above. He crossed to the desk and retrieved the screwdriver he had seen earlier, then returned to the shredder to carefully unscrew and remove the lid that covered the paper feeder. And there, jammed between the teeth that shredded documents delivered by the rollers, was the crumpled top third of a sheet of paper.

Very delicately, Mackenzie eased it free, then smoothed it

out on top of Cleland's desk. Cristina peered over his shoulder as he bent over it. 'What is it?' Even she didn't know why she was whispering.

'A letter or a bill of some kind. The bulk of it's gone, but we have the letterhead. A name and address.'

She read aloud. 'Condesa Business Centre. That's at the port.'

'What port is that?'

'Puerto de la Condesa. It's ten minutes along the coast, just before you get to Santa Ana.'

CHAPTER TWELVE

Puerto de la Condesa was clustered around a sheltered inlet between Santa Ana de las Vides to the east and Castillo de la Condesa to the west. Built in the style of a traditional Spanish pueblo, with white-painted walls below red Roman tiles, colonnades and arches on three levels led to shaded plazas jammed with bars and restaurants. Reflecting white and red in the still blue waters of a crowded marina, the port derived a distinctive identity from a blue and white faux lighthouse at the open end of its breakwater.

Cristina told him that most people thought the *puerto* dated back to the sixteenth century, like Marviña itself. In fact it had been built in the 1980s by a developer trying to add a touch of class to what had become known as the new Golden Mile.

Apartment complexes built around tropical gardens dotted the surrounding hillsides, spoiled only by the later development of ugly serried blocks of jerry-built apartments more reminiscent of 1960s British council estates – sunshine being the only differentiating factor.

Cristina parked at the entrance to the port and she and

Mackenzie climbed to the second level, passing bars that advertised large-screen football for British and Scandinavian holidaymakers, a fish-and-chip shop, a laundry, a café advertising full English breakfast. Through an archway they emerged into the Plaza de la Fuente, with its fountain sparkling in the slanting evening sunlight. Tables belonging to Argentinian and Italian restaurants were laid out in the square, and the smell of food reminded Mackenzie just how hungry he was. He had still not eaten since the morning.

They entered a colonnade mired in shadow and felt the temperature drop. The Condesa Business Centre was set back on the right, behind sandwich boards offering tours to Gibraltar and Ronda and Tangier. Its windows advertised a variety of services, from internet access and mailboxes, to passport renewals, photocopying and fax.

Tourists in shorts and open sandals sat huddled over computers in its dingy interior, indulging in their daily fix of the worldwide web. From behind a counter a tanned young man with a crop of sun-bleached hair offered them a cheery greeting in a very English accent.

'Evening folks. What can I do for you good people today?' But Mackenzie couldn't help noticing the slightly apprehensive eye he cast over Cristina's uniform. He placed the crumpled and torn top third of the Condesa Business Centre letterhead on to the counter top. 'Yours?' he asked.

The young man glanced at it. 'Looks like it.'

'You have a client called Ian Templeton.'

'Do I?'

'You tell me.'

'I have hundreds of clients. I don't recall them all by name.' He paused. 'And you are?'

'Investigator John Mackenzie of the National Crime Agency. I'm working on secondment with the Spanish police.' He tipped his head towards Cristina, and both men dropped their eyes to the diminutive figure of the young Spanish policewoman. She breathed in to puff up her chest and try to look taller.

'Okaaay . . .'

'And you are?' Mackenzie said.

'Dickie Reilly.'

'This your place?'

'It sure is.'

'Well, Mr Reilly, we would very much appreciate it if you would check your customer list and tell us if you have an Ian Templeton on your books.'

Both men were startled by the force with which Cristina slapped a photograph of Cleland on to the counter in front of him. She seemed immediately abashed and said quickly, 'This might help.'

It was the first time Mackenzie had heard her speak English. In an oddly rough voice with a thick accent, as if she were a smoker.

Reilly turned it around to look at it. 'Oh, yeah, him. He's a regular. Couldn't have told you his name, though.' He searched under the counter for a large hardback notebook and flipped through it until he found the name. 'Lives up in La Paloma.'

'Yes,' Mackenzie said. 'Does he have a mailbox here?'

'He certainly does.' Reilly gave him what he clearly believed to be a winning smile. Mackenzie did not return it.

'We'd like to see the contents.'

Reilly's smile didn't waver. 'I'm afraid that wouldn't be possible, Mr Mackenzie. At least, not without some kind of warrant. Customers' mailboxes are private.'

Cristina said, 'You've been in Spain long, señor?'

Reilly looked uncomfortable for the first time. 'About five years, officer.'

'Official resident?'

He attempted a laugh, and waggled his outstretched palm. 'Sort of.' But his smile was fading.

Mackenzie said, 'Either you are or you aren't.'

'Well . . .'

Cristina interrupted. 'This place . . .' She waved her hand vaguely around the office. 'You have many computers here. You have health and safety certificate?'

Reilly raised his hands in submission. 'Look, okay.' He glanced nervously along the rows of computers and lowered his voice. 'But this is strictly unofficial. My business is dependent on confidentiality.' He turned to a board on the wall behind him. It was hung with rows of keys, each with its own tab. He selected one and handed it to Mackenzie. 'Number one-two-seven.'

An entire wall beyond the counter was lined with numbered mailboxes. Reilly busied himself, pretending to ignore them, as they found and opened the mailbox Cleland had rented in the name of Templeton. There were five envelopes inside it. One contained an advertising circular from a wine store in Puerto Banus, another a quarterly subscription reminder from a gymnasium here in the port. The other three were bank statements.

Mackenzie opened them with a sense of anticipation. Three accounts. Three different banks. A cumulative total of nearly two million euros. He heard Cristina's tiny gasp at his side. He turned towards her. 'We can have this money seized. It'll hurt him. Maybe cut off his source of ready cash. But it's not all of it, that's for sure.' He lifted the subscription reminder. 'Let's go see who he pumped iron with.'

Condesa Fitness was accessed from the rear of the port, stairs leading up to a large fitness room with floor-to-ceiling windows giving on to the most spectacular view across the *puerto* and its marina. Sunshine angled in through smoked glass, and lay in strips across a carpeted floor that absorbed the grunts and strains of the half-dozen customers lifting weights and performing curls. The perfume of stale sweat hung in the air, along with discordant notes of cheap aftershave and supermarket deodorant.

They were approached by a tanned, muscular young instructor wearing a black singlet and shorts. He eyed them warily.

'Can I help you?' he asked in Spanish.

Cristina showed him the photograph of Cleland. Mackenzie said, 'A customer of yours, we believe. Behind in his subscription.'

Muscle man looked at the picture and shrugged. 'So?'

'You recognize him?'

'Of course. Señor Ian.'

'He was a regular?'

'Two, three times a week maybe.' He cocked one eyebrow. 'Very fit.'

'Did he come in with anyone else?'

'No. Always alone. Nice guy. Great calf muscles.' He glanced ruefully at his own. 'I asked him how he managed to get muscles like that. He laughed and told me it was genetic. Me? I could work those muscles for years and never have calves that good.'

'It's a Scottish thing,' Mackenzie said. 'You need good calves if you're going to wear a kilt.'

The young man looked at him quizzically. 'You are Scottish?'

'Yes.'

'And you wear the kilt?' It was Cristina this time. She couldn't keep the curiosity from her voice.

Mackenzie shuffled uncomfortably. 'No,' he said. 'I don't have the legs for it.'

The gym instructor nodded, as if he suspected it all along. 'So what's this guy done?'

'Killed a lot of people,' Mackenzie said. 'So if you can think of anything about him, anything at all that might help us track him down, you let us know.'

The young man was clearly shocked. He shook his head. 'Honestly señor, I couldn't tell you the first thing about him. We would chat, you know, just blah. He told me he liked to sail. But I could have guessed that from his tan. You don't get to be that colour from lying on a beach.'

'Well if anything else comes to mind, give my colleague here a call.' He turned expectantly towards Cristina. It took a moment for her to realize he was waiting on her to hand over a business card. She fumbled through the pockets of her uniform before finally finding a dog-eared card for the Policía Local, Marviña, which she thrust at the instructor.

As they went back down the stairs Mackenzie said, 'So already we're getting a sense of this guy. He likes designer clothes, eats out a lot, but likes to keep himself fit. He goes sailing, buys expensive wine in Puerto Banus, and has two million stashed away in secret bank accounts.'

He patted the pocket into which he had folded the bank statements.

'We want to get these to your financial people as quickly as possible. The sooner we shut down his access to cash the sooner we start putting pressure on him. He can't use Templeton's credit cards, or cards from these accounts now either. So where's he going to stay? With friends? How many of Templeton's friends knew he was really Cleland? And I can't see him shacking up in some drug dealer's seedy apartment. He's red-hot untouchable right now. Let's squeeze him.' He paused. 'But above all, please, can we get something to eat?'

CHAPTER THIRTEEN

The light faded rapidly on the drive back up to Marviña. The sky beyond the mountains to the west glowed a deep crimson along a jagged horizon, the moon already visible in a deepening blue. Mackenzie looked back towards the sea that spread itself out below. It lay in narrow bands of blue and grey and green. There was not a hint of wind to ruffle the surface of the gentlest of swells, the Mediterranean slow-breathing in preparation for sleep at the end of a long day.

Mackenzie realized he was tired as well as hungry. The first rush of adrenalin which had accompanied his initial attempts to pick up Cleland's spoor had passed, leaving him hollow and depressed. Right now he should have been listening to Sophia singing to an audience of appreciative parents. He was very probably the only dad not to be there.

As they were leaving the port, Cristina took a call on her mobile, then told him that the *Jefe* had booked him into a small hotel in the newly pedestrianized Marviña main street. She would, she said, take him there once she had faxed the contents of Cleland's mailbox at Condesa to the *Juez de*

Instrucción who was coordinating the search for the fugitive from Estepona. He would, she assured him, be able to get something to eat at the hotel.

Now, as they left the police station, she pointed their SUV up the hill to where the main street wound slowly through the heart of this ancient hill town. White buildings with doors and windows picked out in ochre, black-painted wrought-iron Juliet balconies overlooking the newly paved street, a network of fine cabling stretched between yellow-tiled roofs to support a mosaic of coloured sails to shade pedestrians during the heat of the day.

In gaps between buildings, where streets fell away left and right, Mackenzie could see a patchwork of fields dipping into the valley, then rising again to where the Sierra Bermeja pushed its rugged peaks up into a darkening sky.

The Hostal Totana stood near the end of the street, on the corner of an alley that dropped down to the church below, next door to a *farmacia* and opposite a bar whose patrons sat out at tables on the pavement, drinking beer and wine, smoking and indulging in rowdy conversation that echoed along the street.

Cristina dropped him at the door and told him that someone would contact him in the morning.

'Not you?' Mackenzie was almost disappointed. Getting used to one person was bad enough. Having to break new ground with someone else was a prospect he did not relish. Better the devil you know.

'I have to take my sister to hospital in the morning. Usually

Paco would do it, but right now he is in hospital himself with a bullet in his leg.'

Mackenzie watched her drive off before lugging his new purchases and overnight bag into reception. His room was on the top floor. There was no lift, and he was breathing heavily by the time he got there. It was tiny. A small double bed with head- and foot-boards. And he knew that it would not be long enough to accommodate his height. Meaning a night curled up on one side, or the other. A constant process of leg-bent rotation and very little sleep.

He sat disconsolately on the edge of the bed and supposed that at least it would have clean sheets. They had told him downstairs they served food in the bar, though a glance at the menu had revealed an unappetizing choice of fast foods and tapas, and he wondered if he could summon the energy to go back down. But the rumblings in his stomach told him that fasting was not an option. Wearily he stood up again and carefully hung his new shirts and trousers in the wardrobe, wire coat hangers rattling on the rail. He put his socks and pants in a drawer and propped a couple of pairs of trainers on the shoe rack.

French windows led to a small balcony that looked down on to the street. He could see and hear the drinkers across the way, but those at the tables immediately below were obscured by a canopy above them.

Darkness had fallen suddenly. Street lights illuminating white buildings in burned-out patches snaked off in two long strings down the hill. He slipped his phone from his breast pocket and checked the time. It was likely that Sophia would be home by now.

His attempt to reopen his previous conversation with her on the Messenger app failed. Neither was he able to open a fresh window. After restarting the phone he tried rebooting the app, but each time it would only take him back to her final message – a sad face.

In frustration he opened his Facebook app and quickly discovered that she had unfriended him. A terrible sense of melancholy welled up inside to exclude all other emotion. Unfriended by his own daughter! When he had told Beard that no one liked him very much, he had never imagined that might also apply to Sophia.

A burst of raucous laughter rose from the street below on the warm night air, and he wondered if he had ever felt quite so lonely.

He turned back into his room to shut out the sound of other people's happiness, and made his way downstairs to try and find something on the menu to feed his appetite. But he had little relish for anything other than alcohol to drown his sorrows. As he stood at the bar waiting to be served, a small boy entered from the street and stood looking around. With little hesitation he headed directly for Mackenzie the moment he saw him.

'Señor Mackenzie?' he asked.

Mackenzie looked at him in surprise. He was a slight-built

boy of around nine or ten. An unruly tangle of jet-black hair fell across a high forehead above a wide smile. He made Mackenzie think of Alex. 'Yes.'

The boy stuck out his hand. 'I'm very pleased to meet you. I'm Lucas.'

Mackenzie shook the boy's hand, and was surprised by the strength of his grip, as well as by the quality of English for one so young.

'Cristina is my mother. My father says you are to come and eat with us.'

Mackenzie was taken aback. 'You live nearby?'

'Just across town. It's only five minutes. My father sent me. My mother didn't want me to come, but my father said it would not be hosp . . .' he struggled with the word, 'hospitable, to let you eat alone on your first night in Spain.' This time he held out his hand for Mackenzie to hold, and gave him a wide smile. 'I will take you.'

Lucas led Mackenzie down the length of the main street and into the Plaza del Vino above the fire station. A colourful town plan was mounted on one wall opposite a massive mosaic of winemakers trampling grapes. Everything about Marviña seemed related in some way to wine. On the far side of the square, whitewashed apartment blocks stepped down the hill like terraces in a vineyard. Cristina lived at the top of the hill in a street called Calle Utopía. In Marviña, utopia was a tiny two-bedroom apartment on the first floor with a view of other apartments out back, and a row of shops out front.

The planners had contrived somehow to build homes without views in a town surrounded by them.

When Lucas opened the door to the apartment and called out to announce their arrival, a young man with startling blue eyes in a deeply tanned face hurried out from the living room to greet them.

'*Holà, holà*,' he said, and he grasped Mackenzie's hand in both of his to pump it enthusiastically. 'I'm Antonio, welcome. Excuse me for not speaking English, but Cristina says your Spanish is impeccable.'

Mackenzie raised an eyebrow in surprise. 'Did she?'

Antonio ruffled Lucas's hair, and Mackenzie wondered if the boy had inherited the gene which was already leading to early hair loss in his father. 'Come in, come in.'

They squeezed past a coat stand laden with jackets and hats and scarves and into a cramped, square living space with a dresser and dining table, and an oversized L-shaped settee gathered around a coffee table. A small TV on a stand burbled in the corner beside French windows leading on to a small balcony. What little floor space remained was booby-trapped with discarded toys and shoes.

Antonio was suddenly self-conscious, as if seeing for the first time his own living space through someone else's eyes. 'Excuse the mess,' he said, and started scooping away jackets and laundry to create sitting space on the settee. 'Lucas, put those toys away in your room.'

Obediently the boy did as he was told, gathering plastic

trucks and models of Star Wars characters and a couple of footballs into his arms to carry away to his bedroom.

Through a door opening off the living room, Mackenzie saw into a tiny kitchen. Cristina, pot in hand, swung into view. She wiped a forearm across her forehead and glared at him. She was out of uniform now, and if anything seemed even smaller in jeans and a T-shirt. Her hair tumbled freely around her shoulders, and she looked harassed. Mackenzie thought that if he'd met her like this in the street he might not have recognized her. 'Sit at the table, I'm about ready to serve up,' she said, and vanished from view again.

Antonio grinned at him. 'Always chaos in here,' he said, and waved Mackenzie into a seat. Lucas returned from his bedroom to claim the seat opposite Mackenzie and sit watching him with unabashed curiosity. Antonio drew in a chair beside his son and said, 'Didn't seem right that you should be eating on your own up at the hotel. Where did you learn your Spanish? At university?'

'Never went to university,' Mackenzie said. 'I taught myself all my languages.'

Antonio's eyes opened wide. '*All* your languages? How many do you speak?'

'Four if you include English.'

Antonio whistled softly. 'That makes me feel very inadequate. My English is very poor. Lucas speaks it better than I do. Don't you, son?'

Lucas blushed.

'We send him to a private Catholic school near Estepona. They teach half his subjects in the medium of English. It costs an arm and a leg, and we have to drive him there every day. But you have to make sacrifices, don't you? Can't put a price on your children's future.'

Mackenzie felt a stab of guilt, and wondered if it could be said that he had made sufficient sacrifices for his.

Almost as if he sensed it, Antonio said, 'Do you have any yourself?'

Mackenzie nodded. 'Two.' But he didn't want to elaborate. That would only lead to the subject of his marriage and his separation from Susan. Subjects he did not want to discuss with strangers, but would feel obliged to do so if they asked. He was rescued by a flustered Cristina carrying two steaming plates of spaghetti bolognese to the table. She placed one each in front of Mackenzie and Lucas and hurried off to get another two, while Antonio poured red wine into their glasses.

He laughed '*Boloñesa*. An Italian dish for your first night in Spain.'

Cristina returned with the other plates, but was not amused. 'Pasta is quick and easy,' she said, 'when you have been out working all day.'

'We all work all day, *cielo*.'

'But we don't all have to make dinner when we get home.'

Antonio's smile was strained. 'Except when your wife's on the night shift being shot at.'

Mackenzie sensed the tension between them and took a mouthful of spaghetti to avoid having to speak.

'Nobody shot at me.'

'No, just threatened to kill you and your family after you made him shoot his girlfriend.'

Cristina glared at him, and flicked her eyes pointedly toward Lucas, as if to say *not in front of the boy*! But Lucas appeared not to be paying any attention, his eyes fixed on the TV screen in the corner, and Mackenzie thought he must have heard this script before.

Antonio tried to laugh it off. 'It's a tough town this,' he said to Mackenzie. 'You wouldn't think so to look at it. Especially since the *ayuntamiento* spent taxpayers' money on the make-over. Tourists flock here in the summer. Beautiful buildings, wonderful views, delicious wine. Unaware of the gangs that operate out of the derelict housing developments on the outskirts. Boom town Marviña until the financial crash. You'll have seen the consequences everywhere, all over the valley. Unfinished apartment blocks. Concrete skeletons. Cranes standing over them, like dinosaurs frozen in time. Most of them haven't moved in over ten years, the companies that owned them long since gone bust.'

'Breeding grounds for crime,' Cristina said gloomily. 'Squatters. Illegal immigrants. Drugs gangs.'

Antonio used his fork to wind spaghetti into a ball in his spoon. 'The kind of people the mother of my son has to mix with every day.' He flashed a glance towards his wife.

'Not really,' Cristina said. She seemed weary. This was a well-rehearsed argument. 'The men get to do all the fun stuff. I get to do paperwork, traffic duty and search female suspects. A little ironic since I actually topped my year at the police academy.'

Antonio said to Mackenzie, 'Her parents were dead set against her joining the police.'

Mackenzie was so far out of his comfort zone he had no idea how to respond. 'They must be very proud of you,' he said. It seemed like the right kind of thing to say.

'They're dead,' Cristina said flatly, and Mackenzie wanted the ground to open up beneath him. But neither of his hosts seemed aware of it. Mackenzie wished Lucas had never found him, and that he was still sitting in the bar up at the Hostal Totana, enjoying a beer and a sandwich.

He made a clumsy attempt to change the subject. 'So what kind of area do the police here cover?'

Cristina shrugged. 'In Marviña we're responsible for policing halfway to Estepona and all the way down the coast to Torreguadiaro. As well as a good swathe of territory inland. Just the mundane stuff. The juicy crimes go to the judicial police in Estepona or get referred to the homicide or drugs squads in Malaga.'

'But drugs are your biggest problem?'

'The root of all evil,' Antonio said.

Cristina nodded her agreement. 'The users steal to feed their habit. The dealers diversify. Prostitution, people-trafficking.

We know who most of them are, but it's hard to get solid evidence. Usually we only ever nail them for personal possession or DUI, then they're back on the streets again in no time. The big stuff . . . they hide that well. Safe houses up in the hills.'

Mackenzie frowned. 'Safe houses? What do you mean?'

Antonio said, 'Farmers get coerced into keeping the stuff for them. Innocents with no connection at all to the gangs. Drugs get hidden in barns and cowsheds. The really big stashes. And if it's your farm they choose, you only object if you've grown tired of life.'

Lucas slipped off his seat and started towards his bedroom. His spaghetti was only half-eaten. Cristina said sharply, 'Where do you think you're going? You haven't finished yet.'

'I've got homework to do.' He looked back at them and delivered his coup de grâce. 'Unless you want to help.'

Antonio pulled a face. 'Maths again?'

Lucas nodded.

Cristina sighed. 'I think we're going to have to get you a tutor, Lucas.'

Lucas shrugged. 'Whatever.' And headed off to his room.

'We can't afford a tutor.' Antonio looked at her pointedly.

Cristina turned towards Mackenzie. 'He's a bright boy. Doing really well in most subjects. But maths . . .' She shrugged hopelessly.

'Must be in the genes,' Antonio said. 'Neither of us are remotely equipped to help him. I mean, I sell cars down in Santa Ana. The extent of my arithmetic is subtracting the trade-in value from the asking price and adding on the extras.'

'Maybe I could help,' Mackenzie said. 'I have a degree in mathematics.'

An astonished silence fell across the table. Cristina said, 'You have a degree in maths?'

'Among other things.'

Antonio said, 'Four languages and multiple degrees! What on earth are you doing in the police?'

Cristina flicked him a look, but Mackenzie said simply, 'My dad was a cop.'

Cristina said, 'Well, if you're around long enough, maybe you could see if there's anything you could do to help the boy. But here's hoping we get Cleland sooner rather than later.'

Not least, Mackenzie thought, because it would take the strain off this whole family. Even he could see that living with Cleland's threat of reprisal was taking its toll. He stood up. 'I should be going.'

'Already?' Antonio seemed disappointed.

Mackenzie said to Cristina, 'You told me you're taking your sister to the hospital in the morning.'

She nodded. 'Yes.'

'I hope it's nothing serious.'

'She has breast cancer.'

'Oh.' Again he was at a loss for how to respond, and scared

to say anything in case it was the wrong thing – as Susan had so often accused him of doing.

'I'm picking up Paco, too. He's getting released tomorrow.'

'All one big happy family,' Antonio quipped, though his smile said it was anything but.

CHAPTER FOURTEEN

The Colegio Cánovas del Castillo comprised a collection of square white buildings set someway back from the road to Estepona, behind Burger King and the Mercadona supermarket.

Cristina turned off the A7 at Aldi and followed the cracked tarmac surface of a tree-lined dual carriageway back into the dusty sun-bleached hills that rose in random undulations towards the mountains. Unfinished roads branched off to the left and right, petering out in the dust.

Cranes loomed over abandoned concrete apartment blocks on the rise, and in the valley beyond the school empty terracotta villas sat in rows among the gorse, facing on to the parched fairways of a tawdry-looking golf course. She spun the wheel and turned the battered family Seat down towards the school gates, past the shuttered sales office of a developer peddling homes that had never been built.

The road was lined with the cars of parents dropping off their children, a slow procession in both directions, the pavement crowded with chattering children in shirtsleeves and regulation skirts and shorts, satchels slung over shoulders or hanging from little hands. It was already hot, and Cristina had all the windows down.

She was embarrassed by her car, easing its way between all the shiny new SUVs: Mercs, Audis, BMWs. Many of which Antonio had probably sold. Even with two incomes it was all they could afford. Although Antonio was fortunate in being able to bring home a car from the second-hand lot every evening. Neither Cristina nor her husband earned very much, and the bulk of their disposable income went on providing the best education for Lucas that money could buy. Still, he was not doing as well as they had hoped.

She glanced in the rearview mirror and saw him sitting anxiously in the back seat. After Mackenzie had gone the previous evening, she had done her level best to help him with his homework, but knew she wasn't really up to it. And so did Lucas. Only, it was he who had to face his teachers, not her.

Almost as if she had read her sister's mind, Nuri put a hand over Cristina's and offered her a pale smile from the passenger seat. Cristina could have wept. How was it possible that her little sister, stricken with breast cancer and on her way to Marbella for yet more chemo, could find sympathy for *her*? It was all so unfair.

She turned in a circle at the bottom of the hill and drove back up to the gate to let Lucas off. He gave his aunt a sunny wave, but offered his mother only a quick sullen glance, before running off to find his classmates. They drove up the road, past a white tower with long crosses on each face, and Nuri said, 'Thanks for this. I know you have a lot of things on your mind.'

Cristina shook her head and smiled, doing her best to hide the tears gathering in her eyes. 'Family first,' she said. 'You know I'd do anything for you, sis.'

'I know.'

Neither of them paid the least attention to the black SUV parked next to the chunks of concrete that blocked the road beyond the deserted sales office. Obscured by smoked glass, Cleland sat behind the wheel and breathed his satisfaction. Now he knew where the boy went to school. Knew where the bitch lived. And her sister. It was just a matter of time, and patience.

CHAPTER FIFTEEN

The HC International hospital in Marbella was set in sprawling gardens just off the A7, two hundred metres from the sea. Treatment rooms in Roman-tiled cottages overlooked an area of extensive lawns peppered by shady trees and flowering shrubs, recliners set out on stone terracing around a large turquoise-blue swimming pool.

Cristina had often wondered how much Nuri's treatment here was costing. But just as she and Antonio were investing everything in the future of their son, so Nuri and Paco were gambling everything on her sister's life. What point was there in having money in the bank if you were dead? There was a risk, too, that if she survived the treatment she would be infertile, and Cristina knew just how desperate Nuri was to have children. Although even if it turned out that she couldn't have any of her own, Cristina suspected that Nuri would adopt. She adored children, and doted on her nephew.

First the nurses drew blood, and would only begin the latest treatment if her blood count was suitable: a surplus of white blood cells would postpone it. While the sample went to the lab for testing, Cristina and Nuri wandered through the gardens in the somnolent heat of the morning, listening to the cacophony of bird call coming from the trees, almost unaware of the distant rumble of traffic from the motorway.

It had always seemed to Cristina that Nuri was far too young to have been struck down by the curse of breast cancer at the age of just twenty-six. But her little sister had met the challenge with silent courage and very little complaint. Cristina knew that after each treatment she spent several days throwing up, exhausted and resting most of the time in bed.

They had gone together to a shop in Marbella to pick out a suitable wig to cover her increasing baldness. It was the only time Cristina had seen a crack in her sister's brave facade. She had found her sitting facing the mirror in the little changing room at the back of the store, the chosen wig lying sadly in her lap, tears running down a face ravaged by the poison they had been pumping into her body. When Cristina sat beside her, putting an arm around her shoulders to pull her close, all she had said was, 'I'm so scared, Cris. I don't want to die.'

It was late morning by the time Nuri was summoned to begin her chemo. There were almost a dozen other patients in the treatment room, each in their own recliner, each with their own TV. Most of them knew each other by now and would ignore the television to exchange gossip and the latest family news.

There was a turnover, of course. Some patients reaching the successful completion of their treatment. Others dying. None of these women ever knew which of those two eventualities lay in wait for them. Cancer treatment was a lottery and the stakes were high. If you won you lived.

Cristina watched as a nurse expertly inserted a needle into a vein in the back of her sister's hand. She taped it down, then began an initial flow of saline solution from an overhead bag to flush out her vascular system. Cristina saw the resignation in Nuri's eyes. That psychological balancing act between what would make her sick and what would keep her alive.

But typical of Nuri, her mind was elsewhere, thinking of others. She said, 'Obviously I'm not going to make it to Aunt Ana's today. Would you . . . ?'

Cristina squeezed her free hand. 'Don't worry about Ana, I've got that covered.' She stood up and glanced at her watch. 'I'll leave you to it for the moment, sis. The ambulance from the Costa del Sol should be dropping Paco off about now.'

Paco was waiting for her in the car park. The ambulance from the Hospital Costa del Sol had already been and gone, a trip out to Marviña saved by the unhappy coincidence of his wife being in town for cancer treatment. He looked deathly pale, and shrunken somehow in his jog pants and T-shirt. In spite of having shaved, the shadow of his beard never left his face and seemed darker in contrast with his jaundiced pallor. His right leg was heavily strapped, and he was balancing unsteadily on crutches.

'Hey Cris.' He managed to drop one of them as he attempted to give her a hug. She stooped to pick it up, aware how much his sense of macho pride would be offended by the need of physical help from a woman.

She tipped a raised eyebrow towards his leg. 'How is it?'

'Hurts like hell. I'll be off work for weeks. They say I was lucky. The bullet missed the femoral artery by a whisker. I'd have bled to death in minutes otherwise.'

Cristina looked with concern into his sad dark eyes. 'Do you think he knew that? I mean, do you think he missed it on purpose?'

Paco curled his upper lip in anger. 'I don't think he gave a damn, one way or the other. If I died, I died. If I didn't I would deliver his message.' He met her eye for a moment, before quickly averting his gaze in embarrassment. 'I'd be dead for sure, like the others, if I hadn't been your brother-in-law.' Then his eyes connected again with hers. 'I guess I should be grateful.'

Cristina shook her head. 'But how did he know? That you were married to my sister, I mean? Where would he get that kind of information?'

Paco looked as if he wanted to spit. 'Someone on the inside, obviously. How else did they know what route the truck was taking?'

'The *Jefe* said it didn't seem like the truck had been forced off the road. That the driver had voluntarily turned off on to that dirt track. Could he have been in on it?'

Paco shrugged. He said bitterly, 'If he was, he wouldn't have been expecting a bullet in the face as pay-off.' He drew a deep breath. 'How's Nuri?'

'In good spirits.'

'She always is by the time the chemo has worn off. But it won't take long to drag her right back down again.' There was a break in his voice and for an awful moment Cristina thought he was going to cry. A man like Paco would never have been able to live that down, and would no doubt have found some way to blame Cristina for his moment of weakness. Fortunately for them both he controlled himself. 'It's been tough, Cris, you know? And it'll be tougher now with this.' He flicked his head angrily towards his leg. 'I'll not be able to do stuff for her, like before.'

'You know I'll help any way I can.'

He nodded and managed a grudging half-smile. 'I know. But you guys are both working, and you've got a kid to worry about. At least I'll be home for a while.' He sighed and shook his head. 'I just hope it doesn't mean they're going to put me on reduced pay.' He jerked his head towards the hospital. 'This place is costing a fucking fortune. We're in enough debt as it is.' He breathed his frustration. 'Without the least idea if we're going to survive. Physically or financially.'

It would have been Cristina's instinct to offer financial help, too, but that was beyond her. All she could do was nod her sympathy. She said, 'It'll probably be another couple of hours before Nuri's finished. Do you want me to take you to get something to eat?'

He shook his head. 'Nah. This pain killer they're giving me has totally ruined my appetite.' He paused. 'I could do with a drink, though.'

CHAPTER SIXTEEN

Mackenzie woke late, sun streaming through the French windows to fall in burning bands across his bed. He had managed to kick off all his covers, and was lying in a twisted heap, naked apart from his boxer shorts.

The shortness of the bed had not inhibited his sleep as he had feared. Fatigue had overcome all obstacles to comfort. But now he had a bad taste in his mouth and a growling in his belly.

The shock of looking at his watch to see that it was after ten o'clock propelled him out of bed and into the shower. He dried and dressed quickly. A pair of jeans, a T-shirt, pristine white sneakers. He felt oddly starched in his new clothes as he went downstairs to the bar. There he wolfed down a couple of *churros* and washed them over with two large cups of *cafe con leche*. No one, they said, had called for him, and he wandered out into the street wondering what the hell he was doing here.

The town had already come to life. Locals sat out on the pavement terrace, and at the bar across the street. A couple of mini-markets were doing brisk business, and pale people clutching doctors' prescriptions came and went from the pharmacy next door. A little further down, a couple of old men perched on a bench seat, leaning forward on gnarled sticks to exchange observations on life in the shade of the colourful overhead sails. The sun was already striking heat off stone pavings where sunlight fell between the shadows. Everything, it seemed to Mackenzie, was covered in a fine dust. It had barely rained in weeks.

Impatience turned to irritation, and he set off along the street in the direction Lucas had taken him the previous evening. He remembered his embarrassment at the strained atmosphere between Cristina and Antonio, and his failure to steer a smoother social course out of troubled family waters. He sympathized with Lucas, recalling how alienated he himself had felt when his aunt and uncle fought over the dinner table – or rather, when his uncle had picked a fight and shouted at his wife.

The lower end of the street was dominated by the town hall – *ayuntamiento* as it was called in Spanish – with its mosaics around the entrance and its flags hanging limply in the airless heat. A terrace rose above the road, as the narrow thoroughfare fell away, and steps took him down into the Plaza del Vino. Although there were cars parked along both sides of the street, there were few people in the square.

Half a dozen liveried and unmarked vehicles sat outside the police station, beyond the fire station with its loitering *bomberos* and Mackenzie ran up the steps to the main entrance.

The duty officer looked up from his desk as Mackenzie entered the foyer. 'Is the *Jefe* around?' The policeman flicked his head towards the hall and the open door to the *Jefe*'s office. Mackenzie went through, knocked and entered.

The *Jefe* looked up from a pile of paperwork which had been engaging his concentration and seemed pleased to see him. 'Señor Mackenzie.' He stood up and held out a hand. 'Did you sleep well?'

'Too well, *Jefe*, and half the day is gone already.'

The *Jefe* shrugged. 'It is Spain, señor. We start early and work late. It is too hot once the sun is up.'

'Crime doesn't wait for the weather, *Jefe*.' Mackenzie's disapproval was clear.

The other man laughed. 'You always say what you think, señor. I like that.'

Mackenzie said, 'Most people don't.' He hesitated. '*Jefe*, since Cristina is away this morning, I wondered if I might borrow a car. It feels like I'm just wasting my time hanging about up at the hotel. I could be checking out Cleland's haunts down at the port.'

The *Jefe* shook his head. 'Not possible, I'm afraid. We would need permission from a higher authority. And then there is the question of insurance.' He sat down and waved Mackenzie into the seat opposite. 'Cristina will be back this afternoon.'

'Have there been any developments at all?'

'The financial police in Malaga have frozen those three bank accounts you uncovered yesterday, so Cleland will be feeling the pinch when he starts running out of ready cash. We're tapping every underworld source we can to try and get some notion of where he might be hiding out, and who's helping him.'

'And how seriously do you take the threat on Cristina's life?'

The *Jefe* laughed. 'I don't. Cleland's just looking to scapegoat his own conscience. I'm sure he has other more important things to occupy him now.'

'What about the message he asked her brother-in-law to deliver?'

'Amateur dramatics. Just trying to scare her.'

'He's succeeding.'

The *Jefe* leaned forward on his desk. 'Señor, if I really thought she was in danger I would have her confined to the house under armed guard until Cleland is caught. Trust me, he has bigger fish to fry.' He sat back. 'You're Scottish, Cristina tells me. I spent two weeks in Scotland once. Salmon fishing in the Outer Hebrides. Best fishing of my whole life. Of course, conservation being what it is these days, we had to throw back all the salmon we caught. Do you fish?'

'Unless I was fishing to feed myself I would consider it a waste of time. Catching fish only to throw them back with their mouths half torn open, seems pointless and cruel.'

The *Jefe* raised his eyebrows in amusement. 'I take it that's a no.'

Mackenzie nodded solemnly.

'Do you like whisky, then?'

Mackenzie smiled finally. 'I have been known to sip the odd dram.'

'I love the stuff. I have a wonderful collection at home. Everything from Lagavulin to Glenmorangie. I prefer the peaty kind myself.'

'I'm a glens man,' Mackenzie said. 'Softer, sweeter whisky, aged in old sherry or madeira casks. Balvenie Double Wood is my favourite.'

The *Jefe* beamed. 'I have that very one. The triple wood, too. You must come up some evening and we'll sample a few. I'm all on my own these days.' And his face clouded. 'Since my wife passed.' But the cloud cleared quickly and he added, 'If you're here long enough, that is. We'll both be happy to get that bastard sooner rather than later.'

Mackenzie nodded his agreement. 'We will.'

The *Jefe* sat back in his chair and regarded Mackenzie for several long thoughtful moments. 'Ah to hell,' he said. 'Just don't crash the bloody thing. And we'll not tell anyone upstairs.'

Mackenzie opened his eyes in surprise. 'You're letting me have a car?'

The chief heaved himself out of his chair. 'One of the privileges of being the *Jefe*. Come on,' he said, and Mackenzie followed him out through the hall and foyer to the steps outside, stopping only to retrieve a set of keys from the front office. 'Take the Seat at the end of the line. It's just a little car, and with your long legs you'll have to tuck your knees under your chin, but it'll get you from A to B.'

Mackenzie nodded towards the car immediately below

them. A shiny black Audi Q5. 'I was hoping you might offer me that one?'

The *Jefe* laughed uproariously. 'That's my car, you cheeky bastard! You'll take what I give you, or you can hoof it down to the port under your own steam.'

Santa Ana was an ugly utilitarian town that had grown up around a quaint little fishing village stretching between Condesa and Casares Beach. Remnants of the original village were still to be found along the shore, which was littered now with the fishing boats that went out early each morning to supply the dozens of fish restaurants on the coast.

Mackenzie drove quickly through the Santa Ana agglomeration before turning off the A7 to double back through a tunnel that ran beneath it and out into the Port of the Countess. He parked under palms fibrillating with the chatter of tiny green parrots barely visible among its fronds, and walked through the burgeoning heat of the day into the cool shade of an arcade that led him along to the Condesa Business Centre which had proved so fruitful the day before.

He'd had a thought. It had come to him the previous night after turning out the light. It had haunted him through all his dreams and still been there when the sun woke him belatedly this morning. Now it was burning in his brain and he wanted to put it to the test.

The sandy-haired Dickie Reilly was standing behind his counter. He looked at Mackenzie with undisguised dismay when he stepped out of the shade of the arcade and into the gloom of the business centre. He kept his voice low when Mackenzie approached. 'Repeated visits from the police are not good for business.'

'Oh? Why's that?'

'Because people don't like the police, Mr ... Mackenzie, was it?'

Mackenzie smiled. 'Well, who's to know? I'm on my own today, and not a uniform in sight. All I'm looking for is a simple answer to a simple question.'

'Which is?'

'Where would I go to find out if someone owned a berth at the marina?'

'Ian Templeton, you mean?'

Mackenzie shrugged. 'Anyone. It's hypothetical.'

'The tower,' Reilly said.

'Where's that?'

'It looks like a lighthouse, but it's not. At the entrance to the breakwater. A blue and white building. That's where you'll find the port authority.'

'And they can tell me who owns what berth?'

'They can, but they won't. That's privileged information. Unless you have some kind of official authorization. But, as you say, not a uniform in sight. And no warrant either, I'd guess.' He smiled smugly.

'Thank you for your help,' Mackenzie said.

*

The sea was almost painfully blue as Mackenzie walked squinting into the sun towards the far end of the marina. A constant stream of white-sailed yachts came and went. They littered the water beyond the breakwater like scraps of paper blowing in the breeze. A speedboat cut noisy arcs out in the bay, washing white circles in sparkling azure. *Pantaláns*, or quays, branched off at right angles, yachts and motor boats and dinghies berthed along either side, bobbing almost imperceptibly on the gentlest of swells, the air filled with the sound of steel cables chapping on metal masts.

Access to the *pantaláns* was barred by locked gates, surveillance cameras mounted on each. Berths were expensive, security was high.

Mackenzie saw a young girl in a bikini taking buckets and mops and cartons of cleaning materials from the boot of a car parked opposite *Pantalán* 4. She was lithe and muscular with deeply bronzed skin and hair bleached blond by the sun. She smiled at Mackenzie as he passed. He nodded. '*Hola*,' he said. He imagined that if he spent his days cleaning boats in full sunshine, he too would end up the colour of teak. And maybe the sun would find some blond in even his dark hair.

He noticed that the deeper into the marina he walked, the larger the boats. Only smaller ones were berthed close to the port itself.

The port authority sat right at the end of the access road, where the breakwater offered protection to the inner harbour. A collection of blue-and-white-painted buildings from which the tower itself rose above the breakwater, designed by some fanciful architect to look like an old lighthouse. Mackenzie climbed steps to an office at the foot of the tower. A middle-aged woman looked up from her desk, peering at him from behind a computer monitor. A large TV screen mounted on the wall behind her segued through a carousel of images from security cameras around the port.

'*Buenas días, señor.* Can I help you?'

Susan had always told him that when he faked a smile it was like the grimace of a chimp behind bars in a zoo. He trusted he was doing a better job of it today. 'I hope you can,' he said. 'A friend of mine, Ian Templeton, told me that the berth next to his was for sale. Or rent. He wasn't sure which. I wondered if you could clarify that for me, and tell me how much it would cost.' His jaw ached from his chimpanzee smile.

She gave him a curious look. 'What's the number of his berth?'

'I have no idea.'

She sighed. 'Templeton, you said?'

'Yes. Ian.'

She tapped her keyboard and manoeuvred her mouse around the desk, peering myopically at the screen in front of her. 'Yes, here we are. *Pantalán 4*, berth 405. Which side of it did he say was for sale?'

'He didn't'

She glared at him. 'He didn't tell you very much, did he?'

He tried to factor apology into his smile. 'Sorry.'

She frowned at her screen. 'Well, neither of them are for sale *or* rent. Are you sure it wasn't one opposite?'

He shrugged unconvincingly, certain that she could see right through him. 'Eh . . . maybe.'

She shook her head again. 'There's nothing available on *Pantalán* 4 at all. I can give you something on 3.'

'Oh.' He hadn't been expecting that. 'No, no . . . it's alright.'

'Well what kind of boat do you have?'

He hesitated. 'A . . . A big one.' Which was what this excruciatingly lie was turning into.

She frowned. 'Can you be more specific?'

'No,' he said. 'Not really. Just, you know . . . big.' His smile, he was sure, would have turned milk sour by now. 'But it's okay. I'll talk to him again. Thank you very much for your help.' And he hurried out before she could ask him anything else, force-feeding the lie to grow from big, like his fictitious boat, to unbelievable.

As if in punishment for lying, the sun seemed to strike him a blow as he stepped again into its relentless heat. He breathed a long sigh of relief. Deception was not his forte. Still, he had established one thing. Cleland kept a boat here, registered to Templeton, at berth number 405 on *Pantalán* 4.

A motor launch had pulled in to *Pantalán* 5 to refuel from the Repsol pumps, and he glanced down the quays that stretched away towards the port, gates all locked. No way to take a look at Cleland's boat without going through official channels. He began to walk back along the access road towards the port and took out his phone, resigned to reporting his discovery to the *Jefe*. He stopped at *Pantalán 4* and saw that the nearside berth was number 401. Counting along, he saw Cleland's boat berthed at 405. It was a sleek white motor yacht with a long nose like a shark, an impressive superstructure rising towards the stern of the vessel. The sweep of its smoked-glass windows wrapped around the front of the cabin and either side, hiding its interior from the casual observer. Clip and zip canvas covers sealed off the rear entrance. He saw a maker's name printed high up beneath an external cockpit. Princess 52.

He looked at his phone and saw that he had a 4G signal, so initiated a Google search for the make and model. A second-hand boat for sale came up on his screen almost instantly. This was an expensive beast, 15.95 metres long, or 52 feet 4 inches, which was the source of its model name. It had twin 630-horsepower Volvo diesel engines with a cruising speed of 22 knots. This one had been built in 2000, and still commanded an asking price of €200,000. He had no idea what vintage Cleland's boat might be, but it looked brand spanking new, so was worth, perhaps, anything up to a million. The Princess 52 had three cabins with room for six guests.

Mackenzie swiped through photographs of the interior. This was a luxury vessel. Beneath the external cockpit, a generous lounge and kitchen area of white leather and polished wood gave on to the internal cockpit. Stairs led down to sleeping quarters below, where the three cabins shared two bathrooms and a shower room.

He stood gazing at it through the bars of the gate with something like awe. He could never have dreamed of owning something like this, but had never aspired to. Boats, he knew, were notoriously expensive to run and maintain, and for most owners would provide only occasional use. A measure of the affluence that Cleland had accumulated by trading in other people's misery, the price of all the ruined lives he had left in his wake. Mackenzie felt his hackles rise.

'Hello again.'

He turned, startled, to find the teak-coloured girl in the bikini smiling at him, a bucket and mop in one hand, a box of cleaning fluids beneath her other arm. There was a key dangling from a tab held between her clenched front teeth.

'Open the gate for me?' She had difficulty with the p and the f and the m.

It took a moment for him to realize what she meant. He blushed. 'Of course.' He removed the key delicately from her mouth to unlock the gate and hold it open for her.

'You can just drop it in the bucket,' she said, indicating the key in his hand, and it occurred to him for the first time that she was speaking English. 'My name's Sally.' She glanced at him, inviting a response.

'John,' Mackenzie said reluctantly.

'Dreaming, were you?' She nodded towards the yachts.

For once the lie sprung quickly to Mackenzie's lips. 'No, I just came down to check on my boat and realized I'd left my key at home.'

'Oh. Which is yours?'

'The Princess 52.'

She looked along the *pantalán* and picked it out. 'Nice one, John. You don't fancy taking out a little cleaning contract on it, do you?'

'That's what you do, is it?' he said. 'Clean boats?'

She started walking along the quay and he fell in step beside her.

'It pays for me to spend the whole season down here. And get a great tan at the same time. I sleep on the boats, too, so I have no accommodation costs. Next year I might go back to Cambridge and finish my degree.' She smiled. 'Or the year after. Or maybe I'll meet some rich yacht owner who'll sweep me off to some distant blue horizon and I'll never need to graduate.' She cocked a mischievous eyebrow in his direction.

He laughed. 'You're looking at the wrong man.'

She feigned disappointment. 'Gay?'

'Married.'

'Aren't they all?' She gave him a cheerful grin. 'See you later.' And she headed off along the *pantalán*, leaving Mackenzie standing at the stern of the Princess 52. He watched her walk to the far end and climb aboard a long, sleek-looking sail boat. When she had disappeared below, he turned towards Cleland's boat and saw that it was called *Big Rush*, one of the many street names for cocaine. It rekindled his anger. But an unzipped flap of the canvas cover that weather-protected the rear deck stilled it before it took hold, replacing it instead with a sudden stab of disquiet. Was it possible that this is where Cleland had been hiding out the whole time, right under their noses?

On full alert now, he stepped carefully from the quay on to the exposed lip of the rear deck and felt the boat dip a little in the water from his weight. He stood listening intently, but all he could hear was the gentle purr of motors propelling boats in and out of the harbour, and the cries of seabirds swooping and wheeling overhead. Across the water, at the far side of the marina, the Varadero la Condesa boatyard was winching a boat from winter storage to take its first dip of the year. Its pristine keel cut into mirrored water sending concentric rings off in light-catching circles.

Mackenzie lifted the flap and peered inside. The door to the lounge stood open, and the carpeted luxury beyond it simmered in semi-darkness. He breathed in deeply, smelling leather and aftershave, and all his instincts told him there was somebody there.

He waited several long seconds for his eyes to adjust to the dark after the glare of sunshine on water outside. Very cautiously he moved forward, passing through the open door to feel soft carpet underfoot. The lounge with its open-plan kitchen and the cockpit beyond appeared empty. The hatch to the lower deck stood open. Mackenzie ran a practised eye around every surface. A pair of well-worn boat shoes sat under a dining table strewn with maps and charts. A pullover lay discarded on the settee.

From nowhere a shadow materialized from the darkness, taking form and sudden human shape to deliver a disabling blow to the side of Mackenzie's face. Light filled his head and his knees buckled beneath him. His full dead weight hit the floor with a sickening thud that expelled the remaining air from his lungs in a single long sigh.

His attacker stepped swiftly over him towards the door and from somewhere Mackenzie summoned coherent thought and sufficient strength to reach out and catch an ankle. It was enough to unbalance the other man, who toppled face-forward to strike his head on the doorframe and roll over on to his back. Mackenzie fought to suck air into his lungs and fuel his lunge towards the supine figure on the floor, only to feel the full power of a flat-footed kick in his chest. It felt as though his rib-cage had been crushed by the blow and he fell back again to cry out in pain, rolling to one side to avoid further blows.

The other man got to his knees as Mackenzie tried to get to his, and they found themselves staring straight into each other's eyes, breathless and perspiring. It was Mackenzie's first face-to-face with Cleland and he saw the crazed light in his psychotic blue eyes. How was it Cristina had described him? *Quite mad.*

'You fucker!' Cleland screamed, and his voice resounded deafeningly in the enclosed space of the cabin. Mackenzie lunged again, catching him off guard. He fell backwards with

Mackenzie on top. Mackenzie could smell coffee on his breath, and garlic from yesterday. And something else. Something rank.

Mackenzie hissed in his face, 'You're claimed, Cleland. I'm taking you all the way down.'

For a moment Cleland went limp, and he looked into Mackenzie's face, surprise writ large on his. 'Scottish!? You're fucking Scottish!? You came all the way down here just to get me?'

'That's right, Cleland. And take you back, too.'

'Like fuck!' He bucked hard beneath Mackenzie, and with an enormous effort rolled him off to the side. He was a big man, physically stronger than Mackenzie, and his fist felt as if it were clad in chainmail as it smashed into Mackenzie's face. Blood bubbled into Mackenzie's mouth, and he felt the bitter iron taste of it. He lashed out with his own clenched fist and felt pain jar through his arm all the way to the shoulder as it made contact with Cleland's head.

Cleland cursed, and staggered to his feet. Mackenzie could do nothing to stop him. Nor could he prevent the other man from sinking a foot hard into his solar plexus. He doubled up, gasping with pain, and felt the searing heat of the midday sun as it spilled momentarily into the back of the boat through the open canvas flap. Cleland was through it and gone.

With an enormous effort of will, Mackenzie dragged himself to his knees, supporting himself on the corner of the built-in settee. His eyes settled on a flare gun clipped to the fascia beside the wheel in the cockpit. He scrambled to his feet and staggered across the cabin to wrench it free, then ran to the stern of the boat and out into blinding sunlight.

He blinked fiercely to focus on the fleeing figure of Cleland as he sprinted along the *pantalán* towards the gate. The fugitive had to stop and fumble for a key to open it. Then with a backward glance he was out and pounding along the access road towards the port. Mackenzie limped after him, holding his side with one hand, clutching the signal pistol with the other. He caught the gate before it closed and stumbled into the road. He had a clear shot at Cleland's back as he ran towards steps that rose in two flights towards the road behind the port. He levelled the pistol. There was a good chance that the flare would bring him down. It might do him damage, though it probably wouldn't kill him.

But there were holidaymakers on the road. A young couple with a baby in a pram, a family with a dog, a boy on a bike, Cleland brushing them aside as he sprinted past. Mackenzie clenched his teeth and bellowed through them in pure frustration. There was no way he could release the flare. God only knew how accurate the pistol might be, or what kind of injuries it could inflict on innocents.

Instead, he raised the gun above his head and fired it angrily into the air, sending an arc of pink smoke soaring into the sky above the *puerto* to explode in a bright flash of red that cast its reflection like blood across all the still waters of the marina.

He caught a movement in the corner of his eye and turned to see Sally standing at the far end of the *pantalán*, mop in hand, gawping at him in astonishment.

CHAPTER SEVENTEEN

The excitement occasioned by a flare exploding high above Puerto de la Condesa and seen for miles along the coast had long since subsided.

Mackenzie sat on the concrete box that supplied power and water to Cleland's Princess 52 from the *pantalán*, and winced as a medic in dark green and yellow uniform applied antiseptic to his damaged face. The medic had previously removed Mackenzie's T-shirt and felt carefully around the bruising on his ribs. He didn't believe there was anything broken, but suggested an x-ray and support-strapped it in the meantime.

A forensics team from Estepona had arrived, sweltering beneath plastic jumpsuits as they worked their way systematically from one end of Cleland's boat to the other, taking fingerprints, scrapings from a bloodstain found on the carpet, hair, nail clippings from one of the toilets, a razor, a toothbrush.

The *Jefe* stepped off the boat on to the quay and glared at Mackenzie. 'You couldn't have called for back-up? We'd have caught him red-handed.'

Mackenzie winced as the medic applied fresh antiseptic. 'I was about to,' he said. 'Then this girl unlocked the gate and I thought I'd just take a look.'

'What girl?'

Mackenzie flicked his head towards the far end of the *pantalán* where Sally was giving a statement to a couple of Policía Local. 'She cleans boats.'

'Not Cleland's, apparently,' the *Jefe* said. 'It's filthy. A treasure trove of forensic evidence. Unfortunately, there's just one thing missing. Cleland himself.' He paused. 'What possessed you to fire off a flare?'

Mackenzie shook his head. 'I don't know. I was going to try to shoot him with it. But there were too many people around. I just fired it in frustration.'

'You'd have been in big trouble if you'd hit him.'

Mackenzie nodded his acknowledgement. 'I know.'

The *Jefe* sighed and hooked his thumbs into his belt. 'I don't know that he's been here much. None of the beds have been slept in. There's some dirty laundry tossed on to one of them. Looks like maybe he just came for a change of clothes, something to eat and a coffee. There's a half-drunk cup in the kitchen and the remains of a sandwich on the counter top. Seems you disturbed him before he could finish it. There might also have been some cash on board. He's very probably running out.' He glanced along the quay to where a phalanx of police vehicles, blue lights flashing, clustered around the open gate to the *pantalán*. An ambulance stood on the other side of the access road, engine idling. A large crowd of onlookers, managed by a couple of uniformed Guardia, waned and waxed in turns, holidaymakers and locals exercising their curiosity. 'You know what really hacks me off?'

Mackenzie squinted up at him in the sunlight. The chief was silhouetted against the sky, and Mackenzie couldn't see the expression on his face. 'No,' he said.

'That none of our people thought to check if the bastard had a boat here.' He turned a disapproving gaze on the Scotsman. 'It was a good thought, señor. Just a poor execution.'

Mackenzie could not disagree. His eye was caught by the movement of a diminutive figure pushing through the crowd. It was Cristina. Mackenzie's heart sank. He could only imagine what she would say. She strode along the *pantalán* adjusting her hair in the band that gathered it at the back of her head. She nodded to the *Jefe* and glared at Mackenzie. 'Can't leave you alone for five minutes, can I?'

Mackenzie attempted a smile. 'Apparently not.'

The *Jefe* said to her, 'Get him out of my hair. Take him for something to eat. Tell him we don't operate like cowboys here. There's a meeting at the station called for five this afternoon. We'll go over everything we know then. Just make sure he's back in time.'

'I *am* here, you know,' Mackenzie said. 'I can hear you.'

The *Jefe* glowered at him. 'Not sure I feel like talking to you right now.'

*

154

As they walked back along the access road to the port, Cristina said, without looking at him, 'That was a smart piece of work.'

He kept his eyes on the tables and chairs outside the cafes and restaurants that flanked the harbour ahead of them. 'Thank you.'

'The first part. Not the second.'

'I think the *Jefe* already made that clear.'

'You're lucky he didn't throw you into the harbour.'

Mackenzie pressed his lips into a grim line.

'I think he likes you,' she said, and Mackenzie turned a look of surprise in her direction. She flicked him a glance. 'God knows why.'

The Nissan SUV was parked at the top of the steps which had been Cleland's escape route from the port. As she opened the driver's door Cristina said, 'Are you hungry?'

Mackenzie nodded.

'Well, you'll have to wait. I have to go into Estepona first and call in on my aunt. We can grab something to eat afterwards.'

CHAPTER EIGHTEEN

Ana's excitement is palpable. It consumes her every thought, fills her physical being. It is a feeling she has not known in all the years since the shutters came down on her world. A feeling that brings back hope, like stumbling upon water unexpectedly in a desert. A feeling that perhaps life might just be worth rekindling.

Her fingertips tingle from the braille that she has read and reread on her screen. He will not have heard her voice, and she has no idea how it might have sounded to the operator who passed it on in text on a screen. Whether she spoke too loudly, or too softly, or if it still has that husky little catch that always surprised her when she replayed a recording of it. Something she never heard herself in real time.

Had the operator, she wonders, discerned at all the emotion conveyed in the brief exchange of words for which she had been the conduit?

Sergio's call was so unexpected, so undreamt of, Ana still finds it hard to believe it really happened. All those years ago she had been able to hear *his* voice, and now has to imagine it from the patterns that raise themselves beneath her fingertips, capable only of drawing its rich soft cadences from recollection. Whatever hesitation it might have contained was impossible to interpret from the braille. Whatever apprehension lost for ever in the ether. Just his words in cold, hard little dots.

'Hello, Ana. It's Sergio.'

She had responded to the call, prompted by the buzzer that vibrated at her breast. Never, in any lifetime, expecting to read those words. At first she had been at a loss as to how to respond.

'Sergio?' Which had seemed so inadequate, given how laden this call was with its own history.

'I want to say sorry to you a million times over, Ana. But not in a phone call.'

No words had come. She had sat frozen with disbelief, then fear that somehow this was some wicked hoax. It was more than twenty years since they had last spoken.

'I have only now discovered where you are living. I cannot believe it. All this time, and only a few streets away. Oh, Ana, say you'll see me. Let me come and tell you myself. You owe me nothing, I know. But I owe you everything. Not least an explanation. I could come later this afternoon, or early this evening. It depends when I can get away from work. Please, Ana.'

Finally she had found her inner voice and let it speak

through the operator. 'I'm not going anywhere, Sergio. And even if I could there's nowhere for me to go.'

'I'll come as soon as I can. I'll tell you everything then.'

And so the call had ended, leaving her to thrash about in a sea of emotions, drowning in her own past.

CHAPTER NINETEEN

Ana remembered the first time she ever set eyes on Sergio. He had not immediately endeared himself to her.

It was 1997. She was in her final year at secondary school and facing an uncertain future. The hearing problems which had dogged her from early childhood were getting worse. School had been a hostile environment. As her auditory perception deteriorated and she was forced to wear hearing aids, so the friendships she had made in the early years fell by the wayside. One by one. No one wanted to be friends with a girl who couldn't hear, as if they too might be tainted by her disability. It wasn't *cool*. It made her seem stupid, and slow. Besties became bullies, playing tricks on her behind her back, indulging the apparently endless capacity of children for cruelty. Relentless mimicry, humiliation. And her tearful response only encouraged further ridicule, somehow whipping former friends into a frenzy of heartlessness.

Her teachers were just as bad, or perhaps worse, since they were at least adults. Their cruelty came more in the form of thoughtless neglect than cold-hearted design. Ana had been refused a place at a special needs school. Her hearing deficiency was not deemed serious enough, and from the earliest age the only concession to her problem was to place her in a seat at the front of the class. Her teachers would then proceed to address the others over her head, or speak while facing the blackboard, so that Ana could not even read their lips.

For Ana herself it had resulted in slower than average progress and disparaging report cards.

Ana doesn't pay attention.

Ana is clever, but she just doesn't try.

Ana is lazy.

Ana doesn't do her homework.

So unfair! Ana only ever missed her homework when it was delivered verbally to class, and she either misunderstood, or didn't hear at all. Not one of her teachers took the trouble to write it down for her, or ensure that she understood what was being asked. She was just an irritation, an additional problem they didn't need. A lumpen girl who sat at the front of the class. A girl who never responded, never participated, failed her exams and forgot her homework.

A girl who ached inside, hiding her misery and her loneliness from the world – even from her parents.

Her father was loving in his own way, but hardly ever there. A travelling salesman, he spent days on end, sometimes weeks, away from their home in a small apartment in Marviña old town, leaving Ana in the sole care of her mother. Although her mother came from a poor working-class family in a village in Catalonia, she had a certain conceit of herself, and always stood on her dignity. She adored Ana's elder sister, Isabella, who was everything Ana was not. Pretty, clever, socially adept. And the ten-year age difference between the girls meant that they had virtually nothing in common, sharing very little of the childhoods that were always at very different stages of development. By the time Ana was nearing the end of secondary school, Isabella was already married with two young girls of her own.

Ana was viewed almost with embarrassment by her mother, as if her deafness were somehow her own fault, contrived to reflect shame on her family. When her husband was away she frequently chastised her daughter for failing to listen or understand, shouting at her quite unnecessarily when Ana was perfectly able to hear. Then, overcome with regret, she would smother the girl with love and tears, only to revert to type when Ana next frustrated her.

It was with some trepidation that Ana received the news her father brought home with him one night that he had obtained a place for her at a voluntary centre for the deaf in Estepona. Her mother was none too pleased either. It would be like announcing to the world, she said, that their daughter was disabled. Ana herself was less than happy. She was hard of hearing, she said, not deaf. But her dad had been insistent. The centre was run by a charity, but received government money in the form of a grant from the *Junta de Andalucía*. They provided facilities for the visually impaired, as well as the – and he chose his words carefully – hard of hearing. But it meant that Ana would get the opportunity to learn sign language, and that could only be a good thing. Ana was not so sure.

The centre was tucked away in a back street off the Plaza de las Flores in the old town of Estepona. Ana's father drove her there on the first evening. After parking his car he took her by the hand and led her through the square up into a gloomy side street. 'I'll come and get you at nine, *cielo*,' he said. 'If you like it, you can get the bus next time.' The centre was open three evenings a week, but Ana didn't think there would be a next time.

An unprepossessing entrance led to a dark hallway that in turn opened into a large room set with tables and chairs, a couple of settees and several old armchairs. A hatch leading to a small kitchen released the smell of freshly brewed coffee into the crowded room. A young woman with short dark hair shook her father's hand, and then Ana's. 'Welcome, young lady,' she said. 'Your father tells me you have hearing difficulties, but that you're not deaf.' Ana saw her eyes wander to the hearing aids in each of her ears. She nodded. 'Good. Then that'll make things much easier when it comes to learning sign language. We have an instructor who comes twice a week.' Again Ana nodded. She didn't want to let on that she had no intention of learning sign language. It would be like admitting that she was deaf. Perhaps, she thought, there was more of her mother in her than she might have wanted.

When her father had gone the young woman led her to a table and told her that someone would come shortly to speak to her and take down all her details. Ana sat and looked around with dismay. This was a gloomy room, with scarred and damp-stained yellow-painted plaster, and there was almost nobody here, she decided, under sixty.

'*Hola*, how are you doing?'

She looked up to find herself gazing into the eyes of a young man in his early twenties. A shock of unruly brown hair tumbled across a strong brow with thick, dark eyebrows. He possessed a long aquiline nose, and full lips that seemed pale set against the deep tan of his face. He was tall and quite skinny and smiled at her, and for the first time in her life Ana felt her stomach flip over.

'I'm alright,' she said uncertainly.

'Good,' he said. Then made a series of signs with his hands that left her mystified.

She shrugged helplessly.

'You lip-read?'

She nodded. Reading lips had never been a conscious process, simply something she had learned to do over the years out of pure necessity. She said, 'But I'm not completely deaf.' She saw him watching her lips intently.

He said, 'I am stone deaf. I could hear perfectly well until I was seven years old, then a virus damaged my auditory nerves and I've been unable to hear anything since. I don't like to speak now, because I'm always afraid I sound like a deaf person.' He laughed. 'Which I am, of course. But it's safer to sign.' He paused. 'Have you come to learn?'

She shook her head. 'I'm here because my father brought me. I doubt very much if I'll be back.'

His smile faded, replaced by a look of disappointment. 'Oh, you must. You can't leave me here on my own with all these old people.'

She glanced around self-consciously and he laughed again. 'Don't worry, they can't hear me. They're deaf.' Which made her laugh, too. Of course they were. 'Blind people come on Thursdays to learn to use the white stick. The lucky ones get guide dogs.' He paused. 'I sometimes wonder which is worse – being deaf or blind. But I think losing your sight would be the worst of all. I can't imagine not being able to see the world around me.' He glanced towards the kitchen hatch. 'Someone will likely come and take your registration details shortly. Can I get you a coffee?'

She nodded. 'Please.' And she watched him cross to the hatch. He had an easy gait, and she could see from his T-shirt that he had well-developed arms and pectorals, in a wiry sort of way. He wore tight-fitting jeans, and she found her eyes drawn to the lean but well-rounded buttocks that filled the seat of them.

He returned with two mugs of black coffee. 'I forgot to ask if you wanted black, or . . .'

'I prefer it with milk.'

'No problem.' He set the mugs down on the table and hurried

away to the kitchen, returning a few moments later with an open carton of milk. He poured milk into her coffee until a wave of her hand indicated that it was enough. But as he put the carton down he was too busy looking at her, and caught it on the edge of the table. It slipped from his grasp, and milk went cascading down the front of her blouse and over the legs of her jeans. He leapt back as if he had been burned, and her chair toppled backwards as she jumped to her feet. Both mugs of coffee went flying.

'Oh my God, oh my God,' he said. 'I'm so sorry. Wait, I'll get a cloth.' He hurried off again to the kitchen.

Ana stood with milk dripping on to the floor and running in white threads through dark pools of coffee. She looked around with embarrassment, expecting all eyes to be on her. But apart from an old lady at the far side of the room, no one seemed to have noticed. The young man returned with a tea towel and began feverishly wiping it up and down the front of her blouse. Before suddenly realizing that his fingers were brushing her breasts.

'Oh my God!' he said again, and once more jumped back. 'I'm sorry, I didn't mean . . .' He held out the tea towel for Ana to use for herself. 'Honestly, it was an accident.'

Ana fought hard to keep a straight face. In truth she was furious at him for ruining her blouse and her jeans. But she had also quite enjoyed the sensation of his fingers touching her breasts. Only once before had a boy put his hands on them. It was after a school dance and he had offered to walk her home. There had been a kiss, and then his hand sliding slyly beneath her blouse. She had slapped his face.

The young man blushed furiously.

She tried to soak up the milk from her blouse then glared at him. 'Well, since you have managed to ruin almost everything I'm wearing, the least you can do is tell me your name – if only so I can take it in vain.'

It was clear from his face that he was not quite sure if she was being funny or not. 'I'm Sergio,' he said, and held out an awkward hand.

She thrust the milk-soaked tea towel into it. 'I'm Ana. And maybe this time you'd like to get me a proper *café con leche*, without spilling milk all over me!'

They spent the next two hours just talking and drinking coffee. His lip-reading was better than hers, and she had at least some hearing to augment her comprehension. After ten minutes Ana had completely forgotten that either of them was anything other than a normal young person having a normal conversation. It was the first time in her life that she wasn't aware of her handicap. That it didn't seem to matter. That there were no obstacles to communication.

Sergio told her he had just turned twenty-one. He was studying online for a degree in Spanish. The internet was relatively young, but was already opening up possibilities for the deaf that could never have been imagined. The relationship with his tutors was conducted entirely onscreen, and they had no idea that he was deaf. 'It makes me feel like a normal person again,' he said. 'There's something about being deaf that seems to scare people. As if it's a disease they might catch. Others think you are just stupid, and they treat you like an imbecile.' He smiled. 'But why am I telling you? You must know.'

Ana nodded sadly. 'I know that I've lost all my friends. You sort of get used to just being on your own.' She smiled. 'After a while I kind of got to like it. You start relying on yourself, because you can't rely on anyone else.'

'Exactly right. But that's why I love the internet. You can just be yourself, and nobody's judging you. Nobody knows that you can't hear them, cos you don't need to. We could meet online in a chat room if you like.' The idea seemed to excite him.

Ana's smile faded and her eyes turned down towards the table.

'What's wrong?'

'We don't have internet at home.'

'Oh.' Sergio was crestfallen. 'Maybe you could ask your dad?'

'I don't think he can afford it.'

'Well, then, you'll just have to come here three nights a week, and we can make this our real-life chat room.' He grinned. 'And I'll teach you proper sign language.'

She pulled a face.

'No, honestly, it's good. When you get the hang of it you can really express yourself. You forget that you're not actually speaking out loud.'

She shrugged. 'Maybe.' She paused. 'Still not sure I'm coming back, though.' She watched his face fall again – an odd expression, but for the first time she realized how apposite it was. His face really did fall, and she didn't have the heart to keep playing hard to get. It made her laugh. 'But if you ask nicely . . .'

His relief was patent, and he grinned. 'I'll do better than that. I'll take you out for tapas. I don't just have to see you here.'

'Woah!' she raised her hands. 'Not so fast. We just met, remember?'

'Life's too short for wasting time.'

'Maybe. But it seems to me that you're asking me out on a date when you really don't know anything about me.'

'Well, how am I going to get to know you if I don't see you again?'

'You can see me here.'

His face lit up. 'You're coming back then?'

She saw how he had trapped her into that. 'I'll think about it.'

He beamed. 'Well, think about tapas, too. And maybe a beer. We don't want to spend our whole time surrounded by a bunch of old deaf people.'

She laughed out loud. 'One day, Sergio, we'll be old deaf people, too.' And she realized how much she liked saying his name, and how much she really did want to get to know him better. And she decided there and then that she would accept his offer to take her on a date. But she wouldn't tell him just yet.

It was a couple of weeks before Ana plucked up the courage to tell her parents that she had been asked on a date by a young man at the centre. She needed a lift into Estepona. But she was completely unprepared for the reaction it provoked. She had been five times now to the centre, and on her previous visit had told Sergio that she would go for tapas with him.

It was a hot summer's night. Her father sat at the table wearing only a singlet and shorts, the local newspaper open in front of him. A pair of half-moon spectacles rested halfway down his nose and sweat darkened the white cotton of his vest where it stretched itself over his ample belly.

He looked up, frowning, and said simply, 'No.'

Ana bristled. 'What do you mean, no?'

'Well, which part of the word don't you understand?'

She turned belligerent. 'I understand that I'm seventeen years old and that if I want to go out with a boy, I'll go out with a boy.'

'As long as you're under my roof you'll do what I damned well tell you.'

Her mother appeared at the kitchen door. 'What do you even know about this boy?'

'A lot.'

'What age is he?' her father said.

'He's twenty-one.'

'Hah!' He folded his newspaper shut and slapped a palm on the table. 'Well, that settles it. Only one thing on *his* mind.'

'How could you possibly know what's on his mind?' Ana was aware of her voice rising in pitch.

'Because I was twenty-one myself once. I know what a young man thinks when he looks at a seventeen-year-old girl. The answer is no. And that's an end to it.'

Her mother cast a judgmental eye over her husband, wondering perhaps if those same things still went through his mind when he looked at a seventeen-year-old girl. She refocused on Ana. 'You met him at the centre?'

'Yes.'

'So he's deaf?'

'Yes, he is.'

She gasped her frustration. 'Holy Mary mother of God, Ana, could you not find yourself a normal boy?'

Ana's simmering anger started to boil over. 'What do you mean, "normal"? Are you saying *I'm* not normal?'

Her mother realized her mistake. 'No,' she said hastily. 'But you need someone with normal hearing to make up for your lack of it. You know the doctor said it's only going to get worse. One day you'll not be able to hear at all. Then you'd be two deaf people.'

Now her father slammed both palms down on the table. 'Enough!' he bellowed, and Ana was sure they must have heard him down on the coast. 'You are NOT going out with him.'

Ana felt hot tears fill her eyes. If only Isabella had been

there to speak up for her. She was sure her parents would have listened to her sister. But the only one who was going to stand up for Ana was Ana herself. She got to her feet. 'What are you going to do, tie me up? If I want to go out with Sergio, I'll got out with Sergio. And if you won't give me a lift into town I'll just get the bus.' She lifted her bag, slung it over her shoulder and stormed out of the living room, slamming the door behind her.

Sergio was waiting nervously for her outside the post office on the *Paseo Maritimo*, an elegant tree-lined promenade that ran the length of the seafront in Estepona. The *chiringuito* beach bars were full and the smell of fresh fish grilling on wooden embers filled the evening.

She was nearly half an hour late, and had done her best on the bus to repair the damage to her face.

'I really thought you'd stood me up,' Sergio said. 'Another five minutes and I'd have been off.' Although Ana suspected he would have waited a lot longer. He peered at her in the fading light. 'Have you been crying?'

She shrugged it off. 'Some bad news at home,' she said. 'But it's okay, I don't want anything to spoil our evening.'

Concerned eyes lingered on her face for several long moments before Sergio took her hand and they began strolling slowly along the *Paseo* in the direction of the old port.

Apartments rose on three and four levels above the shops and restaurants lining the broad Avenue del Carmen that swept down into town from the west. A fine, sandy beach stretched away to their left, and a gently foaming Mediterranean washed up along the shore, breathing softly into the night. It was cooling now, but the air was still soft on their skin.

Ana liked the feel of her hand in his. It felt big and protective. Their arms swung together a little as they walked in an easy silence. Lip-reading, since they were both facing in the same direction, was not an option. And their hands were otherwise engaged.

Ana had taken her first few lessons in signing, and spent most of her time with Sergio practising it. To her surprise it had come much more easily than she expected. But for now she was content just to feel close to him. Words were unimportant, and she let all memory of the row with her parents slip away.

Sergio took her to a tiny tapas bar in the port, squeezing past crowded tables on the terrace to find a quiet spot in the dark interior. The walkway outside was jammed with tourists and locals finding seats in restaurants and bars. The smell of woodsmoke and barbecued meats suffused the night air, and yachts bobbed gently in the dark on the moonlit waters of the marina. They ordered the house selection of tapas, and a waitress brought them seemingly endless plates of *patatas bravas*, *albóndigas*, *langostinos*, *empanadas*, *tortitas* . . . Sergio asked for two glasses of Rioja, and they sipped on its smooth velvety vanilla as they ate.

Ana spoke and signed at the same time, Sergio correcting

her as she went. Tea-light candles burned on their table, and tiny pinpoints of light danced in his dark eyes. 'So,' she said. 'Once you have graduated, what is it you want to do?'

'I want to teach,' he said. 'In a school for the deaf, or special needs pupils. I want to bring the world to children with problems and teach them that they are no different from anyone else. That there's nothing to stop them from being whoever it is they want to be.'

Ana felt her heart swell. 'I wish I'd had someone like you to teach me. Maybe I wouldn't have grown up believing that everyone else was better.'

'Oh, Ana . . .' He placed both of his hands over one of hers. 'You mustn't ever think that. You're beautiful inside and out. You're clever, you're articulate, you're funny.' He paused and she felt his hands tighten their grip on hers. 'I think you're wonderful.'

She blushed and glanced away, embarrassed by his directness, but filled with pleasure. And feelings of – she wasn't quite sure what. Just feelings she had never had before.

They ate their way through every plate, washing it all down with a second glass of wine. They talked and laughed and Ana thought, this is how it must be for ordinary people. For the first time in her life she forgot about her hearing difficulties, forgot that Sergio was deaf. Simply felt the pleasure of being alive, and enjoying the company of the person she was with.

When it came time to go, and Sergio paid the bill, she got up from the table with reluctance, for the first time allowing thoughts to enter her mind of what might await her when she got home. In the port outside, bright lights obliterated the darkness, turning night into day, air filled with the sound of humanity at play. Sounds Sergio would never hear, and which registered only distantly for Ana. As they wove their way through the terrace Ana stumbled on someone's bag lying on the floor and almost fell.

Sergio caught her, and for a moment she found herself in his arms, safe from all the dangers that the night presented. He made sure she was steady on her feet before letting her go. She laughed it off. 'I'm getting so clumsy. Tripping over things that I don't seem to notice, bumping into people as I go past them.'

Sergio laughed. 'It's the wine. I feel a little heady myself.'

He took her hand and she leaned in to his side as they walked up out of the port to the bus stop in the Avenue del Carmen. They stood waiting for the bus and for the first time that night could find nothing to say. Something about the anticipation of parting silenced tongues and hands. They had spent many hours together at the centre, but this was their first time out alone, and Ana wondered how they would end it. Her mouth was dry, and her heart beat a little faster when she saw the lights of the bus turning on the roundabout. But she had no time to think about it before she felt Sergio's arm around her waist, his face lowering itself to hers, his lips soft and warm brushing her mouth. She strained on tiptoes to kiss him, and they very nearly let the bus go past.

When it came to a stop, Sergio held her hand as she stepped up into it, and she slumped into a seat at the front ignoring the lecherous grin of the driver.

The twenty-minute drive back to Marviña passed in a blur, a confusion of thoughts and emotions. She tried not to think about her parents, but focus instead on the time she had spent with Sergio. But as her bus turned up the hill from the round-about at Santa Ana de las Vides, she couldn't prevent fears of what awaited her from creeping into her conscious thoughts.

It seemed profoundly dark as she stepped off the bus into the Plaza del Vino. The square, she knew, was ringed with street lights, and she wondered for a moment if there had been a power cut. She heard rather than saw the bus pull away and the hand of fear closed around her heart and filled her with dread. Why couldn't she see anything? It was as if the whole town was smothered in black dust. She was gripped almost immediately by a complete sense of disorientation. It was only a five-minute walk to the apartment, but she had no idea which way to go. She turned left, then right, stumbling over a kerbstone and nearly falling. She put her hands out ahead of her to avoid walking into a wall or a building or a lamp post and wanted to call out for someone to help her. But at this hour the town was deserted. Shutters closed, bars emptied, lights out.

Her fear was so great now it took almost physical form, rising up from her chest and into her throat, very nearly choking her. She staggered forwards, hearing the approaching vehicle before becoming aware, even more distantly, of its headlights turning towards her. She spun around in a panic, heard the screech of tyres, and the impact of the car as it sent her careening sideways. The world tilted, the falling sensation ending abruptly as her head hit the tarmac and true darkness enveloped her.

When light finally penetrated the black, she became aware of a softness enfolding her, almost as if she were suspended in it. But with the light came pain, a searing pain that spiked through her skull and violated her consciousness. She opened her eyes, startled, only to be blinded by the light in her bedroom.

Beyond initial confusion, shapes took form around her. Silhouettes against the light. Faces crystallized into familiarity. Her mother, her father. Isabella. A man who it took her some moments to realize was their family physician, Doctor Celestino. A small and balding man with large, horn-rimmed glasses. They leaned into her field of vision and she could see concern on all their faces.

The doctor's voice came to her faintly. Her hands shot instinctively to her ears, but her hearing aids had been removed.

'She's lucky,' Celestino was saying. 'Some cuts and bruises, but nothing broken, I think. The driver said he had come to a virtual standstill before he hit her.'

Then her father's voice, tight with anger. 'I can smell alcohol on her breath. She was out drinking with that boy!'

Anger gave Ana the strength to pull herself up on to one elbow. 'I am not drunk!' she shouted, only convincing everyone in the room that she was. 'I couldn't see when I got off the bus. Everything was dark, like they'd turned out the lights.' The effort of speaking exhausted her and she dropped once more on to her back. 'I couldn't even see the stars in the sky.'

'So you were *blind* drunk!' her father growled.

'*Papi*!' It was Isabella's voice, trying to calm their father.

Doctor Celestino leaned in close to peer into her eyes. 'Has that ever happened to you before, *mi niña*?' he asked.

'I've never let her drink in this house.' Her father was defensive now. 'Not once.'

But Celestino ignored him. 'Ana,' he said. 'Has it?'

Ana tried to bring clarity to her confusion. 'No. Not like that. I never see well at night. Never have.' She paused. 'It's like that for everyone, isn't it?' Then, 'It's as if I was blind. I just couldn't see.'

Ana's mother's voice now. 'Is there something wrong with her, doctor?'

But Celestino kept his focus on Ana. 'Do you have trouble seeing things in your peripheral vision, little one?'

Ana didn't understand. 'What do you mean?'

'Bump into things or people on either side of you that you just don't see. Trip over stuff on the ground.'

Ana remembered what she had told Sergio only an hour before. 'Yes,' she said. 'All the time.'

Celestino turned towards Ana's parents, his voice laden with concern. 'I think maybe Ana should see a specialist.'

Resentment simmered in Ana's house for the next ten days. Neither of her parents could forgive her, nor she them. She did not go back to the centre while she waited for her appointment with the ophthalmologist in Estepona. School had closed for the summer, and it had not been decided whether Ana would return for a repeat year or apply for a place at college. Her results were not yet in, and everything would depend on how good, or bad, they were.

The days dragged and she wished there were some way she could contact Sergio to tell him what had happened. But she had no idea where he lived, or even his family name.

Nights were worse. She had noticed, with an increasing sense of disquiet, that her night vision was deteriorating rapidly, and she did not even want to venture out of the house after dark.

She spent most of her time shut away in her room listening to music, or reading, or simply daydreaming. Anything to avoid facing the uncertainty of a doctor's diagnosis and a future whose clarity was obscured by doubt.

Her father took the day off work to drive them into Estepona for Ana's appointment with Doctor Esteban at his private consulting rooms in the healthcare centre on the Avenida Juan Carlos Rey de España. Ana never thought to ask how much it might be costing, but her parents had been told that an appointment with a health service specialist could take weeks, even months, and so her father had decided to go private.

She spent more than an hour with the doctor, undergoing tests for both sight and hearing. He asked her endless questions about her apparent clumsiness and invited her to perform various tasks that tested her spatial awareness. He took blood samples to be sent for analysis, performed standard eye tests, and took an electroretinogram to measure the response of her retinas to light stimuli.

Afterwards she sat for what seemed like an age in a waiting room with her parents until Doctor Esteban called them into his office. His manner was very matter-of-fact, but there was a certain gravitas in his tone when he addressed them that somehow telegraphed the bad news to come. He directed his comments directly to her parents as if she were not there.

'I believe your daughter is suffering from something called retinitis pigmentosa, sometimes known as RP. When considering this in conjunction with the continued deterioration of her hearing, I am inclined to believe that she has a condition known as Usher Syndrome.'

It was a name that meant nothing to any of them, though it was one that would come to haunt Ana, not only in the days to come, but for the rest of her life.

He said, 'Assuming my diagnosis is confirmed, Ana will become not only profoundly deaf, but will also lose her sight. She will become deaf *and* blind.'

Ana was devastated. She had more or less come to terms with the possibility that she would at some future time lose her hearing altogether. But to become blind as well? It was unthinkable. Unimaginable. She remembered Sergio's words from their first meeting. *I think losing your sight would be the worst of all. I can't imagine not being able to see the world around me.* And when, a week later, the diagnosis was confirmed by a senior consultant in Malaga, she was plunged into the deepest depression. An abyss from which she could never imagine any way out.

It was a genetic condition, the consultant said. There was no cure. Nothing to be done. And the prognosis itself was uncertain, impossible to predict how quickly or slowly her sight would deteriorate. The only certainty was that blindness, along with eventual deafness, would come. Whether it was weeks, months or years was in the lap of the gods.

He had suggested that Ana start preparing for it immediately. There was, he told them, a form of sign language specifically designed for deaf-blind people. It was called tactile signing. A little like sign language for the deaf, except that the movement of the hands was conveyed by touch rather than sight.

It was with considerable reluctance that Ana's father allowed her, then, to return to the centre in Estepona. They could, they had told him, obtain the services of a special instructor to teach her the basics of tactile signing, preparing her for future blindness. And so with great trepidation Ana went back for the first time in weeks. She had not seen or heard anything of

Sergio since the tapas they had shared that fateful night, and with the knowledge that her future promised only darkness, she was afraid to face him. Afraid that when he realized how dependent she would be on him in any future relationship, he would turn away. After all, who in his right mind would want to take on that kind of responsibility for another human being? Living your own life was hard enough.

Her father drove her to the centre and told her he would return to collect her later, before it got dark. She was taken into an office at the back of the building, where the centre's administrator told her that they had applied on her behalf for the services of a touch-signing instructor. But the instructor would not arrive for another week, and could only come once a fortnight. So it was important for Ana to have someone to practise with in between times.

When her session with the administrator was over, Ana ventured back out into the big lounge. It was busy tonight. Elderly deaf men and women gathered around tables, signing and laughing and drinking coffee together. But her eye was drawn, almost involuntarily, towards the little group of blind people who sat near the door, white sticks resting against chairs, a guide dog sleeping against the back wall. They had no need to sign, for none of them was deaf. However bad it might be for any one of them, it would be worse for Ana. She felt tears of self-pity gathering in her eyes.

'Hello stranger.'

She spun around to find herself face to face with Sergio. She could see the uncertainty behind his smile, and she blinked away her tears.

'It's been a while.'

She nodded.

'I thought you were never coming back.'

She shrugged and attempted a smile. 'Neither did I.'

They stood in awkward silence, then, unsure of what to say next. Finally Sergio said, 'I have a little car now. I could run you home at the end of the evening, if you want.'

'My father's coming to get me.'

'Oh. Okay.' He looked disappointed. 'How have you been?'

She shrugged noncommittally. How could she tell him about her night blindness, that soon it would extend to daylight hours too, that the only future she faced was one of darkness? 'I had a fall,' she said. 'Nothing serious. I'm okay now.'

He seemed concerned. 'What kind of fall?'

She shook her head. 'It doesn't matter.'

He gazed at her with apprehension, aware that somehow all the intimacy of that evening spent together in the tapas bar at the port had dissipated, like smoke in the wind. 'Can I get you a coffee?'

She shook her head. 'No.' She hesitated. 'I'm not staying.' What was the point? The instructor would not come for another week. No reason for her being here, or coming back until then. It was light until much later in the evenings now. She could walk down to the Paseo and telephone her father from a call box. She saw the disappointment in Sergio's face.

'Why not?'

She looked him very directly in the eye. 'Forget about me, Sergio. We weren't meant to be.' And she turned to walk briskly to the door. Moving carefully through the darkness of the hall, and then out into the evening sunshine that slanted across the street from the clearest of blue skies.

She had reached the Plaza de las Flores before Sergio caught up with her. Tables around the perimeter of the square were filled with people enjoying drinks and tapas. The warm air was filled with their voices, like the chatter of birds. Trees in full leaf were laden with oranges, and flowers in bloom suffused the evening with their fragrance. He grabbed her arm, and she turned, surprised, and pulled it free of his grasp.

'What do you want?'

He couldn't hear the tone of her voice, but he could see the anger in her face, and he recoiled from it, hurt, like a dog suddenly slapped by a trusted master.

'What did I do?' he said. 'All this time I've been thinking I must have done or said something to offend you. Why else would you have stopped coming to the centre? Was it the kiss? Did I cross a line?'

His obvious distress felt like someone plunging a knife into her heart. She fought hard to stop the tears. 'No,' she said. 'No. It's not you. Nothing to do with you.'

He was, quite patently, completely bewildered. He put his hands on her shoulders. 'Well, what, then? What? What's wrong, Ana?' Heads turned, drawn by the pitch of his voice, which had risen beyond his ability to control it.

And quite suddenly her tears came. Welling up from deep inside, and spilling down her cheeks in large, quivering drops. 'You don't want to know.'

'I do!'

She shook her head. 'You won't want to be with me anymore.'

He threw his head back in despair. 'Why in God's name would I not want to be with you?'

More heads turned towards them.

'Because I'm going blind, Sergio. Soon I won't be able to see you, or hear you. You'll just be a touch in the dark. And you won't want anything to do with me.'

He was shocked. Staring at her in disbelief. 'I don't understand.'

'I have a genetic disorder. It's called Usher Syndrome. And it's going to take away my sight, as well as the rest of my hearing. It's already begun.'

He closed his eyes. 'Oh, dear God.' And she let him gather her into his embrace, drawing her head to his chest, fingers laced through her hair. 'Oh, Ana. I'm so sorry. I'm so sorry.' Then he held her again by the shoulders, at arm's length, and absolutely trapped her in his gaze. Earnest eyes staring determinedly into hers. 'How could you think, even for one minute, that something like that would drive me away? That somehow I wouldn't want to be with you any more?' Now he raised his eyes to the heavens. 'For God's sake Ana. It's you I love. The person you are inside. Not what you can see or hear.'

But the only thing she heard was *It's you I love*. Words that replayed themselves in her brain like an echo on a loop. And she saw that he did not even realize what he'd said.

He was oblivious. 'We'll find a way to communicate. It'll only bring us closer.'

She wiped the tears from her face, but couldn't stop the flow of more. 'An instructor is coming next week to start teaching me touch-signing while I can still see and hear. I don't know exactly how it works, but . . .' Her voice trailed away.

'I'll learn it with you,' he said quickly. 'We'll be fluent in it in no time.'

And she imagined how intimate that might be. Communication by touch alone. She couldn't think of anyone she'd rather have touch her. And for the first time since receiving the diagnosis, a glimmer of light shone somewhere in the darkness of her future.

The next weeks passed in a blur, and in equal measures of hope and despair. Learning tactile signing was easier than she had thought, since in many ways it was like a sensory extension of the signing for the deaf that she had already started to adopt. But as each session required her to close her eyes, she began to get a sense of what it would be like to be blind, and the shadow that cast upon her future was deep and depressing. By contrast, hope came from the regular and intimate contact with Sergio. They attended the lessons together, and there was something arousing about feeling his hands on hers when she couldn't see him. His fingers on her face, and hers on his. Something she had never known before.

Since the evenings were still light, she persuaded her father that she could travel to and from the centre by bus, and she thought he was relieved to be excused from the obligation of driving her there and back. But, in fact, she and Sergio only attended the centre on the days that the instructor came, and two evenings a week they would go and eat together at a little fish restaurant on the beach front at Santa Ana.

The proprietor was a small bald man with no teeth who greeted them every evening with a gummy smile and a bottle of white wine that he set open on the table almost before they sat down. They ate salad with tuna, and *boquerones*, and *calamares* and *abadejo*, and watched the sea wash pink phosphorescence upon the shore as the sun dipped towards the west. They closed their eyes and practised touch-signing with fingers greasy from anchovies and olive oil, and Ana thought she had never laughed so much in her life.

It was a desperate idyll. Desperate because it could not last, idyllic because they were sharing themselves with each other in ways that most people would never experience.

On the nights they ate at the restaurant, Sergio would drive her home, dropping her in a quiet street just around the corner from the apartment. Always before darkness fell, although already she was struggling to see in the twilight.

Nearly two months of tuition in the basics of tactile signing, and the regular practice she achieved with Sergio, was paying dividends. Already she was quite comfortable with it, spending sometimes hours on end with her eyes closed, the world reaching her only through Sergio's fingertips. But the summer was coming to an end, and with it the nights were drawing in. There was less and less light, and Sergio was forced to take her home earlier. Soon, as the evenings grew darker, Ana's father was going to insist on picking her up from the centre, and their idyll must come to an end.

It was a hot evening in mid-September when a thunderstorm rumbling across the Mediterranean from North Africa brought the meal at their little restaurant in Santa Ana to a premature end. They saw the storm approaching across the water, like a giant rolling cloud of mist, blotting out the blue of the evening sky, and finally the sun, before the wind that accompanied it began whipping large stinging drops of rain in under the awning. Day turned to night in the space of only a few minutes.

Sergio took her hand and they ran to where he had parked his car in the narrow Calle Condesa de Arcos. But, still, they were soaked by the time they had thrown themselves into the seats and slammed the doors shut. Rain streamed down the windscreen, and all the windows in the car quickly misted.

Ana was alarmed by how little she could see as they drove up the hill towards Marviña. The storm seemed to be following them, surging up the slope in their wake. The rain hammered out a deafening tattoo on the roof, and even though her hearing was fading, Ana felt it fill the car.

Marviña was deserted as they drove past the police and fire stations before turning down to their right, the view across the valley to the mountains obliterated by the storm. Sergio wanted to take her as close as he could to her apartment. It was almost dark out there, and the rain was obscuring the far end of the street. But Ana told him to stop. She could make it home from here, she said. It would be dangerous to get much closer because it was likely that in this weather her father would head out to meet her off the bus in the square.

Reluctantly, Sergio pulled in. He reached over to brush the wet hair from Ana's face and leaned in to kiss her. A long, lingering kiss that left the taste of him on her lips. She would have given anything to stay with him, safe and warm in the car. But the threat of an encounter with her father was too great. He would be incandescent if he knew that Ana had continued seeing Sergio, after he had made her promise him that she wouldn't.

She let her fingers trail gently across the fine stubble on his cheeks. 'See you Wednesday,' she said, and slipped out into the night.

She was startled in the rain by a figure that appeared out of nowhere. A shadow disengaging itself from the dark, brushing past her to round the front of Sergio's car and open the driver's door.

'Get out, you pervert!' It was her father's voice.

In the rain and the gloom, it was a shadow play that acted itself out before her. Her father dragging the hapless Sergio from his car, a fist swinging through the night to impact with the face she had so recently touched with loving fingers. She screamed as she saw Sergio fall into the road, raindrops hammering the surface of it, bouncing off the tarmac all around him. She saw her father pull back his leg to swing repeated kicks into the chest and stomach of the now foetal curl of the young man who had just kissed her.

'Stop it!' she screamed, and tried to intervene, to prevent this madness. But she stumbled on the kerb and fell.

'Just stay away from my fucking daughter! If I ever see you with her again, I'll kill you.' Her father's words falling, literally, on deaf ears.

He hurried around the car to pick his daughter off the road and drag her away, weeping, into the rain.

By the time he got her back to the apartment, it was impossible to tell the tears from the rain on her face. She pulled herself free of him. 'I hate you!' she screamed. 'I hate you!' And she fled to her bedroom, slamming the door shut behind her, and collapsing in a sobbing heap on the bed.

It was into October before her father let her return to the centre to resume her lessons in touch-signing. But he was leaving nothing to chance, dropping her off and then going to meet friends for a coffee before returning to drive her home again.

In the intervening weeks, the atmosphere in the house had been febrile, simmering tempers and Ana's bubbling resentment. The tension was palpable, and she could not bring herself even to speak to her father. She would address him only through her mother, and spent most of her days, and quite often evenings too, at the home of her sister, unburdening herself, confiding her secret feelings and deepest fears. Isabella's husband might have resented her constant presence, but for the fact that Ana would babysit the girls, allowing the couple to go out dancing, or for meals at restaurants down on the coast. It was during this time that she formed the bond with Cristina and Nurita that would long outlive their parents.

Ana had been dreading that first night back at the centre, not knowing how she could possibly face Sergio after what her father had done to him. And so it was with a mixture of relief and disappointment that she discovered he was not there. Had not, in fact, been there for several weeks. She feared that perhaps her father had inflicted more serious injury than she had imagined and was filled with concern.

Every night she returned she hoped that he might be there. But he never was, and after a month she went to the administrator to ask for his contact details. The young woman had been very nice, but politely declined. Personal details, she said, were confidential. And, in any case, Sergio had deregistered with the centre, and she had no expectation that he would ever be back.

It was as if the bottom had simply dropped out of Ana's

world. And with the acceptance that in all probability she would never see Sergio again, came the realization that she had been in love with him. Deeply, hopelessly, in love. And that while he, in an unguarded moment, had inadvertently confessed his love for her, those words had never passed her lips. Now they never would, and he would never know. And all that lay ahead in the desert that defined her future was a world of darkness in which the only possible light had already been extinguished.

CHAPTER TWENTY

The little vibrator clipped to her blouse vibrates twice against her chest, alerting her to the presence of someone at the door downstairs. It is too soon to be Sergio, and she supposes it will be Nuri or Cristina. Since Nuri's illness she is never sure which of them will turn up.

She feels for and finds the little panel of rocker switches on the tabletop in front of her, releasing the electronic catch on the door at the foot of the stairs. She sits perfectly still then, eyelids lightly closed, and senses the faintest of footfalls on the wooden staircase.

She is still aquiver with the excitement generated by the call from Sergio, but determines to say nothing about it. Neither Nuri nor Cristina knows anything of her history with Sergio. Both were just children at the time, absorbed in their own worlds, and Ana has not the heart to recount a story that still pains her. And, in any case, Sergio might lose courage and never come. If there is one thing that Ana has learned over all these years, it is that hope only ever brings disappointment.

She breathes deeply as the change of air in the room signals that the door has opened. She knows Cristina's scent by heart, the distant sweetness of orange blossom carried by a single spray of her eau de cologne. But today the air brings her another, different scent. A masculine tone. Distinctive and musky, male hormones transmitted by the oil in perspiration. And she is confused.

'Who have you brought to see me today, Cris?'

It is a moment before she feels the scrape of a chair on the far side of her computer, and the vibration of fingers on a keyboard raising braille on her screen. She scans the dots lightly with sensitive fingertips.

– *It is a policeman from England, Ana. He has come to help us find the man who has threatened me.*

'And does he have a name, this man?'

– *Mackenzie.*

'Ah. So he is Scottish, then.' Ana smiles

– *How do you know?*

'It is a Scottish name, *cariño*.' And she senses Cristina's surprise.

– *But how do you know that?*

'*Tesoro*, when you have all day every day to fill you read a lot. I know many things that I would not know if I wasn't deaf and blind.' And she smiles sadly at the irony of it.

Mackenzie stood a pace or two back. Listening to Ana's soft cadences, little more than a whisper at times. And reading the text produced onscreen by Cristina's quick fingers on the keyboard. It gave him a moment or two to cast curious eyes over the woman seated on the far side of the screens. Ana's black hair was cut short, and fell in a fringe over well-defined eyebrows. Her face was plain, unremarkable. Had he passed her in the street she would not have drawn his eye. But there was a strange serenity in it. In the soft set of her full lips, the almost drowsily half-closed eyes. He tried to guess her age, but she might have been anything between thirty and fifty. He settled on forty as a compromise, and was not so far out.

She wore a black blouse over black jog pants, and a pair of pristine white sneakers. Her frame was petite, although it carried a little more weight than it should. She could not yet be described as plump, but was inclined in that direction, and Mackenzie guessed that so many hours spent trapped each day in a chair would both waste muscle and accumulate fat.

Cristina had warned him in advance that her aunt was deaf and blind, and now as he stood before her he tried to imagine what that must be like. He glanced around the room where she spent her life. Like a cell. No pictures on the walls. No ornaments on the dresser. A table set for one. A corner kitchen with a small breakfast bar. How did she do the simplest things? Make tea or coffee. Or cook a meal. Dress, undress, do her laundry. Obviously she would have help. Family, the State. His eye fell on Sandro eyeing him cautiously from his bed on the far side of the room. Companion, guide, friend.

But for most of her life, she would have only herself to fall back on. Her courage and resilience, her will to be.

And the real prison was not this room. It was her own body. Whoever Ana might be, she was trapped inside it with no way out, and no way of letting anyone else in.

Except that here she was in animated conversation with her niece. Thanks to an extraordinary piece of technology that brought the world to her in dots raised on a screen.

He moved around to Ana's side of the table to watch her fingers scan the braille, and was surprised as her head turned to follow him. Her smile seemed to register his surprise.

She said, 'When fate robs you of your two primary senses, Señor Mackenzie, by way of compensation your remaining senses – taste, smell, touch – become much more highly developed. I can feel the air move as you walk. I can follow your scent, just like Sandro over there. She nodded towards her dog as Sandro raised his head at the mention of his name.

Mackenzie said to Cristina, 'Tell her I'd like to know how her braille works.'

Cristina stood up. 'Tell her yourself.' And she moved aside to let Mackenzie sit in her place. His fingers rattled across the keyboard and he looked up to register Ana's surprise.

'Do you know?' she said. 'You are the first person ever to ask me that.'

He typed. – *I'm interested.*

'Why?'

– *Everything interests me.*

She said, 'Each braille character is made up of six dot positions. These positions are arranged in a rectangle comprising two columns of three dots each. A dot can be raised at any one of six positions, or in any combination. If you count the space in which no dots are raised, there are sixty-four combinations altogether. The alphabet plus contractions.'

Mackenzie sat for a moment absorbing this, visualizing how that would work. He turned back to the keyboard.

– *That's ingenious! Was it difficult to learn?*

'Nothing is difficult when you are motivated, señor. But it requires use of the brain's spatial processors, as opposed to the auditory processors most people use in conversation.'

– *So it helps to be deaf.*

She laughed out loud. 'Señor, there is nothing helpful about being deaf. But, actually, it was my lack of vision that aided me in the learning of braille.'

It was Mackenzie who laughed this time. And text conversations with his daughter enabled him to convey that with an *LOL*. He typed:

– *All temptation to take a peek being removed.*

'Exactly. It was so much easier once I had actually gone blind.' Then she tipped her head in admonition. 'Señor, your Spanish is excellent. But if you want to be strictly correct, you should know that *LOL* is *jejeje*.

– *Correction noted.* He paused, then typed again – *Jejeje.*

Ana raised her head and turned it towards Cristina, a wide grin creasing her cheeks. 'Cristina you can bring your Scottish friend any time.'

Cristina had stood watching with growing astonishment as the conversation between Ana and Mackenzie developed. How was it possible that this misfit foreigner had managed to strike such an instant rapport with her aunt?

Ana eased herself out of her chair. 'I'll make us some coffee.' Something she never did, always allowing her nieces to do the honours when they visited. But it seemed that today she was determined to demonstrate her independence to the Scottish visitor.

Mackenzie watched her move about the room and into the kitchen area with complete confidence. She reached up to open a wall cabinet and took out coffee and sugar before searching out an open bottle of milk from the fridge. She raised her voice above what she knew would be the noise of the kettle.

'Cristina, tell me how Nuri was today, And Paco. I'll catch up on it later.'

Cristina resumed her seat at the computer and typed up an account of her visit to the hospital with Nuri, and her meeting with Paco, while her aunt moved about the tiny kitchen preparing the coffees. When they were ready she placed them side by side on the breakfast bar. She said, 'It makes it easier, señor, that I could see before I went blind. I don't have to imagine the world around me. I can picture it. Recall images from my memories. What's hard about that is that I know just how much I have lost.'

Mackenzie admired that there was no trace of self-pity in this, just a simple statement of fact. He felt unaccountably drawn to her. In the silent darkness of her world, a vibrant intelligence was fighting to get out.

He sat and drank his coffee, watching as Ana resumed her seat and she and Cristina chatted. About family, about the practicalities of daily life – deliveries of groceries, a house-keeper who came once a week but was, in Ana's opinion, taking advantage of her client's disability and skimping on her cleaning duties. Cristina promised to see that she was replaced.

But then he witnessed a certain agitation creeping into the serenity with which Ana had initially greeted them, her fingers straying with increasing frequency to flick nervously over the face of her braille watch. He was not to know that she was expecting Sergio, and worried that this man from her past might arrive before Cristina and Mackenzie left. But he sensed that she wanted them to go.

He placed his empty mug on the breakfast bar and leaned over Cristina's shoulder to interrupt her typing. He brushed her fingers aside and typed himself.

– *Ana, it has been my great pleasure to meet you.* Something he rarely meant, even if social convention demanded he say it. But this time he did. *However, I must drag your niece away. We have a meeting soon at Marviña, and she is yet to take me for something to eat.* Cristina glared at him.

Ana seemed almost relieved. 'Go, children, go. But come again, Señor Mackenzie. Please.'

He leaned once more over Cristina's shoulder.

– *I will.*

Cristina stood up. 'What's the hurry?' she said to him. 'The meeting's not for ages yet. And you two seem to be getting on so well.' He did not miss the sarcasm in her tone.

He inclined his head towards her aunt. 'She wants rid of us.'

Cristina bristled, frowned at Ana then turned towards Mackenzie. 'My aunt does not want rid of us.'

'If you'd been paying attention,' he said, 'you'd have noticed how she keeps fingering her watch, or heard the tension that's crept into her voice. She might be expecting someone.'

'Oh, don't be ridiculous. Ana never has visitors.'

Ana's head was tilted to one side, as if she were listening to them. And, almost as though she had heard their entire conversation, she said, 'I'm expecting a visitor, *cariño*.'

Which took all the wind out of Cristina's sails. She glared at Mackenzie, then stooped to give her aunt a kiss. The older woman squeezed her hand and whispered, 'Trust him.'

Outside, the afternoon sun cast deep shadows across the street. The heat was marked after the cool of the house. The air felt hot to breathe, and the Calle San Miguel was packed with tourists pushing their way past each other in both directions. Distant music drifted across the rooftops, a church bell was ringing. 'Is there something going on in town?' Mackenzie asked.

Cristina seemed distracted. 'What?'

'Music. Crowds. Bells. Is it always as busy as this?'

There was irritation in her voice. 'It's the *feria* of Estepona's patron saint all this week. San Isidro Labrador. There's music and dancing, and there are exhibitions. Tomorrow there will be a procession from the church, with floats and horses. You won't be able to move for people. We don't want to be anywhere near here after six.' She caught his arm to stop him. 'How could you possibly have known she was expecting someone?'

He shrugged. 'An informed guess.'

'Informed by what?'

'Observation. Something you would do well to work on if you ever want to be anything more than a constable.'

He saw anger flare in her eyes and thought he should probably have kept that particular observation to himself. But before she could respond, she was distracted by the sound of a girl's voice calling from the Plaza de Juan Bazán opposite, and they turned to see a group of kids kicking a ball about between the fountains. A girl of around eight or nine waved cheerfully. '*Hola. Buenas tardes, Cristina.*'

Cristina waved back. And she lowered her voice to Mackenzie. 'She lives along the street. Her mother is the housekeeper that Ana complained about.'

Mackenzie smiled at the child and waved also. Sotto voce

he said to Cristina, 'That'll be fun for you, then – sacking her mother.'

Cristina threw him a look. 'I thought you were hungry.'

'Starving.'

When they had moved off through the crowd, a figure emerged from the shadows of a doorway further along the street and sauntered, hands in pockets, into the square. He was tall, with sandy hair flopping across a tanned brow. But his linen suit looked more than a little crumpled, and his white shirt less than pristine. His blue eyes followed the heads of Cristina and Mackenzie until they disappeared among all the others. The football being kicked around the plaza came rolling in his direction and he stooped to pick it up. The little girl who'd had the exchange with Cristina came running up to retrieve it. He held it out, but stopped short of handing it over.

'Who is it who lives in that house there?' he said, nodding towards the door from which Cristina and Mackenzie had emerged only minutes before.

The girl reached for the ball, but still he held it beyond her grasp.

'That's weird Ana's house,' she said.

'Weird Ana?'

'The old blind lady.'

'What would the police want with an old blind lady?' he asked.

'Oh, that's not the police,' the little girl said. 'Not really.

That's Cristina. Weird Ana's her auntie. Can I have our ball please?'

Cleland smiled. 'Of course.' And he let her take it from his hands, before turning to gaze thoughtfully up at the little black-painted wrought-iron Juliet balcony on the first floor.

CHAPTER TWENTY-ONE

Ana feels the buzzer vibrate twice against her chest. Excitement, fear, apprehension. All very nearly stop her from breathing.

Sergio.

She tries to calm herself, and with a trembling hand depresses the rocker switch that opens the door below. Now she places her hands flat on the table in front of her, forcing herself to take long slow breaths.

Immediately she feels better and closes her eyes, waiting for the most distant of vibrations to tell her that he is on his way up the stairs. The change of temperature tells her that he has opened the door and is standing gazing at her.

Only now does she think about how she must look. No make-up, hair unfashionably short. Overweight, frumpy in an old blouse and jog pants. And more than twenty years older than when he last set eyes on her. She finds it hard to picture herself, but is aware with a sudden stab of apprehension that there can be nothing attractive about what he sees in front of him.

There is no clue in all this silence and darkness as to his

reaction. She breathes in his scent, but there is nothing familiar in it. Male hormones, hair oil or perhaps aftershave.

'Hello Sergio,' she says, knowing that he will read her lips. Her voice is the merest tickle in her throat and she knows that she has all but whispered his name. In her mind it thunders in the darkness.

Still nothing. And then a movement of air. The warmth of another body in the cool of the room, shutters drawn against the afternoon sun. She feels the scrape of a chair on the floor. But not at the computer opposite. Much closer. She can feel his breath on her face. Soft, like the gentlest whispering touch of gossamer.

And then his hands, gentle and warm, taking hers in his. A tracing of fingers on her palm, the tactile signing that they had learned together all those years before, and she can feel her breath trembling in her chest.

'Hello, Ana.'

It is extraordinary just how familiar his touch still is, even after all this time, as if it were only yesterday that they had last touch-signed. Only, then she could have opened her eyes to see him, heard his voice. *It's you I love.* She wondered how he would look to her now, if she could only see him.

'I've missed you,' he says.

And a tiny current of anger spikes through her. 'It is you who went away.' And immediately she regrets it.

But she senses the contrition in his words. *'I know, I know. And, God knows, I have spent every minute of every day of every year* regretting it. You are right to be angry, and I have nothing but shame for my lack of courage.'

'I am not angry, Sergio. Not really. Just hurting. Still. You coming here like this today feels a little like having something sharp stabbed into an old wound.'

His hands grip hers, then squeeze them almost too tightly. She can feel his anguish transmitted through every fibre of his body. *Your father contacted my parents. I don't even know how he knew where to find us. And I have no idea what passed between them. But after he had gone my father forbade me ever to see you again.'*

She can feel his tension in the trembling of his hands. 'I always suspected,' she says, 'that my father had something to do with it.'

'You have to understand, Ana, that I was dependent on my parents for everything. For money, the roof over my head, the car that I drove. I could not have continued my studies without their support, and without a job I could not support myself.' His deep, tremulous breath transmits itself to her through the divining rod of his whole body. *'At first I refused. I told them there was nothing they could do to me that would make me give you up. But then my father told me that if I chose you over them I would no longer be welcome in their house, and that he would withdraw his financial support. I knew my father, Ana. He was not a man to make threats lightly. I realized that he meant what he said, and I simply didn't have the strength, or the courage, to defy him.'* He pauses for a long time, and she feels him shake with emotion. *'I was miserable for weeks, and I've regretted it every day of my life since.'*

Ana imagines then the silence that falls between them, hanging heavy in the room. Hands and lips and voices still. Motes of dust suspended in the sunlight that slants in through a gap in the shutters. She has no idea what to say herself, and senses that there is more to come. And she is right. She feels him draw breath.

'One day about two months later, I was still inconsolable and my mother sat me down and told me the story of her first love. A young man she met at university in Madrid. A boy from a poor working-class family in Valencia who had only got to university on some kind of scholarship. Her family was appalled. He was not of the same . . . class. They made her give him up by threatening to take her away from university, withdrawing their financial support. And she always suspected that her family had paid off his family, because the boy himself did not fight it. She was heartbroken at first, she said. But then in time she met my father and never looked back. She said there was no future for me with a girl who was deaf and blind. That I would spend the rest of my life as a carer.' She feels ironic laughter in the movement of his hands. 'The moral of the story, I suppose, was that I would get over you. That I, too, would meet someone else and put you behind me.' He pauses. 'I never did. And there never has been anyone else.' Another pause. 'Never will be.'

His hands raise themselves to her cheeks, long fingers gently brushing away her tears. She lifts her hands to cup his face and feels his tears, too. His pain, and hers, in the hot copious unrestrained flow of them. Two people wilfully kept apart by parents who thought that they knew best.

Gently he takes her hands in his again, and resumes signing. *'My father died five years ago, Ana, but it wasn't until my mother passed away in March that I finally plucked up the courage to try and track you down. It was easier than I thought, though I could never have guessed that all this time we were quite so close. In all my wildest dreams I never actually thought I would find you. But now that I have . . .'* his fingers go still, resting against her palm *'. . . I never want to let you go again.'* Another pause. *'If you'll have me?'*

She extricates her hands from his and raises them to his face again, running her fingers and palms over all its planes and surfaces, fingertips pushing up into his hair. She stops and says, 'You're losing your hair, Sergio.'

He takes back her hands. *'And I'm developing a bit of a belly. I'm happy you can't see how badly I have aged.'*

'While you can see my every fault. Every grey hair, every line, every wobble of my flesh.'

Which made him laugh. *'Ana, you are as beautiful today as the day I met you. Beauty is who we are, not what we look like, and to me you will be beautiful till the day you die.'* Then more hesitation. *'You never answered. Do you . . . do you think you could ever take me back?'*

Ana shakes her head solemnly. 'No Sergio. I don't think I could.' She waits to let the impact of her words sink in. 'I *know* I could. But above all, I *want* you back, more than anything I've ever wanted in my life.'

In an instant, his lips are on hers. His hands on her face. She slips her arms around him and pulls him closer, realizing for the first time that he has dropped to his knees in front of her.

She places a hand behind his head and draws it to her breast, holding him there, feeling his sobs transmit themselves from his body to hers. And all the years since they last touched are washed away like dust in rain.

They remain like this for a long time, bodies generating heat, flushing faces, until finally he draws away and takes her hands again.

'*Ana, I have to go. Having finally found you, I could not wait until this evening to see you. I made an excuse to get away from work, but I'll have to go back.*' He rests his head for a moment on their conjoined hands. '*The irony is that I work just a few streets away at the Banco de Sabadell. When I finish work this evening I will come straight back. I promise.*'

But she doesn't want to let him go. Not just yet. After all the years of hopelessness, on her own in the dark, Sergio has finally brought hope and light back into her life. 'Don't be too long,' she whispers, and when he is gone she weeps unashamedly.

CHAPTER TWENTY-TWO

At the end of the hall in the Marviña police station, a door opened into a large meeting room that was also accessible from the street. Mahogany desks and leather seats stood arranged in a semicircle beneath a drop-down banner at the far end of the room. They faced rows of hard plastic seats set out for an audience. The local council held public meetings here, and one wall was lined with paintings of the men and women who had at one time or another filled the honoured post of mayor. Light flooded into the room from two large windows on the outside wall, and it was already packed by the time Cristina and Mackenzie arrived. They took seats at the back.

The *Jefe* was leaning, half-sitting, on one of the desks, his arms folded across his chest. Another man was addressing the assembly. He was tall, thin and bald. Sweat patches darkened the armpits of his white shirt. His suit jacket lay draped over a chair behind him.

Mackenzie leaned towards Cristina and lowered his voice. 'Who is everyone?'

'The man speaking is the *Juez de Instrucción* from Estepona.

The examining magistrate. I guess, nominally, he's in charge of the case. But really it's homicide in Malaga who're handling it.' She nodded towards a group of plain-clothes officers lounging on seats near the front and breathed her derision. 'These guys think they're starring in a Hollywood movie. All designer suits and sunglasses.' She turned her gaze towards the other side of the room. 'That's UDYCO over there, also from Malaga. They specialize in drugs and organized crime.' Then she leaned forward to look along the back row towards a group of young men in jeans and T-shirts. '*Instituto Forense de Malaga*. Forensics. But these ones are from Marbella.' She cocked an eyebrow at Mackenzie. 'Notice how many women there are among them.' She sat back. There were none. 'The rest are Policía Local from here in Marviña. But we're just the foot soldiers.'

The examining magistrate was perspiring freely. 'We have established that the boat in the marina at Puerto de la Condesa did indeed belong to the criminal Cleland, under his alias of Ian Templeton. But he doesn't appear to have been sleeping there. We're assuming he risked a visit to the boat perhaps to get money, or weapons, or drugs. It's anyone's guess. But at any rate, he was interrupted by the British investigator Mackenzie who failed to apprehend him.'

Mackenzie felt the hackles rise on the back of his neck, and without looking at her was aware of Cristina's eyes turning in his direction. He shifted uncomfortably in his seat, and a sharp pain in his ribs reminded him of his encounter with Cleland.

'UDYCO report that sources are telling them the rumoured handover of drugs is scheduled within the next two days, and that the merchandise is already in the country. Somewhere in this area. But we have no intelligence as yet on where and when the exchange is going to take place.' He held out an open palm towards a well-groomed middle-aged man in a dark suit who sat in the front row. 'Captain Rodríguez?'

As Rodríguez stood up Mackenzie whispered to Cristina, 'Who's he?'

'Head of GRECO – *Grupo de Respuesta Especial para el Crimen Organizado*. That's the organized crime special-response group based in Marbella.'

Unlike the *Juez de Instrucción* Captain Rodríguez was the embodiment of cool. He slipped his shades into the breast pocket of his suit jacket and ran a tanned hand back through jet-black hair. 'We are confident,' he said, 'that we will find out exactly where and when this is all going down. We have had a number of suspected traffickers on our radar for some time. Not little fish by any means. And almost certainly involved. One or other of them is almost certain to lead us to the rendezvous. But I can't stress enough the importance of total discretion in every department. A leak of any kind could compromise the whole operation. We're only going to get one chance at this.'

When the meeting broke up, the *Jefe* waved Mackenzie forward to be introduced to the examining magistrate. Cristina trotted after him. Although the *Jefe* had hosted the meeting, he had played no active part in it, and Mackenzie realized that instructions coming down from the *Jefe* were simply being passed on from a higher jurisdiction. This was all happening on his patch, but he had no real authority except in the direction of his own people.

'Señor Mackenzie, meet Judge Aguado. It was he who requested your services from the NCA in London.'

'Oh?' Mackenzie said, 'Now I know who to blame.' And shook the proffered hand. It was cold and clammy, and when Mackenzie retrieved his own he wiped it absently on the leg of his trousers.

The *Juez de Instrucción* did not miss it. He said stiffly, 'Presumably you are aware how our system works here in Spain?'

'I am,' Mackenzie said. 'Very similar to the French. A Guardia Civil which is part of the army, like the French Gendarmerie. A fragmented civilian police force which doesn't talk to the military, and a system of judges who know nothing about police work but somehow contrive to direct investigations.'

Judge Aguado's pallor darkened, and a clenching of his jaw was betrayed by the depressions that appeared in each of his cadaverous cheeks. He said, 'While the British police divide and subdivide themselves into so many different forces that they lack any coherence.'

'I couldn't agree more,' Mackenzie said, oblivious of the judge's intention to offend him in return. 'They are unco-ordinated and completely disjointed. Criminals are slipping through the cracks all the time.'

No one knew what to say. And it was only when Mackenzie caught Cristina's smirk out of the corner of his eye that he suspected he might have said something out of turn.

When they stepped from the basement of the police station out into the underground car park, tyres were screeching on concrete, motors revving, detectives and forensics officers from Estepona and Marbella and Malaga all heading back to their respective offices post meeting.

Mackenzie disapproved of meetings. He thought they were just an excuse for the brass to show off to the troops and make themselves feel important. Any relevant information would already have reached the people who mattered. But he was more concerned about his apparent faux pas with the judge.

'What did I say?'

He struggled to keep up with Cristina, who, for all her lack of height, was striding at speed across the car park. 'What didn't you say?' she said.

'*What*?' He was at a loss.

She stopped and turned to face him. 'Would you go into someone's house and tell them their baby was ugly?'

His brow furrowed in concentration as he ran the question through his mind, wondering at its relevance.

She rolled her eyes. 'Oh, for God's sake, if you have to think about it . . . !' And she marched off again to where she had parked the Nissan.

He followed and climbed into the passenger seat to sit looking at her. Both her hands gripped the wheel and her face was set. He decided not to pursue his evident blunder with the judge, and instead changed the direction of their conversation entirely, towards something minor which had struck him during the meeting.

'When the *Juez de Instrucción* said that *sources* had provided UDYCO with information about Cleland's drugs deal, what sources was he talking about?'

She looked at him as if he had two heads. 'Sources,' she said, as if repeating the word would explain it. 'You know, informants, *soplones*, or whatever you call them in English.'

'Snitches.' Mackenzie said the word as if it left a bad taste in his mouth.

'So you know what I'm talking about. Criminals who feed information to the police in return for . . . well, usually immunity.'

'And sometimes money.'

She shrugged. 'Most detectives have a snitch. You must have had one.'

Mackenzie shook his head. 'Never! I don't believe in them. A crook is still a crook whether he tips off the cops or not. A crime is still a crime. You can't pick and choose the ones you're going to prosecute. We're not arbiters of the law, we're enforcers of it.'

Cristina was taken aback by his vehemence. She lifted one eyebrow. 'Sounds like there's something personal there.'

Mackenzie realized he had said more than he intended, and sat back in his seat, turning to stare through the windscreen and draw breath.

But she wasn't going to let it go. 'Is there?'

He was silent for several long moments, debating whether to tell her or not. Finally he said, 'I arrested and charged an informant working for another officer in my division.'

She gazed curiously into his eyes. 'And?'

He hesitated. 'I had been warned not to by my commanding officer.'

'So why did you?'

'Because the snitch had been complicit in a murder. An underworld hit. My boss argued that without his information we'd never have got the actual killer.'

'But you still arrested him because . . . ?'

'Because if he had provided us with the same information before the killing rather than after it, we could have stopped it from happening. Which made him as responsible for the death of the victim as the guy who pulled the trigger.'

Cristina chewed on that for a moment. Then she said, 'So what happened?'

'To the snitch?'

She nodded.

'He was convicted and sentenced to fifteen years.' Mackenzie took a deep breath. 'They found him dead in his cell six weeks later. Throat slit from ear to ear.'

'Someone got their revenge.'

Mackenzie nodded. 'And I got the blame. Effectively ended my career with the Met.'

'They fired you?'

'No. But they made it impossible for me to do my job. It was only a matter of time, they reckoned, before I would quit.'

'And that's what you did?'

'Yes.'

She remained sitting for a long time, both hands still gripping the wheel. Without looking at him she said, 'You really don't understand the concept of discretion, do you?'

'What do you mean?'

'You have an opinion, you give voice to it regardless of who it might offend. You decide a course of action, and you follow it regardless of the consequences.'

He was defensive. 'When you know you're right, what else are you supposed to do?'

'And you're always right?'

'Yes.' He thought about it. 'Well, nearly.'

A tiny explosion of laughter escaped her lips. 'Of course you are.' She looked at him and shook her head. 'I'll take you back to your hotel.'

He nodded and seemed disappointed. She turned the key in the ignition and started the motor. But sat letting it idle.

'Had you thought about what you are going to do for dinner?'

'Actually, I'm torn between sandwiches in my room or sandwiches in my room.'

'Spoiled for choice, then.'

'It's just a question of which sandwich I'll go for. Ham. Or ham.'

'I hear the ham's pretty good.'

'I'll take that as a recommendation.'

She sighed and turned the key in the ignition again to cut the motor, and swung the driver's door open. 'I suppose you can eat with us again.'

'With an offer like that,' he said, 'how could I refuse?'

She laughed. 'Come on. It's just two minutes across the square.' And she jumped down into the car park.

CHAPTER TWENTY-THREE

Ana has barely been able to contain herself. Never has she known time to move so slowly. Quite deliberately she has kept her fingers away from the face of her watch. There is nothing quite so frustrating as counting hours that refuse to pass.

She has tried reading, but her concentration is shot, and she has allowed her memories to transport her back through time. She is eternally thankful for her mind's eye, because it allows her to see Sergio as he was all those years ago, when they were both young and she could still see and hear him. She smiles, picturing his impudent grin, his youthful good looks.

She has never understood what it was he saw in her. At best she had been a plain girl. Her parents had struggled financially to bring up two daughters, and Ana had never worn the designer clothes of her contemporaries, or listened to music on the latest Sony Walkman, or had her hair styled in the fashionable salons of Estepona. But for some reason that Ana still cannot fathom Sergio had fallen for her, and all these years later he has come back into her life like a beacon of hope. If there is a God, perhaps He has been saving her for just this moment.

The buzzer vibrates against her chest, and she feels a charge of electrical excitement fork through her body. He's back.

Her usually assured touch deserts her for a moment, and she fumbles to find the rocker that will release the catch on the door downstairs.

Now she sits still, trying to calm herself. Eyes closed, waiting for the tread of his feet on the stairs. Then the movement of air in the room that signals the opening of the door. She cannot hear the low growl that emanates from Sandro's throat in the corner of the room as the old lab struggles on arthritic legs to get to his feet.

And now nothing. No footsteps crossing the floor to greet her, no change of temperature as he nears her. She breathes deeply, aware instantly that something is wrong. This is not the scent of the man who held and kissed her just a few short hours ago. But it is a male scent, made noisome by sweat. And it fills the air around her.

'Who's there?' she asks sharply, the steel in her voice belying the apprehension fluttering in her breast and the fear that has started to crawl in her belly.

Cleland stood stock-still in the open doorway, assessing the small middle-aged woman in black sitting beyond the computer screens. He canted his head to one side, mentally stripping away the awful blouse and jog pants, the pudding-bowl haircut, and somehow saw something sensuous in the fullness of her lips, an almost Asian slant in her almond eyes. In another world, he thought, she could perhaps have been beautiful. And maybe once she was. Or perhaps it was just a trick of the light.

The last rays of sunlight lay in lengthening stripes across the whitewashed walls of the square opposite the house, and reflected in a soft pink light falling through the gaps in the shutters. Otherwise the room simmered in late evening gloom, the heat of the day thickening the air so that it was almost tangible.

His eyes flickered towards the guide dog standing watching him cautiously from the far side of the room. No danger, he thought, from that old boy. He returned his gaze to the little lady in the chair by the window. Blind, the girl in the square had said. The eyes that stared at him from across the room lacked any animation and he knew that the child had not been wrong. He sighed.

'Hello, Ana,' he said. 'I suppose you've probably heard about me.'

Nothing. Not a flicker. He frowned.

'Ana?'

'Who's there?' she said again, a quiver of barely controlled hysteria in her voice now.

A single clap of his hands resounded in the silence of the room. But it brought not the least response, and he whistled softly to himself. She was deaf, too. Blind *and* deaf.

Cleland was not accustomed to feelings of empathy. He

never placed himself in others' shoes, wondering what it might be like to be them. But for the first time since a distant childhood that he had long since banished from memory, he recalled standing in the playground being physically and verbally abused by his peers. Closing his eyes and ears to it all, as if somehow that could make it go away. Letting the pain wash over him like water, so that it would pass more quickly. Retreating into himself, a safe place where he was invulnerable, a place where he could hide until it was time to come out again and exact revenge.

Only Ana, he realized as he stared at her, could never come out again. She was trapped in there, locked away for ever. She could never exact revenge. And even if she could, from whom would she seek that retribution? God? Fate? How unfair was that? It occurred to him then, with something almost like shock, that for the first and only time in his life he was feeling sorry for someone else.

Which brought a further sigh. For he knew that no matter what he might feel in this moment it would not stop him from doing what he had come to do.

He took several steps towards her to look at the computer screen that faced him. Then he rounded the desk to peer at the screen which faced Ana. He recognized the patterns of raised dots as braille, and marvelled at this technology that would allow him to penetrate her darkness and speak to her silence.

Her head was slightly raised as he walked around her, turning to track his movements, like some feral animal following his scent. And he realized that's probably exactly what she was doing. He returned to the screen with the winking cursor and sat down in front of it. Nobody had typed on it since Mackenzie earlier in the afternoon.

– *Ana, it has been my great pleasure to meet you. However, I must drag your niece away. We have a meeting soon at Marviña, and she is yet to take me for something to eat.*

Cleland knew instinctively that these were the words of the Scot with whom he had fought on the boat at the marina. Hadn't Cleland himself been standing in a doorway out there in the street when Mackenzie left with the bitch?

He scrolled quickly back and scanned Cristina's account of her visit to the hospital with Nuri, her conversation with Paco. And he smiled. Such a tight little family. All gathering themselves before him to facilitate his feasting from that dish best served cold.

'What do you want!' Ana's voice raised itself to an almost hysterical pitch, sudden and startling in the silence of the room.

He scrolled back to the cursor and typed.

– *Hello.*

He was aware of some faint vibration alerting her to text on her screen. Trembling fingers lifted to read the dots that had raised themselves there. He watched as she recoiled in fear and confusion.

'Sergio?' she said, more in hope than in any real expectation that it might be him.

– *Try again.*

'Who are you?' Full-blown hysteria now. And he enjoyed her fear.

– *I think, perhaps, your niece might have mentioned me. She and her colleagues are having such trouble finding me.*

The blood drained from Ana's face, leaving it ghostly pale. She said, 'Cristina is not responsible for that young woman's death. You shot her.'

She was unprepared for the force of the open hand that slapped hard across her face and very nearly knocked her from her chair. She cried out, as much in fear as in pain. Then more dots were raised on her screen.

– *She made me do it! And you are going to help me make her pay for that.*

CHAPTER TWENTY-FOUR

The smell of barbecued meat filled the tiny apartment. Sliding glass doors to the balcony at the rear of the block were open, and the chatter of swallows dipping and diving in the warm night air outside was nearly deafening. The room itself resounded to the blare of a television whose volume was set far too high.

Antonio was in the kitchen. Lucas sat at the table amidst a pile of books and jotters, his head tilted into an open palm, a pen twirling absently in his other hand, his eyes drawn towards a cartoon flickering on the TV screen.

Mackenzie followed Cristina into the apartment as she strode across the living room to switch off the television. With only the birds now for competition, she shouted, 'For God's sake, what's wrong with you people? Are you deaf? If the neighbours report us again we'll be asked to leave.'

Antonio appeared in his bare feet at the kitchen door wearing a T-shirt and jeans. His smile was less than welcoming. 'And how was *your* day, darling?' He nodded at Mackenzie.

Cristina released her belt with its empty holster and let it fall on to the settee. 'What are you cooking?'

It sounded more like an accusation than a question.

Antonio stuck his jaw out defensively. 'I thought you might be pleased, not having to make dinner for once.' His head tilted in Mackenzie's direction. 'Only I didn't know we were going to have company.'

Cristina sniffed the air. 'What is it?'

'Barbecued ribs.'

She looked at him in astonishment. 'You prepared them yourself?'

His look turned sheepish, but still defensive. 'I bought them at Mercadona. Oven-ready. They take just twenty minutes.'

'Jesus, Antonio! We can't afford to go buying pre-packaged food. It's crazy expensive.'

'It's a treat,' he said. 'Just this once. I got commission on a sale today.' Then, deflecting further argument, he nodded towards Lucas. 'You'd be better off paying more attention to your son. He came home with his report card today.'

'Is it bad?'

But Antonio had already turned back into the kitchen. He called over his shoulder, 'Take a look for yourself.'

Cristina brushed past the embarrassed Mackenzie and found the report card half-buried under her son's books. The boy assiduously avoided her eye as she scrutinized it.

But a commentary on it came from the disembodied voice in the kitchen. 'English and Spanish good. Maths and science well below average. Take a look at the teacher's comments.'

Cristina read aloud, 'Lucas is a clever boy, but he just doesn't try. His concentration is poor. He's a daydreamer.'

Mackenzie recalled similar comments on the report cards he took home from his teachers. Only, he could silence them all with his exam results.

Cristina looked at her son accusingly. 'A daydreamer, Lucas? What are you daydreaming about?'

The boy's simmering resentment bubbled to the surface. 'About getting away from school,' he shouted, his lower lip trembling. 'Other kids have parents who help them. My dad wouldn't know a prime number from a right-angled triangle. And my mum's never here!'

Mackenzie cleared his throat and said, 'A prime number is a whole number greater than one, whose only factors are one and itself.' And was startled by disbelieving eyes that turned in his direction. Antonio had reappeared at the kitchen door. But the silence occasioned by his outburst lasted only a moment. Lucas was on a roll.

'And now you're sending strange foreigners to pick me up from school.'

Cristina frowned. 'What are you talking about? What strange foreigners?' She glanced at Mackenzie. 'You?'

Mackenzie shook his head, perplexed.

'No,' Lucas said, surly now. 'At lunchtime. When I was walking back from Burger King.'

'Burger King?' Antonio was astonished. 'What the hell were you doing at Burger King?'

'Everyone else gets burgers for lunch. I get some crappy sandwiches that Mum makes.'

But Cristina was not going to be deflected. 'What happened when you were walking back from Burger King?' Her voice was tight with tension.

Lucas shrugged, as if it was nothing. 'This guy in a big black car pulls up beside me and says he's a friend of yours. He says he's going to be picking me up from school someday soon and that I shouldn't be afraid of him.'

'Oh, my God!' Cristina's open palm was pressed to her chest. Then she grabbed the boy, almost pulling him from his chair. 'Lucas, don't you ever talk to that man again. Or anyone! I will *never* send anyone you don't know to pick you up from school, do you understand me? Never!' She held him by the shoulders, shaking him as she spoke.

Antonio crossed the room and pulled her away. 'Stop it, you're frightening him, Cris.'

Cristina's voice rose in pitch. 'He *needs* to be frightened, Toni.'

Mackenzie kept his focus on Lucas. 'How did you know he was a foreigner?'

'He spoke to me in English.'

'And did he give you his name?'

Lucas nodded.

'What was it?' Cristina demanded. 'What did he say his name was?'

227

Lucas shook his head, tears welling in his eyes as he tried to remember. 'It was Señor Clee . . . Clo, or Clan . . . something.'

'Cleland?' Mackenzie said.

'Yes, that was it.' Lucas seemed relieved to have remembered it finally.

A cry of fear tore itself involuntarily from Cristina's throat, and she drew Lucas into her arms, wrapping them around him and holding him so tightly he could barely breathe.

The house phone rang shrilly, piercing its way through the charged atmosphere of the tiny apartment. Antonio crossed the room in two strides and picked it up. 'Yes?' he barked, then after a moment put his hand over the receiver and thrust it towards Cristina. 'It's Miguel.'

Very reluctantly she released her son and took the phone. 'Yes, *Jefe*?' She listened intently, then closed her eyes in something like despair. 'Yes, *Jefe*.' A pause. 'We'll call for back-up if I think it's necessary.' She hung up and looked at Mackenzie. 'Residents in an urbanization in the hills above Casares Beach have reported a blond-haired foreigner coming and going at night from an unfinished complex across the street. The *Jefe* wants us to take a look. He doubts if it's Cleland, but . . .' She shrugged.

'If it is?'

'We'll call in the cavalry.'

Antonio said, 'And we'll eat when?'

'When we get back. You can keep the ribs warm, can't you?'

He shook his head. 'Lucas and I will eat now. You can reheat whatever's left.'

Cristina said, 'Just don't let that boy out of your sight, Toni. Not for one minute. I'll be back just as soon as I can.'

Antonio's anger finally burst through the veneer of constraint he had fashioned to save Mackenzie's embarrassment. Clearly he didn't care any more. 'The boy's right, Cris, you *are* never here, are you? And if it wasn't for you and your fucking job there wouldn't be any need to watch him like a hawk. The kid wouldn't *be* in any danger.'

An element of guilt spurred the anger in her retort. 'And we're supposed to live on what you earn, is that what you're saying?' But she wasn't waiting for an answer. 'If it wasn't for my *fucking* job we couldn't afford to send him to a half-decent school. We couldn't afford to run a car.' She saved the best for last. 'And we couldn't afford your membership of that fucking golf club. Think about that the next time you're teeing off.'

Husband and wife stood glaring at each other. Lucas gathered his books and ran in tears to his bedroom. Mackenzie stood awkwardly, wondering how to break the tension.

'What's your handicap?' he said. And both heads turned towards him.

CHAPTER TWENTY-FIVE

It was almost entirely dark by the time they reached the abandoned development on the hill. Mackenzie had followed Cristina in silence across the square to retrieve her SIG Pro from its lock-safe drawer in the downstairs gun room at the police station. They picked up the Nissan, and she had driven like a woman demented. Down to the coast and then east on the A7 to where a road branched off at a brightly lit family restaurant, before cutting its way up into the foothills of the Sierra Bermeja.

Away to the west, beyond the shadows of jagged peaks that cut themselves darkly against the stars, the sky glowed faintly red in strips between layers of cloud.

High up beyond the remains of what had once been some developer's dream sat a walled and gated complex of villas and apartments assembled around tropical gardens and two swimming pools. In the darkness it shimmered in patches of hard light cast by lamps lining streets and walkways. Warmer light glowed in the windows of holiday apartments and permanent residences. It stood in sharp contrast to the abandoned and semi-derelict construction built into the hillside below.

Cristina parked in the street opposite, and they climbed out of their SUV into the thickly fragrant night air. A warm wind blew gently across the hill, carrying the invasive chirrup of cicadas and the throaty croak of tree frogs. A plastic sign fixed to a wire fence advertised high-speed internet. *Don't pay the months you don't use. 20MB download speed, wifi router + setup from 50€*. Beyond it rows of apartments, some completed, others abandoned, followed the undulating contours of the Andalusian countryside. Red, yellow and white Lego-like cankers on a once agricultural landscape.

Mackenzie sniffed the night air and realized that something more incongruous was also borne on the breeze. Woodsmoke. Who, he wondered, lights fires on a warm night like this?

Behind a concrete retaining wall on the far side of the road, the part of the development exposed to view appeared almost complete. Tiled roofs, white-painted columns and arches. But like a smile without teeth there were no windows, and nature had reclaimed what must once have been intended as gardens. Tall grasses, bamboo, small trees and overgrown shrubs threatened to engulf the building. Its retaining wall was stained by the weather and smothered in graffiti, sidewalks crumbling where weeds had broken through the paving tiles.

Cristina removed a torch from her belt and retrieved one from the glove compartment for Mackenzie. Their beams cut arrows of light through the darkness as they followed a rusted fence along the perimeter of the unmade road that ran below the inhabited urbanization above. As they rounded the curve of the street, white dust rose in the torchlight with every footfall. The construction behind the fence became more skeletal, like something assembled by children with plastic rods and buildings blocks. A shallow-pitched roof stood above the empty structure, supported only by brick walls and concrete columns. A labyrinth of stairways, empty lift shafts, corridors and apartment shells all stood open to the night. Beyond the fence, a ramp disappeared down into the darkness of what must have been intended as an underground car park.

Broken glass crunched underfoot in the still of the night. The smell of woodsmoke was stronger here, more pungent. Ahead, the security fence stretched across the dusty white road preventing further progress. But someone had cut a hole through it with wire cutters, and a well-worn path beyond it led through the undergrowth to an area laid out for covered parking on the ground floor.

Cristina stepped carefully through the hole in the fence and Mackenzie followed as she made her way to the top of the ramp they had seen from the other side. Their torches barely penetrated the darkness below. They stood for a moment, listening. But there was nothing to be heard above the racket of the cicadas. Mackenzie could see the torch trembling in Cristina's hand. Her face was bloodless in its reflected light. She glanced at him briefly, before setting off down the ramp. He walked a metre or two behind.

The ridged concrete descended steeply, and curved away to their left. As they reached the bend, the car park opened up below them. A vast area delineating the footprint of the building itself and supported on rows of square columns. Its surface remained unfinished and strewn with debris. Black pools of stagnant water reflected the light of their torches. There was no sign of life or habitation, and it was almost with relief that they climbed back up into the night.

In a sky studded by stars, a three-quarters moon rose to cast its colourless light across the abandoned ambitions of the previous decade. Cristina and Mackenzie picked their way through the rubble and into the building. A staircase built around an empty elevator shaft climbed through two floors to the roof. They followed it up to the first level where it opened out into a square concrete hall. A graffitied corridor ran off into the dark heart of the building. Gaping doorways, left and right, led into skeleton apartments. White powdery efflorescence crept from unsealed brick walls, rusted steel reinforcement causing floors and columns to crumble from creeping concrete cancer.

Smoke hung now like mist in the beams of their torches. But the smell of it couldn't mask the invasive stench of faeces and urine. Although it was still hot outside, it felt cold in here.

A long way ahead, at the far end of the passageway, a pale light flickered in the darkness. A sinister murmuring reached them on fetid air.

Cristina's free hand rested on her holster. Although she was reluctant to draw her SIG, as a precaution she had unclipped the holster catch.

They drifted cautiously along the corridor, side by side, apprehension burgeoning as the light grew stronger and the murmur louder, until they turned at the end of it into a large open area where brick dividing walls had been crudely demolished leaving only their footings to denote the layout of a dozen or more apartments. Umpteen fires burned among the rubble, huddled groups of ragged people gathered around them for light and warmth.

The murmur of voices quickly faded as Cristina and Mackenzie raked the beams of their torches across the bizarre scene that unfolded before them. Only the crackle of dry wood on a dozen fires broke the echoing silence.

'What the hell . . . ?' Mackenzie's voice was barely a whisper.

Cristina glanced at him, then quickly refocused on the thirty or forty people grouped around the open fires. There were women with shawls and headscarves, *hijabs* and *khimars*, and men with beards and dark gaunt eyes. There were children who stared back at them from haunted faces, and babies that gurned for food. 'Illegal immigrants,' she said. 'They arrive by the boatload from North Africa almost every day now. Washing up on the beaches, then hiding out in these abandoned developments. There are literally thousands of these places lying empty along the coast. Impossible to police.'

She fumbled in the breast pocket of her tunic to take out

one of the crumpled photographs of Cleland that she carried and hand it to Mackenzie.

'Better if it's a man showing them this. I'll check out the next level.'

She set off back along the way they had come and Mackenzie stood for a moment before making his way apprehensively through the rubble to wave the picture of this white-faced, blond-haired Scotsman in front of frightened Arab faces. Suspicious eyes fixed on his and barely glanced at the photograph. He knew it was a waste of time. If Cleland was to be found here at all, it would not be among these sad homeless people in search of a better life.

Not a word was exchanged as he moved from campfire to campfire holding his breath. He was met with blank faces, or the merest shake of the head, and he couldn't help but wonder where these people would go from here. Who they had paid to bring them this far. Who was waiting somewhere in the shadows to take them on to the next stop of this hopeless quest. And the next. And the next. If there was one thing worse, he thought, than people who dealt in drugs, it was those who trafficked in people. Pedlars of misery and the cruellest of false dreams. And it was, he knew, only going to get worse. More and more criminal gangs were abandoning the lucrative but dangerous traffic in drugs in favour of people smuggling. People were a cheap, reliable and endless source of revenue, the authorities spent less time and effort in trying to prevent the flow of illegal immigrants, and the consequences of capture were far less punitive.

From somewhere far off in the building he heard a woman scream. He froze, listening intently, only to become aware of every eye in this hellish place turned in his direction. He hesitated for just a second before sprinting back through the rubble, and along the hallway which had brought them here. On the landing he stopped, gasping for air, and strained to hear above the sound of his own breath echoing back at him off cancerous concrete. He heard a clattering of footsteps from the next floor up and took the stairs two at a time. Only to have his heart very nearly stop. Two teenage boys came hurtling down and parted only at the last moment to stream either side of him. Like water around a rock. Then they vanished into the night.

Mackenzie stood breathing hard, trying to recover his composure. No point in going after them. If Cristina was anywhere, she was on the next floor up. And so he continued the climb, playing his torchlight on the stairs ahead of him.

On the next landing a mirror image of the hall downstairs opened off into a corridor mired in darkness. A crude door had been fixed to the hinges of the first apartment on his right. It stood ajar, and light fell into the dark. Grit and detritus crunched beneath his feet as he moved towards it, one careful step at a time. He reached out and pushed it open with the flat of his hand. Candles and an oil lamp burned in here on a table pushed up against the far wall. There were several chairs around it, one tipped on to its back. Several plates of unfinished food had been abandoned, and a cigarette still burned in an ashtray. Three old metal bedsteads stood side by side against the right-hand wall, makeshift mattresses thrown across rusted sprung frames, tortured sweat-stained sheets lying crumpled on each. But there was no one here.

Mackenzie turned quickly back towards the stairway and heard a muffled cry from the top floor. He shone the beam of his torch ahead of him as he climbed into darkness, becoming aware that there were no longer any walls around him. The tower that housed the stairwell, and what would have been the lift shaft, was completely open to the elements on three sides. Moonlight flooded in now, casting oblique shadows across the steps. Out there, where stars shimmered in the night sky, seemed a world away, and the ground below a dangerous drop into the dark.

As he stepped out on to the topmost level he realized that there was nowhere else to go. An unfinished doorway to his left led on to a small square of roof terrace. Turning to his right he stepped on to the top landing, dusty concrete laid on four sides around a square opening intended to house the lift mechanism. Concrete pillars at each corner supported the roof above.

A gathering of three men and a stricken Cristina stood with their backs perilously close to the drop at the far side of the empty shaft. One of the men held her from behind, his hand over her mouth, the barrel of her SIG Pro pushed against her temple. He was dangerously thin, wearing a torn singlet and filthy sneakers. A soiled red bandanna wrapped itself around greasy hair that fell to his shoulders. The other two dangled scarred baseball bats from arms that bulged beneath stained white T-shirts. They faced off to Mackenzie across the gap, and he could see the terror in Cristina's eyes by the light of the moon that angled in across his shoulder.

He realized that having light behind him gave him an advantage, and he raised the beam of his torch to shine directly at the group opposite. He would barely be visible to them, but could see almost every pore on the unshaven faces of Cristina's captors.

In what seemed to Mackenzie like a stage whisper one of them said to the man holding Cristina, 'What do we do?'

'Has he got a gun?'

'Can't see.'

And Mackenzie realized it wasn't Spanish that they spoke. But Arabic. He relaxed a little and started moving cautiously around the perimeter of the lift shaft towards them.

'Listen,' he said. 'We don't have to do this the hard way. No one has to get hurt here.' And he registered their surprise. This strange pale Caucasian was speaking to them in Arabic.

Cristina's fear morphed into confusion as Mackenzie appeared to engage her captors in conversation. A language that she didn't understand. He seemed unnaturally relaxed as he and the man pressing the gun to her head swapped several short exchanges. Then to her astonishment she felt the hand around her mouth relax its grip, and as her captor let her go he stepped forward to lay the SIG Pro carefully on the concrete floor.

Mackenzie approached along one side of the opening, and all three men moved warily along the facing edge. When Mackenzie stooped to pick Cristina's gun from the floor, they made a break for the stairs. She heard their footsteps clattering down into darkness and thought she was going to faint with relief. But Mackenzie was there with a hand on her arm to steady her. He smiled and handed back her gun.

'You should be a little more careful about who you let play with this,' he said.

It took her a moment to find her voice. 'What . . . what just happened?'

Mackenzie shook his head. 'When I said I was going to learn Arabic, people told me I was an idiot. The only use I would ever have for it, they said, was if I joined the foreign office or became a spy.' He laughed. 'But I always figured it would come in handy someday.'

'What did you say to them?'

'I told the fella with the gun at your head that your weapon was faulty. That the safety catch had jammed and that if he fired it, not only would it blow your head off, it would take his hand and probably half his face with it.'

Cristina gawped at him in astonishment. 'And he believed you?'

Mackenzie shrugged. 'Apparently.'

'So why didn't you hold them at gun point once you'd got it back?'

Mackenzie said, 'I'm not authorized to use your gun. And

if I had, you'd only have got into even bigger trouble.' He started steering her towards the stairs. 'As Sun Tzu explained in his *Art of War*, if we do not wish to fight we can prevent the enemy from engaging us if we throw something odd and unaccountable in his way.'

'A jammed gun?'

'Well, here's the thing . . . one way or another these guys were illegals. Involved in people-trafficking or drugs. Who knows? But they didn't want a fight any more than we did. They were just scared. So I gave them a way out. Whether or not they believed the story about the gun doesn't matter. They accepted the chance it offered to escape. So now you can call this in, and it's someone else's problem.' They started down the stairs. 'It's just a pity we've wasted our time here.'

Cristina stopped halfway down to the next landing. 'But we haven't. Before I met the charmers who dragged me up here, I caught a couple of teenagers spray-painting walls. Showed them a photograph of Cleland and told them I'd turn a blind eye if they could give me any information about this guy. It was obvious they recognized him. Not exactly someone you'd expect to stumble across in a place like this. They said they'd seen him here a few times in the last couple of days. In the company of some unsavoury characters. Not the ones who took my gun. Spanish, apparently. So at least we know where he's been hiding out.'

They stepped on to the first landing, and Mackenzie glanced back along the corridor towards to where poor people fleeing conflict were no doubt collecting their belongings and preparing to move on before the police arrived. He said, 'If this is the best Cleland can do, he can't have many friends left. And he must be pretty desperate.'

CHAPTER TWENTY-SIX

Ana is dying a little inside. Cleland has been moving around her house. She is aware of the smell of him, of his body heat as he comes and goes, of the movement of air as he passes. At one point she feels his breath on her face. Not realizing he is quite so close she cries out.

She is terrified. For herself. For Cristina. But more imminently for Sergio. She knows that sometimes they work late at the bank, even if it is not open to the public. The dots raised on the surface of her braille watch tell her that it is nearly nine. If he is coming, as he promised, it will be soon, for people will start eating at ten.

She hopes against hope that something will prevent him from returning tonight. Even that he has taken cold feet after meeting her earlier, and reconsidered. Yes, even that.

A vibration alerts her to a new message on her screen and she raises her fingers to read the braille.

– *Who is Sergio?*

Fear runs through her bones, chilling her to the very core. It's as if he can read her mind. 'Who?'

– Don't play games with me, Ana. When I first arrived you asked if I was Sergio.

'He's just a friend.'

– But you were expecting him.

'No, not really. He drops by from time to time.' She tries to keep calm, control the trembling in her voice.

– You're lying to me, Ana.

'No. Honestly, I'm not. I'm not expecting anyone.'

And as if to make her a liar, fate chooses that moment for the bell to ring downstairs. Her hand flies to the vibration on her chest, as if somehow she can stop it.

– So who would that be, then?

'I've no idea.'

– Open the door.

She is desperate now. 'Why involve anyone else? It's me you want.'

– And Cristina. Is it her?

'Not at this time of night, no.'

– Well, answer it, then, and we'll find out just who it is.

Ana reaches towards the panel of switches on the table and fumbles unconvincingly with the rocker. 'It's not working.' Then feels Cleland brush her hand aside, before the vibration on her chest tells her that he has successfully unlocked the door below. 'Don't harm him. Please.' It is out before she can stop herself.

– Who is he?

'Just a friend.'

– *We'll see.*

Then nothing. She feels the heat of Cleland's body recede and is only too painfully aware of the tread of Sergio's feet on the stairs. Never has the silence and darkness that traps her felt so imprisoning. She wonders about calling out a warning. But would Sergio even understand? It would make no sense to him, until it was too late.

She is aware that the door has opened, then nothing.

What is Sergio doing? Where is Cleland? Has Sergio seen him? Are they speaking?

And then she feels him crossing the floor towards her. The heat of his body. He is very close. The scrape of a chair vibrating faintly through hers, his now familiar scent. Then suddenly his lips on her forehead. She recoils, startled. A quite involuntary response. She can almost feel his hurt.

Several long moments pass before he takes her hands in his. His signing is hesitant.

'I'm so sorry, Ana. I was held up at the bank. I should have been here ages ago.'

All she can think is that he won't hear Cleland if he approaches him from behind. She turns her head in desperation, as if looking for her captor. Where in God's name is he?

'Ana, what's wrong?'

She can feel through the hands his distress at sensing hers.

'GO, SERGIO!' Her hands sign urgently on his. She is more used to others signing for her than she signing for them. But if she speaks aloud Cleland will hear her. 'LEAVE NOW. DON'T ASK WHY. YOU ARE IN DANGER.'

She can feel his consternation. If fills the air around them, as tangible as if she could reach out and touch it.

Then suddenly his hands are gone. She feels a deep vibration run through her body. Something heavy striking the floor. She cries out.

'Sergio!'

But there is no response of any kind. Nothing. Just the darkness and the silence of her world. There is the sense of someone close. The faintest warmth in the cool air of the room, then it is gone.

She sits trembling, tears spilling silently from stinging eyes. Something awful has happened. She knows it. But she daren't speak, hardly dares even to breathe. And she waits, as she has waited half a lifetime, for the world to come to her. It seems like an eternity before she feels the vibration against the skin of her chest, and raises her fingers to the screen with dread in her heart.

– *What were you doing with your hands?*

'Where's Sergio?'

– *Don't worry about Sergio. Tell me what you were doing with your hands.*

Ana can barely draw enough breath into her lungs to allow her to speak. 'Touch-signing.'

– *What's that?*

'It's a way of communicating letters and words by touch.'
Then, 'Where's Sergio?'

– *He's gone. Don't worry about him.*

'I don't believe you.'

– *I don't care.*

'Don't hurt him, please.' Her voice breaks as she pleads with
the dark. She cannot hear her own sobbing, but feels each
sob tearing itself from her chest. Then pain fills her world. A
stinging, burning pain on the side of her face. He has slapped
her again. She feels his breath in her face, tiny specks of spittle
on it as he shouts at her. It smells rank and she almost gags
on it.

Then nothing once more. For several long seconds. Before
she senses the other chair being drawn in close, Cleland's heat,
his earthy masculine smell. Another vibration at her chest.

– *Show me.*

She doesn't understand how he can be typing when he is
sitting next to her. Then conjures a picture of him with the
keyboard on his knees. It is wireless, so perfectly possible.
'Show you what?'

– *How to touch-sign.*

She feels her breath trembling as she fills her lungs to try
to stop herself from sobbing. All she can think is, *what has he
done to Sergio?* Her voice catches in her throat. 'You can't learn
to touch-sign just like that. It takes weeks, months.'

– *Ana, I have all the time in the world.* A pause. *At least until
Cristina comes again. Will she be here tomorrow?*

'I . . . I don't know.'

– I think you do, Ana. But don't worry, I have endless patience. I learned at school that revenge is a dish best served cold. It's a maxim I have lived my life by.

She doesn't know what to say.

– I want you to teach me to touch-sign. It was intriguing, what I saw passing between you and Sergio. It looked . . . A longer pause while he searched for the word. *Intimate. I want that, too. I want to be intimate with you, Ana.*

She could not stop the shudder that shook her body. A wave of disgust. And she wonders if it shows.

– But not right now. I have to leave for a while.

Her heart leaps. If he leaves, then somehow, some way she will be able to raise the alarm. A call to the operator. An email to Cristina. But his next words send fear spiking into her soul.

– He's a nice kid, your niece's boy. What's his name, Lucas? And such a good school they send him to. What a shame if anything were to happen to him. You'd be to blame. You know that, Ana, don't you? If that little boy were to come to any harm. So you'll just sit here quiet and wait till I get back. Or do I have to tie you up?

With lead in her heart Ana knows that she will do exactly as he wants. The threat of harm to Cristina's little boy binds her more efficiently than any rope he might use to secure her. But if Cleland has patience, then so does she. She's had twenty years to nurture it, to make it a virtue. Her time will come. Of that she is now determined.

CHAPTER TWENTY-SEVEN

Sophia stood at the top of the staircase watching him as he lifted one weary leg after the other and climbed towards her. He had been waiting so long for this chance to tell her how sorry he was about the concert, to put his arms around her and hold her close and tell her he loved her.

He wouldn't say anything about her unfriending him on Facebook, but he would watch his page for her friend request to reunite them again across the ether. It was just a temporary huff. She couldn't hate him for ever. Could she?

He was almost there. Three steps, two steps. He reached out his hand towards her. She turned and fled across the landing, into her room, slamming the door behind her. He summoned all his strength to reach it before she could turn the key in the lock. But even as his hand closed around the handle, he heard the click of the deadbolt slipping into place.

'Sophia!' His own voice sounded distant, desperate.

Hers on the other hand thundered in his head. 'Go away!'

'Sophia, let me in.'

'I hate you!'

As tears came to his eyes he started hammering on the door with his clenched fist. 'Sophia!' Nothing. No response. He hit the door harder. 'Sophia, please . . .'

He sat bolt-upright in the darkness, heart pounding in his throat, the echo of his own voice dying around him. He was soaked in sweat, bedsheets twisted about his body, sticking to his legs and chest. But the banging on the door had not stopped. His confusion lasted for only as long as it took him to realize where he was. A room at the top of the Hostal Totaña in Marviña. And someone was banging on the door. He heard Cristina's voice from the other side of it.

'Señor Mackenzie! For God's sake, *hombre*, what's going on in there?'

He blinked and took in the blurry red numerals on the bedside clock. It was a little after 6 am. He scrambled from the bed, boxer shorts bought in Estepona clinging to every perspiring contour, and unlocked the door. Cristina stood on the landing looking at him. She was in full uniform, no make-up, sleep still in her eyes, hair pulled back in its customary ponytail. Severe, unforgiving. Her gaze wandered down to the boxers and quickly back to meet his eye.

'Who's Sophia?'

'My daughter.'

She peered beyond him into the empty bedroom. 'Why were you shouting at her?'

'Was I?'

'I'd be surprised if there's anyone still asleep in the whole of Marviña.'

Mackenzie looked sheepish. 'It was a bad dream.'

She looked at him for a curious moment, then said, 'Get dressed. We've got a multiple homicide up in the hills.'

His brow creased in a frown. 'And what does that have to do with Cleland?'

'They think it's drug-related.'

The headlights of Cristina's Policía Local SUV picked out great swathes of undeveloped countryside, dusty and deserted in the moonlight, before the road began climbing and winding its way through the forest in the foothills of the mountains. They passed lonely farmhouses, and the occasional family restaurant tucked into folds in the hills – Venta García, Venta Victoria.

The moon had disappeared from view, and the first light was burgeoning in the east, reflecting pink light on dawn cloud over the sea.

They turned off the asphalt road on to a concrete track that cut its way through overhanging cork oaks. It almost glowed in the early light, like the trail left by some giant drunken slug. The SUV bounced and rattled its way over an uneven surface made worse by wholly unnecessary speed bumps. Climbing, climbing, sometimes dropping sheer away into dark bottomless gullies, until they reached a fork in the road, where a signpost dating back to at least the early part of the previous century had been struck by some errant vehicle, and lay twisted and half-buried in the hillside. Originally intended to guide drivers towards two different destinations – Cabezas del Río and La Peña – it was no longer clear which way led to which.

Cristina pulled the SUV to a halt, and it sat idling at a precarious angle while she leaned over Mackenzie to search for a map in the glove compartment. When she found the one she was looking for she opened it against the steering wheel and flicked on the dash light. Mackenzie squinted at the map to see her tracing their route with her finger. She stabbed it at a tiny winding road that headed north-east into the hills. 'That's the one we want. Finca Los Fernández is on the road to La Peña.' She pushed the map at Mackenzie, released the handbrake and swung the wheel to their left, lurching off through the half-dark towards the lost village of La Peña.

After a couple of kilometres the concrete ran out, and the road became little more than a dirt track, rutted and potholed, throwing the SUV and its occupants forwards and sideways, and reducing their progress to a snail's pace. Finally they emerged from the forest into grassy uplands that swept away to the left and right in bold strokes through valleys and ravines towards the mountains. Nothing much grew up here except grass for grazing, almond trees in pink and white blossom, and the odd wild olive. An even narrower track took them off to the left, and down into a tiny sheltered valley where a whitewashed finca and a collection of agricultural outbuildings huddled in the shade of a copse of fig trees.

Two Guardia Civil vehicles and an ambulance stood in the yard, blue and amber flashing in the dawn light. Mackenzie expressed his astonishment. 'How in God's name did anyone even know that something had happened way up here?'

Cristina pulled up behind the other vehicles and jumped out. 'A local goatherd. He was in the habit of dropping in early for coffee. They're up and working at four or five in the hills to avoid the heat of the day.'

They walked towards the house. This was a traditional Andalusian finca, a farmhouse on one level with rough white-painted walls and a red, shallow-pitched Roman-tiled roof. It was built half into the hillside to provide cool cellar space beneath the house, and an adjoining barn was roofed, surprisingly, with rows of brand-new solar panels. Blue and white crime-scene tape had been stretched across the entrance to the property and hung limp in the still morning air. The ambulance driver and a medic leaned against the front of their vehicle, catching a final smoke before heading back down the hill. Nothing for them here. Everyone dead. A private contractor would be sent by the judicial coroner to take the bodies down for autopsy.

A figure familiar to Cristina detached itself from the group of Guardia standing in the yard. Paco hobbled towards them on his crutches. Cristina raised an eyebrow in surprise.

'What are you doing here?'

Paco balanced on his supports to kiss her on each cheek. 'Can't sleep since I got home,' he said. 'So I sit up and drink coffee and listen to the Guardia bandwave. Heard this one called in and asked the guys to collect me on the way up.'

Cristina nodded and half-turned towards Mackenzie. 'Paco's my brother-in-law. The one Cleland shot. Señor Mackenzie is with the British police.' Mackenzie and Paco shook hands. Paco sighed and Mackenzie saw deep sadness in his dark eyes. 'I know these people,' he said. 'Friends of my folks going way back.'

'How bad is it?' Cristina asked.

'It's bloody. You don't want to go in there if you don't have to.'

Cristina nodded grimly. 'I think we probably have to. How long before homicide arrive?'

'Well, the pathologist's already here. He came straight up from Marbella. Homicide are coming from Malaga. It'll be a while yet.'

'We don't want to waste time, then.' She went into the back of the SUV to remove plastic shoe covers and latex gloves for Mackenzie and herself.

The lights in the house were all turned on, and yet it still seemed dark. The front door took them into a single large room with an open fireplace at one end. An old porcelain sink stood against the facing wall, flanked by rough wooden work-tops hung with curtains. A window above the sink leaked early light into the room. A table where the family had no doubt eaten for a generation sat square in the centre of the room.

An old dresser and wooden drawer units crowded surrounding walls that were hung with old black-and-white family portraits dating back a hundred years or more. There was a photograph of the house taken in another lifetime. Also black-and-white. It hadn't changed. The same fig trees, the tendrils of their sinewy roots snaking out across the front yard, cast shade from the same sun. The only difference between then and now was that the family were all dead.

Drawers had been ripped out of cupboards and wall units and contents strewn across the floor. Glass and china lay shattered on cold Andalusian tiles among upturned chairs where blood congealed in great dark pools.

A pathologist in white Tyvek crouched over one of three bodies. A young man who Mackenzie guessed was probably in his late twenties or early thirties. But it was difficult to tell. This was a hard life, and people aged quickly under a relentless and unforgiving sun. Also, his face was a bloody, pulpy mess.

An elderly couple lay nearby. His parents, Mackenzie thought. The old woman's skull had been cleaved almost in two, and there was a gaping hole in the old man's chest.

Cristina, standing beside him, made a muted gagging sound, and Mackenzie guessed she was fighting to keep down the bile rising in her throat. A smell of blood, like rust, hung heavy in the air.

The pathologist was a young man, hood pushed back from a head of finely cropped dark hair. No doubt he had seen some harrowing things in his time, but even he had paled. He turned his face up towards them. 'Poor bastards,' he said. 'Whoever did this was merciless. Almost as if they'd been tortured.'

'Why do you say that?' Mackenzie asked.

'All three have multiple injuries, Señor. Hands, arms, legs. Brutal stuff. Not enough to kill. Not immediately. But you'd have to be a sadist, or trying to get them to talk. Or both. In the end it looks like they either got what they wanted or ran out of patience. The old man took two barrels of a shotgun in his chest. Seems like they used a machete on the mother. And the son . . .' He looked down at the sorry mess on the floor. 'They just beat him into oblivion.'

Mackenzie said, 'Why do you say *they*?'

The pathologist shrugged as if it was obvious. 'The extent of the injuries. The use of multiple weapons.' He paused. 'And then there are all the footprints in the blood. I'd say there were at least four, maybe five. I'll know exactly how many by the time I'm finished here.'

Cristina's voice was a hoarse whisper. 'So whatever they knew, or whatever it was their attackers wanted, was beaten out of them.' She turned towards Mackenzie. 'This was almost certainly a safe house for drugs.'

But Mackenzie shook his head. 'Unlikely.'

Both Cristina and the pathologist looked at him. 'What makes you say that, señor?' the pathologist asked.

Mackenzie said, 'If these people had been coerced into keeping drugs, what pretext would they have for not just handing them over? And even if for some reason they had hidden them, how long would it take to beat the hiding place out of them? An old couple like that? And their boy.' He looked around the room. 'And if their attackers had got the information they wanted, why would they have had to tear the place apart?' He hesitated. 'It doesn't feel right. Any of it.'

The pathologist said, 'They're bringing sniffer dogs up. If there were drugs here they'll know soon enough.'

Mackenzie nodded and picked his way to the door, back out into the early morning light. He had seen enough. The sun was just below the line of the trees now, and he stepped over the crime-scene tape and into the yard. Cristina followed gratefully behind him. He stopped and scratched his head thoughtfully.

'What is it?'

He glanced at her. 'Remember that busted signpost on the road. If we hadn't had a map we might have taken the wrong turning.' He turned to look back at the house. 'I don't think these poor people had the first idea what their attackers wanted. They came to the wrong bloody finca.'

Realization broke over Cristina like cold water. Her hand flew to her mouth. 'Oh my god, we need to get over to the finca at Cabezas del Río.' She started running for the SUV and Mackenzie had trouble keeping up with her.

'Hey!'

They looked back from the open doors of their vehicle to see Paco hobbling after them.

'Where are you going?'

Cristina said, 'We think they came to the wrong house, Paco.'

A frown of confusion clouded his face before sudden understanding swept it away. He paled. 'Jesus.' Then, 'Take me with you.'

The sun had risen fully over the shoulder of the mountain as they lurched down a potholed track to the Hacienda Familia Castillejos, dust rising behind them like smoke in the still morning air.

Hacienda was a grand name for what was really just another finca. The home of Familia Castillejos was built from local stone, a simple single-story house with a vine-shaded terrace at the front. The road, such as it was, ran on a short way beyond the house to a broken-down collection of barns. Hens scattered in the yard as Cristina brought their SUV to an unceremonious halt. The front door lay open, and they could see beyond it that there were lights still burning in the kitchen.

Cristina was first inside, Mackenzie just behind her. It took Paco a good half-minute to catch them up.

In contrast to the kitchen at Finca Los Fernández, this room was neat and clean and well-ordered, lit by several lamps and an overhead light. The smell of a recently cooked breakfast still hung in the air. A weather-worn middle-aged couple sat at the table, breakfast only half eaten in front of them, fat congealing around eggs and ham, coffee long since gone cold in chipped and discoloured mugs.

The woman wore a dark blouse beneath a shawl that hung down to a creased three-quarter-length skirt. Mackenzie could see woollen stockings beneath it, and tattered trainers that might once have been white. The man's skinny frame was clad in grubby blue overalls, silvered black hair like fuse wire contained beneath a sweat-stained cap. Their faces were turned towards the door with the dread of expectancy. The woman's face was stained and still shining from tears. She took in Cristina's uniform. 'It's true, then?' she said.

'Is what true?' Mackenzie asked quickly.

The woman flickered dead eyes in his direction. 'They killed the Fernández family.'

Cristina said, 'How do you know?'

The man scratched a silver-bristled chin, the sound of it rasping in the stillness of the room. His face was the colour and texture of leather, his eyes so deep set they were like black holes in his face. 'Diego.'

'Who's Diego?'

'The goatherd. He came here after the Guardia arrived at La Peña. He usually calls in after he has had coffee with the Fernández people.'

Señora Castillejos shook her head. 'It was all a terrible mistake. We had no idea they had gone to La Peña first. Those poor folk would have had no idea what they were looking for. The drugs were here all the time.'

Mackenzie walked into the room, drew a chair up to the table and sat down. 'Tell us what happened,' he said.

Castillejos shook his head. 'We had no choice, señor. They threatened to kill us if we did not keep their packages for them.'

'What were they like, these packages?'

'Big plastic sacks, señor, like they use for animal feed. About thirty of them. A couple of tons, I'd say. And I should know, they made me unload and stack them in the barn when they first brought them.'

'Do you know what was in them?'

He shrugged. 'Drugs.'

Mackenzie looked at Cristina. 'If it's cocaine, a couple of tons would have a street value running to hundreds of millions. And if this is Cleland's stash then it's the deal of a lifetime. Money like that . . . he'll be gone. History. We'll never find him.' He turned back to the Castillejos. 'What happened this morning?'

She sat wringing her hands on the table in front of her. 'They didn't say they had already been to the Finca los Fernández by mistake. Just ordered Carlos to load the bales into their big covered pickup while they stood around watching and smoking and laughing. Four of them. I'll never forget their faces.'

Her husband cast grave eyes in her direction. 'It might be better, Mariana, if you did.'

But she shook her head. 'When I think of what they did to those poor people . . .' She turned tearful eyes towards Cristina. 'Before they left one of them said we should get our road sign fixed. It would be too easy, he said, to take a wrong turning. Only now do I know what he meant.'

Cristina looked at Mackenzie. She could see Cleland slip-ping through their fingers. 'If they have come for the drugs this morning, it must mean they are planning the handover today or tomorrow.'

'Or just moving it somewhere safer.' Paco's voice made them all turn towards where he stood silhouetted in the doorway. 'With all the police activity to find Señor Cleland they are probably very nervous right now.'

CHAPTER TWENTY-EIGHT

When Ana wakes she is fully dressed, and lying on top of the bed rather than in it. She knows it is morning from the heat of the sun falling across her bed through the shutters, and is surprised that she has slept at all.

It was late when Cleland returned the night before, and she had persuaded him to let her walk Sandro to the end of the street and back. At first he had resisted, telling her it would be unwise to step out in the dark, before she pointed out that her whole life was spent in the dark.

He had accompanied her, a hand hooked through her arm, and they had walked slowly the length of the Calle San Miguel, right down to Calle Caridad and back, stopping only to let Sandro lift his leg against flowerpots and doorsteps.

The untrained eye might have thought them to be just some couple out for a late evening stroll with their dog. They would have realized, of course, that Ana was blind, but the intimacy of Cleland's arm through hers, and their comfortable silence, would have aroused nothing but sympathy.

In fact, their silence had been anything but comfortable.

Behind it, Ana's mind had been in turmoil, desperately seeking some way to escape. But he held her entirely in his power, and she sensed that he was enjoying it.

Back at the house he had told her that she should sleep, and taken her to the bedroom. For a long time she had stood in the silent darkness of her inner prison trying to determine whether or not he had left the room. She did not want to undress with the thought that he was standing watching her every move. So in the end she had simply lain down on the bed fully dressed.

But thoughts of Sergio had kept sleep at bay. Remembering every word of their conversation, his touch, his scent. Then his return, their interchange cut short by the deep vibration of something heavy landing at her feet. Poor, poor Sergio. What had that monster done to him?

It is the first thing on her mind when she wakes, and the cold fingers of fear close around her heart as the full recollection of the previous day's events flood back.

She sits upright, breathing hard, trying to hold herself still. Is there anyone in the room? She cannot tell. Slowly she slips off the bed and makes her way to the small en-suite bathroom, where she sits on the pan to relieve herself, then splashes her face with cold water in the sink. She does not have the heart even to brush her teeth, and feels her way to the door, and out into the sitting room.

Immediately she smells fresh coffee and hot *churros*. A hand on her arm startles her, and she recognizes Cleland's earthy scent. He guides her quickly but gently towards her computer and eases her into her seat. She feels for and finds the small vibrating disk that she pins immediately to her blouse. Almost at once she feels it vibrate against her skin.

Fingers on her screen decipher his message.

– *Good morning, Ana. I hope you like churros. You'll find a plate of them and some coffee on the table in front of you.*

'I'm not hungry,' is her instinctive response. Even although she is.

– *Well, that's a pity. If you don't want them I might have to eat them myself. I love churros, don't you?*

No response.

– *I've eaten far too many of them since I've been in Spain. Much better than porridge! But fattening, don't you think? So much here is fried. A bit like Scotland. I've put on too much weight.* He paused. *Angela, on the other hand, could eat anything and never put on an ounce. Oh, I'm sorry, imperial measures. What would you say? A gram?*

Ana sits in silence, fingers dancing across the screen to read his rambling. None of it, she thinks, requires a response.

– *Of course, there's no danger of Angela ever putting on weight now, is there?*

'Where's Sergio?' She isn't going to play his game, and can almost hear him sighing in the pause before his reply.

– *He's gone.*

'What did you do to him.'

– *I didn't do anything.* Pause. *Well, I did. I hit him over the head.*

I'm sorry. He's going to have a bad headache this morning, but he's probably more upset by what I told him.

'What did you tell him?'

– That you didn't want him to come back. Ever.

She knows he is lying. How could he possibly have explained to Sergio why he had struck him? And then just let him go. She is consumed by fear for her teenage amour. But knows she has to keep Cleland talking. About anything. The more she can build a rapport with him the less likely he is to hurt her. She hopes.

'Why are you doing this?'

– Because your niece killed the woman I was going to marry. The woman who was carrying my child.

This is news to Ana. Did Cristina know that Cleland's woman was pregnant? But she wants to steer him away from that. 'No, I mean, everything you do, everything you are. After Cristina told me about you, I searched the internet for more information. There is plenty out there about you. Newspaper articles. Police bulletins. Even a page in Wikipedia.

– Really? I didn't know that.

She somehow detects pleasure in this response and decides to play on his ego. 'I suppose you're a little bit famous in your own way.'

– Just a little bit?

Which only confirms for Ana that Cleland is more than just a little bit self-obsessed. Image is a skin people wear to hide their real selves. And Cleland is clearly concerned with his.

Even to the point of lying to himself about who was actually responsible for Angela's death. Because, after all, how could he live with himself if he were to admit responsibility for killing the mother of his child, along with the child itself? It wouldn't fit with his own carefully cultivated self-image. Invincible dealer in drugs, respected and feared in his own circles, always one step ahead of the police. Living the life of a wealthy retiree on the Costa del Sol, right under the noses of the authorities. She says, 'Quite a lot, I suppose.' Then hesitates. 'What I don't understand is why.'

– *Why?*

'Your parents were wealthy.'

– *So?*

'They sent you to the best schools, paid your way through Oxford. You never wanted for anything.'

– *Nothing material, no.*

'So what possible reason could you have for turning to crime?'

There is a very long pause.

– *That's a good question, Ana. And I don't pretend there's any easy answer.*

His subsequent response is peppered with long pauses as he reflects, perhaps for the first time, on why he has taken this particular route through life.

– *It all sounds very grand, doesn't it? Wealthy parents, private schools, an Oxford education. The reality was something else. Parents who never wanted me in the first place. A mother and father who* couldn't wait to shuffle off responsibility to nannies and schoolmasters. I was just an inconvenience. We lived in Edinburgh, for God's sake, and yet they had me board at Fettes, less than a mile from the family home. Lavished with everything money could buy. Except for love. Which, of course, you can't buy, as The Beatles so eloquently pointed out to my parents in their youth.

A very long pause now. So long that Ana begins to wonder if he is still there.

– I have no doubt you could regale me with tales of growing up in impoverished southern Spain. But you could never understand how hard it was for a boy abandoned by his parents to spend all his young years in a series of soulless dormitories. Where if you weren't bullied to tears by the big boys, you were punished for crying by the masters. On my 17th birthday my father had a car delivered to my door. A red Porsche 911. The envy of every other boy in the school.

Again he pauses.

– I'd have given all the Porsche 911s in the world for just a little of his time. But, oh no, my father never had time. At least not for me. Packed me off to Oxford with a generous allowance and the keys to my own apartment. God, how lucky was I?

Although she could neither see nor hear him, she could feel the bitterness in his words.

– It became clear to me, Ana, that if no one else was going to have time for me, then I would just have to make the time for myself. Amazing how quickly the calluses grow and the hurt goes away. Extraordinary how you can segue from being the receiver of pain, to being the giver of it. And what pleasure there is in that.

She can visualize the cursor blinking on his screen as he composes his thoughts for what is to come next.

– *Those bullies . . . the ones who made my life so bloody miserable . . . I came across a few of them in later years. Well, actually, I sought them out. And they found out pretty fucking fast that dealing with the adult Jack was a whole other experience from beating up on some pathetic kid. That's what you call taking back power, Ana. And there are very few feelings in this world quite that good.*

She does not know now if he has finished, if he has spent his ire. Or whether there is more to come. So she prompts him.

'I read that you were one of the top traders in the biggest commercial bank in London.'

– *Best trader on the floor.*

'You couldn't have been short of money, then.'

– *If there's one thing I learned from my folks, Ana, it's that money isn't everything. But there I was, Mr Dealmaker, buying and selling just seconds before stocks soared or plummeted. Making fortunes – for someone else. So it was back to the old axiom. Look after Number One. Along came a different kind of deal. One in which I controlled everything, including the profits.*

'Drugs.'

– *A street commodity,* he corrects her. *Following the basic precepts of Capitalism. Supply and demand. There was a demand, I supplied it. But it's a very different environment from the trading floor. Get it wrong and people want to kill you. So you get tough. You learn that there's no place for sentiment. If someone wants to kill you, you kill them first.*

Law of the jungle. And I was good at that. Mad Jock, they called me. Still do, for all I know. We Scots have a certain reputation to maintain.

She doubts very much if it is a reputation that John Mackenzie would approve of. And almost as though he has heard the thought echoing in her darkness, she detects vitriol in his next words.

– *They've sent another Jock to catch me. But he's no match for me, Ana. I smelled his breath, and his hair gel and his aftershave. I heard his Glasgow brogue. Some knucklehead cop looking to make a reputation at my expense. I'm going to kill him, too.*

For the first time, Ana feels despair wash over her. The skin of Cleland's self-image fits him so tightly there is no room for reason. The calluses so thick he has no sense of other people's pain, never mind his own. She says, 'I grew up in a religious family, and though I've never had any time for God I would never knowingly hurt another human being, or take from him or her what is not mine. I've heard that abused children often become abusers themselves. I have never understood that. Surely no one better knows the pain of abuse? I find it hard to have sympathy for you.'

– *I'm not asking for any!*

'I've had none of your advantages in life, señor, but would never have projected my own misfortune on to others as you have done.'

Again the long pause. Is he analysing her words or simply controlling his anger? When it comes, his reply surprises.

– *You are right. Fate has dealt you a hand much worse than mine.*

I can't imagine how it would be to have my sight and hearing taken away. That is unimaginable, Ana.

She feels no compulsion to reply.

– Tell me about you and Sergio.

She feels a constriction of the muscles all around her heart, but says nothing.

– Tell me.

'No.'

– Tell me, Ana.

Although they are only raised dots on her screen, she can feel his frustration in them and realizes that she cannot afford to excite his anger. 'Why?'

– I'd like to know.

She draws a deep breath. And tells him. Everything. Meeting Sergio at the centre. Her parents' disapproval. The diagnosis of Usher Syndrome and Sergio's offer to share the learning of touch-signing with her. Their blossoming romance, the meals at Santa Ana, and then her father's physical attack on the young man.

'I learned only yesterday that my father had gone to Sergio's parents, and that they had threatened to withdraw support and patronage if he didn't stop seeing me.'

– And he agreed?

'I never saw or heard anything of him again until yesterday. I thought . . .' She chokes on the thought and feels tears welling.

– You thought what?'

'I thought that finally I might have someone to spend my life with. Someone to share the darkness, and the silence.'

Cleland's silence lasted so long she really did believe that this time he had gone.

'Hello . . . ?'

Nothing.

'Señor?'

Finally a vibration at her breast.

– *What was worse? Losing your sight or your hearing?*

No reaction to her story. Nothing. Just a change of subject as if, in spite of his asking, her story was not the one he wanted to hear. She realized she would have to respond.

'I was always prepared for the fact that one day I would lose my hearing completely. But nothing prepares you for blindness.' She pauses and runs the rule of recollection back over the years. 'Though perhaps, strange as it seems, the thing I miss most is music. I loved my music as a kid. Everyone else has a soundtrack to their lives. Mine is silence.' And she can almost hear the silence in the room that follows. Finally, her buzzer vibrates once more against her chest.

– *One day, Ana, if we both survive this, I'll see that you never want for anything again. That's a promise.*

She has not the least idea how to respond.

– *I have to go out for a while.*

And she finds herself suffused with relief. Space to think. Time to try and find a way out of this.

– *Just don't even think of trying to alert anyone. People can die too easily. Especially little children.*

*

Cleland sat looking at the sightless woman perched on the chair opposite. Two screens between them. Conduits of communication. Her way of reaching the world beyond silence and darkness. His way of reaching into hers.

He recalled slapping her yesterday. Twice. And felt immediate regret. Like striking a helpless animal. No way for her to hit back. Which made him no better than those bullies who had so relentlessly tormented him through all his miserable childhood. He wanted to reach out and take her hand and tell her he was sorry. Such an alien impulse that he was completely unable to act upon it, and sat just staring at her face. And thought about Sergio.

He had not meant to hit Sergio so hard. If he had known then just how much he meant to Ana . . . It was just one more thing taken from her. God had robbed her of her sight and her hearing. Cleland had stolen her freedom. And her love.

And Angela. He had taken her life. He screwed his eyes tight shut and felt hot tears squeezing out between the lids to track their way down a tanned face starting to show the ravages of stress. If it hadn't been for that stupid bloody policewoman . . .

He reached over to grab the untouched plate of churros in front of Ana, and the mug of cooling coffee, and hurled both at the wall with a force only matched by the strength of the roar of pure frustration that rose from his throat and resonated in the still morning air.

CHAPTER TWENTY-NINE

Outside the police station the sun beat down mercilessly on the pavements of Marviña, the early morning freshness long since burned off. Here in the interview room, where there were no windows, LED strips on the ceiling reflected a bright unforgiving light back off every hard surface. It was sticky hot, and Carlos Castillejos dripped sweat from the end of his long nose on to the plasticized pages of the book of mug shots they kept in the evidence room of the Policía Local. A gallery of rogues scowling at the lens, faces that in some cases reflected defeat, in others defiance. All taken at the moment of arrest and maximum vulnerability.

Carlos displayed no interest in identifying any of the faces that slid by in front of him. He knew what it could cost to get on the wrong side of any of these people. But his wife leaned in against him, scrutinizing each one. She knew the Fernández family well, she had told Cristina. She had been at school with the wife, and as teenagers they had gone to dances together down in Marviña, staying over at the house of her cousin, often sharing a bed, as well as tales of romantic encounters. She was riven with grief.

Suddenly she stabbed a finger at a swarthy face that stared at her with simmering resentment from the pages of the book. 'Him!' she said. 'That's him. He was the leader.'

Carlos threw her a warning look. 'Mariana,' he said quietly, but with an underlying menace. She was oblivious.

'Are you sure?' Cristina asked.

'That face will be etched in my memory till the day I die,' she said.

'Which might be quite soon if you don't shut up,' Carlos growled. All pretence of cooperation with the police had vanished in an instant.

'He was the one who said we should get the signpost fixed.' Mariana was clearly back at the finca looking into this man's ugly face as he sneered at her. 'He thought it was funny. After what they had done to the Fernández family, he thought it was a joke!' She couldn't keep the disgust from her voice. 'Who is he?'

Cristina said, 'You don't need to know.' She turned the book towards herself and looked at the details on the reverse of the page. Roberto Vasquéz. A petty criminal with a string of convictions for possession. Suspicions of dealing unproven. She unclipped the ring binder and removed the page, then returned the book for the Castillejos to continue looking.

Within half an hour they had exhausted the station's photographic record of petty criminals. There were no further identifications. Cristina herself had looked at each face with every turn of the page and thought how, after a while, they all started to look the same. Different faces, but the same dead eyes.

She left Carlos and Mariana in the interview room to vent their domestic disharmony while she took the mug shot of Vasquéz to the front office, where she composed a request for further information from UDYCO in Malaga, then faxed it along with the photograph to the drugs unit in the provincial capital. She headed along the corridor to the meeting room where the *Jefe* was chairing a briefing.

As she came through the door the *Jefe* was saying, 'Information is gold dust here. I want you to lean on every source and every resource we have. Someone knows something, that's for sure. It's the where and the when we're interested in, and we're running out of time. The drugs are on the move, so we can assume that everyone involved is too.'

A dozen or more officers sat upright in hard, uncomfortable seats listening to the chief with mixed feelings. Mackenzie sat among them watching faces that betrayed ambivalence. This was a small community. Police officers lived locally with their families, and were known to everyone. Getting on the wrong side of the drugs lords could bring unwanted attention. And retribution. On the other hand, here was the chance to be a hero. The one to supply the missing piece of the jigsaw. It could lead to commendation, promotion.

Cristina marched to the front of the room and handed the mug shot of Vasquéz to the *Jefe*. 'The ringleader,' she said.

'Señora Castillejos recognized him straight away. I've shared with UDYCO and asked for more info.'

The *Jefe* took the clear plastic folder containing the photograph and stuck it with Blu-tack to a whiteboard on a tripod behind him. 'Okay,' he said. 'Some of you will know this guy. Let's get every bit of info on him that we can. Last known address, known associates, where he drinks, where he takes a piss. Everything. And let's bring him in.'

He reached for a pile of printed sheets on the desk beside him and started handing them out.

'And these are the places Cleland in his persona as Templeton is known to have frequented. Bars, restaurants, golf course, marina. Again we're looking for anyone with connections to Templeton. Fellow diners, drinking buddies, golf companions. Divide them up among yourselves.' He turned towards Mackenzie. 'It would be useful if you checked out the expat haunts.' He smiled. 'Your English is a little better than most of ours.'

As the meeting broke up, Mackenzie scanned the list and approached the *Jefe*. 'What about the golf course, chief?'

He nodded. 'Yes, take that, too. Lot of foreigners with golf club membership. That's what most of them come here for, after all. I'll be up there myself later.' He sighed. 'The police sponsor an annual competition at Balle Olivar to coincide with the festival of San Isidro in Estepona. My turn to make a little speech and fire the starter gun on the first tee. A damned inconvenience, and I'd get out of it if I could, but it won't take long.'

He clapped his hands together briskly to cut through the lethargy of the officers trooping out of the room.

'Okay guys, come on, let's move it!'

CHAPTER THIRTY

Cristina hurried across the Plaza del Vino, past the tobacconist and the newsagent, and the little music shop which was just a stone's throw from the music school on the far side of the plaza. The mini-market would be open till three, and she thought about running in quickly to get some provisions, but there really wasn't time.

She glanced up at the front window of her apartment. It was Antonio's day off and he would have returned long ago from taking Lucas to school. She recalled with embarrassment their row in front of Mackenzie the previous evening. Relations between them had been deteriorating in the last few months. Financial pressures, the problems with Lucas and his schoolwork, the demands of her job. And now all this with Cleland. It was something they had to address before it began to get out of hand.

She saw with some dismay that his car was not parked out front. She was returning home for half an hour on the pretext of showering and changing, after spending half the night out on the job. But really, she just wanted the chance to spend a quiet ten minutes with Antonio. To say sorry. And hold him. And tell him they had something special that she didn't want to lose.

The apartment was empty when she went in. A shambles, as it always was. She simply couldn't stay on top of her job and keep house at the same time. And Antonio never lifted a finger.

The air seemed heavy still with the bad feelings of the previous evening. Few words had passed between them on her return from the abandoned development on the hill where she and Mackenzie had found the illegal immigrants. And then just a few hours later, as she dragged herself out of bed to take the *Jefe*'s call, only a handful of terse and bad-tempered exchanges had been required to establish that Antonio would have to take Lucas to school. Something he resented on his day off.

She went into their bedroom to take a freshly laundered uniform from the wardrobe and search for clean underwear in the chest of drawers. In the shower she turned her face up to the stream of hot water and let it cascade over her body, washing away the dust and the tension. Though nothing, she knew, could ever erase the bloody scene in the finca at La Peña. Like Mariana's recollection of the smirking Roberto Vasquez, it was an image that would stay with her for the rest of her life.

She dried her hair roughly with a towel – no time to blow it dry – and slipped into her clean clothes. It was only as she went through to the living room, pulling her hair back into its habitual ponytail, that she noticed Antonio's golf clubs missing from the corner of the hall where they usually languished. For all her good intentions to kiss and make up, an involuntary anger surged through her. With everything that was going on between them, and the threat from Cleland to Cristina and everyone in her family, all that Antonio could think of was playing golf. 'Fuck you, Toni!' she shouted at the empty apartment. 'Fuck you!' And was startled by the sudden ringing of her mobile phone. She unclipped it from the holder on her belt.

'Officer Sánchez Pradell.'

'Cristina. It's Captain Rodríguez from GRECO.'

Cristina was astonished that the head of the Organized Crime Squad in Marbella would even know her Christian name. 'Yes, Captain.'

'UDYCO forwarded the information you passed on to them about Roberto Vasquéz. That was good work, officer. There have been developments. I've spoken to your *Jefe*. You and the Englishman need to meet with one of our people . . .'

CHAPTER THIRTY-ONE

An avenue of palm trees led up the hill from a derelict sales office just off the A7. The golf course at Balle Olivar itself was immaculately kept, and meandered across the hillside with stunning views towards the sea. But rows of pueblo-style white apartment blocks beyond the clubhouse had failed to sell as the developer had hoped, and now lay half empty, slowly crumbling in the southern sun. It had been a question of timing. The financial crash of 07/08 had come at just the wrong moment, and huge billboards now offered apartments at absurdly low prices.

Mackenzie had spent a fruitless hour-and-a-half trudging from bar to bar in the overcrowded streets of festive Estepona, waving Cleland's photograph in front of barmen and customers in a vain search for associates of the fugitive. On more than one occasion he found himself regarded with suspicion by dodgy characters with south London accents. He thought it more than likely that half the villains on the NCA's wanted list were lurking in the darker corners of some of these establishments. But no one admitted to knowing or recognizing Cleland, or Templeton as he had called himself. And no one was very keen to engage Mackenzie in conversation.

Hunger gnawed at his stomach. He had barely eaten in the last twenty-four hours and it would be another two hours before the Spanish sat down to lunch. In an attempt to get cooler air into the car he wound down the window of the unmarked vehicle they had given him, but the air that blew in was just as hot. He checked his phone. It was almost at full charge. The battery had died after he'd failed to charge it the night before, and he'd been forced to leave it plugged into the cigarette lighter while doing his tour of the bars.

The clubhouse sat on the brow of the hill, set among a profusion of palm trees and semi-tropical flowering shrubs. It was a low, two-storey building with a shallow pitched yellow-tiled roof. There was a great deal of smoked glass and chrome and polished woodwork, and men and women in polo shirts and colourful shorts and slacks stood about in the shade of the veranda, nursing pint glasses and watching entrants in the annual competition teeing off on the first hole. A huge leader board had been erected for the occasion, and adjudicators sat in the shade of an open-sided canvas tent updating it with the latest scores coming in from the course.

Empty apartment blocks overlooked manicured greens peppered with baseball-capped competitors, the undulating course itself punctuated by shimmering bunkers and dusty mature olive trees.

There was not a breath of wind as Mackenzie found a place in the crowded car park and stepped out into the blazing heat of the early afternoon. The Pro Shop in the basement of the clubhouse was crowded, and half a dozen covered golf buggies stood in parking slots out front.

As Mackenzie headed for the steps he spotted the *Jefe*'s black Audi Q5 glinting in the sunlight. So he hadn't managed to get away as quickly as he'd hoped.

Air conditioning brought blessed relief from the heat as he stepped inside. Tables were set with crisp linen cloths for a lunch that would not be served for some hours yet, although Mackenzie could smell something good cooking in the kitchen and his stomach issued an audible complaint. Staff were setting out a long buffet with cold meats and salads. He was tempted to help himself surreptitiously as he passed, but controlled the urge. He spent the next half-hour talking to barmen and serving staff, and the club secretary who told him that Templeton had been a generous contributor to club fund-raisers.

He showed everyone photographs of Vasquéz and Cleland. Predictably, no one recognized Vasquéz. He would have stood out here like a tramp at a cocktail party. Everyone remembered Templeton. And no one had a bad word to say about him. The waitress who brought Mackenzie his coffee said, 'He's a lovely man, Señor Templeton.' She had the look in her eyes of someone smitten. 'Always buying drinks for his friends. And the staff. A good tipper, too.' A group of golfers that he played with regularly was out on the course somewhere, she told him, participants in today's match play. Mackenzie debated whether or not to hang about until they came back in, but it could have been a long wait, and this all felt like a waste of time anyway. He decided to leave.

By the time he got back to the car park the *Jefe*'s Audi was gone. A loud cheer drifted across the cars from the eighteenth green as someone sank a hole in one.

Mackenzie was about to get into his car when he saw Antonio and Paco emerging together from the side entrance to the locker rooms. Antonio, a set of clubs over one shoulder, was walking at pace and Paco was having trouble keeping up with him on his crutches. It was clear to Mackenzie, even from a distance, that the two men were arguing. He stood for a moment watching as Antonio turned suddenly, confrontational, and Mackenzie could hear his raised voice above the excited hubbub from the course. He was curious, and decided to add himself to the mix.

With as casual an air as he could muster, he strolled towards them, hands in pockets. 'Well, hello,' he said, affecting what he hoped was a genuine smile of surprise. 'Didn't expect to see either of you two here.'

Both men started almost guiltily and turned towards him. Paco recovered himself more quickly, although to Mackenzie's eye his smile never got beyond his lips. 'Señor,' he said. 'Good to see you again.' He waved a crutch vaguely towards the course. 'In this better circumstance.'

Mackenzie nodded towards the walking aids. 'You'll not be playing much golf with those.'

Paco inclined his head in wistful acknowledgement. 'I'm afraid I won't. But I still enjoy watching. Not much else to occupy me at the moment.' He laughed. 'I can just about afford the hire of a golf buggy.'

Mackenzie's eyes drifted towards Antonio, and the golf bag slung over his shoulder. Antonio forced a smile that, like Paco's, didn't quite reach his eyes. 'I usually play on my day off, Señor Mackenzie. But I forgot it was the San Isidro competition today.' His smile turned rueful. 'A waste of a journey.'

'You won't stay to watch?'

'I prefer to play.'

Paco looked at Mackenzie. 'You're not here to play, though.'

Mackenzie's laugh was genuine now. 'No. That would not be a pretty sight.' But he decided not to elucidate on the real reason for his being there. 'Maybe see you later.'

And he turned to head off back towards his car.

When he slipped into the driver's seat he unplugged his phone and switched it back on. He could see beyond the reflections on his windscreen that the two men had resumed their argument. But he was immediately distracted by an alert from the phone. It was a text from Cristina. *Where have you been? Meet me ASAP in the car park of Zhivago's. It's a restaurant in Marbella. Find it on Google maps.*

When he looked up again Paco had vanished, and Antonio was striding angrily towards his car, where he raised the boot and threw in his clubs before slamming it shut. Mackenzie watched as he drove off with a squealing of tyres, and wondered exactly what it was that had passed between the brothers-in-law.

CHAPTER THIRTY-TWO

Zhivago's was located in a leafy north-west corner of Marbella known as Little Russia. Wealthy Russian expats hung out here in exclusive clubs and bars among a proliferation of palm trees. They built themselves beautiful bodies in luxury gymnasia, treated their wives to prohibitively expensive sessions in stylish beauty parlours, ate in any one of a number of restaurants offering international haute-cuisine. There was even a school of Russian ballet where daughters could be deposited while parents sipped French wines in upmarket Russian cocktail bars. All within a few hundred metres of some of the most expensive marina real estate in Europe. There they could park their luxury yachts for the purchase of a mere 400,000-euro lease, and dine easy in the knowledge that there would be no parking ticket waiting for them on their return. It was rumoured that Putin himself owned a hacienda in the hills less than five kilometres away.

Mackenzie squinted towards his iPhone resting in the passenger seat, trying to decipher Google maps and listening to computerized instructions from an anodyne female voice. He turned off the motorway and followed an access road down to a roundabout before turning on to a winding access road that took him into the heart of suburban Marbella.

You have reached your destination, his phone told him, and he saw the single-storey white-painted building angled around lush gardens behind a hedge designed for ultimate privacy. Advertising hoardings sat on the shallow pitch of the Roman-tiled roof advertising a *galería* of wines and a *bodega* for fine food. The restaurant's name, Zhivago's, was inscribed in discreet letters below an imperious image of Bacchus gazing skywards.

The food and wine complex sat directly across the road from a private Russian club called Azure Beach. The club stood at the entrance of what appeared to be a gated labyrinth of suburban streets filled with luxury apartments and elegant villas that shimmered mirage-like in the heat of the afternoon sun. Somewhere beyond the palms and willows and bougainvillea that draped themselves over fences and walls, the same streets sloped gently away towards the port below, where the Mediterranean lay coruscating across the bay.

As he turned his Seat into the car park, Mackenzie noticed Cristina's SUV parked some way down a side street leading towards the marina. He stopped, and was about to reverse out again, when Cristina stepped from a dark grey Kia Sportage and waved him over.

He parked and walked across to the Kia. Without a word she opened the rear door for him and slipped back into the front passenger seat. A perspiring and overweight middle-aged man with precious little hair half-turned in the driver's seat and nodded as Mackenzie climbed in.

'Detective Gil,' Cristina said by way of introduction. 'He's with GRECO here in Marbella.'

Mackenzie nodded. He remembered Gil from the meeting at Marviña the day before. He stretched forward a hand and received a damp one in return.

'He's got a video you need to see.'

Gil reached for his Samsung Galaxy and started a video playing, then held it up for Mackenzie to watch. Mackenzie recognized the entrance to Zhivago's and realized that the footage must have been taken on a long lens from somewhere across the street, a hidden vantage point beyond the Azure Beach.

Gil said, 'Surveillance footage. Taken a couple of months back. We were watching a guy called Rafa. Long suspected of laundering drug money. He has this business selling yachts.' His laugh contained not a trace of humour. 'You and I couldn't even make a living on the handful of transactions he does each year. But somehow he manages to turn a handsome profit.' He jabbed his finger at the screen. 'That's him going in. The one in the middle.'

Mackenzie leaned forward for a better look. Three men in designer suits were climbing out of a black Porsche Cayenne. Rafa was the tallest of them, elegant in shiny Italian shoes, dark hair gelled back in crinkled curls from a handsome brow.

'Fancies himself, does Rafa,' Gil said. 'Smart guy. He buys his yachts at trade prices, then sells them to wealthy Russian clients for astronomical profits.'

'And the Russians don't mind being ripped off?'

'No they don't. In fact, no sooner have they bought the yachts than they sell them again for millions less than they paid for them.'

Mackenzie said, 'So effectively paying Rafa for goods or services unknown.'

Gil nodded. 'Exactly. And without the recòrding of any transaction other than the buying and selling of the yacht. We'd been trying to establish exactly what these payments were for. Almost certainly drugs. But we had no proof. The only real drugs connection came in the shape of the agent who was bringing Rafa and the Russians together. Alejandro Delgado.' Again he pointed at his screen. 'He's the one on Rafa's right.' A much shorter man, prosperously round, a cigar burning between big-knuckled fingers. 'We've got nothing at all on Delgado, except that his brother got caught smuggling a shitload of cocaine into the country two years ago. The two brothers ran a yacht-rental agency, and although Delgado himself was never implicated in the drugs bust, it's inconceivable that he didn't at least know about it. He and his brother were like that.' He interlaced fore and middle fingers.

Mackenzie was interested now. 'How did you catch the brother?'

'The cocaine came in first by boat to Gibraltar. There the

contraband was divided among several smaller vessels which were meant to head up the coast and offload at various Spanish ports. But we had been watching it all the way from North Africa by satellite, courtesy of the US. A fleet of coastguard vessels intercepted the transfer boats as they sailed out of Gibraltar into Spanish waters. Delgado's brother was on one of them. The ringleader.' Gil glanced at the video still playing on his phone. 'We'd been hoping that by keeping both Rafa and Delgado under surveillance we could start making connections, not just between them, but with others we didn't yet know about.'

'This is all very interesting, Detective Gil,' Mackenzie said, 'but what's the connection with Cleland? That's what I'm here for after all.'

'Patience, Señor Mackenzie, patience.' Gil found a hanky in one of his pockets and wiped away the beads of perspiration quivering along the line of his brow. His fingers were steaming up the screen of his phone. 'When Officer Sánchez Pradell made her request for further information on Roberto Vasquéz a little alarm bell went off in my head. Vasquéz dined here at Zhivago's a few times at gatherings hosted by Rafa. A very unlikely dinner guest, given the somewhat classier company that Rafa and Delgado usually kept. Local businessmen, politicians, the odd Russian oligarch. This is not a cheap restaurant, señor. And Vasquéz is the epitome of cheap. A low-life hoodlum.' Gil used his handkerchief to clear the condensation from the screen of his phone and only succeeded in smearing it. He scrubbed at the glass in annoyance. 'So, anyway, I went back and had a look at some of the surveillance footage to refresh my memory, and suddenly another face jumped out at me.'

He scrolled forward to a point where a group of ten or twelve men wearing dark suits and white shirts open at tanned necks was emerging from the restaurant, presumably having just eaten. The mood was cordial. There was laughter and back-slapping. Here was a group of men that embodied the quintessential nature of money and power. Sleek and well-groomed and self-satisfied. With the standout exception of Vasquéz, who was unshaven and uncomfortable in his cheap suit. Someone's pet Rottweiler.

Gil pointed his finger at different figures on the screen and rattled off a handful of names. 'But we still haven't been able to identify everyone in the group.'

Suddenly Mackenzie spotted what it was that had jumped out at Gil, and he felt goosebumps raise themselves on his arms and shoulders. Emerging from the back of the group, in deep conversation with Rafa himself, came the familiar smirk of Jack Cleland. The two men were sharing a joke, and Cleland looked as if he didn't have a care in the world.

Gil said, 'I only know the face now because of what's happened in the last few days. At the time we checked him out and he came up clean. Ian Templeton, an expat Englishman enjoying an early retirement along the coast at La Paloma.'

'A Scotsman,' Mackenzie said quietly, and felt a sense of

shame that he should share a nationality with this man. A dull pain in his ribs reminded him of their encounter as he shifted uncomfortably in the back seat.

'Whatever. British. Now, of course, we know exactly who he is.'

'And these are his associates.'

'So it would seem.'

'Is the surveillance ongoing?'

Gil sighed. 'I'm afraid not. Resources are limited and we weren't getting anywhere.'

Mackenzie said, 'We need eyes on all the principals in this group ASAP. Cleland's deal is imminent. The drugs are on the move. Almost certainly someone in this gang of charmers is involved. And my feeling is it's going to be goods for cash. Cleland's not going to want to leave any kind of electronic footprint in his wake.'

'I've already put in the request,' Gil said.

Mackenzie leaned into the front to stab his finger at the phone and pause the video. 'And what about trying to put names to some of these? The ones you couldn't identify at the time.'

'How?'

Mackenzie nodded towards the restaurant. 'We go in and ask.'

Gil laughed. 'No one in there's going to talk to us.'

'Why not?'

'Fear, señor.'

Mackenzie said, 'We're the cops. They should be afraid of us.'

Gil leaned confidentially towards the back of the Kia, lowering his voice as if someone might overhear them. 'What you don't understand, señor, is that like everything else around here, Zhivago's is Russian-owned. Our financial people looked into its business background and found that it actually trades as an escort agency. A classic money-laundering scam. It's almost certainly mafia-owned. So the staff will be a lot more frightened of their employers than they are of us.'

But Mackenzie was not to be deterred. He opened the back door and stepped out. 'Well why don't we go and see?' He held open the passenger door for Cristina. 'And it might help to have a uniform along.'

A shiny wooden walkway bordered by two hedges led through open glass doors to a bar that simmered in semi-darkness. It was flanked on either side by dining areas extending under canvas into the gardens, qualifying them as *outdoors*, and therefore legal smoking areas. Behind the bar, rows of high-value wines nestled side by side on tiered racks lit by hidden spots. No prices on display. If you could afford to drink these, you didn't need to know how much they cost. The place was deserted except for a solitary barman polishing glasses behind a shiny dimpled zinc counter. It was still too early for the Spanish to eat.

Gil showed him his ID. 'I want every member of staff out here now. Kitchen included.'

The barman was a pale thin man in his early thirties, prematurely balding. He cast them a surly look. 'What . . .?'

Gil slapped his palm on the counter. 'Now! No questions asked.' Mackenzie admired Gil's authority but thought that he was probably showing off for Mackenzie's benefit.

Within three minutes seven kitchen workers, including the chef, a maître d', two servers and a sommelier had joined the barman. They regarded the three police officers in sullen silence from behind the bar. Gil placed his phone on the counter and started the video at the point where Rafa, Delgado and Cleland were leaving the restaurant along with Vasquéz, as part of the bigger group.

'These people are all regulars here. There must be a record of bookings, credit-card payments . . . I want names.'

Dead eyes turned in silence towards the video. Not a flicker in any of them. Of recognition or anything else. Mackenzie could hear the tick-tock of a clock somewhere behind the bar.

'Well?' Gil's raised voice forced eyes to lift themselves again and look at him blankly. All he got for his trouble was a surly shaking of heads.

But the younger of the servers, a female in her late teens with the pallid pan-faced features of a Russian country girl, couldn't keep her eyes from straying towards one of the tented eating areas. Cristina followed her glance but could see nothing until she took a step to her right, and realized for the first time that the restaurant was not as empty as it had seemed. A solitary diner sat in the smoking zone, obscured by an enormous lacquered cabinet with a large-screen TV playing info videos about Italian wines. A thick-set man with his hair shorn to a bristling black stubble, he was eating alone at a table for two. His muscular torso stretched a white T-shirt with camouflage patches to bursting point. Oversized gold-rimmed sunglasses sat on a squat nose, a chunky gold watch on a thick left wrist. He had a cigar in one hand, his mobile phone in the other, and was trying very hard not to be noticed. Cristina recognized him immediately as one of the group in the video. In her mind's eye she saw Gil's finger stabbing at his phone screen and immediately pulled back a name. Alvarez.

As soon as Alvarez realized she had seen him he was on his feet. So quickly that his table crashed to the floor, dark glass smashing to spill syrupy green olive oil on red terracotta tiles.

'Hey!' she shouted after him.

But already he was pushing aside a canvas flap and barging through the hedge beyond it, ripping his T-shirt and drawing blood from taut biceps. Cristina saw now that he was wearing long khaki shorts and Roman sandals, his skin the colour of mahogany. He sprinted off across the lawn. Without thinking, she started after him. Running out across the boards between the hedges, capsizing one of two menu stands that stood on either side of the entrance, and feeling the sudden heat of the afternoon sun hitting her like a club. She screwed her eyes against its sudden glare and saw Alvarez running at speed down the long avenue that led towards the port, arms pumping like pistons. Here was a man who did not, at any cost, want to talk to the police.

Cristina had covered less than 50 metres in pursuit before the taller fitter figure of Mackenzie overtook her, flying past in the afternoon heat, long legs devouring the ground and quickly reeling in the gap between himself and the fugitive.

Sunlight strobed between the shadows of trees lining the avenue. Another 20 metres and Mackenzie could hear the distress of the man he was chasing. Desperate lungs gulping in air and pumping it out again, oxygen spent. His muscle mass gave him strength, but neither speed nor stamina. Mackenzie was catching him.

Alvarez glanced over his shoulder and the fronds of an overhanging willow swept the sunglasses from his face, revealing the fear in his eyes, and the realization that he was never going to outrun his pursuer. He veered right into a narrow street lined with cars, and then left into a service lane running between villas.

Mackenzie felt the discarded sunglasses crunch beneath his foot as he followed Alvarez into the narrower street. But by the time he turned into the service lane there was no sign of him. It was fully shaded here under thick foliage in fragrant purple blossom, almost dark after the blaze of sunlight in the street behind him. He stopped, thinking that the other man must somehow have turned off, and was quite unprepared for the shape that emerged from the shadows, swinging a fist like a Belfast ham full into his face. Even as he fell backwards and his head struck the paving stones he felt blood flooding his mouth. Light filled his head. As he blinked to clear it he looked up and saw Alvarez standing over him, legs apart, a pistol held two-handed at arm's length and pointing directly at his chest.

All thirty-eight years of Mackenzie's life spooled backwards through his mind so fast that they were gone in a moment. How short life really was, how insubstantial and fleeting all those burdensome memories, scattered in an instant like the ashes of his aunt in the flower garden at the cemetery. Breath escaped from his lips in a long sigh and he screwed his eyes tight shut in preparation for the bullet that would kill him. He wondered if it would hurt. Did pain outlast life, straddle the divide? And what next? Darkness and silence? Like Cristina's aunt?

But a shout pre-empted the bullet. So piercing and prolonged that it forced him to open his eyes again. Alvarez was still there, the gun still pointing at Mackenzie's chest. But the man's eyes had lifted and were focused beyond them both, back along the lane. Mackenzie craned his neck and saw Cristina silhouetted against the sunlight in the street behind her, pistol drawn. She held hers too in a double-handed stance, its muzzle directed straight at Mackenzie's would-be killer. She could shoot him before he could raise his weapon to fire at her. If he shot Mackenzie she would kill him. It was a classic stand-off. And Mackenzie found himself an almost neutral observer. Having already accepted death, he had somehow banished fear.

He looked back up at Alvarez. The man was caught in an agony of indecision that seemed to last a lifetime, before finally he took a calculated risk and simply turned and ran, sprinting off into the gloom, almost certainly fearing the bullet in his back that never came.

Cristina arrived to kneel beside the prone figure of Mackenzie, breathless and glistening with sweat. Fear and darkness dilating her pupils so that they almost obliterated the irises. She holstered her gun. 'Señor, are you alright?'

Mackenzie wiped blood from his face with shaking fingers. 'Apart from a busted nose and a split lip, I think I might live.'

She helped him to sit upright and produced paper hankies from somewhere for him to hold to his nose. He spat out blood and his words were muffled by his hand and the hankies. 'You know they say that if you save a life you are for ever responsible for it?'

'Do they?' She seemed unimpressed.

'Apparently.'

'Well, Señor, I think you are big enough and ugly enough to look after yourself.'

He shook his head. 'Except today. When you did it for me.' He felt a huge wave of gratitude towards her. '*Gracias* señora. For my life.'

She helped him to his feet as a perspiring Detective Gil finally appeared, fighting for breath, at the far end of the lane. When he saw them he leaned forward to support himself on bent knees. 'He got away then?' he gasped.

PETER MAY

Mackenzie said, 'No, we gave him a business card and he promised to call.'

By the time they got back to Zhivago's, both the restaurant and the wine store were closed. There was no sign of the staff. Everyone had gone. Mackenzie had stopped the blood leaking from his nose, and from somewhere Cristina managed to produce wet wipes to clean the dried smears of it from his face. They stood in a disconsolate knot under the blazing sun in the car park, certain that eyes were trained upon them from behind smoked glass windows in the Russian club across the road.

Gil said, 'If the financial branch can make the money laundering stick, then maybe we would have leverage against the owners of this place to reveal the identity of their customers.'

'No time,' Mackenzie said. People always quoted the maxim, *follow the money*. And they were right. But it always took too long.

Gil nodded. He knew it, too. He shrugged. 'Well . . . I'll get back to the office and see what I can do.' He fished a business card from a back pocket and held it out for Mackenzie. 'You can get me at this number.' Mackenzie took it, and a look passed between them. Gil found a reluctant smile. 'You can pass it on to Alvarez when he calls.'

As the Kia slipped out of the car park, leaving Cristina and Mackenzie leaning against the bonnet of his car, Mackenzie's phone rang. He lifted it from his breast pocket.

'Yes?'

'Señor, is Cristina with you?' He recognized the *Jefe*'s voice at once, and something in its gravitas put him on immediate alert.

'Yes, she is.'

'Shit!'

'What's wrong?' He glanced up to see Cristina looking at him apprehensively.

'What is it? she demanded. Mackenzie held up a finger to silence her.

The *Jefe* said, 'I was hoping to make this easier for her, but I don't see how. It's Antonio. Her husband. He's . . .' Mackenzie heard him gasp his frustration. 'There's been an incident.'

CHAPTER THIRTY-THREE

Ana is close to hysteria. Cleland has been gone for hours, leaving her in the dark and silent world which only technology can penetrate. A world into which she has been plunged alone once more since his departure. She doesn't know if he simply unplugged her computer, or whether he turned off power at the mains. But living without her technology now is almost like trying to breathe without oxygen.

Her distress is heightened by an increasingly pervasive and unpleasant odour. Sandro has not been over the door since early this morning, and it is just possible that he has been forced to empty his bowels somewhere in the house. In the last half-hour he has been repeatedly pushing his nose against her leg. Finding his head with her hands she has felt his anxiety. He is almost certainly whining, perhaps barking too. Though it would be so unlike him. And he is not responding to her attempts to calm him.

She gets out of her chair and feels her well-travelled path to the kitchen to fill his bowls with food and water. He follows her, but is making no attempt to eat or drink. His front paws are up now on her thighs and her waist, very nearly knocking her over. He never jumps up.

She pushes him away and speaks sharply. Something *she* never does. And immediately regrets it. But it must have brought a response, for she can no longer feel him within touching distance. As she makes her way in the dark to her bedroom she is terrified that somehow she might trip over him.

The odour is less invasive here. She crosses to the window and fumbles for the catch to open it. But it is already open. She can feel the hot air from outside seeping into the room, and is aware that she is having trouble breathing.

A prickle of perspiration stings her face as she makes her way into the tiny hallway at the top of the stairs. Out here the smell is much stronger. The heat is nearly overpowering, and the air seems to fibrillate almost tangibly against her skin. She feels Sandro pushing hard against her leg again and reaches down to place a hand on his upturned head. She is certain now that he is barking.

An overwhelming sense of dread slowly envelops her. Invisibly invasive, like nuclear fallout. She reaches forward and finds the handle on the door to the box room where Cristina or Nuri sometimes stay over on the fold-up single bed against the far wall.

The stench hits her immediately, like a physical blow, and it is all she can do not to be sick. A heavy scent, like rotten eggs. And something else, almost sweet, like sugared ammonia.

She feels flies battering against her face. There has been a problem in here before with regular hatchings, but these are frenzied. She feels several crawl into her mouth and spits in disgust, stumbling forward waving her hands about her face. But somehow Sandro has insinuated himself between her feet and she falls heavily to the floor.

Her hip and shoulder are bruised from the fall, and it is with difficulty that she overcomes the pain to get to her hands and knees. Crawling forward now, seeking some leverage to help her back to her feet. Until her hands find something soft beneath them, smooth and abnormally cold in this heat.

The stink is so all consuming now that her olfactory senses have very nearly shut down. It has ceased to be so much an odour as a wholly engulfing sensation of fear.

With both hands she explores the planes and curves of the softness emerging from the miasma that consumes her, only now admitting that it is a body lying on the floor before her. A body from which all warmth has long since departed. Muscles stiffened by rigor mortis, skin crawling with maggots. Her trembling fingers track up along the buttons of the shirt to the neck, and the faintest stubble on the chin.

She knows the features of this face. Features etched in her memory from twenty years ago, and remembered again from only yesterday. The smooth curve of the brow, the hair thinning now across the crown. The face of the man who had come looking for her again after all these years, only to meet his fate at the hands of a psychopath. His blood sticky like glue on her hands.

Her scream is filled with horror, and pity, and pain. A cry in the dark heard by no one. Not even herself.

CHAPTER THIRTY-FOUR

Mackenzie's foot was pressed hard to the metal, engine screaming, and still it was all he could do to keep his underpowered Seat in touch with the blue and orange flashing lights of Cristina's SUV.

It had been a roller-coaster drive from Marbella on the AP7, vehicles pulling over at the sound of the siren to let Cristina past on the off-ramp from the motorway, and at the Estepona roundabout. Now they flew under the overpass at the Condesa Golf Hotel, and the lights of a whole body of police vehicles and ambulances became visible in the parking area outside the Eroski Centre. Advertising hoardings stood atop a double-storey yellow building with red shutters on the second level. *Dia Maxi. Supermercado. Helicopteros Sanitarios. Marlows Fish and Chips.* Behind it, brick-coloured apartment blocks stepped up the hillside, and palm fronds rattled in the heat of the late afternoon breeze.

Cristina nearly overturned her vehicle as she wrenched the wheel hard right at the roundabout and turned down into the car park. She was out of the SUV and running for the ramp to the underground car park before Mackenzie had even brought his car to a stop.

A dozen or more police officers and Guardia Civil stood around in huddled groups. They moved silently aside as Cristina sprinted down the ramp. Inquisitive shoppers from the supermarket crowded hastily erected crime-scene tape. Restaurant staff from *Mini India*, and medics from the *Helicopteros* medical centre stood along the first-floor walkway, staring down with naked curiosity. Medical assistance had been instantly to hand, but there was nothing to be done.

Mackenzie ran down the ramp after Cristina. Into the fetid gloom of the subterranean parking lot. Half the roof lights were broken. The rows of red and white pillars supporting the roof itself were chipped and scored. A single vehicle sat on flat tyres in dusty abandon at the far end of it. Beyond the wreck, a colourfully graffitied wall was nearly obscured by darkness. The underground entrance to the supermarket itself was shuttered, and looked as if it might have been that way for some time.

Almost in the centre of the parking slots, lamps had been erected to cast a surreal light on a scene of carnage. A car, which Mackenzie immediately recognized as Antonio's, sat skewed at an angle, the driver's door lying wide open. Antonio himself lay in a twisted heap beside it. The force of the bullets ripping him apart had propelled him backwards against it. His blood smeared down the rear passenger door where he had slid to the floor. A large pool of it spreading around him, turning brown now, sticky and oleaginous in the airless heat. The same pathologist who had attended the finca killings at the start of the day was ending it crouched over the deceased husband of the police officer he had met on the hill just hours before.

Cristina's howl of anguish reverberated around the scarred and naked walls of this desperate place. Mackenzie felt it chill him to the bone, and tears sprang unexpectedly to his eyes. He wanted to grab her and hold her and tell her it would be okay. But it wouldn't. It never would.

It was the *Jefe*, perspiring and pale, who stopped her from getting any closer to the body. She fought against the arms he put around her, screaming and sobbing, flailing in hopeless desperation until his strength prevailed over hers and she subsided weeping against his shoulder.

Mackenzie saw his distress as he closed his eyes tightly, before opening them again to look over her head in despair towards the Scotsman whose life this woman had saved less than an hour before. There was an almost imperceptible shake of his head as he spread the fingers of his big hand across the back of her head and held her close to his chest.

Rarely had Mackenzie felt so powerless to influence or change the course of events. Here was human tragedy in the raw. Nothing to be done, no comfort in empty words – even were he able to find any. All he could do was stand and stare. Unable to offer solace, and certainly not reason.

He let his eyes drift across the scene illuminated by the pathologist's lamps. There were fresh skid marks on the concrete three metres from Antonio's car, spent shell casings scattered across the floor. A lot of them. He looked back to see more rubber left by spinning tyres at the turn on to the ramp. He could almost hear the echo of those tyres, even above the painful sobs that reverberated around the car park.

A policewoman from Marviña and a female Guardia Civil prised Cristina gently loose from the *Jefe*'s arms, and led – half-carried – her towards the exit. Mackenzie could still hear her pain manifesting itself in the tears that tore themselves from her lungs long after they had taken her back up the ramp.

The *Jefe* wiped his own grief from wet cheeks as Mackenzie approached. Behind them a white van slowly descended the ramp, and half a dozen forensics officers in protective plastic suits spilled out to start a detailed examination of the scene. Mackenzie said, 'Do you have any thoughts?'

'Plenty of thoughts, señor. Not so many ideas. And, anyway, it will be out of our hands when homicide arrive from Malaga.' He paused. 'Did you meet Antonio?'

Mackenzie nodded. 'A couple of times. In fact, I saw him just a few hours ago up at Balle Olivar.'

The *Jefe* nodded. 'Yes, so did I.'

'He and his brother-in-law seemed to be having some kind of altercation.'

The *Jefe* looked up. 'Paco?'

'Yes.'

The chief sighed and cast his eyes across the crime scene.

'Well, this wasn't the result of some domestic dispute. Whoever killed Toni put nine bullets in him. Could have been more than one shooter. Ballistics will tell us that. But no one heard any shots, so they could have been using silencers. Which would make it a professional hit.'

He saw Mackenzie's gaze wander towards the CCTV camera at the entrance to the supermarket.

'Defunct,' he said. 'That entrance has been closed for over a year. No one uses this car park any more. Too many muggings and break-ins. I've got officers questioning shoppers who were in the supermarket in or around the time of the shooting, or in the car park outside, but no one seems to have seen the killer's car leaving. Although, from those tyre marks I'd say they must have left in quite a hurry.' He gazed thoughtfully at Mackenzie. 'So what do *you* think?'

Mackenzie shook a despairing head. 'I have no idea what to think.'

'Cleland?'

Mackenzie shrugged. Somehow he didn't think so. But he had no logical way to express that.

'It would make sense,' the *Jefe* said. 'This is how he gets back at Cristina. Why kill her when he can murder her husband instead and make her suffer like him?'

Mackenzie's eyes wandered again back to the body of the young man lying in his own blood. The curl of dark hair on his forehead, the crook of the bloodied finger that wore his wedding ring. Blood-stained blue socks that he had pulled on just that morning without the least expectation that he would never again pull on a fresh pair. A life broken and ended in a few fatal seconds.

He thought of Lucas who had just lost his dad. He thought of Cristina, who had saved his life while others were taking the life of her husband. Three lives shattered. One lost. Two that would never be the same again.

He allowed his head to drop, and saw a single tear make a crater in the dust of the floor at his feet.

CHAPTER THIRTY-FIVE

Cleland heard the buzzing as soon as he opened the front door. For a moment he thought it might be some electrical fault. But then the few stray flies which had made it downstairs, along with the stink of decomposing flesh, brought him sudden horrified realization. He closed his eyes and cursed himself. He should have disposed of the body during the hours of darkness. Everything decayed so quickly in this heat. It was the reason the Spanish always buried their dead within twenty-four hours.

He took the steps two at a time, up into the thick air of the upper floor. It was filled with flies. He screwed up his eyes with disgust, forced to keep his mouth closed and breathe in noxious air through his nose. He saw immediately that Ana was not at her computer and turned back into the hall.

Sandro's barking fought to be heard above the din of the flies, but he was hoarse now, and his bark carried little force. It was coming from the room where Cleland had dragged Sergio's lifeless form the day before. The door stood open. Ana lay sobbing on the floor, half-sprawled across the body of the dead Sergio. A sight that sickened him almost more than the stench. He stepped quickly into the room, stooping to lift the prostrate form of the deaf–blind woman from the floor. Beyond an initial stiffening of her body she offered no resistance. She seemed surprisingly light as he pulled her out of the room, arms folded under her breasts, dragging her heels across the floor of the hall and into the living room.

He laid her down carefully and hurried back into the box room to open the window, then retreat to the hall and close the door behind him. Sandro danced and barked around his feet as he went through the house opening every window wide to let out the flies and the smell. In the kitchen he found scented candles and lit them along the counter top.

Ana's sobbing had reduced itself to a whimper, but deep trembling inhalations still racked her body as she lay curled up on the floor where he had left her. Impossible now, he realized, to stay here much longer. In two strides he crossed to the table with the computer screens and got down on his knees to reconnect them to the mains. Then he hooked his arms under Ana's shoulders and dragged her to her chair. She slumped into it, eyes open but unseeing. He brushed maggots from her face and hair. Nature wasted no time in employing death for renewal. The worst of the stench of Sergio's decaying body had escaped through the open window. But the corpse in the back room, he knew, would continue to generate noxious gases. All that Cleland could do now was keep the door closed on them, and the windows open, for as long as it took to get Ana and himself out of here.

He fumbled on the table for Ana's buzzer alert and pinned it to her blouse, waiting with impatience for the computer to boot up. It was infuriatingly slow. He circled to the other screen and saw finally that he had a blinking cursor. He pulled up a chair and typed.

– *Ana. Ana, I need to talk to you.*

She did not respond. He was almost overcome by an urge to slap her again, but he didn't like the unaccustomed guilt that went with that and restrained himself.

– *Ana. I'm sorry. I didn't mean to kill Sergio. Please believe me. If I could undo it I would.* He could barely believe that these words were tripping from his fingertips. *He would never have been good enough for you anyway. What took him so bloody long to come back? Twenty years, for God's sake! If he'd been half a man he'd have stood up to his parents, and yours, all those years ago. He wasn't worthy of you. You deserve better.* Some part of him was desperate for her understanding. Although he had no idea why.

Finally she stirred, pulling herself more upright in her chair to pass her fingertips over the braille. Her eyes moved as if searching the room to locate him. Her voice was a hoarse whisper. 'Take me to the church. I have not been for two days. And we must take the dog out.'

The church? Why the hell did she want to go to the church? He had never understood this impulse that people had to seek solace in God. And hadn't she told him herself that she'd never had any time for religion? As for the dog . . . he wished now that he had dealt with Sandro as he had with Sergio. The animal had retreated to a corner of the room and was glowering at him darkly.

– *There are too many people out there. It's the feria. The town is crowded.*

Her voice was insistent now. 'I want to go to the church. It's the least you owe me.'

Owe her? What did he owe her? He screwed his eyes shut. Jesus, who was the hostage here? He forced himself to calm down and steadied his fingers on the keyboard.

– *Okay. I'll take you to the church. I promise. But I have some business to take care of first, some phone calls to make.*

'Don't leave me again!' The plaintive appeal in her voice both surprised and touched him. And he couldn't begin to imagine what kind of turmoil she was facing alone in the prison that was her body. He reached out to place his fingers on her hand. She pulled it sharply away, an instinctive response to his unexpected touch, and to his consternation he found that he was hurt by it.

– *I'm still here. I won't leave you. I'll use your phone. And then, I'll be as quick as I can.*

CHAPTER THIRTY-SIX

Marviña was deserted in the late afternoon heat. Sunlight struck off dusty bleached stone, reflecting light into the darkest shadows. Sensible folk snoozed in cool rooms behind closed shutters after a late lunch. Not a soul, not even a dog, stirred in the shimmering furnace of the Plaza del Vino. But in the ill-named Calle Utopía the blue lights of umpteen police vehicles flashed intermittently, and half a dozen officers stood around smoking and speaking in hushed tones. The entrance to Cristina's apartment block was wedged open, and the darkened stairwell breathed cool air into the baking heat of the street.

Mackenzie cast sad eyes across the scene in the narrow road as the *Jefe* drew his Audi into the kerbside and the two men stepped out of its air-conditioned interior to be assaulted by the Spanish sun. At almost the same moment, a solitary figure cast a short shadow on the flagstones of the square as it made erratic progress towards the group at the top of the hill. Paco took a couple of minutes to reach them, hobbling on his crutches.

'What the hell are you doing here?' the *Jefe* said. 'You should be resting up with that leg.'

Paco's face was putty-coloured with pain. He said, 'Cristina needs support. Where is she?'

The *Jefe* tipped his head in the direction of the police station on the far side of the square. 'Giving a statement.'

'Jesus Christ, *Jefe*! It's a bit fucking soon for that. The woman's just lost her husband.'

'And you were having a bit of a row with him just a few hours ago from what I hear.' The *Jefe* cocked an eyebrow to ask the unspoken question. But Paco just glowered at him, before turning his glare on Mackenzie. When he didn't respond the *Jefe* was forced to frame the question in words. 'What were you fighting about, Paco?'

'It wasn't a fight!' Paco was defensive. 'It was a disagreement.'

'About what?' Mackenzie said.

Paco released a long sigh of resignation. But he addressed his response to the chief. 'Toni and Cris have been going through a bad patch, *Jefe*. Apparently they had a big row last night. She threatened to leave him, and take Lucas with her. Toni told me there was no way he would allow that to happen. If they split up he was going to contest custody. He said any court would see that he could offer a more stable home environment. The hours she works, her shifts, the dangers of the job. No way she could be a single mother *and* a cop.'

The *Jefe* scratched his chin. 'So what was the disagreement?'

Paco shrugged. 'What do you think? I told him not to expect

any support from me. I'm married to Cris's sister, for God's sake. Toni and me might be golfing buddies, but Chris is family.' He paused then, as if suddenly remembering only now that Antonio was dead. He pulled a face and shook his head. 'Jesus . . . I can't believe someone did this to him.' He looked at the chief. 'That bastard Cleland?'

The *Jefe* just shrugged.

'*Jefe*!' A young forensics officer, running with sweat beneath protective plastic, appeared in the doorway to the apartments. Unusually for a Spaniard, he had ginger hair, and his face was puce. 'Something you need to hear, chief.'

He vanished back inside, and Mackenzie and the *Jefe* climbed the steps to follow him. A couple of Guardia Civil stood sentry on the landing at the entrance to the apartment on the first floor. The three men squeezed past and into the apartment. Mackenzie heard Paco grunting and panting in their wake as he fought his way up the stairs.

A faint reminder of last night's barbecued ribs still clung to curtains and soft furniture. The apartment itself seemed marginally tidier since the forensics officers had been through it. The officer who had called them in picked his way across the living room to lift the phone from its base. He held it between the thumb and forefinger of his latexed left hand and carefully depressed several numbers on the keypad with a pen held in his other. 'Messages,' he said. 'This one timed at 14.47 today.' He pressed another key to put it on speaker.

They waited through a series of beeps before a voice that

was unmistakably Cristina's said cryptically, *Toni, meet me in the car park at Eroski. I'm there now. We've got to talk.* The quality of the recording was bad, as if she had called from a mobile with a poor signal.

Mackenzie frowned and glanced at his watch. 'Cristina was with me in Marbella when that call was made. It's not her.'

The *Jefe* looked doubtful. 'It's her voice.'

'I agree it sounds like her.'

Paco said, 'But if she was with you . . .'

'She was.'

The *Jefe* sighed. 'Then what the hell was Toni doing in the underground car park at the Eroski Centre?' He hesitated. 'And Jesus Christ, it sure as hell sounds like Cristina.'

Paco said, '*Jefe* I don't care if she's finished making her statement or not, I'm going across the road to get her out of there and take her back to our place. Nuri's already gone to pick up Lucas from school. Cristina's going to have to tell the boy before he hears it elsewhere. And she's going to need our support.'

The *Jefe* nodded gloomily.

'And something else.'

A sigh of exasperation escaped his lips. 'What now?'

'Someone's going to have to go into Estepona and tell Ana. I'd do it, but I can't drive.'

The *Jefe* raised both palms to rub his eyes. Fatigue and frustration wearing him down. Mackenzie said, 'I'll do it. I don't know what else I'm going to do. I met her yesterday. And maybe it would be better coming from someone who isn't family.'

The *Jefe* looked at him gratefully. 'Would you?' Mackenzie nodded and the chief put a hand on his shoulder. 'Good man,' he said.

CHAPTER THIRTY-SEVEN

Estepona resounded to the sounds of the *feria*. Although shadows were starting to lengthen, the heat of the day still lingered, and the air was filled with music and voices and the clip-clop of hooves on cobbled streets. The smell of barbecued pork, and grilled fish and hot burning sugar floated on the evening breeze.

Mackenzie found space in the underground parking beneath the promenade. He skipped through the traffic on the Avenida España and shoved his way through the crowds thronging the narrow streets of the old town. Across Calle Real and Calle Caridad into the Calle San Miguel, where red and white and purple geraniums poured from pots that hung from balconies on whitewashed houses.

People clogged the street. Locals and tourists. All slow-flowing towards the Calle Zaragoza where the main procession of floats and carriages was scheduled to pass. Mackenzie found himself carried along on the current. Up ahead he saw the Plaza de Juan Bazán, a calm eddy in the circulation of people, fountains glittering in the last of the sunshine that slanted across the roof of Ana's house. Was it really only yesterday that he and Cristina had visited her? So much had changed in that short time. So many lives ruined.

A familiar face in the crowd caught his eye, and it took him a moment to realize that it was Ana herself, tiny and swamped by the people around her. Like a piece of flotsam carried on turbulent water she vanished, appeared, then vanished again in all too fleeting glimpses. Swept away from him towards the Calle Portada. He called her name at the top of his voice, before remembering with embarrassment that she could not hear him.

And then his heart stopped. Another face caught in the fading sunlight. Then gone. At first he couldn't be sure, then there it was again. Cleland! And he was with Ana. He bellowed her name again, this time for Cleland's benefit. It turned the man's head sharply around, and for the most transient of moments their eyes met. Fifty metres apart. But the electricity between them passed at the speed of light. And then he was gone again. Ana, too.

Mackenzie started ploughing his way through the bodies ahead of him to a chorus of protests and cursing.

Ana is hopelessly confused. She has lost control of everything. Her whole physical being, it seems, swept along on a sea of turbulent noisome humanity. All she can feel with any certainty is the iron grip of Cleland's fingers around her arm. Pulling, dragging her through the tempest. She feels elbows in her ribs, a shoulder in her back. Someone's foul breath in her face. She blenches, then panics, realizing suddenly that she has lost hold of Sandro's harness. Gone is his warmth against her legs, his gentle navigation through troubled waters. She calls out his name, but feels only a tightening of Cleland's grip.

They are almost running now. She is breathless and fighting to keep her feet. The ground is sloping beneath them. Fewer people here, she thinks, but Cleland is relentless in forcing them on. Down, down. Another wave of bodies parting to let them past. Something is terribly wrong. She has no idea what, but she can feel Cleland's anxiety.

Then suddenly she collides with something unyielding and Cleland's grip on her arm is broken. Her only security in this nightmare. She feels herself falling, as if through space. An age goes by, it seems, before she hits the ground. Hard, unforgiving asphalt that knocks all the breath from her lungs. Pain shoots through her shoulder. When she gasps for air it is the smell of deep, dark fear that she inhales. The stink of sweating horses. Manure. She can feel the clatter of hooves on cobbles all around her, and realizes with terror that she is in danger of being trampled to death.

Then strong hands close around her arms and she feels herself lifted bodily from the ground and propelled forward. Her face brushes the secreting flank of a horse, the smell of it for a moment overwhelming all her other senses.

*

Perspiration almost blinded Cleland as he steered the help-less Ana through this maelstrom of neighing, rearing horses. Images dazzling him as he turned this way and that, avoiding flanks and hooves. Flat-brimmed Cordobés riding hats, red button-up tunics, ladies riding side-saddle in black and white flamenco skirts, heels scratching at his face. Horsemen screamed at him in a fury, a chorus of angry shouts rising from the crowd as one rider was almost unseated. But like the Red Sea, the passage he had cleaved through the proces-sion closed again behind them. Straw-roofed floats drawn by tractors following on, a brass band belting out its discordant refrain, drums banging, cymbals crashing. A cacophony of horns and klaxons blasting into the hot air of the early evening.

Only as he cleared the crowd lining the route did he dare to look back. There was no sign of Mackenzie. And the pro-cession, in full flood, cut off his path of pursuit. Had the Scots copper made it through the procession, then Cleland might have been forced to abandon Ana to her fate. Which would have meant relinquishing his power over Cristina. But worse, he realized, it would have meant losing Ana herself. And for some reason beyond his understanding he did not want to do that. In any circumstance. In taking the life of Sergio he had somehow made himself responsible for her. Whether he liked it or not. It was the strangest feeling, being beholden to someone else.

*

A burly uniformed Guardia blocked Mackenzie's path, stepping in his way to stop him from trying to break through the procession. Mackenzie saw Ana's guide dog wandering bewildered among a forest of legs. Sheaves of hay passed before his eyes, children in white shirts riding on tractors, Policía Local in black uniforms and white helmets revving the motors of their Suzuki motorcycles. Sunlight angling between the rooftops reflected on their visors. All these cops within touching distance of Cleland and no way for Mackenzie to explain. No point in even trying.

He shoved his way back through the crowds lining the procession, and started running along the narrow Calle Silva which followed a parallel course. With luck he would find a crossing point further along. This street was almost deserted, everyone pushing into the Calle Papuecas, one block north, to glimpse the procession. Toddlers hoisted on parental shoulders, children stretching on tiptoes.

Two junctions further along, Mackenzie managed to cross the path of the parade before the horses arrived. He ran the length of another block, then cut back towards the street where Cleland and Ana had forced their way through. He found himself standing in a semi-deserted *calle*. The sounds of the *feria* carried to him from a block further over. He could see the throng pressing along the route of the cavalcade. But there was no sign of Cleland and Ana. And no indication of which way they might have gone. He bellowed his frustration into the jagged strip of sky between the buildings overhead and closed his eyes.

From nowhere came an image of his father storming the psychiatric patient and his hostage in the close of some dark tenemental Glasgow street. The blade of a knife caught in his flashlight. Then blood, bright red and spurting, drawn in a smile across the soft flesh of a white throat.

He opened his eyes in a panic to banish the image of his father's folly. And all he could see was Ana's pale face as it was carried off on the current of the crowd. The sins of the father, the failure of the son. A wave of fatigue and defeat surged through him and his legs very nearly gave way. He reached out to press his hand against a wall to steady himself, and felt the heat of the sun retained in the stone.

What to do? With reluctance he turned to make his way back to Ana's house. If Cleland had been there, then perhaps he might have left some clue as to where he was going. And more importantly, where he was taking Ana.

Ana is aware of the change in temperature as Cleland leads her up the stone steps from the Plaza de San Francisco and into the cool of the Iglesia Nuestra Señora de Los Remedios. She can actually feel the space opening up around her. In her imagination she can hear their footsteps echoing around the vaulted ceilings, can picture the golden candlelit altar. The air raises goosebumps on her naked arms, and she feels Cleland's tension easing as his grip on her arm relaxes.

'Light a candle for me,' she says, and he leads her down the central aisle towards where she knows the candles burn in serried rows. They stop, and she can feel the warmth of the flames, and realizes that Cleland now has no way to communicate with her.

She feels his surprise as she reaches for and finds his hand, taking it into both of hers. Slowly, carefully, she uses her index finger to trace on his palm the letters of the words she speaks. *My name is Ana. What is yours?* And waits to see if he has understood. It is not the tactile signing she took that teenage summer to learn. But it is simple, if slow, and anyone can do it.

The holding of hands is reversed, and he traces his response in gentle letters on her palm. She almost smiles. Of course he understood. Whatever else he may be, he is not stupid.

– *My name is Jack.*

So now they are on first name terms. 'Light two, Jack. One for each of us.'

– *What's the point? You don't believe in God. Neither do I.*

'I never said I didn't believe in God, Juanito. Only that I had no time for Him. I light candles in the hope that one day He might burn in the same hell to which he has sent me.' She pauses. 'And you. We share the same hell, you and I.'

She can tell by the hesitation in his fingers that he has no idea how to respond. Finally, he lets go of her hand, and she knows that he is lighting the candles. The tiniest increase in the warmth that they generate. No matter how small, their two flames make an impression in the cold air of the church.

A strange serenity suffuses her soul, and she closes her eyes to let the air escape her lungs in a long, slow draught. Now she knows what she must do. She reaches for and finds Cleland's forearm, resting her hand upon it before giving it the gentlest of squeezes.

The Calle San Miguel was almost deserted now. The sounds of the festival a distant and discordant revelry carried on the cooling night air. The *despacho de pan* and the *carnicería* had closed early. A solitary elderly couple sat on one of the benches in the Plaza de Juan Bazán, the perfume of the flowers draped all around its walls hanging sweet and fragrant in the dying light.

Mackenzie tried the handle on the door to Ana's house, prepared to kick it open if he had to. But the door was unlocked and swung into darkness. To his right a door opened into a shuttered storage room whose barred windows gave on to the street. The staircase straight ahead of him climbed up into gloom.

The first thing he became aware of was the smell. The fetid stink of decay, like opening a fridge where meat has been left to fester for weeks beyond its sell-by date. In his pocket Mackenzie found some bloodied tissues from earlier in the day and held them to his nose. This time to staunch the smell rather than the blood. And he began to climb the stairs.

In the upstairs living room he found all the windows opened wide. The same in the bedroom. But the smell lingered in the confined windowless space of the upstairs landing, and hit him with the force of a physical blow when he opened the door to the box room. A plague of houseflies in here had been feeding on the corpse that sprawled on the floor beneath the open window. They had laid their eggs perhaps eighteen hours before and already there had been a hatching of maggots clustering in the mouth and nostrils. In a few days the maggots would generate more flies to feed on the secretions of decomposition and lay yet more eggs.

Mackenzie kept his mouth firmly shut, pressing the tissues to his nostrils, and stepped carefully into the room. He crouched to turn the face of the cadaver towards him. A man maybe not that much older than himself. Dark hair starting to thin. It was not a face he knew. He let the head fall back to the side and saw the blood matted thickly in the hair around a wound on the back of it. The depression in the skull was so deep Mackenzie could only assume that this was the blow that killed him. There was very little blood on the floor. A smear of it, suggesting that the body had been dragged in here. But in any case, Mackenzie knew that if the blow had killed him, then the heart would have stopped pumping blood almost immediately. His skin was already marbling and tinted green.

He stood up, shaking. Who was he? What was he doing here? And where in God's name was Cleland taking Ana? And why?

He moved back out on to the landing, taking care now not to touch anything. Ana's whole house was a crime scene. He crossed the living room to the open window and breathed in fresh air, then fished out his phone to call the *Jefe*.

In less than twenty minutes the house was crawling with cops and forensics officers from the Estepona HQ of the Policía National. Mackenzie was immediately sidelined and told he would be required to give a full statement later.

It took the *Jefe* under thirty minutes to get there from Marviña. He was accompanied by the homicide officers from Malaga who had earlier arrived at the Eroski Centre to open the investigation into Antonio's shooting. He greeted Mackenzie in the street, where the chief of the Policía National stood barking instructions into his mobile phone. When he hung up he approached the *Jefe* and the two police chiefs shook hands. 'They found the blind woman's dog wandering about down town, and we've had several sightings of a couple answering to the description of Cleland and Señora Hernandez entering the church.' He shook his head gravely. 'But nothing since. They're gone, Miguel.'

The *Jefe* said, 'What about the dead guy?'

The Estepona chief drew a clear plastic evidence bag from his pocket. It contained a laminated DNI card. *Documento Nacional de Identidad*. Mackenzie could see a photograph of the dead man on the front of it. He looked younger than the man he had seen upstairs. 'ID card in his wallet. Sergio García Lorca. Aged forty-three. Certified deaf.'

Certified dead, Mackenzie thought. He said, 'What was his relationship with Señora Hernandez? Or Cleland?'

The chief shrugged. 'No idea.' He did not like answering questions from Mackenzie. He nodded curtly and went back into the house.

The *Jefe* flicked Mackenzie an apologetic glance. He said, 'Shell casings at the Eroski Centre confirm two shooters.'

'Or one shooter, two guns.'

'Perhaps. But unlikely. The body's been brought here to Estepona for autopsy. They'll release it to the relatives tonight and he'll be buried tomorrow.'

Mackenzie raised an eyebrow in surprise. 'That fast?'

'Bodies don't last long in this heat.' The *Jefe* nodded towards the house. 'You should have figured that out for yourself by now.'

But all that Mackenzie could think was that last night Antonio had been preparing a dinner of barbecued ribs for his family. Tomorrow his family would be putting him in the ground. Life was such a fragile and insubstantial thing, and you never knew when the candle lit by birth would be doused by death.

The *Jefe* said, 'Cristina's taking it hard.'

'I wouldn't expect her to take it any other way.'

Then the *Jefe* hesitated. 'Do you think there's any truth in what Paco said? About Cristina wanting to leave him.'

Mackenzie remembered the fractious exchanges on each occasion he had been at the apartment, but it was not something he was going to share with the *Jefe*. 'I don't know.'

'That phone call still bothers me, señor. You say she was with you. But was she with you *all* the time? Could she not have made that call without you knowing? It would only have taken a few moments.'

Mackenzie tried to recall if there had been a few such moments. But he shook his head. '*Jefe*, even if she had made the call, it wasn't Cristina at the Eroski Centre.'

'No.' He hesitated a long time. 'But someone there doing her bidding?'

Mackenzie looked at him. 'Do you really believe that?'

The *Jefe* pursed his lips and shook his head in resignation. 'No.' He examined the backs of his hands. 'Will you go to the funeral?'

Mackenzie recalled the singularly impersonal ceremony for his aunt at the Glasgow crematorium. His uncle's later tears. His own lack of grief. 'No,' he said. 'I don't think that would be appropriate.'

The other man nodded. 'I hate funerals.' Then made a determined effort to shake off his mantle of depression. He drew a deep breath. 'Why don't you come up to the house tonight, like we talked about. I could do with some company.' He smiled sadly. 'And someone who is going to appreciate sharing a good single malt.'

Mackenzie thought that in the circumstances whisky sounded like a fine idea.

CHAPTER THIRTY-EIGHT

Streetlights snaked off up the hill from the simmering darkness of the empty hotel complex. Tiles flaked from rain-streaked walls. Unpruned palms and overgrown shrubs climbed the building, obscuring windows and doorways. Weeds poked a metre high from cracked tarmac in covered parking lots out front. And beyond the bridge that straddled the dual carriageway below, headlights raked the night, southbound towards the distant silhouette of Gibraltar.

What little light remained in the sky glowed pink verging on purple. It lay in narrow bands along the distant horizon, where a bank of cloud obscured North Africa beyond a Mediterranean Sea that mirrored infinity. The moon had not yet risen.

Cleland drew his black SUV into the cover of an overgrown gateway hidden beneath the main entrance to the hotel. When he had first arrived in this part of Spain the Condesa Golf Hotel had been a thriving business, its Thalasso Spa a popular attraction for holidaymakers and wealthy locals. Water drawn from the Mediterranean purified for the various treatments offered. Its restaurants serving Michelin-quality food.

But something, Cleland knew not what, had gone wrong. A change in financial fortunes. The hotel had closed and lain empty for years, quietly decaying on the edge of the port without any indication that it would ever reopen.

He grabbed a black bag from the back seat, then helped Ana down from the vehicle. She had shown no inclination to resist since leaving the church, following all his instructions with a quiet acquiescence. Holding her by the arm, he led her carefully past the entrance to the spa. Something opaque had been painted over glass doors to prevent anyone from seeing in, but vandals had used it as a base to scrawl their names, and the names of their lovers, and all their pointless profanities. An unbroken sticker pasted across the doors read *Protegido Por Seguridad*. It was impossible to see in beyond the reflections of willows and bamboo that pushed up from the dry river bed opposite.

They hurried around a proliferation of uncut hedging that hung down over the pavement, to follow a curving walkway almost completely engulfed by advancing regiments of trees and bushes. Paint-peeling walls and glass balconies rose above them through three floors, and they had to fight their way past overhanging branches and trailing root systems to find the short flight of steps that led up to the main entrance.

Cleland tore away red tape stretched across a gateway to the turning circle in front of revolving doors which had once swept guests into an impressive reception. Approaching from this angle avoided the security cameras. He had no idea if they still functioned, but he wasn't going to take the risk. A side door was secured with a padlock and chain. He released Ana and set his bag down on the cracked pavings to take out a pair of heavy-duty wire cutters. They sliced through the chain like a hot knife through butter, and within seconds he was leading Ana into the fusty interior of the hotel.

He shone a torch into darkness and saw footprints in dust which had accumulated like frost on marble tiles. Old footprints. He stopped for a moment to shine his torch on the plans he had been given. Downstairs, through the spa, then out by the rear entrance to the rooms and up the fire stairs that wrapped around the lift shaft. The bedroom he was looking for was on the second floor. No. 233. It would be unlocked, they had said. He would find a bed with clean linen, a working toilet, bottled water, candles, matches. A safe room. A place to lie low for thirty-six hours until the exchange.

'Where are we?' It was the first interest Ana had shown. He took her hand in his.

– *No matter. We're safe.*

This time he held on to her hand and led her down into pitch blackness. By the beam of his torch he saw spa baths raised above floor level, the size of swimming pools laid side by side. They filled a vast echoing space that must once have resounded to the carefree voices of wealthy patrons. All gone. In another era these pools had frothed with clear blue Mediterranean waters. Now they were filled with dust and debris, Roman pillars stained by time and damp. Doors led off along one side. Changing cubicles, and massage rooms where hot stones wrapped in soft towels had once been laid on aching backs.

They circumnavigated a tiny labyrinth of stairways leading to and from the baths, disturbing dust as they walked. It hung in the air like mist in their wake. Until they found the exit door at the far end and climbed the stairs to the second floor.

Room 233 was carpeted. Even though its south-facing windows were shuttered, it had trapped the warmth of the day and was stifling hot. Cleland led Ana to the bed and sat her down while he rolled up the shutter and slid open glass doors leading to the balcony. Fresh air flooded in and he took a deep breath.

'Don't hurt me.' Her voice was tiny.

He looked at her and frowned. He had sat her on a bed. Did she really think he was going to rape her? He sat beside her and took her hand again. As a means of communication this was frustratingly slow.

– *Not going to hurt you. Here for a while. Don't call for help. No one to hear. I'll be gone some of the time. Day after tomorrow I'll take you to The Rock. You know it?*

'Gibraltar?'

– *Yes.*

'I've never been.'

– *A shithole. Strategic for the British. And for us.* He paused. *It'll all be over then.*

CHAPTER THIRTY-NINE

The *Jefe*'s villa lay at the end of a long bumpy track that wound up through gnarled cork oaks and the fleshy overhanging leaves of sprawling banana trees. Mackenzie's ancient Seat strained on the gradient, tyres spinning and throwing up clouds of dust in the moonlight. It was little wonder that the police chief had splashed out on a four-by-four. Otherwise the approach to his home would be impassable when it rained.

Finally the track levelled off, then descended steeply to the faux finca below. This was a beautiful house, with arches and shaded terracotta terraces on three levels. Built in the style of a traditional white Andalusian farmhouse, Mackenzie thought that it was probably no more than fifteen or twenty years old.

Beyond banks of azaleas and bougainvillea, Mackenzie saw a swimming pool reflecting moonlight, and after parking next to the Audi, he followed steps down to a lower terrace. From here a spectacular view of the distant coastline opened up a long way below, lights like glowing beads on a string stretched intermittently along its sweeping contour.

The *Jefe* sat under a bamboo canopy, a glass in his hand, a half-empty bottle, some water and a second glass on the table beside him. Concealed lighting spilled subtle illumination across the terrace, catching highlights of amber in his glass. He stood up to shake Mackenzie's hand, then waved him into a chair on the far side of the table.

'Welcome to my humble abode.'

'Not so humble,' Mackenzie said as he watched the chief fill his glass then dilute it with a little water.

'Extravagant now, I suppose. For a man living on his own. But when I built it there were three of us.'

'Your wife and . . . ?'

'My son.' He raised his glass. '*Salud.*' They touched glasses and drank. 'How did you get on with the Policía Nacional?'

'They kept me waiting for over two hours before they took my statement. I don't think they liked me very much, *Jefe.*'

'Why not?'

'Well, for a start I'm a foreigner.'

'And?'

'They didn't appreciate my pointing out the mistakes made securing the crime scene.'

The *Jefe* threw back his head and roared with laughter. 'I bet they didn't.' He looked at Mackenzie with amusement. 'You just say it like it is, señor, don't you?'

Mackenzie shrugged, not quite sure what was so amusing. 'What other way is there to say it, *Jefe*?'

The chief chortled. 'With tact, my friend, with tact.'

Mackenzie allowed himself a wry smile. 'You sound like my wife. Or, rather, ex-wife. Well . . . soon to be ex.'

'You have children?'

'Two.'

'Then you owe it to them to fix whatever is broken in your marriage. You might be feeling pain, but it is your children who are the real victims.'

'What was it you were saying about tact?'

The *Jefe* smiled sadly. 'Not my strong suit either.'

They sat in silence for a while then, sipping the lifeblood of Mackenzie's native soil, gazing wordlessly at the stars that glittered across a crowded sky. There was no light pollution here, and the clarity was startling.

'What happened to your wife?'

The *Jefe* glanced at the Scotsman. 'Oh, the usual. Cancer.' He sighed deeply, and some of the bitterness that resided in him seeped out. 'A diagnosis that comes out of the blue. Shattering your dreams, your hopes and all of your certainties. Then there are the pedlars of false optimism, the doctors with their toxic treatments that are worse than the malady itself. All they can really do is prolong life for a few miserable months. What's the point in that?' He sipped his whisky and gazed into his glass for a long time. 'The thing I have never quite got used to is being on my own. Especially here. Rattling about in this big empty house. At first I wanted to throw everything of Maria's out. Burn it. Get rid of it. I'm glad I didn't. At least it feels like a part of her is still here.' He chuckled and flicked an embarrassed glance towards Mackenzie. 'There are times when I find myself talking to her. I've lost count of just how often I've come into the kitchen in the morning and found her at the sink. The kettle boiling on the worktop.' He hesitated. 'Not. Or climbing into bed at night and turning to kiss lips on an empty pillow.' He half-turned in his chair to look back at the house, soft light on white walls against the impenetrable black of the mountain behind it. 'I love this place. And I hate it. So many happy memories. So many bad ones.'

'You wouldn't think of selling, surely?'

'I'd leave here in a heartbeat, señor. My only future is in looking back.' He leaned forward to top up their glasses. 'What do you think of the whisky?'

Mackenzie took the bottle to look at it for the first time and raised an eyebrow. 'I knew it was good,' he said. 'But I'd no idea it was that good.'

'Sixty-nine Glenfiddich. One of my prized bottles.'

'I feel privileged.'

'Don't. I've had it for years, and I'd have finished it long ago. But a whisky that good needs someone to share it with.'

Mackenzie savoured its oaky velvet smoothness. 'What is it your son does?'

'He doesn't do anything, señor. He's dead.'

Mackenzie closed his eyes momentarily. He could hear Susan whispering in his ear that he should have seen that coming. 'I'm sorry,' he said, aware of his inadequacy. 'What happened?'

'Joachim was a cop. Following in his old man's footsteps.

I think he was hoping that one day he would carry on the family tradition and take over here as *Jefe*. And, who knows, he probably would have. Except for a terrorist shooting in Madrid that took him from us at a criminally young age. Just twenty-four years old.'

Mackenzie saw the tears in his eyes catch the light of the rising moon.

'Amazing how quickly those who give their lives are forgotten by their country. The very people for whom they made their sacrifice.'

Now Mackenzie didn't know where to look. And he was frightened to speak for fear of saying something crass or stupid or just offensive. It seemed he never knew what to say, and when he tried he usually got it wrong. Or so Susan always told him. Silence spoke with more discretion.

It was the *Jefe* who broke it. He forced a laugh. 'I'm sorry, señor, I didn't mean to be maudlin. It's been an emotional couple of days.'

Mackenzie nodded. 'Has Cristina worked under you for long?'

'Not so long. But I've known her since she was a child. Knew her parents.' He shook his head. 'Gave her away at her wedding after the death of her father.' He paused. 'It's a tragedy what happened to Antonio. And I haven't told Cristina about Ana yet. Seemed like that might just be more than she could cope with right now.' He blinked back the threat of more tears. 'Sometimes . . . sometimes things just never turn out the way you want them to.' He forced himself away from the thought. 'I don't know how much longer they'll want to keep you here. I suppose until either Cleland is caught, or he gets away. One way or another, that's likely to be in the next forty-eight hours.'

Mackenzie emptied his glass. 'I should have had him. Twice! But today was worse. I let him get away with Ana. If anything happens to her ...' His uncle's words about his father still resonated, even after all this time. *He was a total waster, your father. Thought that nothing was beyond him. Well he learned the hard fucking way just how wrong he was.*

'Not your fault, son.'

Mackenzie didn't miss the paternal undertone. There was something very Scottish about the *Jefe*'s use of the word *son*. And when he thought about it he realized that the *Jefe* was probably just about old enough to be his father.

The chief also seemed to realize the implication of what he'd said and quickly shrugged it off. 'Anyway, don't beat yourself up. We'll get him. I'm just really pissed off that I've got a conference in Malaga the day after tomorrow. I've tried to get out of it, but obviously they think I'm more value there than here.' He pulled a self-deprecating face. 'I just hope I don't miss all the fun.'

CHAPTER FORTY

First light slanted in through a window at the back of the cemetery, falling across the half-open casket, throwing shadows across the serenity fixed by some mortician on Antonio's face. Cristina sat on a hard settee, as she had through most of the night, Lucas stretched out asleep beside her, his head resting in her lap.

Nuri and Paco had kept her company on the vigil, greeting the stream of visitors arriving to pay their respects, until at last their numbers dwindled to zero around midnight. People had brought food. Soup, and tapas. But Cristina had been unable to eat. Nuri had spent much of the night throwing up in a toilet two doors along, the fruit of the toxins they had drip-fed into her body just the day before. Everyone had heard her retching. Paco slipped out just after sunrise to make final preparations for the service.

More than her grief, more than the desperate desolation she felt for the son who had just lost his father, Cristina had obsessed through all the long hours of darkness about the message they had found on the answering machine at the apartment. How was it possible? How could anyone even believe it had been left by her? Ever since Paco had brought news of it back with him, she had wanted to hear it. To play it at volume through loudspeakers for everyone to hear and scream, *See? It's not me!* How could anyone who knew her think it was? And why, in God's name, did Antonio believe for one moment that she would want to meet him in an underground car park at the Eroski Centre? It made absolutely no sense.

And so she had passed a night divided equally between grief and anger. And frustration. By morning the tears had all been spilled, leaving her drained. Eyes stinging, throat swollen. She had barely heard the procession of muttered commiserations the night before. What did it matter? Her life was over.

The sounds of a car engine idling out front came with the opening of a door somewhere in the building. And voices. Before Paco returned to push his head into the room. 'We should go and get ready for mass. The undertaker will take Toni to the church.'

It was thought that most of Marviña would be there, the tiny chapel downstairs hopelessly inadequate for the numbers expected.

Cristina looked at her sleeping child, and her heart broke for him all over again. How could she wake him to face the misery of this day when he had found, finally, escape in sleep?

The hearse arrived at the church with flowers trailing from the tailgate. As it lifted, the flowers fell to the ground and the pall bearers slid out the coffin to raise it on sturdy shoulders. They carried it in silence through the central arch and into the expectant hush of the cool crowded space beyond. The narrow streets around the church were thick with parked cars. People had come from miles around for the funeral. Some out of respect, others out of curiosity.

For Cristina it passed in a blur. The sonorous voice of the priest, the flesh and blood of Christ, the tribal nature of psalms sung in mourning. And then they were out again into the incongruity of blue skies and sunshine. Another beautiful day. The first without Toni.

It was a long walk in procession behind the hearse back to the cemetery on the edge of town, where rows of vertical tombs, four deep, stepped down the hillside like terracing in a vineyard. Concrete slots for coffins, bought or rented, bones to be removed to the ossuary in twenty years to make way for future travellers to eternity.

Across the hillside, cars paused briefly at the tollbooth on the motorway before passing on their way, oblivious to one life passing into the next in the cemetery below.

The *Jefe* stood by Cristina's side, holding her hand as he had on her wedding day. In her other hand Cristina felt her son's desperate grip, squeezing tightly as they watched the bearers sliding his father's coffin into darkness, posted to the afterlife. She felt rather than heard the sobs that broke from his chest. And noticed for the first time that Ana was not there.

CHAPTER FORTY-ONE

The town was deserted as Mackenzie walked up the Calle Utopía. Everyone, it seemed, was at the funeral. Most people in town, the *Jefe* had told him, had bought their cars from Antonio.

The heat had risen early today and was already shimmering in the air as church bells rang out across the rooftops, calling mourners to the requiem mass. Mackenzie glanced across the square towards the ceramic mosaic of winemakers trampling grapes. People came and went, but the wine was eternal, grapes the lifeblood of this community. He wondered who would sell them cars now.

A uniformed police officer was stationed outside Cristina's apartment. Mackenzie was not sure why. It wasn't a crime scene, and anyway forensics had already been through it with a fine-toothed comb.

Mackenzie recognized the officer from the briefings. They exchanged nods and Mackenzie asked him to open the door to the stairwell. The apartment itself was not locked and Mackenzie let himself in, feeling a little like an intruder on invisible grief. This was a living, loving place where a family had spent their lives without ever suspecting that tomorrow might never come. For Antonio, at least, it had not. For Cristina and Lucas tomorrow offered only grief. It would be a long healing process.

He thought about Antonio and Cristina, their relationship, the squabbling he had witnessed on each visit. And yet, wasn't that normal? Couples fought. And when things went wrong, conflict even over inconsequentialities seemed inevitable. Certainly, it had for him and Susan. The fighting between them latterly had been vicious, and conducted all too often in front of the children.

He recalled the *Jefe*'s words from the night before. *You might be feeling pain, but it is your children who are the real victims.* And he felt laden with regret. Cristina had fought with Antonio, and now he was dead. No way to say sorry, no second chances. How would he feel if something were to happen to Susan? Whatever might have gone wrong between them, their love hadn't always been broken.

Colourful plastic letters were arranged on the door of Lucas's bedroom, spelling his name and telling the world that this was his space. He thought about Alex and Sophia, and their spaces that he no longer shared. And the weight of his regret turned to an ache. He pushed the door open and saw a collection of soft toys piled together in a basket on a table. Each one, no doubt, with its own significance, its own special memory, a furry history of childhood.

In a graphic on the wall above the bed, a boy flew through a starry universe beneath the aphorism *Me pregunto si las estrellas se illuminan con el fin de que algún día cada uno pueda encontrar la suya.* Mackenzie translated it in his head as: *I wonder if the stars are shining so that one day everyone can find theirs.*

But Lucas had just lost one of the two stars that shone brightest in his life. And again Mackenzie thought of his own kids. And the light that he no longer shone on their lives.

He wandered around the apartment touching things. A coat hanging on the stand in the hall. Candles in the shape of love hearts that sat on a shelf. A scarf draped over the back of a chair. A CD player sitting among a pile of scattered CDs on the coffee table.

The grief was no longer invisible. It was here in everything he looked at, everything he touched. Framed wedding photographs on the wall, a colouring book on the table, an empty spectacle case. All the component parts of deconstructed lives.

Finally he lifted the phone and replayed the message. *Toni, meet me in the car park at Eroski. I'm there now. We've got to talk.* Then he replayed it again. And again. And again.

The quality of it was even poorer than he remembered. Full of pauses and clicks, like a signal interrupted. He was certain she'd had no opportunity to leave that message after they had met outside Zhivago's. It was always possible, he supposed, that she had called before he arrived. He was hazy on the exact timing. But it was his impression that he had got there before 14.47.

The recording certainly sounded like her, and it had been enough to fool Antonio, who had been married to her for ten years. But if it wasn't Cristina, then who was it and how had it been done?

He took out his iPhone and opened the *Voice Memo* app. He replayed Cristina's message and held his phone to the speaker to record it, then listened to it on his own phone. It was a good representation of a bad recording. He saved the file then attached it to an email addressed to a forensic audio expert he had worked with at the Met. Mick Allbright was a geek, as socially inept as Mackenzie, which was perhaps why they had got along. Mackenzie had no idea how much could be gleaned from such poor-quality audio, but if anyone could dissect it with accuracy, Mick could. He tagged it *Urgent*.

Outside the heat struck him anew. The officer on guard had sought shade inside the doorway and looked guilty as Mackenzie emerged. But Mackenzie was preoccupied. Had things really got so bad between Cristina and Antonio that she had threatened to leave him? That's what Paco said Antonio had told him. Mackenzie tried hard to re-conjure the conflict he had witnessed between the brothers-in-law at the golf course. He had been some distance away, but did it really look as if they had been arguing over a marital break-up?

Across the road, the sun reflected off a dark glass globe mounted on the wall above the door of the mini-market. A CCTV camera. There was a good chance it had caught Antonio leaving the apartment. Mackenzie loped across the road, half-running, and was perspiring by the time he stepped into the comparative cool of the shop.

The owner regarded him suspiciously from the far side of the counter and refused to let him review the footage. Some foreigner without so much as a badge or an ID! Mackenzie crossed the street and returned with the officer guarding the entrance to the apartment. This time the owner was reluctantly acquiescent. He led Mackenzie into a back room where an ancient PC whirred and groaned on a scarred table top. Footage from the camera, he said, was recorded on to an external disc and automatically rerecorded every forty-eight hours, wiping the previous recording in the process. It was less than twenty-four hours since Antonio had been murdered.

Mackenzie pulled up a stool and scrolled back to the previous afternoon, pausing the time-code at 14.45 before setting it to play. The camera gave greatest coverage to the front of the shop, but the entrance to Cristina's apartment across the road fell just inside the upper right corner of the frame. If Antonio's car was parked at the kerbside it was out of shot. Mackenzie sat and watched the minutes tick by. No one came or went. A full five minutes passed. Surely after receiving the call, Antonio would have left straight away?

Mackenzie was puzzled. He let the recording run for another five minutes. Nothing. By now Antonio would have had difficulty in reaching the Eroski Centre before the first reports of the shooting. A full fifteen minutes and there was no sign of Antonio. Which is when it occurred to Mackenzie that if

Antonio had actually taken the call, there would have been no need for Cristina to leave a message. So how did he know to go to the Eroski Centre?

He rewound, scrolling back a full ten minutes prior to the time of the call, then set the recording to play again. At 14.40 a scowling Antonio emerged from the apartment block, hands in pockets, fishing out his car keys as he went. He vanished out of shot. The last time anyone had seen him alive, apart from his killer, or killers. And a full seven minutes before the call from Cristina.

Mackenzie left the mini-market with the hard disk in his pocket and the proprietor's complaints ringing in his ears. It took him less than two minutes to cross the square to the police station and climb the steps to reception.

The duty officer looked at him in surprise. Perhaps he thought that Mackenzie should have been at the funeral. Mackenzie laid the hard disk down on the counter. 'I need to enter this in evidence,' he said. 'And I need you to do me a favour.'

CHAPTER FORTY-TWO

It was late afternoon by the time Cristina got home.

The *Jefe* had broken the news to her about Ana after the funeral. She had been furious. Boss or no boss, she laid into him. He had no right to keep something like that from her! But distress had displaced grief in her emptiness, and for a short while fear for Ana had replaced the heartbreak of losing Antonio.

They had all returned to Nuri and Paco's house, and despite her illness Nuri had done her best to feed them all. Neighbours had helped, arriving in constant procession with fish soup and goat stew and paella. But Cristina had been unable to eat. She had grilled the *Jefe* on every detail of Ana's disappearance. Mackenzie's sighting of her in the street with Cleland. The chase through the *feria*. The body found in her house. Neither she nor Nuri had the least idea who Sergio García Lorca might be, or what his connection to Ana was. If any.

Now she was quite simply exhausted. A night without sleep. Twenty-four hours without food. Grief and fear an almost impossible double burden. Lucas had to be her focus now.

She knew that. He had none of the mental and emotional resources to fall back on that she had. And, God knows, she had little enough of either herself.

The officer stationed in the street outside the apartment was long gone, and she dragged herself wearily up the stairs, Lucas trotting at her side, his hand still clutching hers. He had been braver than she could possibly have believed. A day without tears. Few words, and a stoic smile for all the fussing neighbours.

She paused for a moment with her hand on the door handle, closed her eyes and took a deep breath. This was their nest. How empty would it be without the man who had helped her build it? The first of many trials that lay ahead.

As soon as she let herself in she knew there was someone in the apartment. Fear and shock stung the skin of her face and she quickly insinuated herself between Lucas and the living room as she stepped out of the hall to confront whoever might be there.

The glass door to the balcony had been slid aside, and Mackenzie stood with his back to the rail, leaning against it and tapping on the screen of his mobile phone. He looked up, startled, as he heard her come in, and was immediately embarrassed, a physical intruder on her grief.

'Who the hell let you in?' she barked.

'I'm sorry,' he said. 'There's an officer posted downstairs. Did he not tell you?'

'There was no one there when I got here.'

'Oh.' He scratched his head. 'I don't know why they thought they needed one in the first place.' He slipped his phone back in his pocket. 'I'm sorry.'

'How could you let that bastard get away with Ana?'

Mackenzie reddened. Embarrassment and now guilt. 'I didn't . . .' But there were no excuses. 'I'm sorry,' he said again.

'Yes. So am I. Sorry I ever did a colleague a favour. Sorry I ever went to that break-in at La Paloma. Sorry I ever had to set eyes on you.'

Mackenzie lowered his head and wished that the ground would swallow him up. When eventually he raised his eyes again, she was standing in the living room with hers closed. Lucas stood at her side still clutching her hand, gazing at him with unglazed misery, his lower lip quivering. But still he held back his tears.

Finally Cristina opened her eyes and drew a deep trembling breath. 'I'm sorry. None of this is your fault.' She paused. 'What are you doing here?'

He didn't think that this was the moment to discuss the phone message, or the CCTV footage. And again heard Susan's silent commendation for his uncommon discretion. He said, 'I didn't think it would be right for me to go to the funeral. I hardly knew . . .' Now he felt Susan's metaphorical pinch on the arm.

But Cristina had turned her attentions to Lucas. 'Shall I put on the TV?'

The boy shrugged, which she took as assent, and crossed the room to turn it on. There was an animated film playing, and cartoon voices filled the room to displace the awful silence. But Lucas wasn't interested. He disentangled his hand from his mother's, went out to the hall and into the room with his name on it. He shut the door behind him.

Cristina stood for a moment. Helpless. Hopeless. Wondering what to do or say now. She glanced at the phone. All night she had wanted to hear the telephone message she had allegedly left. Now she couldn't bear to listen to it. Maybe tomorrow . . .

Mackenzie said, 'I should go.'

And suddenly she didn't want him to. 'Are you hungry?'

He had not thought about it, but hadn't eaten all day. 'I suppose I am.'

'They've been trying to make me eat for hours and I just haven't felt like it. But I do now. And Lucas will need something.' She tipped her head towards the kitchen. 'I'll see what I can rustle up.' And she went through to rattle pans and forage in the fridge.

Left on his own now, Mackenzie had no idea what to do. He pushed off from the railing and went into the living room, where he began gathering the toys and items of clothing that lay on chairs or scattered across the floor, and piled them on to the table. He found the remote for the TV and turned down the volume. Which is when he heard the faint sound of sobbing from Lucas's room. He glanced towards the kitchen where Cristina was noisily busying herself to avoid thinking, and thought that he should probably do something. He would, if Lucas had been one of his.

He went out into the hall and knocked softly on the door. The sobbing stopped almost at once. He knocked again, and a tiny voice told him to come in.

Lucas was sitting on the edge of the bed, his hands folded in his lap, tears shining on his cheeks. He glanced at Mackenzie then away again. Machismo dictated that Spanish boys didn't cry. Mackenzie went and sat on the bed beside him. What to say? He had never really known how to comfort his own children in distress. Susan had been good at that. Finally he said, 'My father committed suicide.'

Lucas brought his head sharply round to stare up at Mackenzie with big dark curious eyes. Mackenzie had no idea why he'd said it. It was something he had not confided in anyone. Not even Susan. Preferring to perpetuate the myth he had grown up with that his father had died a hero.

'He was a police officer. Tried to rescue a woman being held hostage, but only got her killed. He couldn't live with that and hanged himself.' There was an extraordinary sense of relief in saying it aloud for the first time in his life.

Lucas blinked at him. 'What age were you?'

'Oh, I was just two. I didn't know anything about it at the time. I didn't learn about it until later.'

'So it was just you and your mum?'

'Well, no. They took me away from my mother. I was brought up by my aunt and uncle.'

'Like Paco and Nuri?'

'Yes. But no one's going to take you away from *your* mum.

She'll always be here for you.' He was scared now that he had frightened the boy and looked around the room for something to change the subject. His eyes lit on Lucas's school jotter on the desk below the window. 'Still having trouble with your maths?'

Lucas nodded. And then a sad little smile. 'Dad was hopeless at it, too. Maybe I take after him.'

Mackenzie reached for the jotter and opened it up. 'What are they teaching you?'

'Percentages.'

Mackenzie looked at him in surprise. 'So what's difficult about that?'

'You're kidding, right? I mean, it's easy if its 10, or 100 . . .'

Mackenzie said, 'But if they ask you what is 17.5 per cent of some number that's not a hundred, and you don't have a calculator your brain freezes. Is that what happens?'

Lucas nodded. 'Yeah. Freezes is right. I just can't think.'

Mackenzie smiled. 'I'll teach you a little trick, then. It'll unfreeze your brain and your teacher will think you're a genius.'

Lucas eyed him with naked scepticism. 'How?'

'Well, like you said, it's easy to multiply or divide by 10 or 100. But if you were asked to find 17.5 per cent of say, 416, that would seem really hard.'

'Yeah, it would.'

'Because 17.5 is a really unfriendly number, right?'

Lucas nodded enthusiastic agreement.

'But any unfriendly number is just made up of friendly numbers, numbers that are easy for you to work with. So all you have to do is find friendly numbers that add or subtract to make 17.5. For example 10 plus 5 plus 2.5 make 17.5, right?'

Lucas nodded again. And already light was starting to dawn. '5 is half of 10, 2.5 is half of 5.'

'Exactly. So divide 416 by 10 and what do you get?'

'41.6'

'Right. So half of that is . . . ?'

'20.8.'

'And half of that . . . ?'

'10.4.'

'So all you have to do . . .'

But Lucas was way ahead of him. 'Is add those three numbers together . . .' He grabbed the jotter and a pencil, wrote them down and added them up. 'And you get 72.8.'

'Which is 17.5 per cent of 416.' Mackenzie grinned. 'See? Told you it was easy.'

Lucas's dark eyes shone. It was as if a whole landscape of understanding had just opened up before him. 'Can we try another one?'

'Yes, of course . . .'

Cristina looked at the magnets arranged along the angle of the cooker hood. An ice-cream cone, a jukebox, a couple of minions – Bob and Kevin; a religious icon, a motorcycle. Each with its own memory of Antonio. A sticker for Pollo Pronto in Santa Ana, a carry-out chicken joint where Antonio would often buy them cheap take-home dinner on his way back from work. She wanted to tear them all off, wipe away the memories that right now were only painful. But a part of her knew, somewhere deep inside, they were memories that one day might bring pleasure rather than pain. And she would regret it if she'd thrown them away.

She had improvised a tagliatelle carbonara and ladled it out of the pot on to three plates. The cooking time had been spent thinking about Ana. She wanted to phone the police station to see if there was any news. But she knew that if there were they would have called her. She carried the plates through to the table, and sighed as she saw the detritus that Mackenzie had piled there from around the room. She set the plates down, and with a single sweeping movement of her arm sent it all tumbling to the floor. Then marched through the hall to throw open the door to Lucas's room. The sight that greeted her stopped her in her tracks.

Lucas and Mackenzie were sitting together at the little desk below the window, poring over an open jotter, textbooks all around them. Lucas turned shining eyes towards his mother. 'Señor Mackenzie is teaching me maths, mamá. It's so easy. I'm going to be top of the class. And make papá really proud.'

By the time they had finished the tagliatelle Cristina and Mackenzie had consumed almost a bottle of red wine between them. Lucas had eaten quickly and retired again to his room to do more maths. But when Cristina had peeked in, he had been lying sound asleep on the bed with his jotter open beside him, his pencil still loosely clutched between crooked fingers.

Rather than lubricating conversation between them, the wine had only made things more sticky. Mackenzie had quickly exhausted his very limited supply of small talk, and Cristina seemed less than inclined to speak at all. Only the background burble of the TV filled the silence in the room.

Finally Mackenzie said, 'Why did you and Antonio want to break up? Could you not have talked things through?'

She turned eyes on him that blazed both anger and astonishment. 'What are you talking about?'

'You told Antonio you were going to leave him and wanted custody of Lucas.'

She was on her feet now. 'That is complete rubbish! Why would you even say something like that?'

He was taken aback by her ferocity. 'It's not true, then?'

'No, it's not!'

He was at a loss. 'I was only here twice and you were fighting both times.'

'Oh, for God's sake. Couples fight! Don't you ever fight with your wife?'

He shrugged and tried to find a smile. He didn't want to tell her just how much.

'It doesn't mean a thing.' Almost as if she were trying to convince herself. 'I think maybe it's time you left.'

He stood up, red-faced with embarrassment. Somehow he

had only managed to make things worse, and was desperate to try and make up for it.

'I found CCTV footage from the mini-market across the road. It shows Antonio leaving the apartment seven minutes before you left that message.'

'I didn't leave any message!'

'That's not even the point. How could he know where and when to meet you if you didn't leave the message until after he'd left?'

Which gave her pause for thought. But only for a moment. She glanced at the phone and knew she would listen to the message after all. Once Mackenzie had gone. 'Go señor. Please.'

He glanced awkwardly at his feet, then up again and nodded. 'I'll see you tomorrow, I suppose.'

She followed him to the door. But he turned before she could close it behind him. 'It was Paco who told me.'

She frowned. 'Told you what?'

'That you and Antonio were breaking up.'

Her face creased with consternation. 'Why would he say something like that when it's not true?' She breathed her exasperation. 'Just go.'

And she slammed the door in his face.

Mackenzie's room at the Hostal Totana seemed cold and unwelcoming, in spite of the heat. A question of mood rather than temperature. He knew he had misspoken at the meal with Cristina, and it distressed him to think he had upset her. But still, he knew now that Paco had been lying about the argument with Antonio. Why?

He stripped to his boxers and lay on top of the bed in the dark, but found it difficult to breathe in the airless heat. He swung his legs off the bed and crossed the room to wind up the shutters, sliding open the glass doors and stepping out on to the balcony.

Everything in the main street below was closed up for the night and there was not a soul stirring in the town. He stood gulping down the slightly cooler night air and heard the beep of an incoming email on his phone. He went into the room to fetch it from his shirt pocket and took it back out to the balcony. The email was from Mick, his audio forensic expert at the Met.

Hola my Spanish Warrior,

I'm guessing you don't want the full forensic transcription or the detailed Primeau Forensics analysis, because you never possessed my delight for detail. Such things you may require for future reference, but here for your delectation are the facts in brief.

This is an absurdly amateurish cobbling together of bits and pieces of other recordings. Other phone messages would be my best guess. It would take a matter of minutes with a couple of mobile phones to assemble something this bad, assuming you had the raw material to hand. Wouldn't stand up in a court of law for five minutes. If you want more, I am at your service.

El Cid

Mackenzie smiled at his old friend's childish sense of

humour. But his email only confirmed what Mackenzie had already suspected. That someone had called Antonio to make a rendezvous at the Eroski Centre, then allowed time for him to leave the apartment before calling again to leave Cristina's phoney message. The caller could not have known exactly where Cristina might be at that time, whether she would have an alibi or not. But at the very least it would sow the seeds of confusion. Sometime tomorrow, he hoped, he would be able to identify exactly who had made those calls.

His phone vibrated and pinged in his hand. It was a Facebook alert. He went into the app and saw a red dot attached to the double head-and-shoulders icon that represented friend requests. He tapped it. A single name appeared. Sophia Mackenzie. *Confirm* or *Delete*. His heart filled up with love for the little girl who just forty-eight hours ago had unfriended him.

He tapped *Confirm*.

CHAPTER FORTY-THREE

The persistent single trill of the telephone penetrated troubled dreams that vanished from recollection the moment he awoke. It took a second to remember where he was, and then another to reach for the bedside phone.

'Yes?'

The voice that sounded in his ear could almost have been computer-generated. It was monotone and curiously stilted, as if the speaker were trying to disguise it. And if it was someone Mackenzie knew, he was making a good job of it. He spoke in Spanish. 'Condesa Golf Hotel. Thirty minutes. Come alone. Simple exchange. You for the blind lady.' And the caller hung up before Mackenzie could even respond.

He sat upright on the bed. Perspiring, breathing hard. He could feel his heart punching at an already tender rib cage.

He ran every possible eventuality through his head at high speed, and each one led him to the same conclusion. However clumsily contrived, it was clearly a trap. But an oddly honeyed trap, almost as if its architect knew how irresistible it would be to Mackenzie. The chance to make amends for his father's mistake all those years ago. Sacrificing himself to save the hostage. But how could anyone know about that? And how could anyone think he was stupid enough not to realize that a trap was a trap. In contradiction of the popular aphorism, there was no honour among thieves, so there was no guarantee that the promise of any exchange would be respected. Cleland simply wanted to kill him. He knew it in his bones.

But what to do?

He weighed everything in his mind. He could not involve Cristina. She had more than enough to contend with. But he had a location. The Condesa Golf Hotel. It was just possible that Cleland might actually be there. Mackenzie had noticed it the other day, sitting up above the A7 overlooking the sea half a mile short of the Eroski Centre. Green-smoked glass and pale yellow walls. An air of abandonment. Closed shutters, over-grown gardens, and two letters dangling at odd angles from the name of the hotel above the front entrance. Of course, it was perfectly possible Ana wasn't even there.

But what to do?

He took his own phone from the charger and called the police station. A sleepy-sounding duty officer responded, and took more than a moment to realize who Mackenzie was.

'I need a number for the *Jefe*,' Mackenzie said.

'Well, isn't there something *I* can help you with?'

'No, I need to talk to the *Jefe*.'

He heard the officer sigh, then after a moment he read out

a number. 'He won't be happy to hear from you at this time in the morning.'

Mackenzie hung up and dialled. He was not going to make a decision on this by himself. Unlike his father, he would defer to a higher authority. He closed his eyes and listened to the sound of the phone ringing in the dark of the *Jefe*'s home somewhere up in the hills. He rehearsed what he was going to say. But the phone just rang and rang, until finally Mackenzie hung up and his carefully thought out words scattered in the winds of uncertainty.

'Shit!' His own voice whispered back at him from the walls. He glanced at the bedside clock. It was 4.17 am, a good five minutes now since the call. The caller had said thirty minutes. Time was running out. By the time he got to the police station and explained himself to the duty officer, that thirty-minute window would have closed. He had to go now.

Cursing under his breath, he dragged on a pair of jeans and pushed his feet into white trainers. His only fresh shirt was a white one. He would be seen coming a mile off. He shoved the shirt tails into his jeans and dropped his phone into the breast pocket, then took a moment to steady himself, fingers pressed into the soft flesh at either side of his temples. He forced himself to take a deep breath, then ran silently down the stairs to search for his car in the underground garage.

There was no traffic on the A7 as Mackenzie pulled off it, slipping his car into neutral and drifting to a halt in front of the golf club. He cut the engine. The hotel itself stood at the top of a short rise beyond the clubhouse and languished in profound darkness. He glanced at his watch. The thirty minutes were almost up.

He stepped out of the car and stood listening. All he could hear was the creak of cicadas, and an offshore breeze that rattled the fronds of palm trees overhead. A waning moon and a star-studded sky provided enough light to see by.

He ran cautiously up the hill staying close to the retaining wall, then sprinted for the deep shadow of rusted canopies that raised themselves above the overgrown slots of an empty car park. From here he surveyed the front entrance to the hotel, half hidden by foliage. It all seemed closed and secure. There were no lights inside.

Keeping to the shadows, he moved around the far side of the building to where a spa occupied the basement on a lower level. The hotel was built in wings enclosing an overgrown garden. Steps led up to a gated entrance. Everything was padlocked.

Mackenzie drifted across the access road, and found a path that curved back around the slope towards the front of the hotel. He pushed through tangling bushes to reach steps that climbed to a side entrance. There he stopped and stood quite still. A chain hung from the padlock that Cleland had severed and the door itself stood half open.

He listened intently. But the cicadas, like tinnitus, drowned out everything else. All that he could hear above it was the sound of his own blood pulsing in his ears. He stepped forward to push the door carefully into darkness. And moved silently into the interior.

For several long moments he stood motionless, letting his eyes accustom themselves to what little light there was. Moonlight fell feebly from an atrium high above reception, and in its cold wash he saw the tracks left by many feet in the dust that lay thick on the floor. Some old, some fresh. They led across marble tiles to a staircase that descended to the spa. Mackenzie moved slowly in the footsteps of whoever had gone before him and started down the stairs.

It was darker here. Light from street lamps in the access road filtered through glass doors to cast deep shadows across empty pools. Mackenzie followed the footprints in the dust, past locker rooms and abandoned massage tables, to double doors obscured by gloom at the far side of the spa.

Now he was in one of the residential wings. Hands painted on the walls of the stairwell pointed up towards numbered rooms on the floors above. He stopped on the first landing. A strangely invasive moan penetrated the darkness. Erratic, repetitive. An almost human sound. Although he knew that it wasn't. But like chalk on a blackboard it sent an involuntary chill through his body.

This was madness. What could he possibly achieve by coming here on his own, walking straight into a trap so crudely set? He was unsure if he had ever been in greater fear for his life. Perhaps he should have gone to the police station after all. But it was too late for second thoughts. In the end, it seemed, he had been just as foolish as his father. There was nothing for it now but to push on.

As he reached the second landing the moaning grew louder. It came to him from somewhere beyond double doors that led into what must once have been a guest lounge. Settees and armchairs and coffee tables hid like phantoms beneath discoloured dust sheets, and Mackenzie slalomed between them towards a wall of glass with sliding doors that stood open. Outside, a covered terrace overlooked the garden.

Once on the terrace he identified the source of the almost human moaning. The remains of a flag dangled from a pole overhead and swayed gently back and forth in the breeze that blew up from the shore, causing a steel rope to swing on a rusted retaining hinge. An endless eerie refrain heard only by the ghosts of guests past. And those in whose footprints Mackenzie had followed.

He stepped across the terrace and peered over the rail into the shrubbery below. Weeds pushed up through cracked tiles around an empty swimming pool where myriad blue mosaic tiles had flaked off to lie scattered across its debris-strewn floor like glitter.

The sound of broken glass crunching underfoot brought him spinning around, in time to see the silhouette of a man standing in the doorway. He knew immediately that it was Cleland, but all consciousness was drowned out by the sound of the shot that echoed around the gardens, and by the force and pain of the bullet that struck him full in the chest. It propelled him into the railings behind him, tipping him over backwards into darkness. Falling. Falling. Into silence.

Cleland watched with satisfaction as Mackenzie toppled backwards over the railing into the garden below. His original assessment of Mackenzie as a knuckle-headed cop vindicated by the stupidity of his coming here alone. It had taken no time at all for Cleland to track Mackenzie down on the internet. A tabloid story of heroism thwarting a bank raid in north London. And the background that the journalist had dug up on a family suicide. His father a cop whose bungled rescue attempt had led to a fatality, and later the taking of his own life. Like father like son. Only it was Cleland who had taken the son's life.

He crossed the terrace and looked down into the dark tangle of foliage below. There was no sign of Mackenzie in the overgrown ruin of a garden where guests had once sunned themselves on luxury loungers. But no movement either. Cleland had no doubt that he was dead. He had won prizes for target shooting at his gun club and had directed his bullet directly at Mackenzie's heart. But it never did any harm to be sure.

He turned and saw the shadow of Paco skulking in the doorway. 'Call your boss and tell him the rendezvous is going ahead as planned,' he said. 'Then get down there and make sure that bastard's properly dead.'

*

Ana is cold. She knows that the air is warm. She can feel it on her skin. But the chill comes from within. So deeply that she is shivering.

Her time here has seemed endless, without any means of communication. Cleland has kept her company only intermittently, and with every interaction between them she has felt only more antipathy toward him.

Much of this time has been spent thinking about Sergio. Dwelling on what she realizes now were the days of their lives. Those idyllic evenings passed together so long ago. At the centre in Estepona. At the seafood restaurant on the beach at Santa Ana. And she has found herself wondering what might have become of the toothless proprietor. She supposes he was younger then than her teenage self imagined. Perhaps both he and the restaurant are still there.

Unlike Sergio.

His meeting with the young Ana had brought him only pain and misery. Her father and his so set against their relationship. The denial of what might have been the young couple's only chance at happiness. All those lost years, poor Sergio regretting what had never been his fault. Only to die at the hands of Cleland when finally he had tried to turn back the clock and remake the past.

How very close he had come. So very close.

Tears fill her eyes, fuelled by her pain and anger. How unfair it all is. As if she has been cursed. A curse unwittingly passed on to the man she loved.

A change in temperature signals Cleland's return. When he comes close she smells him. She is sitting by the window, another chair beside her, a table to her left with water and biscuits. All that she has been given to sustain her.

From the adjoining chair his hands take hers, and she feels his finger tracing words on her palm. His breath is rank. And there is a strange smell from his hands, like the odour of nitroglycerine she had identified from Cristina's gun.

– *Leaving now.*

'Where's Cristina?'

– *Never mind.*

'Don't harm her, please. You have me.'

– *Yes.* A pause. *We're going on a boat. Not for long. Don't be afraid.*

'Cristina . . .'

He puts a finger to her lips to silence her.

– *She's at home with Lucas. Safe. No need to hurt her now.*

She raises a hand unexpectedly to his face, taking him by surprise and catching the smile that still lingers on his lips. She knows he is lying.

CHAPTER FORTY-FOUR

Paco cursed his luck. He hated Cleland with a vengeance. Shooting him in the leg had been no part of the deal. 'I had to make it look real,' Cleland had told him later. 'Just a flesh wound. Avoided the bone and the femoral artery. You'll live.'

Yes, in constant bloody pain! The price he was paying for Nuri's treatment. He screwed up his face as he hobbled around the side service road to access the garden. There was no way, it seemed, to reach it from inside. All doors leading out were firmly locked.

He toyed with the idea of going back and telling Cleland that he had found Mackenzie, and that he was well and truly dead. But what if he wasn't? Cleland was unpredictable. Brutal. Mad. There was no telling what he might do.

A service ramp sloped down to a shuttered cellar beneath the gardens where the pumps that powered the spa and the pool were housed. From the pavement, steps led up to a pad-locked gate with spiked railings and barbed wire that gave on to another level. Yet more steps rose to the garden itself.

Paco climbed to the gate, leaned his crutches against the

wall and unclipped Cleland's wire-cutters from his belt. They sliced easily through the chain, and he let the links and padlock fall away. The gate swung open with a rusty complaint, and he grabbed his crutches to help propel himself up the last half-dozen steps to the garden itself.

The grass was almost waist-high here, the dead fronds of untended palms dangling in profusion all around and rustling in the breeze. The moon was rising now over the roof of the hotel, casting deep shadows in the empty pool. Paco pushed his way through barbed branches and tangling hedge. Thorns scratched his face and arms. The hanging leaf of a banana tree slapped him heavily in the face, and he had trouble keeping his balance.

He looked up and saw that he was directly below the terrace from which Mackenzie had fallen. That smug fucking Scotsman. At least he had got what was coming to him. But there was no sign of the body. Just the crushed leaves and snapped branches of thick foliage that must have broken its fall. Where the hell was he?

As Paco looked up again to check that he was in the right place, a shape took shadowed form and emerged from the darkness with such force that it knocked him from his feet, landing on top of him with full crushing weight to force the air from his lungs. A fist slammed into his face. He felt teeth breaking and sinking into the soft flesh behind his lips. Another blow. Blood bubbling into his mouth and spurting from his nose. He swung desperate fists in the dark and struck solid bone. He gasped and gurgled and squirmed his way out from beneath the weight of his attacker. Whatever damage Cleland's bullet had done to Mackenzie, it had not killed him.

Paco scrambled to his feet, crutches discarded, and went charging off through the undergrowth, ignoring the fire in his wounded leg. Fear launched him blindly into darkness until his shins struck a low stone wall at the perimeter of the garden and tipped him forward into space.

His fall ended abruptly and in searing agony. It seemed to consume his whole body for just a second. Before darkness took him. And the pain and everything else went away.

Mackenzie staggered after the hapless Spaniard, legs buckling beneath him. He was half crippled by pain. But unlike Paco's, Mackenzie's pain wasn't going away any time soon. He reached the wall and dropped to his knees and peered down to see Paco staring back at him. The man lay full-length along the top of the railing below, spikes protruding from his chest and stomach and groin, skewered like a sardine in readiness for the flames. Dead eyes gazing into the firmament, and to eternity beyond.

The lights of a vehicle sent shadows firing off into the night as it swung around a bend in the service road below, and by the reflected light of the headlamps Mackenzie saw, as it passed, Ana's pale frightened face pressed against the passenger window.

*

The bleary-eyed medic on the desk at Helicopteros Sanitarios looked up from his computer as the outside door slid open. His eyes opened wide as the dishevelled figure of a tall, fair-skinned man with a blood-stained white shirt staggered in out of the night. He was on his feet in an instant. 'Señor, what's happened?'

Mackenzie responded through clenched teeth. 'I've been shot.'

The medic helped him through to a treatment room at the back and sat him up on the examination table. He was obliged to inform the police of any gunshot wounds, but that could wait until he'd made an assessment of the damage.

Mackenzie winced as the medic peeled away the shirt from his chest, and the ruined remains of his iPhone fell to the floor. It had left an almost perfect reddish-purple bruised impression of itself on his chest.

'Jesus,' the medic whispered. 'Man, have you any idea how lucky you are to be alive?'

'I don't feel so lucky right now.' Mackenzie's voice was hoarse.

The medic grabbed a pair of tweezers from his kit of sterilized tools and started picking tiny pieces of glass and circuit board and phone body from the deepest area of abrasion right behind where the bullet had struck the phone. 'Not seen anything like this since I was with medical staff in Herat.' He glanced up at Mackenzie and clarified. 'Afghanistan. Part of Operation Resolute Support. Saw quite a few injuries like this.

Behind body armour injury. Backface deformation they call it.' He chuckled. 'Never saw a bullet stopped by an iPhone before, though.'

Mackenzie didn't see what was amusing about it. 'Has it busted any ribs?'

'I doubt it,' the medic said. And he pressed gently around the area of bruising, causing Mackenzie to gasp. 'A young guy like you. The cartilaginous portions of your ribs there are still soft. Another fifteen or twenty years and it'll all have turned to bone, and that would almost certainly have shattered.' He smiled. 'The good news is you'll live. The bad news is, once I've dressed up the wound I'm going to have to report you to the police.'

Mackenzie gasped his frustration. 'I *am* the bloody police.'

It was a full forty-five minutes before Mackenzie was back on the road, bandaged and strapped up and feeling like death. The medic had been reluctant to let him go, but couldn't stop him, and Mackenzie had left him phoning to report the incident to the authorities.

He had tried calling the *Jefe*'s number several times from Helicopteros. Without success. He debated going straight to the police station. But that would entail lengthy and complex explanations to junior officers on night shift. God only knew how long it would take to get a more senior-ranking officer involved. He needed to talk to the chief, and decided to go directly to his house.

The moon was well up in the sky now, washing its blood-less light across the hillside. The dust that rose around him as he powered the Seat up the dry forest track drifted in ghostly illumination like mist. At the top of the hill he turned his car down the steep incline to the *Jefe*'s finca only to find the house itself swaddled in darkness. There was no sign of the Audi.

Mackenzie banged the heels of his hands against the steering wheel, then let his head fall forward to rest on it. He closed his eyes and let despair wash over him. Where in God's name was the *Jefe*?

He sat back, then, in the driver's seat and forced himself to breathe at a measured rate. He needed to think clearly. It seemed to him he had two choices. Go straight to the police station and raise the alarm. Or get Cristina out of her bed. At least he had some kind of traction with her.

But he had no idea where Cleland was going, and he had Ana with him. What could any of them do? They would have no idea which way to turn. He knew he was going to have to report the shooting and the death of Paco, but all that was only going to throw up flak and serve as a distraction.

With reluctance he decided that Cristina was his best option. She had a vested interest in cutting through the red tape. He glanced down at the shirt that hung off his shoulders in bloody tatters and realized he would need to stop at the Totana on the way to her apartment for a quick change of clothing.

He swung the Seat through a three-point turn and accelerated back up the hill. The moon seemed to sit on the rise directly above him, shining straight into his eyes. He snapped down the sun visor and tutted his annoyance at the irony.

CHAPTER FORTY-FIVE

Cristina opened her eyes, startled. Something had wakened her, and in that foggy transition from sleep to consciousness she could not identify what it was.

She sat up and realized there was a light in the room. Going to bed the previous night had been one of the most difficult things she had ever forced herself to do. Climbing into the space she had shared in intimacy with Antonio these last ten years. Lying between sheets that still smelled of him, making it harder to accept that he was gone. The shape of his head pressed into the pillow where last he had laid it.

For a time she had debated whether or not to leave the light on. Something about the dark frightened her. Superstitions from childhood. Tales of ghosts. But she had told herself she was being foolish and turned it off. Only to lie sleepless in the dark for what had seemed like all night long, wondering how she would ever sleep again and willing the dawn to come.

But somehow, at some time, she had drifted off, only to be startled awake now, blinking in the unexpected light. It was only when the light vanished that she realized what it was. The illuminated screen of her phone. That's what had wakened her. The alert of an incoming message.

She reached across the bed to lift the phone from its charger and saw that it was a text. It was 5.43 am. She sat up, sweeping the hair from her face and tapped the message preview to open up the window. And suddenly she was wide awake, heart hammering in the silence of the bedroom.

GIBRALTAR SKYWALK FIRST LIGHT. TELL NO ONE – WE WILL KNOW. MACKENZIE DEAD.

In the dark, the light of her screen burned itself on to her retinas, along with the words of its message. She was frozen in disbelief. Mackenzie dead? How? When? Before the full weight of this cryptic message bore down on her. Cleland had Ana. And now he wanted her.

He was telling her not to expect any help from Mackenzie, but in any case she knew that there was no one who could rescue her from this dilemma. How could she not go? How could she simply ignore this message and leave Ana to her fate? How could she live with herself if she did?

But if she went there could only be one outcome. Cleland would kill her, without any guarantee that he would spare Ana. It was perfectly possible that her aunt was already dead. And if Cristina were to die, then Lucas would have lost both his parents. How could she deprive him of his mother after the murder of his father? Who would care for him then? Nuri and Paco?

She had never felt so alone in her life. *Tell no one – we will know*, they said. Which could only mean they had someone on the inside. Which meant that she couldn't go to the *Jefe* or to any of her other colleagues in the police. There was no one to advise her, no one to help. And an impossible decision to make: die and abandon her child, or let Cleland murder her aunt, and live for ever with the guilt.

She dropped her face into outspread palms and felt tears of despair fill her eyes. Her thoughts tumbled one over the other in a stream of confused consciousness. How was it possible that Mackenzie was dead? Maybe they were lying. Because he was the only one left in the world, it seemed, that she could trust.

She wiped the tears quickly from her eyes and fumbled with her phone to find Mackenzie's mobile number and tapped it to autodial. It rang four times before redirecting her to leave a message. Her voice was hoarse as she whispered into the phone, 'Señor, they want to exchange me for Ana. The Gibraltar Skywalk at first light. If you get this, know that I have no choice but to do what they want.'

When she hung up she realized that in crystallizing her thoughts in the words of her message she had made her decision. With a heart that was breaking, she slipped from the bed she had shared all these years with the father of her son, and went to rouse the boy from his sleep.

CHAPTER FORTY-SIX

It was a little after 6 am when Mackenzie pulled up outside the apartment at the top of Calle Utopía. At the hotel he had changed his jeans, and dug a used shirt out of the laundry. It had taken him some minutes to clean the blood from his face and hands. There was little that clung more stubbornly to the skin than dried blood. It got into every crease, insinuating its way into every pore. His right hand was already bruised and swollen from having driven it with force twice into Paco's face. The painkillers given him by the medic at Helicopteros had kicked in and his chest hurt less. But every muscle in his body was seizing up.

He climbed stiffly out of the car. It was still dark.

He pressed the buzzer on the door to the stairwell and waited. No response. He pressed again and held his finger on it for a full ten seconds. Still nothing. A pervasive sense of foreboding took hold.

He stepped back on the pavement and looked up. There were no lights in the windows of Cristina's apartment. But there was a light shining in one of the windows of the adjoining apartment. He went back to the door and pressed another buzzer. An irate voice barked through the speaker at him almost immediately.

'Have you any idea what time it is?' A woman's voice.

'My apologies, señora, this is an emergency. I'm trying to contact Officer Sánchez.'

'She's not here.'

'How do you know?'

'Because I saw her leave with the boy about ten minutes ago. That's how.'

'I don't suppose you know where she's gone?'

'How would I know that?'

Mackenzie reached for his phone to try and call her, before realizing that the shirt pocket was empty. His phone in pieces in the car. He pressed the buzzer again.

'What!'

'Would you call her mobile number for me?'

'For Heaven's sake, señor.'

'Please, señora. Do you have it?'

'Yes, I have it.' Another sigh, then a long pause that seemed to stretch out forever. Then: 'No reply. It went to the answering service.'

'Shit!' Mackenzie's powers of processing went into overdrive. She had the boy with her. If she was going to keep some ill-advised rendezvous with Cleland, as he suspected, she wouldn't take Lucas with her. He pressed the buzzer again.

'If you don't go away I'm going to call the police!'

Mackenzie raised his eyes to the heavens. 'I'm going. I promise. I just need Nuri's address. Cristina's sister.'

The neighbour growled back. 'I know who her sister is.'

Nuri and Paco's apartment was on the east side of town, on the hill below the main street. It was on the fourth floor of an apartment block above a tapas bar, tables and chairs stacked on wooden decking in front of it. It took Mackenzie less than five minutes to get there. He pulled into a parking slot beside the deck and stepped out into cooling air. Finally the oppressive temperatures of the night were in retreat. But with the dawn, and the rising of the sun, the heat would build all over again, and another breathless day lay in prospect.

Across the street, beyond a white wall, a patchwork of fields and vineyards fell away into the night before rising towards the foothills of the distant Sierra Bermeja. The lights of an occasional truck tracked a path through the dark on the motorway that crossed the plain below, its viaducts spanning dried river beds and volcanic valleys.

A sign was pinned to the wall above the door of the stairwell. *Se Vende*, and a telephone number. Mackenzie pressed the buzzer for the top flat. A frightened woman's voice answered almost straight away. 'Who is it?'

'My name's Mackenzie. I've been working with Cristina.'

A long metallic buzz signalled the unlocking of the door. Mackenzie pushed it open and forced himself to run up the four flights of stairs two at a time. He was breathless and perspiring by the time Nuri greeted him on the top landing. She was painfully pale, and Mackenzie saw that she had lost much of her hair. She held a pink nightgown tightly around a wasted body that seemed brittle enough to break if touched.

'Is Cristina here?'

'No.'

His heart sank. 'Do you know . . . ?'

'You missed her by about ten minutes. She came to leave Lucas with me. But wouldn't say where she was going.' Her face crumpled. 'Oh señor. My husband has been out all night without leaving any word. Cristina didn't know where he was.' She hesitated. 'I don't suppose . . .'

Mackenzie's mind was filled with the image of Paco impaled on the railings below the gardens at the Condesa Golf Hotel. How could he tell her that? And yet it bothered him to lie. 'I'm sorry,' was all he could say. And he was. Not for Paco. But for Nuri. 'Was Cristina in uniform?'

Nuri shook her head.

'So she wasn't armed?'

'I don't think so. She was very upset.'

He exhaled his hopelessness. If she had gone to face Cleland without a gun she would stand no chance. But he knew, too, that she would have had to go to the police station to get it. He turned away to go back down to the car.

'You'll let me know, señor? If you hear anything about Paco?'

He hesitated on the top step, and wanted to weep for this fragile creature, widowed without knowing it, and fighting a losing battle against the malignancy inside her. 'Yes,' he said, knowing that he wouldn't.

The duty officer looked embarrassed when he raised his head from the desk to see Mackenzie pushing through the door from the street. He stood up. 'Señor Mackenzie . . .'

Mackenzie looked at his watch. It was 6.15 am. 'When will the *Jefe* be in?'

'He won't, Señor. He's at a conference in Malaga today.' He sucked in his lower lip, steeling himself to make the confession. 'I'm sorry. When you called earlier I forgot that the *Jefe* would not be at home. He left word that he was spending the night in Malaga to save himself an early rise.'

Mackenzie closed his eyes. The time he had wasted! 'Fucking idiot,' he said in English.

The officer frowned. 'I'm sorry . . . ?'

'Do you have any idea where Cristina is?'

He shook his head. 'No señor. I haven't seen her since the funeral.'

'She hasn't been here, then?'

'No.' He hesitated. 'That information you asked my colleague to request for you yesterday. From the telephone company.'

'What about it?'

'It came in late last night from Movistar.'

'Movistar?'

'The telephone company.'

'And?'

'I put it on the *Jefe*'s desk, señor, along with a lot of other stuff. He was here quite late last night, but I'm not sure if he saw it.'

'Let's take a look, then.' Mackenzie pushed open the door into the lobby beyond reception. The duty officer emerged quickly from a door behind the counter. 'You can't just go barging into the *Jefe*'s office, señor.'

Mackenzie said, 'I can, you know. Watch me.' And he opened the door to the *Jefe*'s office and walked in. The agitated duty officer followed him. The heads of two officers on night shift raised themselves from books in the office opposite to glance curiously across the hall.

Mackenzie rounded the desk, and found the faxed information from Movistar on top of the pile. He had requested the source number for the two calls made to Cristina's apartment on the afternoon of Antonio's murder. The first corresponded, time-wise, to the call which must have sent him to the rendezvous at the Eroski Centre. The second to the call leaving the fake message from Cristina. Both came from a mobile number listed to Nurita Sánchez Pradell. Mackenzie closed his eyes and shook his head in disbelief. How inept had Paco been in his attempted deception? He had used his own wife's phone to make the call which had sent Antonio to his death, and then again to leave the message he had somehow cobbled together, probably from messages Cristina had left for her sister.

The duty officer peered at him, concerned for the first time. 'What is it, señor?'

Mackenzie opened his eyes. 'Cristina is in serious danger. I think she's gone to offer herself to Jack Cleland in place of her aunt.' He almost barked his frustration at the Spanish policeman. 'But I have no idea where.' He reached for his phone automatically, before remembering again that it wasn't there. 'I need a functioning phone. Do you have a phone?

'Well, yes . . .' The duty officer's affirmative was reluctant.

'What kind of phone is it?'

'It's an iPhone X.'

'Same as mine. I need to borrow it.'

'But it's not a police phone, señor, it's mine.'

'I'll take good care of it,' Mackenzie said, and had a thought. 'Wait a minute, if my sim card is still in one piece, I could swap it for yours, then I'd also have access to all my contacts. Wait here.'

He hobbled out to the car and returned a few moments later with the shattered remains of his phone. The duty officer had returned to his place behind the counter, and Mackenzie put his phone down in front of him.

'Paper clip!'

But the duty officer couldn't take his eyes off the wreckage of Mackenzie's phone. 'Is that what you call taking good care of your phone, señor?'

'Actually,' Mackenzie said grimly, 'it was the phone that

took good care of me.' He reached over to snatch a paper-clip from the worktop behind the counter, straightened one leg of it, and used it to open the sim drawer in his phone. Miraculously, the card appeared to have escaped any damage. He snapped his fingers at the duty officer. 'Come on, give me your phone.'

Very reluctantly and with a deep sigh, the duty officer handed it over. Mackenzie extracted the sim card and replaced it with his own, then rebooted the phone. Almost immediately an alert sounded to signal a phone message. Mackenzie put it on speaker and tapped play. Cristina's voice was clear and unambiguous, and Mackenzie could hear the fear in it.

Señor, they want to exchange me for Ana. The Gibraltar Skywalk at first light. If you get this, know that I have no choice but to do what they want.

'Jesus!' Mackenzie's eyes flickered involuntarily towards the street outside. It was still dark, but daylight wasn't far away.

The duty officer's eyes were wide with both alarm and astonishment.

Mackenzie said, 'What's the fucking Skywalk?'

'It's a glass platform near the summit of the Rock of Gibraltar, señor. Built around an old fortified lookout post. A tourist attraction. I took my own kids to see it just last week, but it was closed for maintenance.' He shook his head. 'I wish they'd advertised that in advance. It would have saved me a journey.' Then he paused to think about it. 'But Cristina wouldn't have gone to Gibraltar, señor. The Spanish police have no jurisdiction there.'

Mackenzie cocked a despairing eyebrow. 'She hasn't gone as a police officer. How long will it take me to get there?'

The duty officer shrugged. 'This time of day? Probably no more than about thirty-five minutes.'

CHAPTER FORTY-SEVEN

Large silver letters affixed to the wall reflected the light of his headlamps as Mackenzie swung his car through the roundabout. La Paloma. He knew the name at once. It was here that it had all begun, the night Cristina and her colleague went to investigate a reported break-in at what turned out to be Cleland's villa.

He accelerated along the cliffs, the Mediterranean washing phosphorescence upon the beach below, and fumbled with his borrowed iPhone to autodial the number of the NCA in London. It would not yet be 6 am in England. He put it on speaker and dropped it on to the passenger seat. The voice of the night duty officer filled the car. 'National Crime Agency, how can I help you?'

'Investigator John Mackenzie. This is an emergency.'

'Yes, sir.'

'I am on deployment in Spain and I urgently need a name and contact number in the Royal Gibraltar Police. There is a major drugs deal going down on the Rock, and the lives of two women are at risk.'

'I'm sorry, sir. I'll need to confirm your identity and clear this with a higher authority.'

Mackenzie drew a long slow breath to contain his exasperation and fumbled in his back pocket for his wallet and ID. He flicked on the dash light and squinted to read the number off his card and keep an eye on the road at the same time. Then he said, 'Contact Director Beard for authorization and call me back.'

He had no sooner hung up than the phone began to ring. Too fast to be the NCA. He glanced sideways to hit the answer icon. 'Mackenzie.'

'Señor, this is Detective Gil from GRECO in Marbella. I'm sorry to get you out of your bed at this hour, but it is a matter of some urgency.'

Mackenzie was not about to explain why he was not in bed. He said, 'Go ahead.'

'As we discussed a couple of days ago, my boss agreed to resume surveillance on Delgado and Rafa, along with the other principals on our list. One of our teams arrived to install themselves at Puerto Banus early this morning. Delgado's yacht was missing from its berth. The port authority confirmed that it left harbour just after five. So the team conducted a routine check of CCTV footage.' He paused. 'Señor, a truck entered the marina and parked at the *Pantalán* where the yacht was berthed a little after three o'clock. Four men unloaded somewhere in the region of thirty bales, which were then stowed aboard the yacht before it set sail. One of those men was identified as

Vasquez. When the yacht left it was confirmed that Delgado was on board.' Mackenzie heard him sighing. 'Unfortunately, we have no idea where it was headed.'

Mackenzie said, 'I do. It's going to Gibraltar. I'm halfway there right now.' He didn't wait for Gil to register surprise. 'I know that the Spanish and the Gibraltarians don't really talk to each other, detective, but if you don't start right now Cleland and the rest are going to get away.'

There was a brief hiatus. 'You're sure about this?'

'Yes. Cleland has taken Officer Sánchez Pradell's aunt hostage and she is meeting him in Gibraltar to try to secure her release. But you and I both know he's going to kill her.'

Another pause. 'We have contacts in HM Customs in Gibraltar. I'll alert them.'

CHAPTER FORTY-EIGHT

From here the bay of Gibraltar seemed circled by lights. Strings of them like luminous pearls followed the curve of the coastline. Black waters dotted with tankers and freighters sending shimmering spears of light to pierce the depths. Long, illuminated wharves reached out like protective arms from docks and container terminals, providing safe haven in calmer waters for giant ships. At the far side of the bay, tucked in beneath the mountains, lay the Spanish port of Algeciras, and beyond that the ferry terminal at Tarifa where cars and passengers trafficked back and forth between Spain and Morocco. Immediately below, the lights of Gibraltar town cast their pollution into a sky still dark.

Cristina sat in numbed silence in the back of her taxi, trying to ignore the ramblings of the driver, a man more used, so he told her, to conducting circuits of the Rock with a car full of tourists.

The one-way road to the peak was overhung by dark trees and rose steeply through hairpin bends snaking up into the night.

'You see those big metal rings set into the road?' her driver was saying. 'The British used them as part of a pulley system for hauling cannon to the top of the Rock. Sheer brutal manpower.' When she didn't respond he said, 'Spanish?'

'Yes.'

'Thought so.' He sighed. 'So many of the young ones don't even speak it now. My people were from Malta. Lot of Italians came here, too. Only twenty per cent of Gibraltarians are of British descent, you know.'

Cristina glanced at the back of his head for the first time. It was half-turned towards her. She saw dark Mediterranean features. 'But you think of yourself as British?'

'Oh, yes. Born under the union flag,' he said proudly.

They slowed to take a bend in the road where it almost doubled back on itself, and for a moment Cristina had a view out across the strait. The first glimpse of dawn, burgeoning somewhere in the hidden east, cast its pale misted light across brooding waters. The darker outline of the mountains of North Africa were clearly visible, the shadow of a nearer peak cutting its silhouette against the palest of light in the sky beyond.

'Ceuta,' the driver said. 'One of the Pillars of Hercules. Gibraltar is the other. Hercules is said to have cut through the mountains with a single blow of his sword and used his great strength to separate the two continents and create the strait.' He chuckled. 'I leave you to decide whether or not there is any truth in this story.' It probably went down well with tourists, but was lost on Cristina, her mind already wandering.

The driver glanced at her in the mirror.

'You know, there really is no point in going to the Skywalk. Like I told you, it's closed for maintenance work. All you're going to find up there are apes. And nothing else is open yet. St Michael's Cave, the tunnels, the cable car . . .'

'It doesn't matter,' Cristina said. 'Just drop me at the Skywalk.' Her apprehension was so intense now that the shivering which had accompanied her across the border had become a deep, numbing chill. Her whole body was rigid as she sat gripping her seat in the back of the taxi.

The Spanish border town of La Línea was deserted apart from traffic on the arterial road leading to the frontier. As Mackenzie accelerated through a series of roundabouts, street lights cast a ghostly yellow across the dual carriageway, vehicles travelling in one direction only. On his right, beyond the marina, the waters of the Bay of Gibraltar reflected the lights of myriad ships at anchor. Vast areas of covered parking stretched ahead, and beyond that the tail lights of vehicles queuing to cross the border into Gibraltar. The queue had started early, as it always did, to process the more than 23,000 people who came from Spain to work on the Rock every day.

As Mackenzie joined the tail of the queue he cursed and glanced at his watch. If this was how it was early on a Saturday, God only knew what it would be like on a weekday. It was almost 7 am and he could see first light in the sky beyond the black shape of the Rock. He lowered his head to glance up, impressed by the scale of it rising sheer into the night, dwarfing customs and immigration buildings and the airport runway below.

His phone rang and he grabbed it. 'Mackenzie.'

'Sir, pleased to connect with you. Detective Sergeant David Greene. I'm with the serious crime squad of the Royal Gibraltar Police. I've been briefed by the NCA in London, and my colleagues in Customs and Excise have received an alert from GRECO in Marbella. Where are you, sir?'

'I'm stuck in bloody traffic in La Línea, waiting to cross the border.'

'Dump the car, sir, and come through on foot. It's much quicker. I'll meet you on the other side.'

Mackenzie pulled the wheel hard to his right and swung out of the queue. He turned into the entry lane of one of several car parks that sprawled behind mesh fencing, and snatched a ticket from the machine to lift the barrier. He slotted his car into the first available space, then took off on foot, trying to ignore the pain that jarred through his body with every juddering footfall.

People were arriving, it seemed, from nowhere now. Dropped perhaps from cars, or coming on foot from homes in La Línea itself. Gibraltar was a major local employer. Everyone was heading for passport control. Mackenzie pushed his way unceremoniously through the crowd.

On the far side of the entrance to customs and immigration, a huge animated billboard shone its advocacy of *Watergardens*

Dental Care into the dark before dawn. Vehicles backed up in two lanes for several hundred metres, idling and belching fumes into the cool morning air, waiting to pass through laborious checks put in place by the Spanish to irk the British.

Mackenzie ran past rusted fencing, beneath twin arches that marked the crossing point for vehicles, and towards the single doorway that led to the immigration hall. Here a queue had already formed at a row of automated passport control gates. Mackenzie shoved his way to the head of it, ignoring a barrage of complaints, and made for the first available gate. From a window on the far side, inscrutable immigration officers eyed him suspiciously as he held his passport in the digital reader and waited for the flash of the camera to record his image. He endured what seemed like an interminable wait before the light ahead of him turned green and the barrier let him through.

Moving with the flow of people passing through the narrow opening from one hall to the next, he waved his passport at a bored British official sitting at a raised desk, a perfunctory pretence of passport control, and ran through a wood-panelled customs hall where uniformed officials were more interested in chatting than checking.

Immediately outside, in Winston Churchill Avenue, a stocky middle-aged man in a dark suit and open-necked white shirt loitered by an old-fashioned red-painted British telephone box. It seemed strangely incongruous here at the southern tip of Spain, just fifteen kilometres from the continent of Africa. The man glanced down at a faxed ID sheet in his left hand, then up again at Mackenzie. He stepped forward, his right hand extended. 'Mr Mackenzie. Pleased to meet you, sir. DS Greene. I have a car over here.'

Greene's silver-grey Honda Civic was pulled in at the back of a taxi rank where drivers stood around smoking and chatting among themselves, waiting for early morning business. Across the road, a huge expanse of floodlit tarmac stretched away to the new terminal at Gibraltar Airport.

Greene slipped a flashing light on to the roof of the Honda and started his siren as he pulled off into the stream of traffic heading for town. But even lights and siren did not give him precedence over the barriers that fell to stop traffic in both directions where the road crossed the runway. Greene tapped his wheel with impatient fingers as they waited for an early easyJet flight to take-off.

'Fifth most dangerous airport in the world,' he said. 'And not just because the road goes right across the runway. We have terrible cross-winds here. Not too bad this morning.' He leaned forward to peer up at the Rock through his windscreen. 'It'll be windy up there, though. You can count on it.' He glanced across at Mackenzie. 'We've got armed uniformed officers on the way up by car. You and I are going to take the cable car. Much faster. I had to get the operator out of his bed. It's not normally open for another couple of hours, and wind conditions this morning would usually mean a cancellation of service.' He smiled grimly. 'But needs must, eh?'

Lights turned green, the barriers lifted, and Greene leaned on the horn to augment his siren in forcing the traffic ahead out of his way. Mackenzie had the sense that he was enjoying this.

They accelerated through several roundabouts between tall buildings and passed broken-down sections of the old city wall. Dark space opened out on their right, and Mackenzie saw containers lined up along a dock, yachts in a marina, and the lights of Algeciras twinkling distantly eight kilometres away across the bay. The light of dawn cast itself in pale pink across the peaks of the mountains beyond.

Gibraltar old town lay somewhere off to their left, and as they passed the Trafalgar Cemetery Greene said, 'Are you armed?'

'No I'm not. You?'

'Yes sir. I'm a trained firearms officer. And I checked out a sidearm before leaving base.'

Opposite an art deco fire station, he pulled in at the kerb-side, and they jumped out of the car. Mackenzie glanced up to see huge pylons set into the hillside at precarious angles, support for the cables that would haul their car to the summit more than 400 metres above. He followed Greene into the docking station.

Cristina watched the tail lights of her taxi vanish over the brow of the hill to make its way back down to the town below. No need to wait for her. She knew she wasn't coming back. The wind tugged at her hair and yanked at her clothes. It was fresh, almost cold in the first light of dawn.

Above her, the glass platforms of the Skywalk stood on two levels, constructed around an old stone watchtower where the British had once installed a Bofors gun. A lift, not functioning at this hour, climbed to the topmost level. Red and white tape was stretched across the stairs that led up to both, and a red triangular sign announced that the Skywalk was closed for maintenance.

Beyond it, the Rock fell sheer to an arc of coastline almost 340 metres below, the Mediterranean washing white along its contour. On the bay side, it dropped away steeply on a tree-covered slope to the lights of the town and the harbour reflecting in the bay. To her right, the Rock swept upwards on a knife edge to its second-highest peak. On her left it rose towards the cable car station and the highest point of this British overseas territory.

The stars were fading now in a sky that went from blood red along the distant eastern horizon, through the palest of turquoise to the darkest blue of the vanishing firmament.

Cristina breathed deeply. There was something invigorating in drawing on this fresh clean air in the final minutes of her life. Something, perhaps, almost poetic about dying in this most beautiful of places as the sun sent its light scattering across the sea, which had been such an ever-present through all of her days.

But still her heart weighed like a burden in her chest as she stepped over the red and white tape to climb the stairs to the platform above. And all she could think of was the son she was about to orphan.

She reached the lower platform which extended out across the drop. Tourists flocked here during the season to step gingerly over the glass and look at the terrifying drop that fell away beneath their feet.

There was no one there.

She climbed the steps to the observation platform above. It, too, was deserted. The wind battered her here, and she held on to the glass barrier wondering if somehow she had got it wrong. Was it *not* at the Skywalk she was supposed to meet Cleland? Or had she missed him? The Spanish coastline stretched away to the north, before sweeping eastwards. She could see the lights of Estepona, and more distantly the conurbation of Marbella. And somewhere in the dark fold of the hills lay Marviña. Her home. The land of her father and mother. Of her aunt. Another kind of fear gripped her. And she wondered if Ana was already dead.

Then she saw a light flashing from the southern peak, another 60 metres up. Once, twice, three times. A signal. She was certain of it. They wanted her to come to them. Perhaps it was too exposed here on the Skywalk. She slipped a torch from the pocket of her anorak, and in its beam saw steps carved into the rock six metres below. They wound their way up and along the crest of the Rock towards the summit. She climbed down to the foot of the stairs, and began the steep ascent into the dawn to meet her destiny.

Ana feels the wind wrapping itself around her, almost violent in its caress. It fills her mouth, and makes her sightless eyes water as though she were crying. Her hair is pulled back from her face like the repeated strokes of a brush fighting to remove every tug. She has to brace her feet firmly on uneven ground to keep from losing her balance.

The journey by boat had seemed to last for ever. She had not been on water since childhood, and although the sea was not rough, a heavy swell had made her feel quite nauseous. Cleland had sat with her, holding her hand for most of the journey, fetching her water when she asked for it and holding the container to her lips.

When finally they had disembarked, she'd had the impression of a great sense of open space around her. An industrial smell. The stink of motor oil and smoke. Solid ground beneath her feet again had come as a relief.

Then there had been the short journey by car. Climbing ever upward through bends that tipped them in their seats, one way then the other. Cleland's hand ever-present.

Emerging from the car, she had immediately felt the force of the wind, and experienced a great sense of height. She could feel the difference in pressure, the temperature of the air. And then Cleland's hand on her arm, guiding her up endless crooked steps that turned and twisted, up and up until her legs ached and her lungs were close to bursting. Apprehension grew with every step.

She knows that they have come to Gibraltar. Or, at least, that's what he has told her, so now she assumes they are somewhere high up on the Rock. That great monolithic limestone promontory that so characterized the southern skyline of her childhood. She can picture it. It is exhilarating. And were she not so afraid, she would feel almost exultant to be standing here on the roof of the world.

Cleland's hand has never left her, fingers firmly wrapped around her upper arm. She is not quite sure how, but she feels another presence, as if they are not alone. But with all her senses so assailed by the wind, she cannot be certain. Neither can she escape the feeling that if he let go of her, she would blow away. Fly off into the void, an escape to some gentler place.

'Are we on the Rock?' she asks, raising her voice because she knows that otherwise the wind will drown it. She holds out a hand for his response. He takes it. A single tap for yes, two for no, the code that has somehow evolved in the last twenty-four hours. He taps once.

'Describe it for me.' She wants to picture it in her mind, for him to paint that picture with words traced on her palm. But she can feel his hesitation. 'Please.'

– *We're close to the top. 400 metres up. Dawn. Clear sky. A wall to our right, then a sheer drop to the sea. An old watchtower. Below and left, trees hide the road up from the town. In the distance . . .*

But he breaks off now, and she feels his sudden tension. With dread in her heart she asks, 'Is she here?'

– *She's coming.*

'Don't harm her, please. Kill me instead.'

He does not respond and she breathes deeply, attempting to calm the inner turmoil. She tries to complete the picture he did not finish. In the distance she imagines the lights of Algeciras. Her parents took her there once as a child, when they went to visit the windblown beaches of the south coast. She knows that a short way across the water, the Dark Continent lies brooding in mystery. She has seen the distant Atlas Mountains. She has breathed the smell of Africa in the heat of the wind.

She says, 'I saw you last night.'

And the tightening of his fingers on her arm signals his surprise. Then his touch on her palm.

– *How?*

'In a dream.'

– *You can see in your dreams?*

'And hear. Just as if I was a normal person. Except that I can also fly. Last night I flew with you.' She is lost for a moment in thought. 'You cannot begin to know how it feels to wake up and remember that you are deaf and blind, to have your sight and hearing taken away from you every single day of your life. When I am asleep I never want to wake again.' She smiles, a tiny sad ironic smile. 'Maybe this is my dream. Or my nightmare. Maybe I will wake up and see you again and not feel sad.'

– *What did I look like?*

'Hard to describe. Kind, I would say. Yes. Kind.'

But she has lost his attention. She feels his whole body stiffening next to her, and she knows that Cristina has come to die for her.

CHAPTER FORTY-NINE

Mackenzie had little head for heights at the best of times. And this was not the best of times. As the cable car winched higher into the dawn, the wind sent it swinging wildly. He could barely bring himself to look at the distant horizon as it tilted one way then the other.

The far mountains were fully lit now, bathed in early morning sunlight, although he and Greene were still in the shadow of the Rock, and it seemed almost impenetrably dark here. A glance at the other man told Mackenzie that Greene was no happier with this perilous ascent than he. Both men clung to the bars set along the windows, pressing themselves against the walls, listening to the whine and clatter of the cables, willing the car up to the summit.

When finally it slipped into the shelter of its concrete dock, and the door slid open, they tumbled out with shaking legs on to the deck, and a new kind of fear displaced the old.

'Which way?' Mackenzie said.

Greene pointed south. 'You can just see the Skywalk set into the dip between the peaks.' Mackenzie followed his finger and saw low sunlight glinting off the glass walls of the distant observation platform. Then, some way above it, a light flashing on the dark side of the Rock.

'What's that?'

'No idea. We need to get down on to the road.'

They scrambled down steps and through bushes to jump finally on to the single-track road that dipped along the crest of the summit. In the shadow of the rock again, Mackenzie saw the silhouette of a figure leaping from the wall above them. Greene spun around, drawing his weapon from a shoulder holster to level it at their attacker.

'Stop!' Mackenzie shouted, and Greene saw just in time that it was an ape. An adult male. Probably looking for food. Mackenzie's bellow in the wind sent it scampering, and a jumpy DS Greene raised his gun, two-handed, to point at the sky before quickly reholstering.

The two men set off at a run down the road, sending long shadows off to the west in the strangely cold yellow light. They passed a white Mercedes pulled into the side of the road where apes clustered around a semi-covered area set into the rock beneath a crumbling stone arch. A concrete base was littered with orange peel.

'The remnants of last night's meal,' Greene said. 'They'll be up to feed them again soon.'

The usually friendly Barbary macaques hung from wooden beams or balanced precariously on railings, gazing at them with dark, apprehensive, simian eyes. Perhaps they, too, sensed the fear that blew across the summit on this cold dawn.

It took several more breathless minutes to reach the platform, only to discover that there was no one there. Mackenzie stepped out on to the glass deck and felt his insides fall away as he looked down. He retreated quickly to the safety of the stairs, and shaded his eyes against the sky to look up towards the southern peak that loomed over them. 'That's where the light came from. How do we get up there?'

'Steps going up from the foot of the platform,' Greene said, and he clambered back down to the stairs. Mackenzie went after him two at a time.

Cleland canted his head to one side and looked curiously at the slight figure of Cristina as she stepped out on to the tiny stone platform, breathless from the steepness of the climb. Her anorak seemed to inflate in the wind, and although her hair was tied back, strands of it had come free to dance around her head. He almost wondered how he had managed to harbour such hatred for someone so insignificant.

Cristina glanced around, almost as if looking for some means of escape. The ruins of an old guardhouse stood off to her right. On her left, a low wall ran from a small round watchtower to the rocks and spiky maquis plants bordering the remaining steps to the peak. The Rock remained dark on the west side, while sunlight sprayed early colour across the east face and sent diamonds coruscating away across the

Mediterranean towards Africa. The wind was fierce and she had to plant her feet to avoid being toppled by it. It lent her a look of defiance that only served to enrage Cleland.

Somehow Ana sensed her presence and called out her name, taking a step towards her. But Cleland held her arm firmly, a pistol in his free hand pressed against her temple.

'Don't hurt her, please,' Cristina begged him.

Cleland's smile was rueful. 'It's not my intention. It was. But not any more. She's a remarkable lady, your aunt. When this is all over I'm going to take her with me. I will do whatever it takes to restore her sight and her hearing.'

Cristina regarded him with puzzled astonishment. 'You can't.'

'I can do anything I like.'

'Her condition is genetic. There is no cure. There can be no cure.'

'It's amazing what money can buy. And I have money to burn, Cristina. And no one else to spend it on since you killed my Angela.'

'I didn't!'

But he wasn't listening. 'And my child.'

Cristina frowned.

'You didn't know she was pregnant, did you? No one did. The test had only confirmed it two days earlier. You killed them both.'

Cristina shook her head vigorously. 'No! You did.'

He shrugged. 'I'm not going to argue with you. I am assuming you have a weapon. I'd advise you to take it out very carefully and lay it on the ground.'

'I'm not armed.'

There was scorn in Cleland's laughter. 'Of course you aren't.' But the smile wiped itself from his face in an instant, to be replaced by a look so ugly that Cristina felt almost violated by it. 'Put it on the ground or I'll kill her.' The bellow of his voice resounded around this tiny space, and he pressed the barrel of his gun into Ana's temple.

Cristina shook her head helplessly. 'I swear. I don't have a gun. Look . . .' And carefully she unzipped her anorak to hold it open. She wore only a T-shirt beneath it, and felt cold air filling it and chilling her skin.

It seemed to take Cleland several moments to absorb the fact that this woman had come, unarmed, to plead for the life of her aunt. In the full knowledge that Cleland would kill her. He almost admired her for it.

He swung the gun away from Ana's head and pointed it at arm's length towards Cristina. She closed her eyes. 'I have a young son,' she said.

'As I too might have had.'

And she knew that there would be no reasoning with this madman. He would kill her, and orphan her son. And God only knew what would become of Ana.

'Don't fucking move, Cleland!'

The voice was hard and full of menace, and came from behind. Cristina glanced over her shoulder to see Mackenzie and another man standing at the top of the steps, both of them breathing hard. The other man pointed a pistol directly at Cleland.

Cleland immediately returned his gun to push it hard against the side of Ana's head. His confidence was dented, but he still managed the hint of a smile. 'Well, well, Mr Mackenzie. It seems I'm going to have to kill you twice. I was so sure I had sent that bullet winging its way straight to your black Glasgow heart.'

Mackenzie struggled to contain his anger. 'You did. It was my iPhone that saved me.'

Cleland seemed vindicated by this. His aim had not been errant after all. 'Apple has a lot to answer for, then.'

'Lower your weapon,' Greene shouted at him. 'If you pull that trigger you're a dead man.'

A single gunshot pierced the pitch of the wind, and Greene looked down in surprise at the hole in his chest, his failing heart fighting immediately to pump blood into the dawn. He fell forward on his face, then toppled on to his side, and Mackenzie saw blood pooling around him on the stone flags. Less than an hour ago, as Mackenzie placed his call requesting help from the Gibraltar police, he had probably still been in bed.

Mackenzie looked up as a familiar figure stepped from the shadows of the ruined guardhouse.

'*Jefe!*'

It took Cristina's exclamation of astonishment to clear the fog of confusion and disbelief from Mackenzie's mind, and he felt all hope slip away. He was bereft, debilitated by his own sense of failure. His father had ignored his superiors and failed. Mackenzie had put faith in his, and failed too. He was going to die. And so was Cristina, and Ana. And he had been unable to prevent any of it.

He closed his eyes and pictured the *Jefe*'s melancholy as he sipped his Glenfiddich that night at the finca. A dead wife, a dead son. *My only future here is looking back*, he'd said. Loss stealing reason and purpose.

He opened them again to stare at the somehow diminished figure of the chief of police. The gun still in his hand, regret still on his face. And everything fell into place. 'Paco was your man,' he said. 'Obviously I just missed seeing you together at the golf club that day.'

The *Jefe* shrugged acknowledgement.

'That's how Cleland managed to live here undetected all this time.'

Cleland said, 'It helps to have friends at court.'

Cristina was bewildered. 'I don't understand. What are you talking about?'

But Mackenzie kept his eyes on the *Jefe*. 'Why in the name of God did you have to kill Antonio?'

Cristina cast Mackenzie a look of disbelief, then turned her gaze on her boss. The *Jefe* seemed embarrassed.

He said, 'He overheard me and Paco having a row in the locker room. Paco was still pissed off at Cleland shooting him in the leg. And it hadn't been any part of the deal, he said, for Cleland to kill all those Guardia.' He threw a venomous glance towards Cleland. 'And he was right.' He sighed. 'Antonio was incandescent. Said he was going to tell Cristina. Paco was sure he could talk him out of it. But I knew we couldn't take the risk.'

'*You* killed him!' Anger and hurt and disbelief all conveying themselves in Cristina's three words. She made a lunge for him, but Mackenzie grabbed her arm to hold her back.

The *Jefe* couldn't meet her eye. 'Not directly.' Then he looked from one to the other, as if soliciting understanding. 'I never ever thought it would come to this. But . . . you know . . . when things go wrong you have to go where they take you. So much that can't be undone.'

'And where are these things that can't be undone going to take you now?' Mackenzie's voice was laden with sarcasm.

The *Jefe* inclined his head a touch. 'To a yacht in the harbour down there, señor. Enough cash stashed aboard it to make sure I never have to worry about money ever again. A new identity. A new life. And no need to look over my shoulder.'

'Well, anyway, that was the plan.' Cleland spoke for the first time in a while. He had been listening with interest. And now he swung his pistol away from Ana's head and shot the *Jefe* in the face. The force of the bullet jerked the chief's head back, and he spun away across the stone flags, dead before he hit them. A pale smile lit Cleland's face. 'Loose ends,' he said. 'Hate them.' And he brought his weapon around to point towards Cristina and Mackenzie. 'Who's first?'

Ana has felt both shots. Even in this wind, the firing of a gun deforms the air. A physical sensation. An acrid whiff of propellant caught in a gust. She is too late to save Cristina, and a large part of her dies with the realization. She cannot explain the second shot, but has the scent of death in her nostrils, can almost smell the blood.

And now she feels Cleland's grip on her arm relaxing. She has an extraordinary sense of them both, up here in the sky, battered by the wind, drenched by early morning sunlight. A great void beneath them.

His descriptions traced on her palm have brought images to mind from long-ago school days. Photographs of the Rock in history books, Spanish outrage at British theft. The long ridge that sweeps between peaks, and the sheer fall to the sea below.

A sense of freedom from the chains of her disability infuses her whole being. She is an angel. As in her dreams, she can fly. But it is the thought of poor Sergio, and her anger at the death of Cristina, that fuels the ferocity with which she throws herself at Cleland. She feels her face strike the bone of his shoulder. He staggers, taken by surprise, the full weight of her body and her fury driving him towards the void. His panic, arms flailing, as they join in unbalanced union to tip into the abyss.

And now they are flying. Together. She reaches blindly into space to find his hand, holding it in hers as they seem to soar into the morning. It feels wonderful. Transcending all the years of darkness. Winging their way to eternity, and a final reckoning with her maker.

Cristina and Mackenzie watched frozen in horror as the unexpected weight of Ana's lunge caused Cleland to stagger sideways, his leg catching on the low stone wall to propel them together over the edge.

At the last moment, Mackenzie dived to try and catch her. But his fingers closed only around fresh air. And all he could do was watch as Cleland and Ana fell together, hand in hand, towards the tiny strip of beach below. She fell in silence, the same silence with which she had lived for all these years. His scream echoed into the early light, carried off by the wind from Africa.

And Mackenzie felt as bereft as his father must have done before him.

CHAPTER FIFTY

The sounds of a thousand passengers milling in the departure hall rose high into the void, lost in a fog of brilliant sunshine flooding in through tall windows.

Mackenzie had no need to check a bag. The clothes he had bought, laundered by the Totana, fitted easily into the overnight bag he had brought with him. It seemed like an eternity since he had left Glasgow on that wet Tuesday morning after his aunt's funeral. And yet it was only a few days. How his life had changed in that short time.

Cristina walked with him to security. Neither of them was in any hurry.

They had shared the ordeal, singly and together, of a remorseless debrief. Forty-eight hours of it. And the emotional hits just kept on coming. Nuri's discovery that Paco was dead. His betrayal. And his complicity in the death of Antonio. How she and Cristina would ever get over that, Mackenzie could not begin to imagine.

At least Lucas still had his mother. It was the sole consolation.

The bodies of Cleland and Ana had been recovered from

a grassy slope just above the narrow road that followed the contour of the coast below the Rock. Neither recognizable after the fall.

Ana had been buried the following day.

Delgado, Rafa, Vasquez and others had been arrested, and nearly two tons of cocaine recovered, along with almost forty million euros. The Spanish and Gibraltarian authorities would doubtless fight over custody of both for the foreseeable future.

Mackenzie couldn't have cared less.

They reached the queue for the security gates and stood awkwardly at the moment of parting, not sure how to accomplish it without embarrassment.

'What will you do?' he said.

She shrugged. 'What all survivors do, I guess. Carry on, and wonder why I'm the only one left standing.'

'Lucas needs you.'

'I know. That's all that keeps me going.' She paused. 'And you?'

'Go home and kiss the NCA goodbye. It's clear to me now that I should never have been a cop in the first place. Not cut out for it. Just like my father. We both failed.'

Cristina shook her head. 'You succeeded in almost everything, señor.'

'Except saving Ana.'

She gazed at the floor. 'You and I both.' Then she looked up to meet his eye. 'But it was Ana herself who took that out of our hands. Whether she thought she was saving me, or avenging my murder, we'll never know. But she saved both our lives in sacrificing hers.'

He nodded, not trusting himself to speak.

'So what will you do if you quit the police?'

Mackenzie's laugh lacked any humour. 'For a man qualified on paper for almost anything, it seems I am patently unsuited for almost everything. Short answer, I have no idea.'

'You should teach,' she said, remembering how he had sat with Lucas to reveal the mysterious secrets of calculating percentages. 'You'd make a good teacher.'

Self-consciousness coloured his cheeks. 'What I do know . . . what *you* taught me . . . is that your children are everything. So the first thing I must do is try to be the father I've never been. I never had a role model to teach me what a good parent was. Until now.'

Cristina blushed. 'You'll be good at that too.' She pushed herself up on tiptoes and kissed him lightly on the cheek. 'Goodbye, John Mackenzie.'

And she turned to walk briskly towards the sliding doors, and all the uncertainty of the world beyond them. He watched her go with an almost overwhelming sense of sadness, before turning away to join the queue to a future unknown.

ACKNOWLEDGEMENTS

Most of my research for *A Silent Death* was done in situ. I have written my last five books in this part of Spain, where I have an apartment that overlooks the Mediterranean and is eminently suited to winter writing. I owe a debt of gratitude to my many British and Spanish friends who helped me strip away the veneer of beaches, sea and sun that tend to characterise the tourist view of this Andalusian coast to reveal a slightly more disturbing reality in the book. In particular, I owe thanks to the chief of the Policía Local at Manilva, whose name 'Paco' I borrowed for my errant Guardia, and to single mother Isabel Reina Gil, who became my invaluable translator, researcher and font of all things Spanish, whose apartment I used for Cristina and whose son was the model for Lucas. Finally, I offer both thanks and sympathy to all those deaf-blind victims whose testimonies in the book *Deaf-Blind Reality*, edited by Scott M. Stoffel, provided a bleak insight into lives without sight or sound.

Peter May
France 2020